3

D0504804

CANCELLED
FALKIRK COMMUNITY
TRUST LIBRARIES

Praise for J. R. Ward's Black Dagger Brotherhood series

'Now here's a band of brothers who know how to show a
girl a good time'
New York Times bestselling author, Lisa Gardner

'It's not easy to find a new twist on the vampire myth, but Ward
succeeds beautifully. This dark and compelling world is filled with
enticing romance as well as perilous adventure'
Romantic Times

'These vampires are *hot,* and the series only gets hotter . . .
so hot it gave me shivers'
Vampire Genre

'Ward wields a commanding voice perfect for the genre . . . Intriguing,
adrenaline-pumping . . . Fans of L. A. Banks, Laurell K. Hamilton and
Sherrilyn Kenyon will add Ward to their must-read list'
Booklist

'These erotic paranormals are well worth it, and frighteningly
addictive . . . It all works to great, page-turning effect . . . [and has]
earned Ward an Anne Rice-style following, deservedly so'
Publishers Weekly

'[A] midnight whirlwind of dangerous characters and mesmerising
erotic romance. The Black Dagger Brotherhood owns me now. Dark
fantasy lovers, you just got served'
USA Today bestselling author of *Evermore*, Lynn Viehl

J.R. Ward lives in the South with her incredibly supportive husband and her beloved golden retriever. After graduating from law school, she began working in health care in Boston and spent many years as chief of staff for one of the premier academic medical centres in the nation.

Visit J. R. Ward online:

www.jrward.com
www.facebook.com/JRWardBooks
@jrward1

By J. R. Ward

J.R. WARD

THE CHOSEN

piatkus

PIATKUS

First published in the US in 2017 by Ballantine Books, an imprint of Random House,
A Division of Penguin Random House LLC
First published in Great Britain in 2017 by Piatkus

1 3 5 7 9 10 8 6 4 2

Copyright © Love Conquers All, Inc., 2017

The moral right of the author has been asserted.

*All characters and events in this publication, other than those
clearly in the public domain, are fictitious and any resemblance
to real persons, living or dead, is purely coincidental.*

All rights reserved.
No part of this publication may be reproduced, stored in a
retrieval system, or transmitted, in any form or by any means, without
the prior permission in writing of the publisher, nor be otherwise circulated
in any form of binding or cover other than that in which it is published
and without a similar condition including this condition being
imposed on the subsequent purchaser.

A CIP catalogue record for this book
is available from the British Library.

Hardback ISBN 978-0-349-40916-0
Trade paperback ISBN 978-0-349-40917-7

Printed a⸝   ⸝Y

Pap

Falkirk Community Trust	
30124 03068604 4	
Askews & Holts	
AF	£20.00
MK	

London EC4Y 0DZ

An Hachette UK Company
www.hachette.co.uk

www.littlebrown.co.uk

To You:

After all this time,

you have been chosen.

Welcome home.

ACKNOWLEDGMENTS

With immense gratitude to the readers of the Black Dagger Brotherhood!

Thank you so very much for all the support and guidance: Steven Axelrod and Kara Welsh. Thank you also to everyone at Ballantine—these books are truly a team effort.

With love to Team Waud—you know who you are. This simply could not happen without you.

None of this would be possible without: my loving husband, who is my adviser and caretaker and visionary; my wonderful mother, who has given me so much love I couldn't possibly ever repay her; my family (both those of blood and those by adoption); and my dearest friends.

Oh, and my WriterAssistant, Naamah.

GLOSSARY OF TERMS AND

PROPER NOUNS

ahstrux nohtrum (n.) Private guard with license to kill who is granted his or her position by the King.

ahvenge (v.) Act of mortal retribution, carried out typically by a male loved one.

Black Dagger Brotherhood (pr. n.) Highly trained vampire warriors who protect their species against the Lessening Society. As a result of selective breeding within the race, Brothers possess immense physical and mental strength, as well as rapid healing capabilities. They are not siblings for the most part, and are inducted into the Brotherhood upon nomination by the Brothers. Aggressive, self-reliant, and secretive by nature, they exist apart from civilians, having little contact with members of the other classes except when they need to feed. They are the subjects of legend and objects of reverence within the vampire world. They may be killed only by the most serious of wounds, e.g., a gunshot or stab to the heart, etc.

blood slave (n.) Male or female vampire who has been subjugated to serve the blood needs of another. The practice of keeping blood slaves has recently been outlawed.

the Chosen (n.) Female vampires who have been bred to serve the Scribe Virgin. They are considered members of the aristocracy, and previously were spiritually rather than temporally focused. Now freed from the Sanctuary, they are finding themselves and individuating from the cult-like restrictions of their traditional role. In the past, they were used to meet the blood needs of unmated members of the Brotherhood, and that practice has been reinstated by the Brothers.

chrih (n.) Symbol of honorable death in the Old Language.

cohntehst (n.) Conflict between two males competing for the right to be a female's mate.

Dhunhd (pr. n.) Hell.

doggen (n.) Member of the servant class within the vampire world. *Doggen* have old, conservative traditions about service to their superiors, following a formal code of dress and behavior. They are able to go out during the day, but they age relatively quickly. Life expectancy is approximately five hundred years.

ehros (n.) A Chosen trained in the matter of sexual arts.

exhile dhoble (n.) The evil or cursed twin, the one born second.

the Fade (pr. n.) Non-temporal realm where the dead reunite with their loved ones and pass eternity.

First Family (pr. n.) The King and Queen of the vampires, and any children they may have.

ghardian (n.) Custodian of an individual. There are varying degrees of *ghardians*, with the most powerful being that of a *sehcluded* female.

glymera (n.) The social core of the aristocracy, roughly equivalent to Regency England's *ton*.

hellren (n.) Male vampire who has been mated to a female. Males may take more than one female as mate.

hyslop (n. or v.) Term referring to a lapse in judgment, typically resulting in the compromise of the mechanical operations of a vehicle or otherwise motorized conveyance of some kind. For example, leaving one's keys in one's car as it is parked outside the family home overnight.

leahdyre (n.) A person of power and influence.

leelan (adj.) A term of endearment loosely translated as "dearest one."

Lessening Society (pr. n.) Order of slayers convened by the Omega for the purpose of eradicating the vampire species.

lesser (n.) De-souled human who targets vampires for extermination as a member of the Lessening Society. *Lessers* must be stabbed through the chest in order to be killed; otherwise they are ageless. They do not eat or drink and are impotent. Over time, their hair, skin, and irises lose pigmentation until they are blond, blushless, and pale eyed. They smell like baby powder. Inducted into the society by the Omega, they retain a ceramic jar thereafter into which their heart was placed after it was removed.

lewlhen (n.) Gift.

lheage (n.) A term of respect used by a sexual submissive to refer to her dominant.

Lhenihan (pr. n.) A mythic beast renowned for its sexual prowess. In modern slang, refers to a male of preternatural size and sexual stamina.

lys (n.) Torture tool used to remove the eyes.

mahmen (n.) Mother. Used both as an identifier and a term of affection.

mhis (n.) The masking of a given physical environment; the creation of a field of illusion.

nalla (n., f.) or *nallum* (n., m.) Beloved.

needing period (n.) Female vampire's time of fertility, generally lasting for two days and accompanied by intense sexual cravings. Occurs approximately five years after a female's transition and then once a decade thereafter. All males respond to some degree if they are around a female in her need. It can be a dangerous time, with conflicts and fights breaking out between competing males, particularly if the female is not mated.

newling (n.) A virgin.

the Omega (pr. n.) Malevolent, mystical figure who has targeted the vampires for extinction out of resentment directed toward the Scribe Virgin. Exists in a non-temporal realm and has extensive powers, though not the power of creation.

phearsom (adj.) Term referring to the potency of a male's sexual organs. Literal translation something close to "worthy of entering a female."

princeps (n.) Highest level of the vampire aristocracy, second only to members of the First Family or the Scribe Virgin's Chosen. Must be born to the title; it may not be conferred.

pyrocant (n.) Refers to a critical weakness in an individual. The weakness can be internal, such as an addiction, or external, such as a lover.

rahlman (n.) Savior.

rythe (n.) Ritual manner of assuaging honor granted by one who has offended another. If accepted, the offended chooses a weapon and strikes the offender, who presents him- or herself without defenses.

the Scribe Virgin (pr. n.) Mystical force who was counselor to the King as well as the keeper of vampire archives and the dispenser of privileges. Existed in a non-temporal realm and had extensive powers. Has relinquished her role in favor of another.

sehclusion (n.) Status conferred by the King upon a female of the aristocracy as a result of a petition by the female's family. Places the female under the sole direction of her *ghardian*, typically the eldest male in her household. Her *ghardian* then has the legal right to determine all manner of her life, restricting at will any and all interactions she has with the world.

shellan (n.) Female vampire who has been mated to a male. Females generally do not take more than one mate due to the highly territorial nature of bonded males.

symphath (n.) Subspecies within the vampire race characterized by the ability and desire to manipulate emotions in others (for the purposes of an energy exchange), among other traits. Historically, they have been discriminated against and, during certain eras, hunted by vampires. They are near extinction.

the Tomb (pr. n.) Sacred vault of the Black Dagger Brotherhood. Used as a ceremonial site as well as a storage facility for the jars of *lessers*. Ceremonies performed there include inductions, funerals, and disciplinary actions against Brothers. No one may enter except for members of the Brotherhood, the Scribe Virgin, or candidates for induction.

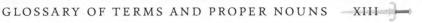

trahyner (n.) Word used between males of mutual respect and affection. Translated loosely as "beloved friend."

transition (n.) Critical moment in a vampire's life when he or she transforms into an adult. Thereafter, he or she must drink the blood of the opposite sex to survive and is unable to withstand sunlight. Occurs generally in the mid-twenties. Some vampires do not survive their transitions, males in particular. Prior to their transitions, vampires are physically weak, sexually unaware and unresponsive, and unable to dematerialize.

vampire (n.) Member of a species separate from that of Homo sapiens. Vampires must drink the blood of the opposite sex to survive. Human blood will keep them alive, though the strength does not last long. Following their transitions, which occur in their mid-twenties, they are unable to go out into sunlight and must feed from the vein regularly. Vampires cannot "convert" humans through a bite or transfer of blood, though they are in rare cases able to breed with the other species. Vampires can dematerialize at will, though they must be able to calm themselves and concentrate to do so and may not carry anything heavy with them. They are able to strip the memories of humans, provided such memories are short-term. Some vampires are able to read minds. Life expectancy is upward of a thousand years, or in some cases even longer.

wahlker (n.) An individual who has died and returned to the living from the Fade. They are accorded great respect and are revered for their travails.

whard (n.) Equivalent of a godfather or godmother to an individual.

THE CHOSEN

PROLOGUE

*F*irelight thrown from a shallow pit clawed across the damp walls of the cave, the rough rock face bleeding shadows. Outside the earthen womb, a great snowstorm raged, howls of bitter wind echoing into the throat of the shelter, joining the screams of the female upon the birthing pallet.

"Tis a male young," she panted a'twix her contracting burden. "A male!"

O'er her recumbent, straining flesh, looming as a curse upon her, the Black Dagger Brother Hharm cared naught for her pain.

"We shall learn soon enough."

"You will mate me. You promised—"

Her words choked off and her face squeezed into ugliness as her innards contorted to expel his progeny, and as he played witness, Hharm reflected how unattractive this aristocrat was in her laboring. She had not been thus when he had first met her and seduced her. Then, she had been proper and satin-clad, an appropriate vessel for his legacy with perfumed skin and shining, bouncy hair. Now? She was nothing but an animal, sweated and stringy—and whyever was this taking so long? He was so bored by the process, offended that he had to attend to her. This was the work for females, not a warrior such as himself.

But he was not mating her unless he had to.

If this was the son he had prayed for? Then yes, he would legitimize the young through a proper ceremony and give this female the status she was calling her due. If not? He would walk away and she would say nothing, because in the eyes of her class, she was be-fouled, her purity lost as her field had been plowed.

Indeed, Hharm had decided it was time for him to settle down. After centuries of debauchery and depravity, his age was setting upon him and he was considering for the first the legacy he would leave behind. At the current, bastards abounded, fruits of his loins that he knew not of, cared not for, associated never with—and for so long, that had been an acceptable by-product of him being accountable to naught and no one.

Now, though . . . he found himself wanting a proper family tree. And there was also the issue of a number of wagering debts, something this female's father could readily discharge for him—although again, if this was not a son, he was not mating her. He wasnae crazed, nor willing to whore himself out for pence. Further, there were countless females from the glymera *who coveted the status that came with mating a member of the Black Dagger Brotherhood.*

Hharm would not commit until he had a male offspring to raise properly from night one.

"Oh, do compose yourself," he snapped as she screamed again and his ears rang. "Be silent."

As with all things, however, she defied him. "It's coming . . . ! Your son is arriving!"

The shift she had on was dragged up to the base of her distended breasts by her twisting, fisted hands, her stretched and rounded belly put on a shameless display, her thin and pale thighs spread wide. What transpired at her core was disgusting, that which should have been a delicate and lovely entry for to accept the arousal of a male leaking all manner of fluid and discharge, the flesh swollen and distorted.

No, he would ne'er penetrate that again. Son or naught, mating or not, the perversion upon his eyes the now was nothing he could unsee.

Fortunately, matings of convenience were commonplace among aristocrats—not that he would have cared if they were not. Her needs were hardly what was important.

"He is upon you!" she shouted as her head fell back and her fingers scratched at the earth beneath her. "Your son . . . he is upon you!"

Hharm frowned and then widened his stare and his stance. She was not misapprised. For truth, there was a thing emerging from her interior . . . it was . . .

An abomination. A terrible, misshapen—

A foot. 'Twas a foot?

"Take your son from my body," she commanded between pants. "Pull him from me and hold him upon your beating heart, know he is flesh of your flesh!"

With his weapons and his battle gear latched upon his form, Hharm sank unto his knees as a second foot emerged.

"Pull him! Pull him!" Blood came forth and the female screamed again and the young did not vary its position. "Help me! He is affixed!"

Hharm stayed back from the straining mess and wondered how many of the females he had impregnated had gone through thus. Was it always so unpleasant, or was she just weak?

For truth, he should have let her do this on her own, but he did not trust her. The only way he could be certain that his young was male was to be at the birthing bed. Otherwise, he would nae have put it past her to swap out a far less desirable daughter for the coveted masculine offspring—of another's loins.

This was, after all, a negotiated transaction, and he knew all too well how such things were readily tampered with.

The sound that next arose from the female's open throat was of such volume and duration that it stopped his thoughts. Then came the grunting, the female's dirty, bloodied hands gripping the insides of her thighs and pulling up and out, widening the gulch at her apex. And just when he thought for certain she was dying, when he debated whether he would have to bury them both—and he promptly decided not, as the creatures of the woods would consume the remains readily—the young popped forward some distance, clearing some internal obstacle.

And there it was.

Hharm lunged forth. "My son!"

Without another thought, he reached out his hands and grabbed hold of the slippery little ankles. It was alive, the young was kicking with force, struggling against the confinement of the birthing canal.

"Come to me, my son," Hharm commanded as he pulled.

The female writhed in agony, but he gave no thought to her. Hands— tiny, perfectly formed hands—appeared next, along with the rounded belly and the chest that even in its nascent form promised great breadth.

"A warrior! 'Tis a warrior!" Hharm's heart beat hard, his triumph thundering in his ears. "My son shall carry forth my name! He shall be known as Hharm as I was before he!"

The female lifted her head, the veins in her neck standing out like coarse ropes under her too-pale skin. "You shall mate me," she rasped. "Swear to it . . . swear to it on your honor, or I shall hold him within me until he turns blue and enters the Fade."

Hharm smiled coldly, baring his fangs. And then he unsheathed one of his black daggers from his chest. Angling the sharp point down, he placed it over her lower belly.

"I will gut you like a deer to free it quite readily, nalla.*"*

"And who would feed your precious son? Your seed shall not survive without me to succor him."

Hharm thought about the raging storm outside. How far they were from vampire settlements. How little he knew of a young's requirements.

"You will mate me as promised," she groaned. "Swear it!"

Her eyes were bloodshot and crazed, her long hair sweated and tangled, her body naught that he could e'er a'rise again for. But her logic arrested him. To lose what he wanted in the face of precisely the arrangement he had been prepared to make, simply because she was presenting it as her will, was not a wise course.

"I swear it," he muttered.

With that, she bore down anew, and yes, now he would aid her, tugging in rhythm to her pushes.

"He is coming . . . he is . . ."

The young arrived out of her in a rush, fluid bursting forth with him, and as Hharm caught his son in his palms, he knew an unexpected joy that was so resonant—

His eyes narrowed as he cast his vision upon the face. Thinking that there was membrane or the like masking the young, he cast his hand down the features that were a mixture of his and the female's.

Alas . . . it changed naught.

"What curse is this?" he demanded. "What curse . . . is this!"

ONE

The Black Dagger Brotherhood were keeping him alive, so that they could kill him.

Given the sum of Xcor's earthly pursuits, which had been at their best violent, and at their worst downright depraved, it seemed an apt end for him.

He had been born upon a winter's night, during a historic blizzard's gale. Deep within a damp and dirty cave, as icy gusts had raked o'er the Old Country, the female who had carried him had screamed and bled to bring forth unto the Black Dagger Brother Hharm the son that had been demanded of her.

He had been desperately wanted.

Until he had fully arrived.

And that was the beginning of his story . . . which had ultimately landed him here.

In another cave. On another December's eve. And as with his actual birth, the wind howled to greet him, although this time, it was a return to consciousness as opposed to an expelling unto independent life that brought him forth.

As with a newly born young, he had little control over his body. Incapacitated he was, and that would have been true even without the steel chains and bars that were locked across his chest, his hips, his thighs. Machines, at odds with the rustic environs, beeped behind his head, monitoring his respiration, heart rate, blood pressure.

With all the ease of unoiled gears, his brain began to function properly beneath his skull, and when thoughts finally coalesced and formed rational sequences, he recalled the series of events that had resulted in him, the leader of the Band of Bastards, falling into the custody of what had been his enemies: an attack upon him from behind, a concussive fall, a stroke or some such that had rendered him prone and on life support.

At the non-extant mercy of the Brothers.

He had surfaced unto awareness once or twice during his captivity, recording his captors and his whereabouts in this earthen corridor that was inexplicably shelved with jars of all kinds. The returns to consciousness had never lasted long, however, the connectivity in his mental arena unsustainable for any length of time.

This emergence was different, however. He could sense the shift within his mind. Whate'er had been injured had finally healed and he was back from the foggy landscape of neither-life-nor-death—and staying on the vital side.

". . . really worry about is Tohr."

The tail end of the sentence uttered by a male entered Xcor's ear as a series of vibrations, the translation of which was on a delay, and whilst the words caught up to the syllables, he shifted his eyes over. Two heavily armed figures in black had their backs to him and he reclosed his lids, not wishing to reveal his change of status. Their identities were duly noted, however.

"Nah, he's tight." There was a soft scratching sound and then the smell of rich tobacco rose up. "And if he slips, I'll be there."

The deep voice who had first spoken became dry. "To chain our brother back in line—or help him murder this piece of meat?"

The Brother Vishous laughed like a serial killer. "Such a dim fucking view of me you got."

'Tis a wonder we are not better aligned, Xcor thought. These males were as bloodthirsty as he.

Such an alliance was never to be, however. The Brotherhood and the Bastards had been e'er on different sides of Wrath's kingship, the line drawn by the path of the bullet Xcor had put into the throat of that lawful leader of the vampire race.

And the price of his treason was going to be exacted here and soon upon him.

Of course, the irony was that a countervailing force had since interceded upon his destiny and taken his ambitions and focus far, far from the throne. Not that the Brotherhood knew any of it—and nor would they care. In addition to sharing an appetite for war, he and the Brothers had in common another core feature: Forgiveness was for the weak, pardoning the act of the pathetic, pity a capacity possessed by females, never fighters.

Even if they became aware that he no longer carried any aggression toward Wrath, they would not release him of the reckoning he had so rightfully earned. And given all that had transpired, he was not bitter or angry at what was coming his way. It was the nature of conflict.

He did find himself saddened, though—something that was not familiar to his makeup.

From out of memory, an image came unto his mind and took his breath away. It was of a tall, slender female in the white robing of the Scribe Virgin's sacred Chosen. Her blond hair waved down o'er her shoulders and trailed off at her hips on a gentle breeze, and her eyes were the color of jade, her smile a benediction he had done naught to deserve.

The Chosen Layla was what had changed everything for him, recasting the Brotherhood from target to tolerable, from enemy to co-existable tenant in the world.

In the short year and a half Xcor had known her, she had had more effect upon his black soul than anyone who had come before, evolving him a greater distance in a lesser time than he would have e'er thought possible.

The *Dhestroyer*, Vishous's fellow Brother, spoke anew. "Actually, I'm down with Tohr ripping him the fuck apart. He's earned the right."

The Brother Vishous cursed. "We all have. Gonna be hard to make sure there's anything left at the end for him to have at."

And herein was the conundrum, Xcor thought behind his closed lids. The only possible way out of this deadly scenario was to reveal the love he'd found for a female who was not his, never had been, and was not e'er going to be.

But he would not sacrifice the Chosen Layla for anyone or anything. Not even to save himself.

As Tohr walked through the pine forest of the Brotherhood's mountain, his shitkickers crunched over the frosted ground and a bracing wind hit him square in the face. In his wake, as tight on his heels as his shadow, he could feel his losses filing along with him, a grim, mournful lineup as tangible as chains.

The sense he was being pursued by his dead made him think about all those paranormal TV shows, the ones that tried to pin down whether ghosts actually existed. What a load of bullshit that was. The human hysteria around supposed misty entities floating up stairwells and making old houses creak with disembodied footsteps was so characteristic of that self-absorbed, drama-creating lesser species. It was one more thing Tohr hated about them.

And as usual, they missed the point.

The dead absolutely fucking haunted you, running their cold fingertips of remember-me up the back of your neck until you couldn't decide whether you wanted to scream from missing them . . . or from wanting to be left alone.

They stalked your nights and prowled your days, leaving a minefield of sorrow triggers in their path.

They were your first and last thought, the filter you tried to push aside, the invisible barrier between you and everyone else.

Sometimes, they were even more a part of you than the people in your life that you could actually touch and hold.

So yeah, nobody needed a dumb-ass TV show to prove the already known: Even as Tohr had found love with another female, his first *shel-*

lan, Wellsie, and the unborn son she had been carrying when she'd been murdered by the Lessening Society, were never further away from him than his own skin.

And now there had been yet another death in the Brotherhood household.

Trez's mate, Selena, had gone unto the Fade mere months ago, passing away from a disease for which there had been no cure and no relief and no understanding.

Tohr hadn't slept properly since.

Refocusing on the evergreens around him, he ducked down and pushed a limb out of his way, and then sidestepped a fallen trunk. He could have dematerialized to his destination, but his brain was banging around so violently in the prison of his skull that he doubted he could have concentrated enough to go ghost.

Selena's death had been one big-ass fucking trigger for him, an event affecting third parties that had nonetheless grabbed his snow globe and shaken it so hard that his inner flakes were whizzing around and refusing to settle.

He had been down in the training center when she had been called unto the Fade, and the moment of death had not been silent. It had been marked by a sound torn from Trez's soul, the audio equivalent of a gravestone—and Tohr knew that one well. He'd done it himself when he'd been told about his own female's death.

So, yeah, on the wings of her love's agony had Selena been carried forth from the earth unto the Fade—

Dragging himself out of that cognitive loop was like trying to pull a car from a ravine, the effort required tremendous, the progress made inch by inch.

Onward through the forest, though, through the woods, through the winter night, crushing what was underfoot, with those ghosts of his whispering behind him.

The Tomb was the Black Dagger Brotherhood's *sanctum sanctorum*, that hidden site where inductions occurred, and secret meetings were held, and the jars of slain *lessers* were kept. Located deep within the earth, in a labyrinth created by nature, traditionally it was off-limits to anybody who hadn't gone through the ceremony and been marked as a brother.

That rule had had to bend, however, at least with respect to its quarter-mile-long entrance hall.

As he came up to the cave system's inconspicuous entrance, he halted and felt his anger surge.

For the first time in his tenure as a brother, he was not welcome.

All because of a traitor.

Xcor's body was in there on the far side of the gates, halfway down the shelved passageway, lying on a gurney, his life force monitored and kept going by machines.

Until that bastard woke up and could be interrogated, Tohr was not allowed inside.

And his brothers were right not to trust him.

As he closed his eyes, he saw his King shot in the throat, relived the moment when Wrath's life had been slipping away along with his red blood, recast that scene as Tohr had had to save the last purebred vampire on the planet by cutting a hole in the front of his throat and sticking tubing from his Camelbak into that esophagus.

Xcor had ordered the assassination. Xcor had told one of his fighters to put a bullet through that male of worth's flesh, had plotted with the *glymera* to overthrow the rightful ruler—but the motherfucker had failed. Wrath had lived in spite of the odds, and in the first democratic election in the history of the race, had then been appointed the leader of all vampires, a position he now held by consensus as opposed to bloodline.

So fuck you very much, you sonofabitch.

Curling his hands into fists, Tohr easily ignored the creak of his leather gloves and the constriction along the backs of his knuckles. All he knew was a hatred so deep it was a mortal disease.

Fate had seen fit to take three from his and his own: Destiny had stolen from him his *shellan* and his young, and then taken Trez's love. You want to talk about balance in the universe? Fine. He wanted his balance, and that was only going to come when he snapped Xcor's neck and gouged the fucker's warm heart out from between his ribs.

It was about time for a source of evil to be taken out of commission and he was just the one to even the goddamn score.

And the waiting was now over. As much as he respected his brothers, he was done cooling his jets. Tonight was a sad anniversary for him and he was going to give his mourning a special little present.

Party time.

TWO

The squat crystal glass was so clean, so free of soap spots, dust, and debris, that its corpus was as both the air and the water within it: utterly invisible.

Half full, the Chosen Layla wondered. Or half empty?

As she sat upon a padded stool, between two sinks with golden fixtures, and a'fore a gold-leafed mirror reflecting the deep tub behind her, she stared at the surface of the liquid. The meniscus was concave, the water licking ever so slightly up the inside of the glass as if its more ambitious molecules were seeking to scale their confines and escape.

She respected the effort whilst mourning its futility. She knew well what it was to want to be free of that which you had been housed in through no fault of your own.

For centuries, she had been the water in the glass, poured unwittingly, by virtue solely of birth, into a role of service unto the Scribe Virgin. Along with her sisters, she had long performed the sacred duties of the Chosen up at the Sanctuary, worshiping the mother of the race, recording the events upon the earth for vampire posterity, awaiting a new Primale to be appointed so she could be impregnated and give birth to more Chosen and more Brothers.

But all that was done and dusted the now.

Leaning over the glass, she looked more closely at the water. She had been trained as an *ehros*, not a scribe, but she knew well the practice of peering into the seeing bowls and playing witness to history. Within the Scribing Temple, those Chosen tasked with recording the stories and lineages of the race had sat for hours upon hours, watching as births and deaths, love and matings, wars and times of peace unfolded, slender hands with sacred quills putting to parchment the details, keeping track of it all.

There were no pictures for her to see. Not here on earth.

And there were no more witnesses up above.

A new Primale had eventually come. But instead of laying with the stable of females, and continuing the Scribe Virgin's breeding program, he had taken the unprecedented step of freeing them all. The Black Dagger Brother Phury had broken the mold, broken tradition, broken the binds, and in doing so, the Chosen who had been sequestered since their planned births had embraced their liberation. No longer living, breathing representatives of rigid tradition, they had become individuals, developing their own likes and dislikes, dipping their toes in the waters of earthly reality, seeking and finding destinies that centered around self, not service.

In doing so, he had set in motion the demise of the immortal.

The Scribe Virgin was no more.

Her birthed son, the Black Dagger Brother Vishous, had sought her out in the Sanctuary above only to find her gone, a last missive written upon the wind for his eyes only.

She had said that she had a successor in mind.

No one knew who that was.

Sitting back, Layla regarded the white robe she wore. It was not the sacred kind she had clothed herself in for all those years. No, this one was from a place called Pottery Barn, and Qhuinn had bought it for her just last week. With the winter coming on hard, he was concerned that the mother of his young be always warm, always cared for.

Layla's hand went to her now-flat stomach. After having carried their daughter, Lyric, and their son, Rhampage, within her body for those many months, it was both strange and familiar to have naught within her womb—

Murmuring voices, low and deep, penetrated the door she had closed.

She had come in here from her bedroom to use the toilet.

She had stalled out after she had washed her hands.

Qhuinn and Blay, as usual, were with the young. Holding them. Cooing to them.

Each evening, she had to brace herself to witness the love, not among them and the young . . . but betwixt the two males. Indeed, the fathers exhibited a resonant, resplendent bond one to another, and although it was beautiful, its radiance made her feel the empty coldness in her own existence all the more.

Brushing away a tear, she instructed herself to pull it together. She couldn't go back into her bedroom with too-bright eyes and a red nose and flushed cheeks. Now was supposed to be a joyous time for their family of five. Now, with the twins having survived the emergency of their birth, and Layla having come through as well, they were all to revel in the relief that everyone was safe and sound.

Now was the happy life to be lived.

Instead, she was as yet the sad water in the invisible glass, clamoring to get out.

This time, however, the jail was of her own making, instead of her luck of genetic draw.

The definition of treason, at least according to the dictionary, was "the action of betraying someone or something"—

The knock on the closed door was soft. "Layla?"

She sniffed and turned on one of the faucets. "Hello!"

Blay's voice was quiet, as was his way. "Are you all right in there?"

"Oh, indeed. I have decided to give myself a bit of a facial treatment. I'm coming out promptly."

She got to her feet, bent down, and splashed her cheeks. Then she scrubbed her forehead and chin with a hand towel so that the flush was more evenly dispersed across her skin. Tightening the sash on her robe, she straightened her shoulders and went for the door, praying that she could keep her composure long enough to hustle them out to Last Meal.

But she had a reprieve.

As she opened things up, Blay and Qhuinn weren't even looking in her direction. They were bent over Lyric's bassinet.

"—Layla's eyes," Blay said as he reached in and let the young grab onto his finger. "Definitely."

"She has her *mahmen's* hair, too. I mean, check out the blond coming in."

Their love for the little one was incandescent, shining in their faces, warming their voices, tempering their movements so that everything they did was with care. And yet that was not what Layla focused on.

Her stare locked on Qhuinn's broad palm as it stroked up and down Blay's back. The caress of connection was unconscious on both sides, the proffer and the acceptance both nothing at all and everything that mattered. And as she played witness from across the room, she had to blink fast once again.

Sometimes kindness and love could be just as difficult as violence to witness. Sometimes, when you were on the outside looking in, watching two in-sync people was a scene from a horror film, the kind of thing that you wanted to look away from, forget about, banish the memory of— especially when you were about to go to bed for the day and facing hours upon hours of being alone in the dark.

The knowledge that she would never have that special love with anyone was—

Qhuinn glanced across at her. "Oh, hey."

He straightened and smiled, but she wasn't fooled. His eyes were going over her like he was profiling her—although mayhap that was not the case. Mayhap that was merely her paranoia talking.

She was *so* over living a double life. Yet, in the kind of cruel irony that seemed to be destiny's favorite source of amusement, the price of relieving her conscience would come at the expense of her very existence.

And how could she leave her young behind?

"—okay? Layla?"

As Qhuinn frowned at her, she shook herself and forced a smile. "Oh, I'm very well." She was assuming that had been an inquiry about her well-being. "Just fine, indeed."

Seeking to prove the lie, she approached the bassinets. Rhampage, or Rhamp, as he was known, was fighting the need for sleep, and as his sister made a cooing sound, his head turned and his hand reached out.

Funny, even at this young age, he seemed to recognize his station and want to protect her.

It was the breeding. Qhuinn was a member of the aristocracy, the result of generations of selective pairings, and even though his "defect" of having one blue eye and one green had rendered him beneath contempt in the opinions of both the *glymera* and his own family, the venerable nature of his bloodline could not be denied. And neither could the impact of his physical presence. At well over six and a half feet tall, his body was braided with great cuts of muscle, his flesh honed by both practice and the actualities of war into a weapon every bit as deadly as the guns and daggers he went unto the field with. The first member of the Black Dagger Brotherhood to be inducted on the basis of merit as opposed to lineage, he had not let the great tradition down. He never let anyone down.

In fact, Qhuinn was an altogether beautiful male, if in a rather raw way: His face was all angles from his having little to no body fat, and those mismatched eyes stared out from under dark brows. His black hair had been cut short recently, all but shaved on the bottom with the top slicked back, and as a result, his neck looked extra thick. With gunmetal-gray piercings in his ears, and an *ahstrux nohtrum* teardrop under his eye from when he had served as John Matthew's protector, he caught stares wherever he went.

Perhaps because people, vampires and human alike, worried about what he might be capable of if displeased.

Blay, on the other hand, was the opposite, as approachable as Qhuinn was best avoided in a dark alley.

Blaylock, son of Rocke, had red hair, and skin that was a shade lighter than most in the species. He was every bit as big, but when you were around him, the first impression he made was of intelligence and heart, rather than brawn. Still, no one argued with how impressive he was in the field. Layla had heard the stories, although never from him, as he was not one to boast, create unnecessary drama, or draw attention to himself.

She loved them both with all her heart.

And the separation she felt from them was all on her side.

"Look at this," Qhuinn said as he nodded at the young. "We got two lights-out specials over here—well, one and a half."

As he smiled, she wasn't fooled. His eyes were continuing to go over her face, searching for signs of exactly what she was attempting to hide. To make his examination more difficult, she backed off.

"They are good sleepers, thank the Virgin Scribe—er, thank Fates."

"You coming down with us for Last Meal tonight?" he asked in an easy tone.

Blay straightened. "Fritz said he'd make you anything you like."

"He is always so kind." She went across to the bed and made a show of lying down against the pillows. "Actually, I got peckish around two so I went to the kitchen and had oatmeal and toast. Coffee. Orange juice. Breakfast for lunch, as it were. You know, sometimes one feels like re-winding the night and starting fresh at the middle."

Pity that could be done only in a metaphoric way.

Although . . . would she really have chosen not to have met Xcor?

Yes, she thought. She would prefer never to have known of his exis-tence.

The love of her life, her Blay, her match of the heart and soul . . . was a traitor. And her emotions for the male had been an open wound into which the bacteria of betrayal had entered and spread.

Thus now she was here, in this prison of her own making, tortured by the fact that she had consorted with the enemy; first because she had been duped . . . and then later because she had wanted to be in Xcor's presence.

They had parted badly, however, him putting an end to their clandestine meetings when she had forced him to acknowledge his feelings. And then things had gone from sad to tragic when he had been caught and taken into the Brotherhood's custody.

At first, she had been unable to gain information on his condition. But then she had traveled in the way of a Chosen, going unto him and witnessing him near death in a stone corridor filled with jars of every shape and color.

There had been naught that she could do. Not without coming forward and exposing herself—and even if she did as such, she could not save him.

So she was stuck here, a ghost haunting a tangled stretch of emotions studded with the poison ivy of guilt and regret, never, ever to be free.

"—right? I mean . . ." As Blay continued speaking to her about something or another, she had to force herself not to rub her eyes. ". . . end of a night when you've just been up here with the young. Which is not to say that you don't like being with them."

Get out, she willed the two males. Please, just go away and leave me be.

It wasn't that she didn't want them with the young or that she held some kind of animus unto Lyric and Rhamp's fathers. She just needed to breathe, and every time either one of the fighters stared at her as they were doing the now, that became next to impossible.

"Does that sound good?" Qhuinn asked. "Layla?"

"Oh, yes, of course." She had no idea what she had agreed to, but she made sure she smiled. "I'm just going to rest now. They were up a lot during the day."

"I wish you'd let us help more." Blay frowned. "We're just a knock away."

"You are both out fighting most nights. Sleep is required."

"You matter, too, though."

Layla shifted her eyes to the bassinets, and as she remembered cradling the young in her arms and feeding them, she felt even worse. They deserved a *mahmen* who was better than her, one uncomplicated and unburdened by decisions that should never have been made, one who was uncontaminated by a weakness for a male who should never have been approached . . . much less loved.

"I do not matter at all in comparison to them," she whispered starkly. "They are everything."

Blay came over and took her hand, his blue eyes full of warmth. "No, you are also very important. And *mahmen* need time for themselves."

To do what? Ruminate on regrets? No, thank you, she thought.

"I shall go to my grave without them and enjoy my own company, then." As she realized how grim that sounded, she hurried forth with, "Besides, all too soon they will be grown. It will happen faster than the three of us know."

There was further conversation at that point, none of which she heard because of the screaming in her head. But then, finally, she was left in peace when the bonded pair departed.

The fact that she was so glad to see them go was one more sadness to carry.

Shifting off the bed, she went back to the bassinets, her eyes watering once again. Wiping her cheeks, over and over, she took a tissue out of a hidden pocket and blew her nose. The young were fully asleep, their lids closed, their faces turned to each other as if they were communicating telepathically in their slumber. Perfect little hands and precious little feet, rounded, healthy bellies wrapped in a flannel sheet. They were such good young, cheery and smiley when awake, peaceful and angelic when at rest. Rhampage was gaining weight faster than Lyric, but she seemed heartier than he, fussing less when being changed or bathed, meeting eyes with greater focus.

As tears dropped off Layla's face and landed on the carpet at her feet, she didn't know how much longer she could do this.

Before she was aware of moving, she went to the house phone and dialed a four-digit number.

The *doggen* she summoned arrived in a moment, and Layla put her social mask in place, smiling at the servant with a serenity she did not feel. "*Thank you for watching my most precious ones*," she said in the Old Language.

The nursemaid replied with happy words and sparkling eyes, and it was all Layla could do to withstand the two or three seconds of communication. Then she was out of the room, and traveling on quick, slippered feet down the hall of statues. When she reached the doors at the far end, she pushed them wide and entered the staff wing.

As with all mansions of its size and distinction, the Brotherhood's home required tremendous servant support, and the *doggens'* rooms lined a number of corridors, the segregations of age, sex, and job titles forming communities within the larger whole. Within the maze of hallways, Layla chose her direction with no particular thought other than the goal of locating a room that was unclaimed—and she found one some three doors forth from some turn she made. Entering the bare, simple space, she went over to the window, cracked the sash, and closed her eyes. Her heart was pounding and her head was swirling, but as she breathed deep and scented the fresh, cold air . . .

. . . she ghosted away through the whistling gap she'd created, becoming one with the night, her molecules scrambling forth and heading away from the Brotherhood mansion.

As usual, the freedom was temporary.

But desperate as she was, she took it in like oxygen to the suffocated.

THREE

huinn was a male's male. And not just because he was a fighter and had a mate who was a dude.

Yeah, sure, before he'd settled down with his Blay, he'd liked fucking females and women well enough. But then again, his data screen for sexual partners had been set so low that even vacuum cleaners and the occasional tailpipe had been candidates.

No sheep, though. #standards

But he couldn't say that females had ever captivated or particularly interested him. It wasn't that there was shit wrong with them or that he didn't respect them in the same way he did anything else rocking the living-and-breathing job descript. They simply weren't his cuppa, as it were.

On a night like tonight, however, he regretted his lack of experience. Just because he'd done some laps with the opposite in the sack didn't mean he was equipped in any way to deal with what was confronting him now.

As he and Blay came to the bottom of the grand staircase, he stopped and looked at his mate. In the background, emanating from the billiards room across the foyer, the sounds of deep male voices, thumping music, and ice hitting crystal glasses announced that the Brotherhood pool tournament was already in full swing.

Qhuinn smiled in a way he hoped looked chill. "Hey, I'll meet you in there, 'kay? I'm supposed to go down and talk to Doc Jane about my shoulder for, like, ten minutes? Shouldn't be long."

"Of course. Do you want me to go with you?"

For a second, Qhuinn got lost just staring at his male. Blaylock, son of Rocke, was everything he himself was not: Blay was flawless with a Michelangelo body, a face to die for, and a head of red hair that was thick and shiny as a pony's tail; he was smart, but also levelheaded, which made all the difference; and he was as steady and reliable as a granite mountain, the kind of guy who never wavered.

In all the ways that mattered, compared to Blay, Qhuinn was the plastic tub to the porcelain bowl, the partial set to the perfect dozen, the crack down the middle to the never-been-broken.

For some reason, though, Blay had picked him. Against all odds, the disowned, bad-seed son of a Founding Family, the sex fiend with the mismatched eyes, the mercurial, hostile, snarling stray . . . had somehow landed Prince Charming, and shit, it was almost enough to make you religious.

Blay was the reason he breathed, the home he'd never had, the sunlight that powered his earth.

"Qhuinn?" Those iridescent blue eyes frowned. "Are you okay?" "Sorry." He leaned in and pressed his lips to the male's jugular. "Distracted. But you do that to me, don't you."

As Qhuinn eased back, Blay was blushing—and aroused. And that scent was a diversion not easily conquered.

Except he had a real problem he needed to deal with.

"Tell the brothers I'll be fast." Qhuinn nodded in the direction of the billiards room. "And I'ma beat their ass."

"You always do. Even Butch."

The words were soft, and backed up with an adoration that made Qhuinn count every one of his blessings.

Giving in to instinct, Qhuinn got up close again and whispered in the guy's ear, "You may want to food up at Last Meal. I'm going to keep you busy all day long."

With a quick lick of the throat he intended to work on later, Qhuinn stalked off before he couldn't leave his mate at all.

Heading around the base of the staircase, he went through a hidden door and down into the tunnel system that connected the components of the estate. The Brotherhood's underground training center was located about a quarter of a mile away from the mansion, and this subterranean pass connecting the two was a broad, concrete expanse lit by fluorescent ceiling panels.

As he stomped along, his footfalls echoed all around, like his shitkickers were applauding his initiative.

He wasn't so sure they were right, though. He had no fucking clue what he was doing here.

The door into the back of the supply closet opened without a sound after he entered the correct code, and then he was passing by shelves of legal pads, printer paper, pens, and other Staples shit. The office beyond presented your typical desk-chair-computer and old-school filing cabinets setups, none of it particularly registering as he punched through the glass door across the way and hit the corridor beyond. With long, impatient strides, he went by all kinds of professional-grade facilities, from the full-size gym and the Dwayne Johnson–worthy weight room, to the locker rooms and the first of the classrooms.

The clinic portion of the training center had a number of treatment spaces, an OR, and several patient bunks. Doc Jane, V's *shellan*, and Dr. Manny Manello, Payne's mate, took care of all manner of war-related injuries in it as well as household-whoopsies, and even the pregnancies and deliveries of L.W. as well as Nalla, Lyric, and Rhampage.

He knocked on the first door he came to, and he didn't have to wait more than a heartbeat.

"Come on in!" Doc Jane called out from the other side.

The good doctor was in surgical scrubs and Crocs as she sat at the computer on the far side of the well-equipped clinical space, her fingers flying over the keys as she updated someone's record, her head bent, her short blond hair sticking up like she'd been dragging her hand through it for hours.

"One sec . . ." She punched the enter key and spun herself around. "Oh, hey there, Dad. How are you?"

"Oh, you know, soaking up the love."

"Those babies of yours are amazing. And I don't even like kids."

Her smile was as easygoing as apple pie. Her forest-green eyes, on the other hand, were laser sharp.

"Thanks to you, they're doing great."

Annnnnnnd cue the quiet. As the conversation stalled out, he wandered around because he couldn't stay still, checking out the shiny, sterile equipment in the stainless-steel cabinets, inspecting the empty gurney under the operating light, jacking up his leathers.

Doc Jane just sat there on her little stool, calmly and quietly letting him thrash around in his own head. And when her phone went off, she let it go to voice mail without even checking to see who it was.

"I'm probably wrong," he said eventually. "You know, what the fuck do I know."

Doc Jane smiled. "I actually think you're a very smart guy."

"Not about shit like this." Clearing his throat, he told himself to get on with it—even though Doc Jane didn't seem in a rush, he was annoying himself. "Look . . . I love Layla."

"Of course you do."

"And I want the best for her. She's the mother of my children. I mean, behind Blay, she's my partner because of those kids."

"Absolutely."

Crossing his arms over his chest, he cut the pacing and faced off at the good doctor. "I'm not saying I know anything about females. Like, about their moods and shit. Except . . . Layla's crying a lot. I mean, she tries to hide it from Blay and me, but . . . every time we go in to see her, I find Kleenex wads in the wastepaper basket, and her eyes are too shiny, and her cheeks are flushed. She smiles, but it never reaches past the surface. Her eyes are . . . fucking tragic. And . . . I don't know what to do, I just know it's not right."

Doc Jane nodded. "How is she with the kids?"

"Great, as far as I can see. She's totally devoted to them, and they are thriving. Matter of fact, the only time I see her even halfway to happy, it's when she's holding them." He cleared his throat. "So I guess what I'm wondering . . . asking . . . whatever, is, like, can't pregnant females, once they're unpregnant, can't they, like . . ."

Jesus, he was winning all kinds of awards here for self-expression. And the technical terms he was throwing around? He was one step away from being an M.D. like her.

Fuck.

But at least Doc Jane seemed to recognize that his conversational airplane was out of runway: "I think you're asking about postpartum depression." When he nodded, she continued, "And I can tell you that it's not uncommon in vampires, and it can be debilitating. I've spoken with Havers about it before, and I'm really glad you're raising the issue. Sometimes the new mom isn't even aware of it becoming an issue."

"Is there a test for the . . . or a . . . I don't know."

"There are a couple of different ways of assessing what's going on, and behavior is a big one. I can absolutely talk with her, and I can run some blood tests to check her hormones. And yes, there are a lot of things we can do to treat her and support her."

"I don't want Layla to think I'm going behind her back or anything."

"Totally understandable. And, hey, I was going to go up and see her and the young anyway. I can frame everything in terms of routine assessments. I won't have to bring you into the discussion at all."

"You're the best."

With his business done, he supposed it was time to go back to his mate and the billiards tournament. But he didn't leave. For some reason, he couldn't.

"It's not your fault," Doc Jane said.

"I got her pregnant. What if my . . ." Okay, yes, she was a doctor, but he still didn't want to say the word *sperm* around her. Which was nuts. "What if my half is the cause—"

The door opened wide and Manny put his head in. "Hey, you ready—oh, sorry."

"We're almost done here." Doc Jane smiled. "And you didn't see the two of us together."

"You got it." Manny knocked on the jamb. "If there's anything I can help with, let me know."

And then the guy was gone as if he'd never been.

Doc Jane got up and came over. She was shorter than Qhuinn was, and not built like a nearly three-hundred-pound male. But she seemed to tower over him, the authority in her voice and her eyes exactly what he needed to calm his irrational side.

As she put her hand on his forearm, her stare was steady. "It's not your fault. This is nature's course sometimes and with some pregnancies."

"I put those young in her."

"Yes, but assuming this is a case of her hormones regulating themselves following birth, no one is to blame. Besides, you've done the right thing coming here, and you can also do a lot to help her by just talking to her and giving her the time and space to talk to you in return. And honestly, I'd already noticed that she hasn't been coming to meals. I think we need to encourage her to join the rest of us so she knows how much we all are there for her."

"Okay. Yeah."

Doc Jane frowned. "May I give you a piece of advice?"

"Please."

She squeezed his arm. "Don't feel responsible for something over which you have no control. It's a recipe for stress that will make you insanely miserable. I know that's easier said than done, but try to keep it in mind? I've seen you be with her every step of the way during the pregnancy. There's nothing you haven't done or wouldn't do for her, and you're a fantastic father. Only good things are ahead, I promise you."

Qhuinn took a deep breath. "Yeah."

Even as his worry persisted, he reminded himself that over the course of Layla's pregnancy, he had learned he could trust Doc Jane. The healer had helped him walk the life-and-death road, and she had never let him down, never led him astray, never lied to him or offered bad advice.

"It's all going to be okay," she promised.

Unfortunately, as it turned out, the good doctor was wrong.

But then she had no control over fate.

And neither did he.

FOUR

The young was ruined. Possessing naught but a mutated, ugly version of Hharm's features, the upper lip all wrong, like that of a hare.

Hharm dropped the babe upon the cave's dirty ground, and the thing made no sound as it landed, the arms and legs barely moving, its flesh of blue and gray, the cord still linking it with the female. It was going to die, as all results against the rules of breeding and nature should—and that outcome was not cause for indignation.

The fact that Hharm had been cheated, however, was. He had wasted these eighteen months, these number of hours, that moment of hope and happiness on a monstrosity that was untenable. And what he knew for sure? It wasnae his fault.

"What have you wrought?" he demanded of the female.

"A son!" She arched back as if in agony anew. "I have brought forth—"

"A curse." Hharm rose to his full height. "Your womb is foul. It has corrupted the gift of my seed and produced that—"

"Your son—"

"Regard it for yourself! See with thine eyes! 'Tis an abomination!"

The female strained and lifted her head. "He is perfect, he is—"

Hharm shoved the young with his boot, causing it to jerk its tiny limbs and let out a weak cry. "Even you cannot deny what is in plain sight!"

Her bloodshot eyes latched onto the young, and then widened. "It is . . ."

"You did that," he announced.

Her lack of argument was an inevitable capitulation, for the defect was undeniable. And then she moaned as if she were in labor still, her bloody fingers clawing at the cold ground, her legs trembling as they split wider. Upon further straining, something passed out of the female, and he thought perhaps there was another. Indeed, his heart caught with optimism as he prayed that the first was the dhoble, the cursed of a pair of twins.

Alas, no, it was some manner of the female's interior, perhaps her stomach or bowel.

And the young cried on, its chest pumping in and out with lesser effect.

"You shall die here and so shall he," Hharm said without care.

"I shall not—"

"Your innards are coming out."

"The young is . . ." she mumbled. "The young . . ."

"Is an abomination of nature against the Scribe Virgin's will."

The female fell silent and went lax as if the process of expulsion were concluded, and Hharm waited for a final paroxysm wherein her soul departed from her body. Except she continued to breathe and meet his stare . . . and exist. What manner of trickery was this? The idea she would not go to Dhunhd for this was an insult.

"This is your doing," he spat at the female.

"How do you know 'twas not your seed that was—"

Hharm put his boot at her throat and pressed down, cutting off her words. As a tide of rage made his warrior body seek mortal action, only the fact that this occurrence could be in punishment for things he'd done previously stopped him from crushing her neck.

She must pay, he thought abruptly. Yes, the fault was hers, and for the disappointment she had caused him, the female had to atone.

Hissing, he bared his fangs. "I shall let you live such that you may raise this monstrosity and be seen with it. That is your curse for cursing me—he *shall e'er be upon your neck, an amulet of damnation, and if I find out that thing has died, I will hunt you down and slaughter you by inches. Then I will kill that sister of yours, all of her progeny, and your parents."*

"What say you!"

Hharm leaned down, the pounding flush in his face and head one that was familiar. "You heard my word. You know my will. Challenge me at your peril."

As she cowered back, he stepped away and regarded the mess of the birth, the pathetic female, that horrid result—and he slashed his hand through the air, wiping them out of his timeline. As the blizzard howled, and the fire died down, he went for his coat of pelts.

"You ruined my son," he said as he swung the heavy weight of furs o'er his shoulders. "Your punishment is to raise that horror as a proclamation of your failure."

"You are not the King," she countered weakly. "To order aught."

"'Tis a social service unto my fellow males." He jabbed a finger in the direction of the wailing newborn. "With that on your hip, no one else will lay upon you and suffer similarly."

"You cannot force me thus!"

"Oh, but I can and I shall."

She was a spoiled, defiant female by nature, and that was what had first attracted him unto her—he had had to teach her the errors of her ways and the instruction had been quite intriguing for a time. Indeed, there had been but one instance when she had attempted to exercise dominance over him. Once, and never again.

"Do not test me, female. You did a'fore and recall the end result."

As she paled, he nodded down at her. "Yes. That."

He had nearly killed her the night he had had to show her that whereas he would be with whomever he wished, whenever and wherever, she would ne'er be permitted to lay with another male whilst she was even tangentially associated with him. It had been shortly thereafter that she had decided her only chance at reining him in would be in providing him with the son he sought, and at the same time, he had begun to think in terms of his legacy.

Alas, she had failed in her endeavor.

"I hate you," she groaned.

Hharm smiled. "The feeling is mutual. And again, I say that you best ensure that thing lives. If I find out you killed him, I shall take his death from your flesh and that of your entire bloodline."

With that, he spat twice on the ground at her feet, once for her and once for the young. And then he strode away as she called for him and the forsaken young wailed in the cold.

Outside, the blizzard raged on, swirls of snow blinding him only to relent like a flock of birds scattering to reveal the landscape. In the valley down below, mountains rose off the shores of a lake basin, the snowdrifts upon the frozen water as waves would be in the warmer months. All was dark, and frigid, and lifeless, but he refused to find portent in what he beheld.

With his dagger hand itching, and his hostility upon its inner charging steed, he told himself to take no mind of this outcome.

He would find another womb.

Somewhere, there was a female who would give him the legacy he deserved and required. And he would find her and have her swell with his seed.

There would be a proper son for him. He would have it no other way.

FIVE

As Tohr approached the mouth of the Brotherhood's sacred cave, he snuck into the damp interior, and once inside, the smell of dirt and a distant source of flame irritated his sinuses. His eyes adjusted immediately, and when he continued on, he quieted the falls of his shitkickers. He didn't want to be heard, even though his presence was going to be apparent readily enough.

The gates were far in, and made of old iron bars thick as a warrior's forearm and tall as trees, a steel mesh soldered on to them to prevent dematerialization. Torches hissed and flickered on either side, and beyond, he could see the beginnings of the great corridor that led even further into the earth.

Stopping at the enormous barrier, he took out a copper key, and felt no remorse that he'd stolen the thing from the drawer of Wrath's ornate desk. He'd apologize for the theft later.

And also for what he was going to do next.

Unlocking the mechanism, he pulled the colossal weight open, stepped in, and relocked things behind himself. Walking forward, he followed the natural pathway that had been expanded with chisel and brute muscle, and then set wtih wooden shelves. On the various planks, hundreds upon hundreds upon hundreds of jars provided a playground for shadows and light.

The vessels were of all different shapes and sizes, and came from different eras from the ancient to the modern, but what was inside each one was the same: the heart of a *lesser*. Since the inception of the war with the Lessening Society, way back in the Old Country, the Brotherhood had been marking their enemy kills by claiming the jars of their victims and bringing them here to add to the collection.

Part trophy, part fuck-you to the Omega, it was legacy. It was pride. It was expectation.

And perhaps it was no more. Slayers were so few and far between in the streets of Caldwell and elsewhere now that they had to be closing in on the end.

Tohr did not feel any joy in the accomplishment. But that was probably due to tonight's terrible anniversary.

It was hard to feel anything but the loss of his Wellsie on what would have been her birthday.

Rounding a subtle curve, he stopped. Up ahead, the scene was like something out of a movie that couldn't decide whether it was *Indiana Jones, Grey's Anatomy,* or *The Matrix.* In the midst of all the old stone walls, and raw-flamed torches, and mismatched, dusty jars, a thicket of beeping and blinking medical equipment was running interference with a body on a gurney. And beside the prisoner? Two massive male vampires covered from head to toe in black leather and black weapons.

Butch and V were the Frick and Frack of the Brotherhood, the former human homicide cop and the son of the race's Creator, the good Catholic boy and the sexual deviant, the wardrobe addict and the tech tsar, united by a common devotion to the Boston Red Sox and a mutual respect and affection that knew no limit.

V tweaked to Tohr's presence first, the brother wheeling around so fast, ashes flew off the lit end of his hand-rolled. "Oh, hell no, no fucking way! You're out of here!"

That opinion, regardless of its volume, was easy to ignore as Tohr focused on the slab of meat on the gurney. Xcor was lying there, tubes going in and out of him like he was a car engine about to be jumped, his breathing regular—wait, not regular.

V stepped to Tohr, going close-up and then some. And what do you know, the brother had taken out his poodle shooter—and the muzzle of the forty was pointed directly into Tohr's face.

"I mean it, my brother."

Tohr looked over that heavy shoulder at their prisoner. And found himself smiling grimly. "He's awake."

"No, he's not—"

"His breathing just changed." Tohr pointed to that bare chest. "Look."

Butch frowned and went across to the captive. "Well, well, well . . . wakey-wakey, motherfucker."

V twisted around. "Sonofabitch."

But that gun didn't move, and neither did Tohr. As much as he wanted at Xcor, he was going to deep-throat a bullet if he took one step further: V was the least sentimental of the brothers and about as patient as a rattle-snake.

At that moment, Xcor's eyes blinked open. In the flickering light of the torches, they looked black, but Tohr remembered they were some kind of blue. Not that he cared.

V put his face in the way, those diamond eyes like daggers. "This is not going to be the birthday present you give your dead *shellan*."

Tohr peeled his lip off his fangs. "Fuck you."

"Not going to happen. Call me all the shit you want, but no. You know how things are going to go down and you are not at bat yet."

Butch grinned at their captive. "We've been waiting for you to join the party. Can I get you a drink? Maybe some mixed nuts before we put you in the upright position and take off? No reason to show you the fucking exit. You ain't gotta worry about that."

"Let's go, Tohr," V said. "Now."

Tohrment bared his fangs, but not at his brother. "You bastard, I'm going to kill—"

"Nope, not doing this." V hooked an arm around Tohr's bicep and all but dragged him into a do-si-do. "Outside—"

"You're not God—"

"And neither are you, which is why you're leaving."

In the back of his mind, Tohr was aware the rat fucker had a point. He was not even halfway rational—and P.S., fuck V for remembering what night it was.

His beloved *shellan*, his first love, would have been two hundred and twenty-six. And she would have had a two-year-old in her arms.

But fate had not provided that.

"Don't make me shoot you," V said roughly. "Come on, my brother. *Please.*"

The fact that the p-word came out of Vishous's mouth was what did it. The shit was just that shocking, disarming Tohr from the swords of his anger and madness.

"Come on, Tohr."

This time, Tohr allowed himself to be led off, his grand scheme deflating, the too-quiet aftermath of his craziness making him shake in his skin. What the fuck had he been doing? What the *fuck*?

Yeah, he had been granted the right to kill Xcor by royal proclamation, but only when he was released by Wrath to do so. And that had explicitly *not* happened yet.

This could have been a mess of treasonous proportions.

Talk about trading places. One dead betrayer for a living, breathing one.

When they came up to the gate that Tohr had unlocked to get access, V put out his gloved hand. "Key."

Tohr didn't look at the brother as he took the thing from his leather jacket and handed it over. After some clanking and a creak, the way was open and Tohr walked forward without prompting, hands on his hips, shitkickers grinding into the dirt, head down.

When there was another round of metal-on-metal, he figured he was being locked out on his own. But then V was right next to him on the far side.

"I promise you," the brother said. "You and you alone will kill him."

Was that going to be enough, Tohr wondered. Would anything ever be enough?

Before they came up to the mouth of the cave, Tohr stopped. "Sometimes . . . life just isn't fair."

"No, it isn't."

"I hate that. I fucking hate that. I go through . . . periods of time, not just nights, but weeks, sometimes even a month or two . . . when I forget about everything. But the shit always comes back, and after a while, you can't hold it in anymore. You just can't." He banged the side of his head with his fist. "It's this worm inside me, and I know killing Xcor won't distract me for longer than ten minutes. But on a night like tonight, I'd take even that."

There was a *shhcht* as V lit up a hand-rolled. "I don't know what to say, my brother. I'd tell you to pray about it, but there's no one up there to hear you."

"Not sure your mother was ever listening. No offense."

"None taken." V exhaled. "Trust me."

Tohr focused on the way out of the cave, and as he tried to take a breath, he was strangely exhausted. "I'm tired of fighting the same fight. Ever since Wellsie was . . . murdered . . . I feel like a limb of mine has never healed, and I can't take the hurt one more second. Not for one more goddamn second. Even if it just migrated to another place, it would be better."

There was a long silence between them, only the muffled howl of the winter wind breaking up the quiet in the cave.

Eventually, V cursed. "I wish I knew what would help you, my brother. I mean, if you need a reassuring hug . . . I can probably pay someone to give you one."

Tohr shook his head as his upper lip twitched into a smile. "That's almost funny."

"Yeah, I'm going for levity." V exhaled again. "It's either that or I shoot you, and I'd hate filling out all of Saxton's paperwork, true?"

"I can see your point." Tohr scrubbed his face. "Totally . . ."

V's diamond eyes shifted over. "Just know that I'm sorry. You don't deserve any of this." A heavy hand landed on Tohr's shoulder and squeezed. "If I could take the pain for you, I would."

As Tohr blinked fast, he thought it was a good thing V wasn't a hugger, or there would be a serious fucking breakdown happening all over the place.

The kind of breakdown a male didn't come back from in one piece.

Then again, was he really whole now?

sHAdoWs Nightclub, downtown Caldwell

Trez Latimer felt a little like a god as he stared out of the glass wall of his second-floor office at his club. Down below, in the converted warehouse's vast open area, a crowd of sexed-up humans established patterns of attraction and disdain in a tumultuous sea of deep purple lasers and pounding bass beats.

In large measure, his clientele were millennials, that generation born between 1980 and 2000. Defined by the Internet, the iPhone, and a lack of economic opportunity, at least according to the human media, they were a demographic of lost moralists, committed to saving each other, preserving the rights of everyone, and championing a false utopia of mandated liberal thinking that made McCarthyism looked nuanced.

But they were also, in the manner of youth, baselessly hopeful.

And how he envied them that.

As they collided and crashed into each other, he witnessed the rapture on their faces, the rampant optimism that they would find true love and happiness this very evening—in spite of all the other nights that they had come to his club and dawn had ushered in nothing but exhaustion, a new STD, and a crap load of shame-based self-doubt as they wondered exactly what they had done and with who.

He suspected, however, that for most of them the cure for that angst was two hours of sleep, a Starbucks venti latte, and a shot of penicillin.

When you were that young, when you had yet to face challenges that you couldn't even begin to comprehend, your resilience knew no bounds.

And there was where he wished to trade places with them.

It was odd to pedestal humans on any level. As a two-hundred-plus-year-old Shadow, Trez had long viewed those rats without tails as an inferior, inconvenient clutter on the planet, rather like ants in one's kitchen or mice in the basement. Except you weren't allowed to exterminate the humans. Too messy. Better to tolerate them than risk a species exposure by murdering them just to free up parking spaces, supermarket lines, and your Facebook feed.

And yet here he was, aching in his chest to be in the shoes of even one of them, if only for an hour or two.

Unprecedented.

Then again, they hadn't changed. He had.

My queen, is it time for you to go? Tell me if it is.

As memories bullied through his brain, he covered his eyes and thought, oh, God, not again. He didn't want to go back to the Brotherhood's clinic . . . to the bedside of his beloved Selena, to him dying on the inside while she expired in fact.

In truth, however, he had never left those events, even as calendar days suggested the contrary. After the passage of well over a month, he could still recall each and every detail about the scene, from her tortured breathing to the panic in her stare to the tears that rolled down her face and his.

His Selena had been struck by a disease known to rarely affect members of her sacred class. Throughout the generations of Chosen, certain of them had had the Arrest, and it was a horrible way to die, your mind left alive in the frozen shell of your body, no escape possible, no treatment to help you, no one to save you.

Not even the male who loved you more than life itself.

As Trez's heart tripped in his chest, he dropped his hands, shook his head, and tried to reconnect with reality. He had been struggling recently with these intrusive episodes, and they were getting more frequent instead of less so—something that made him worry about his sanity. He'd heard that adage that "time heals all wounds," and shit, maybe that was true for other people. For him? His mourning had transitioned from the incandescent pain at the beginning, an agony so hot it rivaled the flames of her funeral pyre, to this chronic racetrack of reminiscing that seemed to spin ever faster around the open-field fulcrum of his loss.

His own voice echoed in his head: *Do I understand you correctly? Do you want this . . . to end?*

By the time Selena's final moments had arrived, she could no longer speak. They had had to rely on a previously agreed-upon communication system that presupposed she would have control over her eyelids right up until the end: one blink for no . . . two for yes.

Do you want this to end . . . ?

He had known what her answer was going to be. Had read it in her exhausted, distant, dimming stare. But that had been one of those times in life when you'd wanted to be absolutely, positively sure.

She had blinked once. And then again.

And he had been by her side when the drugs that stopped her heart and gave her the relief she needed had taken her away.

In all of his years, he never would have imagined that kind of suffering. On both their parts. He couldn't have created a worse death out of any sort of nightmare, and he couldn't possibly have fathomed that he would have to give the nod to Manny to administer the shot, to be screaming in his head as his love faded away, to be left on his own for the rest of his nights.

The only comfort was that her suffering was over.

The only reality was that his was just beginning.

In the immediate aftermath, he had found solace in the fact that he would rather have been the one to have to miss her as opposed to the other way around. But as time had continued, he had overused that panacea, as it was the only one he had, and now it didn't work anymore.

So there was nothing to relieve him. He'd tried drinking, but alcohol only served to uncap what fragile hold he had on his tears. He didn't care for food at all. Sex was completely out of the question. And no one would let him fight—it wasn't like the Brothers and iAm didn't recognize he was unhinged.

So what was he left with? Nothing but dragging himself through the nights and days, and praying for the most basic of relief: a breath unhindered, a stretch of mental calm, an hour's worth of undisturbed slumber.

Reaching out, he touched the angled glass pane that was his window on what he considered was the other world, the one outside his insular hell. Funny to think that what he now considered as "other" had once been "real" . . . and even without the separation of species, age, and this lofty perch above the club's fray, he was so far apart from all of them.

He had a feeling he would always be apart from everyone.

And honestly, he just couldn't keep going like this.

This mourning had broken him, and if it weren't for the fact that those who committed suicide were denied entrance unto the Fade, he would have put a bullet in his brain about forty-eight hours after the death.

I can't keep going one more night, he thought.

"Please . . . help me . . ."

He had no fucking clue who he was talking to. On the vampire side, the Scribe Virgin was no more—and in his current frame of mind, he could totally understand why she would want to drop the mic and walk offstage from her creation. And then as a Shadow, he had been raised to worship his Queen—the only problem was, she had mated his brother and praying to his sister-in-law seemed weird.

A veritable declaration that all of this spiritual stuff was just a bunch of bullshit.

And yet even so, his suffering was so great he had to reach out.

Leaning his head back, he looked up at the low black ceiling and poured his broken heart into word. "I just want her back. I just . . . I only want Selena back. Please . . . if there's anyone up there, help me. Return her to me. I don't care what form she's in . . . I just can't do this anymore. I can't live like this for one more fucking night."

There was no answer, of course. And he felt like a total asshole.

Come on, like the vast emptiness of space was going throw anything but a meteor back at him?

Besides, was there even a Fade? What if he had just been hallucinating during the cleanse and had only imagined seeing his Selena? What if she had just died? As in . . . simply ceased to exist? What if all the crap about a heavenly place where loved ones went and waited for you with patience was just a coping mechanism created by those left behind in the kind of agony he was in?

A mental fallacy to bandage an emotional wound.

Leveling his head, he regarded the human crowd below—

In the glass, the reflection of a huge male figure standing right behind him made him spin around and go for the gun he kept tucked into the small of his back. But then he recognized who it was.

"What are you doing here?" he demanded.

SIX

The five-acre meadow rose from a vacant country lane like something created by an artist with a discerning eye, all natural aspects of hill and dale seemingly subject to the rules of pleasing visual standards. And atop the gentle, snow-dusted ascent, as a crown upon the head of a benevolent ruler, a great maple tree spread its branches in a halo so perfect even winter's barren reveal did not diminish its beauty.

Layla had dematerialized to the base of the field from the mansion, and she made her way up to the tree on foot, her bedroom slippers no match for the frosted ground, the cold wind cutting through her robe, her hair whipping free of its braid and flying around.

When she reached the top, she stared down at the roots that grounded the glorious trunk unto the earth.

It had been here, she thought.

Here, at the base of this maple, she had come to Xcor the first time, summoned by one whom she'd thought was a soldier of honor in the war, one whom she had fed down in the Brotherhood's clinic . . . one whom the Brothers had failed to inform her was in fact foe rather than friend.

When the male had called upon her to provide a vein, she had thought nothing about doing her sacred duty.

So she had come here . . . and lost a piece of herself in the process.

Xcor had been on the verge of death, wounded and weak, and yet she had recognized his power even in his diminished state. How could she not? He had been a tremendous male, thick of neck and chest, strong of limb, powerful of body. He had tried to refuse her vein—because, she liked to believe, he had seen her as an innocent in the conflict between the Band of Bastards and the Black Dagger Brotherhood and had wanted to keep her out of it. In the end, however, he had relented, ensuring that both of them fell prey to a biological imperative that knew no reason.

Taking a deep breath, she regarded the tree, seeing through its bare branches to the night sky beyond.

After Xcor's true identity had come out, she had confessed to Wrath and the Brotherhood what she had done, tearfully seeking their forgiveness— and it was a testament to the King and the males who served him that they had pardoned her for aiding the enemy readily and without punishment.

In turn, it was a poor testament to her that she had gone back to Xcor after that. Consorted with him. Become emotionally attached.

Yes, there had been an initial coercion on his part at the time, but the truth was, even if he hadn't forced her hand? She would have wanted to be with him. And worse? When things between them had finally ended, he had been the one to break their meetings off. Not her.

In fact, she would be seeing him still—and the heartbreak on her side at the loss of him was as crippling as her guilt.

And that was before he had been captured by the Brotherhood.

She knew exactly where they were keeping him because she had witnessed him in his wounded state in that cave . . . knew what the Brothers planned to do to him as soon as he awoke.

If only there was a way to save him. He had never been cruel to her, never hurt her . . . and he had never approached her sexually in spite of the hunger within him. He had been patient and kind . . . at least until they had parted.

He had, however, tried to kill Wrath. And that treason was punishable by death—

"Layla?"

Wheeling around, she tripped and fell to the side—just barely catching herself on the rough trunk of the maple. As pain flared in her palm, she tried to shake it off.

"Qhuinn!" she gasped.

The father of her young stepped forward. "Did you hurt yourself?"

With a curse, she wiped at the scratches, brushing debris away. Dearest Virgin Scribe, it hurt. "No, no, it's fine."

"Here." He took something out of the pocket of his leather jacket. "Let me see."

She trembled as Qhuinn checked her hand and then wrapped it with a black bandana. "I think you'll live."

Will I? she thought. I'm not so sure about that.

"You're freezing out here."

"Am I?"

Qhuinn took his jacket off, and as he draped it around her shoulders, she was swallowed by its size and warmth. "Come, let's go back to the mansion. You're shivering—"

"I can't do this anymore," she blurted. "I just can't keep going."

"I know." As she recoiled in surprise, he shook his head. "I know what's wrong. Let's go home and we can talk about it. Everything's going to be okay, I promise."

For a moment, she couldn't breathe. How could he have found out? How could he not be angry at her?

"How did you . . ." The tears came fast, emotion overriding everything. "I'm sorry. I'm so sorry . . . it wasn't supposed to be like this . . ."

She wasn't sure whether he opened his arms or she clawed herself onto his chest, but Qhuinn held her against him, sheltering her from the wind.

"It's all right." He made big circles on her back with his palm, soothing her. "We just need to talk it through. There are things we can do, steps we can take."

She turned her face to the side and looked out over the meadow. "I feel so awful."

"Why? It's out of your control. You didn't ask for this."

She pulled back. "I swear to you, I did not. And I never want you to think for a second that I would endanger Lyric or Rhampage—"

"Are you kidding me? Seriously, Layla, you love those young with everything in you."

"I do. I promise you that. And I love you and Blay, the King, the Brotherhood. You are my family, you are all I have."

"Layla, listen to me. You are not alone, okay? And like I said, there are things we can do—"

"Really? Truly?"

"Yes. In fact, I was talking about it before I came here. I don't want you to think that I'm betraying you—"

"Oh, Qhuinn! I am the betrayer! I am in the wrong—"

"Stop it. You are not—and we are going to take care of it together. All of us."

Layla put her hands up to her face, the one that he'd bandaged and the one that was bare. And then, for the first time in what seemed like forever, she released her breath all the way, a balming ease replacing the horrible burden she had carried.

"I have to say this." She looked up at him. "Please know that I've been eaten alive with regret and sadness. I swear that I never meant for this to happen, any of it. I've been so alone, struggling with guilt—"

"Guilt is unnecessary." He brushed under her eyes with his thumbs. "You've just got to let that go, because you can't help the way you feel."

"I can't, I truly can't—and Xcor is not evil, he's not as bad as you think he is. I swear. He always treated me with care and kindness, and I know that he would not hurt Wrath again. I just know it—"

"What?" Qhuinn frowned and shook his head. "What are you talking about?"

"Please don't kill him. It's just as you said, there is a way to work this out. Maybe you can let him go and—"

Qhuinn didn't so much step back as push her away. And then he seemed to struggle to find words.

"Layla," he said slowly. "I know I'm not hearing you right, and I'm trying to . . . can you . . ."

Seizing the chance to make her case, Layla hurried to speak. "He never hurt me. In all the nights I went to him, he never once hurt me. He got us a cottage so that I could be safe, and it was only ever just the two of us. I never saw any of the Bastards . . ."

She trailed off as his expression went from confusion . . . to an ice-cold reserve that made him look like a total stranger.

When Qhuinn spoke next, his voice was flat. "You have been meeting with Xcor?"

"I've felt terrible—"

"How long ago?" he snapped. But he didn't let her answer. "Did you go see him while you were carrying my young? Did you willingly and knowingly consort with the enemy while my fucking young were in your body?" Before she could answer him, he held up his forefinger. "And you need to think really long and hard about your answer. There is no going back from it, and it better be the truth. If I find out you lied to me, I'm going to kill you."

As Layla's heart thundered in her chest and panic made her light-headed, her one and only thought was . . .

You're going to kill me anyway.

Back at shAdoWs, Trez tucked his gun away and tried to plug back into reality. "Well?" he prompted. "What are you doing here, especially without a Tony Manero polyester special on?"

Lassiter, the Fallen Angel, smiled in a way that didn't include his strangely colored, pupil-less eyes; the expression only affected the lower part of his face. "Oh, you know, leisure suits are so last week for me."

"Moving on to eighties New Age? I don't have any neon to lend you."

"Nah, I have another new costume to wear."

"Good for you. Scary for the rest of us. Just tell me you aren't going to pull a Borat on the beach."

When the angel didn't immediately reply, Trez felt a set of Freddy Kruegers tease the nape of his neck. Normally, Lassiter was the kind of guy who was so upbeat most folks couldn't decide whether to shoot him to put everyone out of their misery . . . or just grab some popcorn and a Coke and watch the show.

Because even if he pissed you off, it was always hella funny.

Not tonight, though. That bizarre stare of his was about as light and frothy as a granite slab, and his huge body was so still, none of the gold on his wrists and his throat, his fingers and his ears, was glinting in the low light.

"What's up with the statue routine?" Trez muttered. "Someone move your My Little Pony collection again?"

Unable to stand the silence, Trez made a show of sitting behind his desk and shuffling some papers around. "You trying to read my aura or some shit?"

Not that that would require any special skills. Everyone in the household knew where he was at—

"I want you to meet me for dinner tomorrow night."

Trez looked up. "What the hell for?"

The angel took his damn time answering, heading over on a saunter to the glass panes and staring down at the crowd from the exact place Trez had been standing in. In the dim light, the angel's profile was the kind of thing that the females would love, all good proportions and right angles. But that frown . . .

"Out with it," Trez demanded. "I've had a lifetime's worth of bad news already. Whatever it is, it can't compare to the shit I've been through."

Lassiter glanced over and shrugged. "Just dinner. Tomorrow night. Seven p.m."

"I don't eat."

"I know."

Trez tossed whatever invoice or staff schedule or whatever the fuck he'd been busy not looking at back with the rest of the crap on his desk. "I find it really hard to believe you've taken an interest in nutrition."

"True. This gluten-is-the-enemy thing is total bullshit. And don't get me started on kombucha tea, kale, anything with antioxidants in it, and the fallacy that high-fructose corn syrup is the root of all evil."

"Did you hear that Kraft Macaroni & Cheese took out all its preservatives months ago?"

"Yeah, and the bastards didn't tell anyone up front, either—"

"Why do you want to have dinner with me?"

"Just being friendly."

"That's not your style."

"Like I said, I'm changing things up." Annnnnd there was that smile again. "Figure I'd begin with a bang. I mean, if you're going to turn over a new leaf, you should start as you mean to go on."

"No offense, but I'm not in the mood to spend time with people I actually like." Okay, that came out badly. "I mean, my brother's the only one I can tolerate right now, and I don't want to see even him."

That smile Lassiter was popping was something Trez was more than ready to see the last of—and talk about prayers getting answered: The angel headed for the door.

"I'll see you tomorrow night."

"No, thank you."

"At your brother's."

"Oh, for fuck's sake, why?"

"Because he has the best pasta Bolognese in Caldie."

"You know that's not what I'm asking."

The angel just shrugged over his shoulder. "Come and find out."

"The hell I will." Trez shook his head. "Look, I know people are worried about me and I appreciate the concern." Actually, he didn't. At all. "And yes, I've lost weight, and I should eat more. But it's funny how having your chest ripped open and your heart taken out by fate doesn't leave you with much of an appetite. So if you're looking for a plus one so your two-top doesn't feel like a game of solitaire, why don't you start with someone who will actually eat and say more than two words? I can guarantee both you and I will have a better evening."

"See you tomorrow."

As the angel let himself out, Trez called across the office, "Fuck you!"

When the door simply eased shut, he thought, At least we aren't going to argue anymore. And Lassiter would get the picture when he was Bolognesing his pasta by himself.

Problem solved.

SEVEN

here were times in life when the aperture of your attention span narrowed to such a tight focus that your entire consciousness rested upon a single person. Qhuinn was not at all unfamiliar with this phenomenon: It happened whenever he was alone with Blay. When he held his young. When he was fighting the enemy and trying to make sure he made it home in one piece, without leaks or a concussion.

It was happening again now.

Standing at the base of a Harry Potter tree, at the apex of a rolling meadow, in the winter's wind, Qhuinn was aware of absolutely nothing but Layla's right eye. He could count every dark blond lash, trace the perfect circle of the pupil, measure each of the pale green striations that radiated out from the jet-black nucleus. There could have been a mushroom cloud off in the distance, a spaceship overhead, a lineup of dancing clowns right next to him . . . and he would have seen, heard, acknowledged absolutely nothing fucking else.

Well, that wasn't entirely true.

He was dimly cognizant of a roar between his ears, something that was a cross between a jet engine and one of those fireworks that whistles like a banshee and goes in a circle until it exhausts itself.

"Answer me," he said in a voice that didn't sound like his own.

He'd followed her out here to this isolated place when he had sensed she'd left the mansion—and he'd come here to talk to her about postpartum depression. Had had a plan to get her back home, comfort her in front of the fire, put her on a path where she could enjoy what she had worked so hard to bring into the world.

How in the fuck they'd ended up on the subject of Xcor and her meeting up?

No fucking clue.

But there was no misunderstanding anymore. And no retraction coming. Layla's wide stare and silent panic told him that as much as he hoped that this was a miscommunication of colossal and laughable proportions, that wasn't the case.

"I was safe," she whispered. "He never hurt me."

"Are you fucking—"

He stopped himself right there. Just cut that shit right off, like you would the detonator of a bomb.

Before he did or said something he regretted, he stepped off and flexed his fingers wide so they did not curl into fists.

"Qhuinn, I swear to you I was never in danger—"

"Were you alone with him." When she didn't reply, he ground his molars. "Were you."

"He never hurt me."

"Okay, that's like saying you were never bitten—while you were using a cobra as a scarf. Over and over again. Because it was on the fucking regular, wasn't it. Answer me!"

"I'm sorry, Qhuinn—" She seemed to try to compose herself, sniffling back tears. Straightening her shoulders. And the way her eyes begged him for understanding made him nearly violent. "Oh, dearest Virgin Scribe—"

"Cut the praying! There is no one up there anymore!" He was losing it. Totally fucking losing it— "And what the hell are you asking for forgiveness for! You knowingly and willingly put my young at risk because you wanted—" He recoiled. "Jesus Christ, did you have sex with him? Did you fuck him with my children in you?"

"No! I've never been with him like that!"

"Liar," he hollered. "You're a lying whore—"

"I'm all but a virgin! And you well know it! Besides, you don't want me. Why would you care?"

"You're saying you never so much as kissed him." When she didn't answer him, he laughed harshly. "Don't bother denying it. I can see it in your face. And you're right, I didn't want you, I've never wanted you— and don't get it twisted. I'm not jealous, I'm fucking disgusted. I'm in love with a male of worth and I had to be with you because I needed an incubator for my son and my daughter. That and the fact you threw yourself at me in your needing was the *only* reason I was ever with you."

Layla's face got ashen, and as much as it made him an asshole, he was glad. He wanted to hurt her inside, where it counted, because as mad as he was, he could never strike a female.

And that fact was the only reason she was still standing.

Those babies, those precious, innocent babies, had been taken into the mouth of a monster, into the presence of the enemy, exposed to a danger that would have left him shitting himself if he'd known it was happening.

"Do you have *any* idea what he's capable of?" Qhuinn said grimly. "The atrocities? He stabbed his own fucking lieutenant in the gut just to send the male into our hands. And back in the Old Country? He slaughtered vampires, humans, *lessers*, anything that crossed his path, sometimes for the war, sometimes just for sport. He was the Bloodletter's right-hand male. Do you have any conception of what he's done while he's been on this earth? I mean, clearly you don't give two shits that he put a bullet in Wrath's throat—obviously that means nothing to you. That bastard could have raped you a thousand times over, gutted you, and left you for the sun—with my young inside of you! Are you even fucking kidding me with this?"

The more Qhuinn thought about the risk she'd taken, the more his head hummed. His beloved young might well not exist because of the poor choice of this female who, by biological dictate alone, had had to shelter them until they could breathe on their own.

She had put them at risk, by putting herself at risk—with no apparent thought of the consequences or how he, the blooded father, might have viewed the debacle.

His fury, seated in the love he had for those babies, was undefinable. Undeniable. Inexhaustible.

"We both wanted them," she said roughly. "When we laid together, we both wanted—"

In a flat voice, he cut her off. "Yeah, I regret that. Better for them not to be born at all than to have half of you in them."

Layla threw out a hand to catch herself against the tree once more— and as it was the hand that he had wrapped with his bandana, he was struck by a need to rip the cheap cloth from her palm. Then burn it.

"I did the best I could," she said.

He laughed hard at that one, until his throat burned. "Are you talking about when you were sleeping with Xcor? Or when you were endangering the lives of my young?"

All at once, she returned his anger with a blast of her own. "You have the one you love! You lay beside him every day, and you get to build a family with him! Your life has purpose and meaning beyond service to others—whereas I have nothing! I've spent all my nights and days serving a deity who no longer cares for the race she begot and now I am *mahmen* to two young whom I love with all my heart, but who are not me. What do I have to show for my life? Nothing!"

"You got that right," he said tightly. "Because you're not going to mother my young anymore. You're out of a job."

She recoiled with indignation. "What say you? I am their *mahmen*. I—"

"Not anymore you're not."

There was a heartbeat of silence, and then her voice exploded from her. "You can't—you can't take Lyric and Rhamp . . . you can't take them away from me! I'm their *mahmen*! I have rights—"

"No, you don't. You have consorted with the enemy. You have com-

mitted treason. And you are going to be lucky to come out of this alive—
not that I give a damn whether you live or die. The only thing I care
about is that you never see those young again—"

The change in her was as instantaneous as it was consuming.

All at once, Layla went from angry to stone-cold silent. And the shift
was so abrupt that he wondered if she hadn't stroked out.

But then her upper lip curled off fangs that had descended. And the
sound that came out of her was something that made the hair on the
back of his neck stand up in warning.

Her voice, when she spoke, was as deadly as a dagger blade. "I do not
recommend you try to prevent me from seeing my son and daughter."

Qhuinn bared his own fangs. "Watch me."

Her body curled into a springing crouch, and the hiss she let out was
that of a viper. Except she didn't spring at him to claw his face to ribbons.

She up and dematerialized.

And there was only one place she was going to.

"Oh, hell no," he shouted at the cold, uncaring winter landscape.
"You want war, you're going to fucking get it!"

"—times I still crave one," Blay was saying as he took a sip off the rim of
his rocks glass. "I mean, for humans, it's a deadly habit. But vampires
don't have to worry about getting cancer from smoking."

The Brotherhood's billiard room was mostly empty, the tournament
having fallen apart when Butch had had to stay with Xcor, Tohrment had
begged off, Rhage had been injured in the field, and Rehv had decided to
stay up north at the Great Camp with Ehlena. But it was cool. Blay had
still found a game with Vishous, the pair of them circling the middle of
the five tables, edging each other out. The good news? Lassiter was somewhere else, which meant ESPN was on mute on the TV over the huge
stone hearth.

No Disney movies with all that ridiculous singing tonight.

If Blay heard that shit from *Frozen* one more time, he was going to let
it goooooooooooo, all right.

As in emptying a clip, right into his own frontal lobe.

On the far side of the table, Vishous lit up another hand-rolled. "So why did you quit smoking?"

Blay shrugged. "Qhuinn hates it. His father smoked cigarettes and pipes, so I think it reminds him of things he'd rather not think about."

"You shouldn't have to change for anyone."

"I was the one who chose to stop. He never asked me."

As the Brother leaned over the table and lined up his cue, Blay thought back to the beginning of him and Qhuinn. The whole smoking thing on his side had coincided with having to watch the male he was in love with fuck anything that moved. Horrible, that period. No, they hadn't been in a relationship—and every time Qhuinn had gone off with someone else, it had served as a reminder that they never were going to be in one.

Hell, back then, Blay hadn't even come out yet.

The stress and sadness of it all had been tough to handle, but there had also been a simmering, irrational resentment on his side. So yes, he had embraced a coping mechanism that he'd known Qhuinn hadn't approved of or liked. It had been a subversive, petty payback for sins the male wasn't actually committing.

But at least quitting had been simple. Once the two of them had gotten their act together? He'd put the Dunhills down and never looked back.

Well . . . maybe it was more accurate to say that he'd never backslid. Sometimes, when he saw Vishous light up, and that fragrant exhale hit the air, he did get a hankering for one—

Just as V sent the cue ball cracking through the racked setup in the center, a horrible pounding sounded out in the foyer. Loud, repeated, hard enough to shake, rattle, and roll the mansion's solid-as-an-oak front door, it sounded like an entire horde of *lessers* were trying to break into the mansion.

Blay outed his house gun from under his arm as he and V ditched their cues and ran out of the billiards room to the main entrance.

Bam-bam-bam-bam!

"What the fuck?" V muttered as he looked into the security monitor. "What the hell is wrong with your boy?"

"What?"

The question was answered as V released the lock and Qhuinn exploded into the foyer. The male was furious to the point of possession, his face screwed down tight in anger, his body breaking into a full-on run, his state such that he didn't seem to be aware of anyone else's presence.

"Qhuinn?" Blay said as he tried to catch hold of a shoulder or an arm.

Nothing doing. Qhuinn hit the grand staircase and pulled a Usain Bolt, the red carpeted steps being consumed by leaps and bounds.

"Qhuinn!" Blay took off in the wake of the drama, trying to catch up. "What's going on?"

At the top of the stairs, Qhuinn's shitkickers dug into the carpet and all but tire-screeched as he went left to the hall of statues. Tight on his heels, Blay pounded after him, and as the direction became clear, a sudden terror took hold.

Layla and the young must be in danger—

At the door to Layla's bedroom, Qhuinn grabbed the knob and twisted—only to slam right into the locked panels.

Curling up a fist, he started hitting the wood so hard, chips of paint went flying.

"Open this fucking door!" Qhuinn yelled. "Layla, you open this fucking door right now!"

"What the hell are you doing!" Blay tried to stop him. "Are you insane—"

Qhuinn's gun came up from out of nowhere, and as the Brother pulled a twist and shoved the muzzle into Blay's face, it became obvious this was some kind of nightmare, the inevitable result of a second glass of port after Fritz's lamb dinner.

Except it wasn't.

"Stay out of this," Qhuinn snapped. "You stay out of this."

As Blay put both hands up and backed off, Qhuinn turned his shoulder to the door and rammed his body into the thing so hard the wood splintered, the panels splitting under the force of the blow.

What was revealed inside the pretty lavender room was equally terrifying.

As Vishous skidded to a halt next to Blay, and Z broke out of his suite down the hall, and Wrath emerged from his study at the head of the stairs, Blay's brain was forever stained by the inescapable, incomprehensible sight of Layla with one young under each arm, her fangs bared in attack, her face that of a demon, her body trembling—but not in fear.

She was prepared to kill anyone who came at her.

Qhuinn pointed the gun right at her through the hole he'd made. "Drop them. Or I drop you."

"What the *fuck* is going on here!" Vishous's voice was so loud it was like he had a bullhorn. "Have you lost your fucking minds?"

Qhuinn reached in, unlocked the mechanism, and sprung what was left of the door. As he stepped inside, Blay stopped the others from entering. "No, let me do this."

If anyone other than he went in there, bullets were going to go flying and Layla was going to attack, and people were going to get hurt—or worse.

And what the *fuck* was happening here?

"Drop them!" Qhuinn barked.

"So kill me!" Layla shouted back. "Do it!"

Blay put his body right in between the two of them, his torso blocking the path of any bullets. Meanwhile, Layla was breathing hard and Lyric and Rhamp were both wailing—shit, he was never going to forget the sound of those cries.

Facing off with Qhuinn, he put his palms out and spoke slowly. "You're going to have to shoot me first."

He didn't focus on anything other than Qhuinn's blue and green eyes . . . as if he could somehow telepathically communicate with the guy and calm him down.

"Get out of the way," Qhuinn snapped. "This is not your business."

Blay blinked at that. But considering he was staring down the barrel of a forty, he figured he'd shelve that insult for the time being.

"Qhuinn, whatever it is, we'll deal with it—"

That mismatched stare flicked to him for only a split second. "Oh, we will? You mean the fact that she's been consorting with the enemy is just something we can OxiClean out or some shit? Great, let's call fucking Fritz in on this. Fan-fucking-tastic idea."

As the young continued to cry, and more people came onto the scene out in the corridor, Blay shook his head. "What are you talking about?"

"She took my young with her when she fucked him—"

"I'm sorry, *what*?"

"She's been with Xcor all along. She didn't stop seeing him. She's been consorting with a known enemy of our King while she was pregnant with my young. So yes, it's absolutely within my rights as a sire to pull a gun on her."

Abruptly, Blay became aware of a growl rising up behind him, and the horrible sound of it reminded him of what he'd heard about the female of the species being more deadly than the male. Glancing over his shoulder, he thought . . . yup, Layla was clearly prepared to protect her young to the death in this fucked-up parallel universe they'd somehow gotten sucked into.

Xcor? She'd been seeing *Xcor*?

Except he couldn't be sidetracked from the immediate threat.

"All I care about is that you put the gun down," Blay said evenly. "Put the gun down and tell me what's going on. Otherwise, if you want to shoot her, the bullet's going to have to go through me."

Qhuinn took a deep breath, like he was having to force himself not to scream. "I love you, but this is not your business, Blay. Get out of the way and let me deal with this."

"Wait a minute. You've always said I'm the father of these young, too—"

"Not when it comes down to this. Now get the fuck out of the way."

Blay blinked once. Twice. A third time. Funny, the ache in his chest made him wonder if Qhuinn hadn't pulled the trigger and he'd somehow missed the discharge.

Stay focused, he told himself. "No, I'm not moving."

"Get out of here!" Qhuinn's body started to tremble. "Just get the fuck out of my way!"

Now or never, Blay thought as he lunged forward and went for the wrist that controlled the gun. As he punched that forearm away with everything he was worth, the weapon discharged repeatedly, and lead slugs went flying—but with a powerful shift, he managed to tackle Qhuinn to the side. The pair of them went down hard to the floor, and he fought to dominate his mate, his momentum rolling the pair of them away from Layla and the young while keeping that gun pointed into the far corner of the room.

Blay ended up on top, but he knew Qhuinn was going to fix that quick. The gun, he had to maintain control of the—

All of a sudden, it was arctic time.

The temperature in the bedroom dropped to below zero so fast that the walls, floor, and ceiling creaked in protest, everyone's breath coming out in puffs, condensation frosting the glass on the windows and the mirrors, any exposed skin goose-bumping up.

A great roar was next.

The sound was so loud that it was nearly inaudible, nothing but a pain that pierced through the eardrum and made your head go cathedral bell—and that, even more than the climate change, stopped everyone in the suite, in the hall, in the mansion . . . maybe in the world.

Wrath's enormous body dwarfed the doorjamb as he entered the bedroom, his waist-length hair, his black wraparounds, his leather-clad thighs and bulging upper body the kind of thing that would have halted a train in its tracks.

His fangs were fully descended and long as a saber-toothed tiger's. But he had no trouble talking around them.

"Not in my fucking house!" He was so loud that the painting next to him vibrated on the plaster wall. "This is *not* happening in my fucking house! My *shellan* and my son are here—there are young under this roof. There are young in this fucking room!"

Across the way, Layla collapsed onto the floor, her bones absorbing the fall with a loud clatter. She kept Lyric and Rhamp from harm, though, cradling them in her lap, while she dropped her head and began to weep.

Underneath Blay, Qhuinn tried to shove his way free.

"Not till you let go of the gun," Blay gritted out.

There was a metal-on-wood clatter as the forty was released and Blay shoved it away. Then Qhuinn broke free and popped up on his shitkickers. He looked like he'd been in a wind tunnel, his black hair all messed up, his eyes peeled wide, his skin flushed in some places, stark white in others.

"Everyone out of here," Wrath snapped, "except for the three parents."

Well, at least someone was recognizing his role, Blay thought bitterly.

Shifting his eyes back to Qhuinn, he found himself staring across the chaos at a male he thought he knew nearly as well as himself.

At the moment, however? Blay was looking at a stranger. A total frickin' stranger. Eyes that Blay had peered into for hours, lips that he had kissed, a body that he had touched, caressed, entered and been entered by . . . it was like some kind of amnesia had wiped all of their togetherness away, rendering what had once been an intimate reality into a hypothetical that was so dim, it was nonexistent.

Vishous stepped forward into the room. "Weapons check first."

As Wrath's upper lip twitched, it was clear he didn't appreciate the interruption. There was no arguing with the logic, though.

V was efficient about the pat-down, stripping Qhuinn first of a couple of knives and another handgun—and then Blay got up, lifted his arms, and spread his legs even though he knew no one was worried about his trigger finger.

"Done," V announced as he squeezed by the King and went back out into the hall.

"Tell them to get gone," Wrath snapped.

"Roger that."

At the royal command, the crowd disappeared from the doorway, but they didn't go far, their presences lingering as they clearly waited for an aftershock or two. In any event, there was no closing the door. The thing was splintered into a sieve.

Turning in Qhuinn's direction, Wrath let out a curse, and then demanded, "You want to tell me why in the fuck you discharged a firearm in my house?"

EIGHT

As Layla looked up at the three males, she was shaking so badly it was hard to keep her upper body off the floor. What gave her the little strength she had? Lyric and Rhamp were in her lap, the folds of her robe enveloping them and protecting them from the cold in the room, their cries silenced—for now.

Focusing on the King, she wanted to wipe her eyes, but she wasn't letting go of her young for even a second.

"She's been seeing Xcor," Qhuinn said, his breath coming in clouds of white. "Behind our backs. This whole time—while she was pregnant. I want her stripped of her rights to see my young, and I want her out of this house. Whether it's because she's been sentenced to death or because she's been banished . . . that's for you to decide."

Wrath's cruel and aristocratic face cranked in the Brother's direction. "Thank you for carving out my role in this, asshole. And if you're talking banishment, right now it's *you* I'm debating that over, not her."

"You try finding out that Beth has been sleeping with the leader of the Band of Bastards while she's—"

"Watch yourself," Wrath snarled. "You're walking a line here that you're about to fall the fuck off of. In fact, get out. I want to talk to Layla alone."

"I'm not leaving my young."

The King glanced at Blay. "Take him out of here. In a choke hold if you have to—"

"I have rights!" Qhuinn yelled. "I have—"

Wrath jacked forward on his hips. "You have only what I fucking grant you! I am your master, fucker, so shut the hell up, get out of this room, and I'll deal with you when I'm good and goddamned ready. I understand that you're up in your head. I'd even be able to respect it if you didn't keep behaving like you run the world. But right now, my only concern is your young, because clearly, they're not on your radar—"

"How the fuck can you say that—"

"Because you just turned a gun on their mahmen*!"*

Next to Qhuinn, Blay was looking like he had seen death up close and personal, his expression one of distilled horror and sorrow, his hands shaking as he pushed them through his red hair again and again.

"I am the King, this is my house. Get him out of here, Blay—that is an order."

Blay said something to Qhuinn that didn't carry. And then Qhuinn marched out of the bedroom, his shitkickers crunching across the iced-over carpet. As he went, Blay stayed with him, like a bodyguard would.

Except Blay was more likely to protect others from him.

When it was only Wrath and her, Layla took a deep breath that hurt. "Permit me to place the young in their bassinets, my Lord?"

"Yeah, yeah. Do whatever you need."

Her legs felt like they had no bones in them, and with her fury gone, she feared she was not strong enough to stand and keep both young in safe grips at the same time. It was a struggle to decide which one to put aside gently, and in the end, she carefully set Rhamp down on the Oriental rug. Cradling Lyric in both arms, she struggled to her feet and limped over to the bassinets. After she laid Lyric upon the soft nest, she returned and picked up Rhamp, who had begun to fuss with the absence of his sister. Tucking blankets around them to keep them warm, she steeled herself and faced the King.

"May I sit?" she whispered.

"Yeah, you better."

"There is aught before your feet, my Lord. If you should wish to come further inside."

He ignored her efforts to help him in his blindness navigate an unfamiliar room. "You want to tell me what the hell's going on here?"

Qhuinn couldn't remember a goddamned thing.

As he went into the second-story sitting room on the far side of the mansion, he tried to piece together the series of events, because it gave him something to do other than screaming: His last moment of crystal clear was of him nearly breaking down the vestibule's door to get into the house. Everything from that split second on—until now as he prowled around the silk sofas and the side tables—was a blank slate.

And the harder he tried to remember, the more elusive that gap in reality became, as if pursuit made his prey faster.

For fuck's sake, he couldn't fucking think here. He couldn't . . .

Dimly, he was aware of Blay watching him. And then the male was speaking. But all Qhuinn could do was keep pacing, around and around, the territorial urge to protect his young a prime directive that demanded all his concentration.

What the fuck was Wrath going to do? Surely, the King wasn't going to let Layla—

From out of nowhere, Blay stood in front of him, the male stone-faced and stiff backed. "I can't do this."

"Do what?"

"Be in the same room with you for even a minute longer."

Qhuinn blinked. "Then leave. I'm unarmed, remember? And there are fifty million pounds of brother loitering around that goddamn bedroom."

Otherwise, yes, he would still be in there. With his children.

"You got it," Blay muttered. "I'm going home to check on my *mahmen*."

As the syllables hit the tense air between them, it took a minute be-

fore Qhuinn's salad of a brain deciphered them. Home . . . ? *Mahmen* . . .
—oh, right. Her ankle.

"Okay. Yeah."

Blay stayed where he was. And then in a low voice, he said, "Do you
even care if I come back before dawn?"

When there was a heartbeat of pause, the male stepped off, shaking
his head as he went for the exit. Qhuinn noted the departure—and a part
of him knew he should call out, reconnect . . . stop the leaving. But an
even bigger part of him was back in that bedroom, trying to pull out
threads of recollection from the white-hot blind spot that had taken him
over.

Jesus . . . had he really discharged his gun in the mansion? With his
young in the room—

"Qhuinn."

He refocused across the room. Blay was in the doorway, his eyes narrowed, his jaw set.

The male cleared his throat. "Just so you and I are clear, I will never
be able to get what you just said out of my head. And the same goes for
the sight of you with that gun in your hand."

"That makes one of us," Qhuinn muttered.

"Excuse me?"

"I can't remember any of it."

"That's a fucking cop-out." Blay jabbed a finger in Qhuinn's direction. "You don't get to erase a scene like that by claiming you're pulling a
blank."

"I'm not going to argue with you about it."

"Then we don't really have much to say to each other."

When Blay just stared at him, Qhuinn shook his head. "Look, no
disrespect, but the lives of my kids are the only thing I'm thinking about
right now. Layla isn't who I thought she was, and she—"

"FYI, you just told me I wasn't a parent." Blay's voice was stilted, like
he was trying to keep the hurt out of it. "You looked me in the eye and
told me that those kids and their mother were none of my business."

Some distant echo, deep within the recess of Qhuinn's consciousness, rose up through the still-hot anger. But it was a tie that he couldn't hold onto. All he wanted to do was go back to that bedroom and grab his son and daughter and leave. He didn't care where he went—

Blay cursed. "Don't wait up for me. I'm not coming back."

And then Qhuinn was alone.

Fantastic. Now his relationship was also in the shitter.

Leaning to the side, Qhuinn looked out through the open doorway, but it was more to try to gauge if there were still brothers in the hall of statues. Yup, the fighters were milling around—but come on, like any one of them would leave? Even with Wrath ordering them away?

They'd probably sleep outside of that fucking bedroom, protecting a female who didn't deserve it—

The next thing Qhuinn knew, there was a lamp in his hand, and he was holding the converted Oriental vase like he was an MLB pitcher. And huh, go fig—apparently, he'd decided to throw it at himself: He was standing in front of one of the antique mirrors, his reflection distorted in the old glass.

He looked like a monster, like some version of himself that had been sausage'd through the cogs of a nightmare, his face as a fist curled up tight, his features compressed until he could barely recognize them. Staring at himself, he knew without a doubt that if he sent this lamp flying, he would trash the entire room, tearing the paintings off the walls, breaking the windows, taking the burning logs in the fireplace and throwing them onto the sofas to make proper blazes.

And he wouldn't stop there.

He wouldn't stop until someone made him, either with lengths of chains or maybe a bullet or two.

Oddly, his eyes went to the cord that was swinging loose from the lamp's base, the brown tail like that of a nervous dog begging for forgiveness and mercy for something it had no clue it had done.

Qhuinn's whole body trembled as he put the vase with its silk shade down on the floor.

Just as he was straightening, he caught sight of a window, and before he could think twice, he went over, cranked it open, and closed his eyes.

But he couldn't dematerialize. He had nowhere in mind to go, he—

No, wait—he did have a destination. He absolutely fucking had a destination.

All at once, he became calm and focused, and as he ghosted out and away from the mansion, he wished he'd been able to play things cooler. If he had, maybe his restitution would have been more obvious sooner.

As he re-formed, the scent of evergreens was thick in the winter air, and the wind plowed through the pine boughs, making the trees scream. The cave he had come for had an entrance that was hidden by boulders, but if you knew what you were looking for, you had no problem finding its mouth. Inside, he made quick strides to the Tomb's great gates, and as he triggered the granite partition to move aside, he was perfectly composed as he stood at the iron bars, the easy smile on his face like whitewash on a rotting fence.

"I'm here to relieve," he shouted out as he rattled the ancient metal. "Just like Alka-fucking-Seltzer. Tums. Pepcid. You get the deal."

He was praying that for once, word did not travel fast in the Brotherhood. That the brother on duty maybe hadn't checked his phone, or maybe everyone back at the house was still so up in their head about the fucking drama that they didn't think to text the person who was on duty here—

Phury came down the torch-lit hall of shelves, the sound of his shitkickers on the stone floor echoing up among all the *lesser* jars.

"Oh, hey," the brother said. "How we doing?"

In the flickering orange light, there was no suspicion, no alarm on that face, no narrowed eyes. No hands going for a cell phone to call out for backup. No tension like that warrior body was prepared to defend its position even with the gates in place.

"We're fantastic," Qhuinn replied as he tried not to focus on how long the guy was taking to saunter the fuck to him. "Other than the fact that I'm covering Lassiter for today."

Phury stopped at the gate and put his hands on his hips. Which made Qhuinn want to scream.

"Let me guess," the other brother said. "*Golden Girls* marathon."

"Worse. A retrospective on *Maude*. Bea Arthur is hot, apparently. So you gonna let me in?"

The Primale started in with the copper key. "He's awake, by the way."

Qhuinn's heart started pounding. "Xcor?"

Like they'd be talking about someone else?

"Not very communicative, but he is conscious. No interrogation, yet. V had to peel Tohr away and then Butch left when I got here." Phury opened the way in and stepped aside. "And you know the policy. There have to be two of us present to work on him—and I can't stay. I've got to meet Cormia up at the Great Camp. Do you have a number two or are we waiting for nightfall to start the fun and games?"

Ironic, really. Everyone had been worried about Tohr going rogue and taking out his pound of flesh too early.

But that wasn't going to be the problem, was it.

Qhuinn released a breath and made sure he didn't rush inside. "Blay was going to come with me, but he has to go see his *mahmen*."

As they traded places, Phury handed over the key, which he'd almost put into his pocket. "Oh, sorry—you're going to need this. Yeah, I heard about the fall. How's her ankle?"

Qhuinn was so distracted by what had been put in his hand that he lost track of the conversation. What the hell had they been—

"Better," Qhuinn heard himself say as he closed things up and put the key head back into the lock slot. "Anyway, he was going to arrange for coverage."

"I'd stay if I could."

Qhuinn watched from a distance as he cranked the ornate handle to the left, throwing the tumblers so that the lock's gears met and grabbed hold—

"Qhuinn?"

He shook himself and made a show of affecting a pleasant expression—something his features were generally not familiar with, regardless of the crisis he was currently in.

"Yeah?"

"Are you okay? You don't look right."

Making a show of brushing his hand through his hair and jacking his leathers up, he rolled his shoulder—and wanted to high-five the body part as it let out an obliging *crack!*

"To be honest, this rotator cuff is killing me." He reached across and massaged things for show. "Doc Jane thinks she might have to operate on it to clean out the socket. But don't worry, it's low-grade chronic, not acute, and I'm not on any meds. If anything happens with the piece of meat back there"—he motioned behind himself—"I can handle shit."

Phury cursed. "Been there. And I'm not concerned about you. I know you'll take care of business. Do you want me to swing by the mansion and see if Z can come hang?"

"No, Blay's gonna find someone. But thanks."

For the love of all that was unholy, could they *please* stop fucking talking. Any second the brother's phone was going to go off with a text or a call to inform him that under no circumstances was Qhuinn to be within three hundred yards of their prisoner—

"Bye." Phury turned away and lifted a hand. "Good luck with him."

"He's going to fucking need it," Qhuinn whispered to the brother's retreating back.

NINE

I n his blindness, Wrath was both more isolated from, and more connected to, the world than those who were sighted: Isolated, because the lack of visual cues from his environment meant he was forever floating in a galaxy of darkness, and more connected because his other faculties were amplified in his perpetual, internal night sky, stars of other information that he orientated himself by.

So, as he faced off at Layla, and she told him the whole story, he caught and tracked all of her nuances, from the variations in her scent and tone of voice, to every little move she made, to the change in air pressure between them as her mood alternated between anger and sadness, regret and guilt.

"So Xcor found the compound," Wrath concluded, "by tracking your blood. That's how he did it?"

There was a slight creak as the bed adjusted to a shift of her weight.

"Yes," she said softly. "I had fed him."

"Yeah, that first night. When Throe tricked you into coming out to that field. Or did it happen again after that."

"It happened again."

"Your blood was in him," Wrath repeated. "And he followed the signal here."

"He promised that if I continued to see him, he wouldn't attack the compound. I told myself I was protecting all of us, but the truth is . . . I needed to see him. I wanted to see him. It was awful, being trapped between my heart and my family. It has been . . . awful."

Goddamn it, Wrath thought. There was going to be no easy way out of this.

"You committed treason."

"I did."

Wrath had worked hard to reverse many of the restrictive and punitive Old Laws, abolishing things like blood slavery and indentured servitude, and establishing basic due process for offenses among civilians. But the one thing he had adhered to was that betraying the crown was still punishable by death.

"Please," she whispered, "do not take me away from my young. Do not send me unto the Fade."

She was hardly an enemy of the state. But she had committed a very serious crime—and God his head was pounding.

"Why did you need to see Xcor?" he asked.

"I fell in love with him." The Chosen's voice was level and lifeless. "I had no control over it. He was always so gentle with me. So kind. He never once made an advance to me—and when I did to him, he pushed me away even though it was well obvious that he . . . was not indifferent. He just seemed to want to be near me."

"You're sure he wasn't lying."

"About what?"

"Knowing where we stayed."

"No, he wasn't. I saw him on the property. I met him . . . on the property." Now she spoke more quickly, a fervent begging entering her voice. "So he has honor—he could have attacked, but he chose not to. He kept his word, even after he told me to go and never see him again."

Wrath frowned. "You're saying he ended it between the two of you?"

"He did. He cast me out and deserted the cottage we had been meeting at."

"Was there any reason he would have done that?"

There was a long pause. "I confronted him about his feelings for me. I knew he had them, and . . . but indeed, that was when he threw me out."

"How long ago was that?"

"It was right before he was captured. And I know why he ended it all. He didn't want to be vulnerable with me."

Wrath frowned and crossed his arms over his chest. "Come on, Layla, don't be naive. You haven't even once considered it was more a case of him finally having mobilized enough troops and intel to marshal an offensive here?"

"I'm sorry? I don't follow."

"Xcor has been actively working with the *glymera* to form allegiances against me. Before and after he put a bullet in my throat." As she gasped, he would ordinarily have stopped. But reality was ignored at one's peril. "If you're going to sack a fortification like this one, you're going to need months and months of surveillance and planning. You're going to require a well-equipped army. You have to gather supplies and equipment. And you're telling me that you didn't consider, even for a moment, that he was continuing to use you just to buy time? And maybe he blew you off because he was finally ready?"

Her voice became strident. "After he told me to go, I was confused and upset, but I've thought about it. I know what he feels for me is real. I've looked him in his eyes. I've seen the emotion."

"Don't be romantic, okay? Not in matters of war. That bastard is a stone-cold killer and he used you. You're like everybody else to him. You're a tool to get him what he wants. Take your blinders off, female, and get real."

There was a long silence, and he could practically hear her thinking hard.

And then she said in a low voice, "All that aside . . . what are you going to do with me?"

As Xcor listened to the voices far down the corridor, he tested his bounds anew even though he knew naught had changed and he was stuck where he was, pinned upon the table. And then he caught the scent of a new male, heard heavy footfalls approaching, sensed an aggression that was downright rageful.

The time had come. The reckoning was here, and he was not going to live through it.

Flexing his arms and legs once more, he found his strength at an ebb. But it was what it was. Perhaps that meant he would die faster and that was of measurable benefit.

The face that came into his line of sight was a well-familiar one, the mismatched blue and green stare, hard features, and black hair identifiers that made Xcor smile a little.

"You find me amusing?" Qhuinn demanded in a voice flat as a knife blade. "I'd think you'd greet your killer with something other than a grin."

"Irony," Xcor said roughly.

"Destiny, motherfucker."

Qhuinn went for the steel band at Xcor's left ankle, the tugging and pulling making Xcor frown—and as the pressure was released, he strained to lift his head. The Brother went on to remove the one on the right . . . and then proceeded up higher to the wrists.

"What . . . doing . . ." Under no construct could he fathom why he would be set free. "Why . . ."

Qhuinn went around his head and unlocked the last of the binds. "Because I want this to be a fair fight. Sit the fuck up."

Xcor started to move slowly, bending his arms and then lifting his knees. After having been flat on his back for however long, all of his muscles had atrophied and there was an essential stiffness to his joints that made him think of tree branches snapping. But it was amazing how being on the verge of getting attacked made you break through pain and functional barriers.

"Are you not"—he grunted as he rose onto his elbows, his vertebrae cracking along the highway of his spine—"even going to ask me . . ."

Qhuinn settled into a fighting stance about five feet away, his fists raised, his weight down on his legs. "Ask you what?"

"Where my soldiers are?"

Ever since his consciousness had been noted by his captors, all of the wires that had been running between his body and the machines that had kept him alive had been removed, save for the IV in his arm. On instinct, he ripped it out and left the hole to bleed.

"This is not about your Band of Bastards."

With that, the male lunged at him, leading with a right hook that was so accurate and violent that it was like getting hit by a car in the side of the face. With no energy, little coordination, and a naked body that wasn't responding to commands more complicated than those of breathe and blink, Xcor flipped off the table. In mid-air, he reached out to whatever he could grab hold of to stop his fall—and caught the edge of the gurney, pulling it down on top of himself.

Qhuinn went for the shield, picked it up, and threw the thing over his shoulder like it weighed nothing more than a pillow—and the crash, as it hit the shelves and shattered jars, was loud as a bomb going off in the torch-lit corridor.

"You motherfucker!" Qhuinn shouted. "You fucking asshole!"

Xcor felt himself get dragged upright by the hair, and his legs didn't have a chance to fail him—his body went the way of the table, flying through the air, hitting a fresh section of shelving, the jars offering as much cushion as gravel.

As he landed in a heap, the rock floor cracked his pelvis like glass, or at least it felt that way, and he rolled over onto his back in hopes of providing some defensive protection for himself with his hands.

Qhuinn jumped over him, one boot on each side of his torso. Crouching down, the Brother yelled, "She was with my young! Jesus Christ, you could have killed them!"

Xcor closed his eyes against a razor-sharp image of Layla with her changing body, the result of another male's offspring—*this* male's offspring—growing within her. And then worse pictures presented themselves upon his mind . . . that of her flesh bared to another male's touch, her precious core penetrated by someone other than he, a mating occurring between her and somebody else.

From out of nowhere, a surge of power enlivened his body, gasoline flooding what had been a dry engine.

Without conscious thought, he flashed his fangs, the canines descending on their own, his bonding scent flaring against a target that he was going to kill with his bare hands.

Qhuinn's nostrils flared, and he froze as if stunned.

"Are you fucking kidding me . . . you've fucking *bonded* with her?" The Brother started laughing, throwing his head back—but then abruptly, he cut the levity and sneered. "Well, I serviced her in her need. Think about that, motherfucker. I was the one who took her and eased her pain in the way only a male—"

The great wild part of any male vampire took over Xcor, ripping off the claustrophobic blanket of weakness, exposing the warrior in his blood, the killer in his marrow.

Xcor sprung up and hit the Brother with everything he had, tackling Qhuinn and sending them both on a scatter down the opposite wall of shelves, their positions changing one for another as Qhuinn shoved back and punches were thrown. Xcor was by far sloppier and more easily o'erpowered, but he had the bonding on his side, his male need to protect and defend, his innate jealousy, his overwhelming possessiveness providing him with a vital will to attack until he subjugated his competitor.

As they scrambled, his feet got chewed up on the broken pottery, and he bled from his nose, and one of his legs dragged like dead weight, but he nailed Qhuinn with a head butt and then threw all of his strength into shoving his opponent off. As Qhuinn careened back in the direction of the medical equipment, arms pinwheeling for a stability that could not be found, Xcor leaped forth, intending to land upon the Brother and beat him senseless.

But like the trained fighter he was, Qhuinn managed to twist whilst in free fall, and somehow righted himself in time to plant his boots and pick up one of the monitors. Slinging the heavy weight in a circle, he cast it upon Xcor, as one might a boulder.

No time to duck, not with coordination as poor as Xcor's, and the impact cost him his breath and balance, the air forced out of his lungs as the medical device struck him in the side. After a mere beat of recovery, however, he pitched himself into a defensive roll—for Qhuinn had picked up another piece of equipment, this one even larger.

Qhuinn lifted the ventilator high, and Xcor knew that he provided too large and slow a target for the Brother to miss.

So he rushed at the male instead of away from him. And at the last second, Xcor dropped flat, punched his palms into the stone floor, and mobilized every single muscle he had to send his lower body on a swinging ride, his bare legs circling round—

To knock Qhuinn's feet right out from under him.

As the Brother fell, the ventilator slipped from his hold and went down atop him, the curse and grunt suggesting contact had been made in a vulnerable place.

Indeed, he curled into himself as if his gut had been compromised.

Split second. Xcor had a split second to cut through his bonded-male response and analyze the fight with logic. Fortunately, there was not much consideration required. Even with the bonding in his veins, he was going to lose this.

And when facing an opponent who outmatched you, if one wished to survive, one retreated and to hell with ego.

The Bloodletter had taught him that. The hard way.

With Qhuinn torquing onto all fours and clutching his side, Xcor took off on his lacerated feet, tripping and falling over the ruined gurney and careening through the debris field of broken *lesser* jars and the rank, rotting hearts contained therein. He could not run; his stride was more that of a drunk, pitching him all around, the world spinning even though he was fairly sure that the torches and the shelving were static.

Fast as he could go. And then even faster.

He went as quickly as any male who had been immobilized by his enemy for weeks and weeks could.

Which was to say he was all but out for a saunter. Qhuinn, however, had been badly hurt. A quick glance over the shoulder showed the Brother vomiting blood.

Xcor kept going, a brief optimism spurring him onward. Except then he confronted a problem that was of such magnitude that his inefficiency of forward momentum was rendered moot.

In the flickering torchlight, he saw heavy gates up ahead that were made of stout iron bars set into the rock of the cave—and they had a mesh of steel set upon them that was so fine that dematerializing was going to be impossible.

Xcor was panting, bleeding, sweating, and shaking as he came up and tested with his pathetic arms the strength of the barrier. Solid as the cave's walls. Not a surprise.

Looking behind himself, he saw Qhuinn stand up, shake his head as if to clear it, and find an abrupt focus.

As a predator does with its prey.

The fact that there was blood dripping from the male's chin and covering his chest seemed a portent of destiny.

Alas, he was not going to survive this.

TEN

As Layla waited for Wrath to speak of her punishment, she could not swallow for the fear and the shame and the regret. Then again, her mouth was so dry, there was nothing to carry down her throat.

Unable to stay still, but incapable of standing up from the bed, she looked away from the harsh figure of her King—only to catch sight of the bullet holes in the plaster high up in the far corner. Nausea rose from her gut, a vile, burning tide. With her anger spent, she couldn't fathom her previous rage, but she had no doubt of where she had been emotionally. Where Qhuinn had been.

Dearest Virgin Scribe, she was going to throw up.

"I'm not going to have you killed," Wrath announced.

Layla exhaled as she sagged. "Oh, thank you, my Lord—"

"But you can't stay here."

She straightened as her heart began to pound. "And what of the young?"

"We'll work out some kind of visitation or—"

Bolting upright, she put her hands to her throat sure as if she were actually being strangled. "You cannot separate me from them!"

The King's visage, so aristocratic, so commanding, offered compassion, but no quarter. "You can't stay here anymore. Xcor is not going to live through what we're going to do to him, but Throe has fed from you, and even though it's been a while, it's just not safe. We assumed the *mhis* was strong enough to insulate us, but clearly that's faulty logic—and a security risk on a catastrophic scale."

Layla stumbled across and fell to her knees at Wrath's feet, clasping her hands in prayer. "I swear to you, I never meant for any of this to happen. Please, I beg of you, don't take my young away from me. Anything else, I shall abide by, I swear!"

Out in the hall, she knew the Brothers had closed in once again and were listening at a discreet distance, and she didn't care that they were seeing her fall apart. Wrath did, though. He shot a glare over his shoulder.

"Back off—we're good in here," he barked.

No, we're not, she thought. We are not good at all herein.

There was a brief commotion and then there was no one out in the corridor that she could see—and Wrath refocused on her, his deep inhale flaring his nostrils. "I can smell your emotions. I know you're not lying about what you say and what you believe. But there are times when intent is irrelevant and this is one of them. You need to leave now—"

"My young!"

"—or I shall have you removed."

As tears fell, she wanted to wail, but there was naught to argue against. He was correct. Xcor had found her and followed her home, and who was to say Throe could not do the same? Even though she had fed that male but once, with her blood being so pure, the tracking effects could last years, decades, maybe longer. Why had she not considered this? Why had not they?

"Are you extinguishing my parental rights?" she said hoarsely.

The horror of losing her young was so overwhelming, she could barely put her fear into words. In all her worst nightmares, she had never thought it would come down to this. She had never once considered that the ramifications would be so devastating.

But then again, when one was going into a head-on collision, one could not possibly catalog with total accuracy the extent of the upcoming injuries—especially if you were in the midst of evasive maneuvers to try to stave off the accident itself.

Fate had placed her here.

Her own choices had, too.

There was no negotiating with either.

"No," Wrath said abruptly. "I will not cut you off. Qhuinn will hate it, but that is not my problem."

Layla closed her eyes, her tears squeezing out and tangling in her lashes. "Your mercy knows no bounds."

"Bullshit. And now you got to go. I have some properties that are secure and I'll arrange for transport. Start packing."

"But who will stay with them?" She wheeled around to the bassinets. "My young . . . oh, dearest Virgin Scribe—"

"Qhuinn will. And then we'll make arrangements for you to see them." The King cleared his throat. "This is . . . how it must be. I have to think of the other young here—hell, right now, I'm wondering if I don't need to evac every single person in this house. Jesus, why they haven't attacked already, I don't fucking know."

As she imagined not sleeping beside Lyric and Rhamp, not feeding them through the day, not being the one to change them and soothe them and bathe them, she couldn't breathe. "But only I know what they need, and I—"

"Say your goodbyes, and then Fritz will—"

"What the *hell* happened here?"

As Wrath pivoted back around, Layla sniffled and looked up. The Primale was standing in the broken doorway, Phury's brows down low over his yellow eyes, his body strapped with weapons and smelling of the outdoors.

"Are you all right, Layla?" he asked with concern as he entered and stepped around Wrath. "Dearest Virgin Scribe, what—are those bullet holes? Who the hell discharged a weapon here! Are the kids okay?"

"Qhuinn was the one with the happy finger." Wrath crossed his arms over his chest and shook his head. "The young are fine, but she needs to leave. Maybe you can help take her out of here?"

Phury jerked toward his leader, his multi-colored hair swinging on his broad shoulders. "What are you talking about?"

The King was efficient with the story about her and Xcor—and he didn't use the words *betrayal*, *treason*, or *punishable by death*, but he didn't have to. All of that and so much more was implied readily—although Wrath didn't get through the whole story.

Phury cut him off before the end. "So that's why he came!"

"Xcor was using her, yes—"

"No! Qhuinn! Fuck!" Phury put his fingers to his mouth and whistled so loudly that Layla had to cover her ears. Then he started talking fast. "Qhuinn just came to the *sanctum sanctorum*! He told me he was taking Lassiter's place for the day and—shit, he said he was waiting for backup. He didn't look right, so I figured on my way to the Great Camp, I'd stop by here and make sure that whoever Blay got to cover him was going to go there immediately—"

"No!" Layla shouted. "He can't be alone with—"

"He's going to kill Xcor," Wrath snapped. "Goddamn it—"

Zsadist, Phury's identical twin brother, slid into the doorway in the process of pulling a chest holster on. "What?"

Wrath cursed. "He's going to fucking kill him. You two, go now! I'll get Vishous!"

As the Brothers and the King rushed out, Layla hurried into the hall in their wake. Even though there was nothing she could do—nothing she should do—she was enveloped in the nightmare.

Just as they all were.

At the great gate of the cave, Xcor turned his back on Qhuinn's limping, bleeding approach and yanked at the bars, putting all his instinct for survival into the pull. To naught effect.

"I'm going to fucking kill you," Qhuinn said roughly. "With my bare fucking hands. And then I'm going to eat your heart while it's still warm—"

Xcor went to turn around and prepare a defense against his attacker—when something flashed in the firelight and froze him where he stood. At first, he couldn't believe what caught his attention. It was so unexpected that even the prospect of certain death wasn't enough to distract him.

Closing his eyes, he shook his head and then popped his lids wide as if perhaps that would give him a more accurate view.

On the opposite side of where the gate's hinges were . . . there was a lock. And sure as the sun set in the west, there appeared to be a key sticking out of the mechanism.

As the shuffling sound of Qhuinn's uneven gait grew louder, Xcor reached out a shaking hand and wrenched the heavy piece of old metal one way—and then the other—

The tumbler cranked over and suddenly what had been solid as a rock had a remarkable give to it. Xcor pulled the gate open and stumbled out.

Qhuinn tweaked immediately to the colossal security breach, the Brother cursing and sprinting forward whilst holding his side. But Xcor snatched the key, slammed the weight shut, and discovered, yes—*yes!*—the mechanism was a double-sided lock.

As the Brother came into range and pitched his heavy body against the iron bars, Xcor shoved the key home, wrenched it in the correct direction and—

Locked Qhuinn inside the cave.

Xcor shoved himself back as the Brother railed against the iron bars and steel mesh, a snarling, cursing horror that was the Grim Reaper bitterly denied and then some.

Landing on his naked ass, Xcor trembled so hard his teeth clapped together.

"—going to kill you!" Qhuinn screamed as his hands clawed at the mesh until they began to bleed. "I'm going to fucking kill you!"

Xcor looked over his shoulder. Fresh air was coming from that direction, and he knew he had no time. Qhuinn most certainly would call for backup as soon as he stopped wrestling with his iron opponent.

Hobbling to his feet, he listed so badly he had to catch himself on the cave wall. "I shall leave the key here."

His weak and shaky voice cut through the tirade, briefly quieting his opponent.

"I want no part of you or the Brotherhood." He bent down and put the key on the dirt. "I wish you no harm, no ill will. I covet no longer the throne, nor do I desire for war. I leave this key as a testament to my intentions—and I swear on the female I love with all my soul that I shall never enter upon your premises here or any other place again."

He started off, dragging a foot behind himself. But then he paused and looked back.

Meeting Qhuinn's wild, mismatched stare, Xcor spoke with clarity. "I love Layla. And I never once claimed her body—nor shall I. I will never seek her out nor set mine eyes upon her again. You want me to die? Well, I have. For every night she lives with you and your young, I am being murdered for I am not in her presence. So your goal is well-served and accomplished."

With that, he set upon his departure, praying that somehow he might be able to dematerialize. As his vision began to flicker, however, he had little faith that that would be the case.

His strength was failing him now that the bonded male in him was no longer triggered by a rival. Indeed, there seemed little cause to try to run as he was just going to fall back into the very hands he had been in, but there was naught to be done about that. If he was lucky, they would catch him in the wilderness and shoot him like a wild boar.

But luck had rarely been on his side.

ELEVEN

Back at the Brotherhood mansion, down a good four doors from where the drama with the gun had rolled out, Tohr lay back on top of his bed, fully clothed. As he stared up at the canopy overhead, he tried to convince himself that he was relaxing—and it was an argument he lost. From his rock-hard thighs to his twitching fingers to the way his eyeballs bounced around, he was about as chill as an electrical current.

Closing his lids, all he could see was that forty swinging around and bullets flying inside the mansion.

The whole world seemed out of control—

"I've brought you some tea."

Before he could stop himself, Tohr went for the gun strapped under his arm. But instantly, as he caught the scent of his female and recognized her voice, he lowered his hand and focused on Autumn. His beloved *shellan* was standing in front of him, his YETI mug in her hand, her eyes sad and serious.

"Come here," he said, reaching out to take her hand. "You are what I need."

Tugging her to a sit beside him, he thanked her for the tea and put the Earl Grey aside. Then with a shudder of relief, he eased her onto his chest, wrapped his arms around her, and held her to his heart.

"Bad night," he said into her fragrant hair. "Very bad night."

"Yes. I am so glad no one was hurt—and it is also Wellsie's birthday. It's a very, very bad night."

Tohr set Autumn back a little so he could stare into her face. Following the murder of his pregnant mate by the enemy, he had been convinced he would never love again. How could he, after that tragedy? But this kind, patient, steady female before him had opened his heart and soul, giving him life where he was dead, light in his perpetual darkness, sustenance in his starvation.

"How are you like this?" he wondered, tracing her cheek with his fingertips.

"Like what?" She reached up and smoothed back the white stripe that had formed in the front of his hair right after Wellsie had died.

"You've never resented her or . . ." It was hard for him to acknowledge his continued attachment to his dead aloud to her. He never wanted to make her feel lesser. "Or my feelings for her."

"Why would I? Cormia has never been frustrated by her male's lack of a limb. Nor Beth by Wrath's blindness. I love you as you are, not how you would have been if you had never loved another, never lost another, never been cheated out of a chance to be a father."

"It could only be you," he whispered, leaning in to press his lips to hers. "You are the only one I could ever be with."

Her smile was as her heart, open, guileless, accepting. "How convenient, as I feel the same for you."

Tohr deepened the kiss, but then broke the contact—and she understood why he stopped, just as she always understood him: He could not lie with her on this evening or this day. Not until midnight. Not until Wellsie's birthday was over.

"I don't know where I would be without you." Tohr shook his head, thinking about the mood he'd been in as he'd gone to the cave to kill Xcor. "I mean . . ."

As Autumn smoothed the frown between his brows, he went further back in time, to when Lassiter had shown up in the middle of a forest with a bag full of McDonald's and an insistence that Tohr return to his brothers. The fallen angel hadn't listened to reason—the beginning of a trend, natch—and the pair of them had halt-and-lamed it back here to the mansion.

Tohr had been on the verge of death, having survived on deer blood and not much else for however long he had been out in the woods on his own. He'd had a plan back then: Over the course of those months, he'd tried to kill himself by attrition because he'd been unwilling to test the urban legend that people who committed suicide didn't go to the Fade.

Starving himself had seemed, to his addled mind, a different death from putting a bullet in his head.

But that hadn't been his destiny. Just as returning to this house with that fallen angel hadn't been his salvation.

No, he owed that to this female here. She and she alone had turned him around, their love bringing him back from hell. With Autumn, his perspective on staying on the planet had done a total one eighty, and although he still had bad nights, like tonight . . . he also had good ones.

He refocused on his female. "Your love has transformed me."

God, it was almost like Lassiter had known how it was all going to turn out, had been sure that then was the time for Tohr's return and resurrection—

Tohr frowned, sensing a shift in his female. "Autumn? What's wrong?"

"Sorry. I'm just wondering . . . what's going to happen to Layla?"

Before he could answer, someone started pounding on their door—and that kind of urgency meant one and only one thing: a mobilization of arms. Had the Band of Bastards decided to attack?

Tohr set Autumn aside gently, and then leapt off the bed for his dagger holster.

"What's going on!" he barked out. "Where are we going?"

The door flew open and Phury looked like hell. "Qhuinn's down at the Tomb alone with Xcor."

Tohr froze for a heartbeat, doing the math and coming to a conclusion that meant he was getting cheated out of killing that fucking asshole. "Goddamn it, he's mine, not Qhuinn's—"

"You're staying here. We need someone on Wrath. Everyone else is going there."

Tohr ground his molars at getting benched, but he wasn't surprised. And guarding the King himself was hardly a demotion. "Keep me posted?"

"Always."

With a curse, the brother wheeled away and took off along with the others, joining what became a stampede of shitkickers pounding down the hall of statues.

"Go," Autumn told him. "Seek out Wrath. It will make you feel purposeful."

He looked over his shoulder. "You always know me, don't you."

His beautiful mate shook her blond head. "You have mysteries that still captivate me."

As a sudden lust thickened his blood, Tohr released a pumping purr. "Midnight. You are mine, female."

Her smile was as old as the species and just as enduring. "I cannot wait."

Tohr was out in the corridor a moment later—and feeling totally cooped up even though the mansion had how many rooms? But then, as he came up to the open doorway of Wrath's study, the King nearly mowed him over.

"—fucking bullshit, I'm outta here." Wrath shut the double doors behind him and headed for the top of the grand staircase. "Goddamn it, I'm a brother, I'm allowed in there—"

"My Lord, you can't go to the Tomb."

As George, the King's service dog, whimpered on the far side of the closed-up study, the last purebred vampire on earth hit the stairs on a pounding descent.

"Wrath." Tohr fell into a jog right on the male's heels, but didn't bother much with the whole volume thing. "Stop. No, really. Stop."

Yup, he was about as persuasive as an asshole with semaphore flags and two broken arms: He wasn't jumping in front of his ruler. He wasn't reaching out, grabbing onto the guy, and forcing the King to stay inside. And he wasn't, ultimately, going to prevent his ruler from leaving for the Tomb. Where Qhuinn was.

Where Xcor was.

Because, hey, if he were guarding the King, he had to go with the male wherever he went, right? And if that just so happened to take him to where that Bastard was? Welllllllll, that was hardly his fault. Besides, given Wrath's mood? Any argument about staying put was going to be wasted breath. The King was highly reasonable—except when he wasn't. And when that black-haired SOB with the wraparounds decided he was going to do, or not do, something? Nobody, but nobody, was going to change his mind.

With the exception of maybe Beth—and even that wasn't a given.

As he and Wrath hit the foyer and crossed the mosaic depiction of an apple tree in bloom, Tohr said in a bored voice, "Seriously. Let the others handle it. Stop."

Wrath didn't hesitate and did not falter. Even though he was sightless, he was so familiar with the mansion, he was able to anticipate the number of steps, the direction, even the height of the enormous door handle he was gunning for. Things kept up like this and they were going to be at that cave on the northern side of the mountain in a nanosecond.

Except . . . as the entrance to the vestibule got yanked open and cold air rushed in, Tohr took a deep breath.

And instantly, his insanity cleared.

Wait a minute, he thought. What the hell was he doing?

It was one thing to go off the handle himself—another to fail at his job as a private guard and allow the King to put himself into a situation that could endanger his life. And also, P.S., it was bullshit to want to kill Xcor for shooting at Wrath, while at the same time be willing to let the King walk into what could be an ambush. The Band of Bastards was even more of a wild card than ever. What if something went wrong down there with Qhuinn going rogue and Xcor somehow got free? Found his boys? Attacked the Brotherhood?

As Wrath pile drove through the vestibule and headed out into the night, Tohr got back on the job.

Now he did leap in front, shove his hands out, punch the pecs of his ruler.

Glaring into those black wraparounds, he said, "Hold up, I can't let you go to the Tomb. As much as I really want a fucking excuse to get down there and deal with Xcor's fucking ass on my own terms, I won't be able to live with myself if—"

Buh-bye.

Without a single word or hesitation, Wrath up and disappeared. Which proved Tohr had been fucking right about the King doing what he wanted—and really fucking stupid for not tackling the male on the grand staircase.

"Damn it!" Tohr muttered as he unholstered both of his forties.

His own dematerialization cut off the rest of the curses that were running a scrimmage through his no-account brain. And then he was resuming his form in the dense woods, at the place he had been forcibly evicted from no more than an hour before.

Oh . . . *God.*

Blood. In the midst of the gusting, frigid wind . . . he could smell Xcor's blood.

The sonofabitch was out? What the hell? Because that shit was not distilled from a distance, as if it were coming from an injury that was in the cave's interior.

No, it was right at his feet, in the fallen pine needles and the dirt. A trail.

An escape.

Even though his instinct to track the male was nearly overpowering, Wrath was more important. Pivoting on his shitkicker, he jogged over to his ruler.

"My Lord!" Tohr scanned the environs, looking for movement. "What the fuck is wrong with you! We need to get you out of here!"

Wrath ignored him and headed into the cave, where the voices of other brothers were echoing around and clearly providing him with an orientation. Tohr thought about stopping the male, but better in there with the Brotherhood than out in the forest as a sitting duck.

Man, they were going to have words after this, though.

Great night for the household. For fuck's sake.

The scent of the blood was thicker here, and yes, he had a stab of jealousy go through his chest. Qhuinn had clearly had at the bastard. But something had gone very, very wrong. There was the trail of barefoot prints and blood leading out of the cave, and Qhuinn was leaking, too. That scent was likewise strong.

Was the brother still alive? Had Xcor somehow overpowered him and taken the key to the gate? But how would that have been possible? Xcor had been half dead on that gurney.

As Tohr and the King went deeper into the cave, the light from the torches at the gate offered a glow to follow and then he and Wrath came up to everyone else—and Tohr confronted a situation that was as unexpected as it was inexplicable.

Qhuinn was on the interior of the great gates of the *sanctum sanctorum*, sitting on his ass on the rock floor, his elbows on his knees. He was bleeding in a number of places and breathing in a shallow way that suggested he might have some broken ribs. His clothes were all out of order, and stained with blood that was his and had to be Xcor's, too, and his knuckles were busted up.

But that was not the weirdness.

The key to the gate was on the outside. Sitting upon the earthen floor like it had been placed there deliberately.

Three of his brothers were standing around the thing like it might blow up on them, and everywhere else, people were talking over each other. All that chatter ended, however, as Wrath's presence registered on the group.

"What the fuck!" someone said.

"Jesus, Mary, and Joseph!" Okay, that was Butch. "What the hell?"

More brothers jumped on that bandwagon, but the King was having none of it. "What am I looking at! Someone fucking tell me what I'm looking at!"

In the silence that followed, Tohr waited for one of the first responders, so to speak, to do the rundown.

Except no one seemed to want to man up.

Fine, fuck it, Tohr thought. "Qhuinn's conscious, bleeding, and locked inside the Tomb. The key"—Tohr shook his head at the gate—"is on our side of the lock. Qhuinn, is Xcor in there with you or not?"

Even though that trail of blood out through the forest provided answer enough.

Qhuinn dropped his head and rubbed at his dark hair, his palm making slow circles in what was already matted. "He escaped."

Okaaaaaaaaaaaaaaay, you want to talk about f-bombs? It was like each and every one of the Brotherhood had had a piano dropped on his fricking foot and was using the word "fuck" as an analgesic.

A sense of urgency made Tohr unplug from all that. Turning away, he took out his cell phone, initiated the flashlight, and swept the beam around. Tracking those messy prints in the loose sand and dirt was easy and he followed them back out to the mouth of the cave. Xcor had been shuffling, rather than walking, his ambulation compromised clearly both by the month he'd spent on his back as well as by whatever had gone down when he and Qhuinn had done their rounds.

As Tohr reemerged in the thick of the forest, he crouched down, and swung the little light in a circle. Behind him, a huge argument was rolling out between Wrath and the Brotherhood, those deep voices echoing around courtesy of the rock walls, but he let them have at it. Walking forward, he shut the beam off and put his cell phone back into his ass pocket. He hadn't taken a coat or anything with him as he'd left the mansion, but the twenty-five-degree night didn't bother him.

He was too busy making like a bloodhound, sniffing the air.

Xcor had gone to the west.

Tohr fell into a jog, but he couldn't go too fast. With the wind coming and going in different directions, it was hard to keep the trail.

And then it just ended.

Circling around, Tohr back-tracked so he could reconnect with the blood path . . . and then yup, lost it once more.

"Oh, you fucking bastard," he hissed into the night.

How in the fuck that weak, wounded piece of shit had managed to dematerialize, Tohr was never going to comprehend. But you couldn't disagree with the facts: The only possible explanation for the trail getting cut off so abruptly was that the bastard had somehow found the strength and will to ghost out.

If Tohr hadn't hated the motherfucker with such a passion . . . he'd have almost respected the sonofabitch.

As Xcor resumed his corporeal form, it was naked in a heap on some snow-covered brush, deep within a forest that was no longer of pine, but of maple and oak. Gasping, he forced his eyes to get to work, and when the landscape abruptly appeared clear and in focus, he knew he'd made it off the Brotherhood's property. The *mhis*, that protective blurring of the landscape that marked their territory, was gone, and his sense of direction was returned unto him.

Not that he had any clue of his whereabouts.

Over the course of his escape, he had managed to dematerialize three times. Once from about fifty yards outside of the cave; the second, some distance away from that, mayhap a mile down the mountain; and then to here, to this flat portion of parkland, which suggested he was well away from the mountain where he had been held.

Rolling onto his back, he pumped his lungs and prayed for strength.

The immediate threat to his life having passed, an insurmountable weakness came upon him, as deadly as any other kind of foe. And then there was the cold that further compounded the energy deficit, slowing his already poor reflexes as well as his heart rate. But none of that was his biggest concern.

Turning his head, he looked to the east.

The horizon was going to start warming from dawn's imminent arrival within the hour. Even in his state, he could feel the shimmers of warning across his naked skin.

Forcing his head off the ground, he searched for shelter, a cave, perhaps, or a collection of boulders . . . an overturned, rotting trunk that offered a hollow place in which he could hide himself. All he saw were trees, standing arm in arm, their bare boughs forming a canopy that was not going to provide nearly enough protection from the dawn.

He was going to be up in flames as soon as the sun rose fully.

At least then he would be warm, however. And at least then, it would all be over.

Certainly, whatever horrors immolation held for him, they were nothing in comparison to what tortures the Brotherhood would have no doubt put him through—tortures that would have been for naught, assuming information on his Band of Bastards was what they would be after.

For one, his soldiers would have followed protocol and decamped to another locale following his disappearance. After all, death or capture were the only two explanations for any absence of his, and there was no logical rationale to gamble on which one it might be.

For the second, he wouldn't have given up his fighters even if he were in the process of being disemboweled.

The Bloodletter hadn't been able to break him. No one else would.

But again, all of that was moot, the now.

Curling onto his side, he drew his legs up to his chest, wrapped his arms around himself, and shivered. The leaves under him were no soft bed, their frozen, curled edges cutting into his skin. And as wind crisscrossed the landscape, a tormentor in search of victims, it seemed to pay particular attention to him, pushing forest debris into his nooks and crannies, stealing ever more of his dwindling body heat.

Closing his eyes, he found a part of the past coming back to him . . .

It was December of his ninth year, and he was in front of the ramshackle, thatch-roofed cottage in which he and his nursemaid stayed. Indeed, as soon as night fell each evening, he was cast out here and chained in place by the neck, tolerated upon the interior once more only when the sun was threatening in the east and the humans would be out. For most of the lonely, cold hours, especially during this, the winter season, he huddled against the outer wall of his home, moving on his tether only to stay in the lee of the wind.

His stomach was empty, and going to stay that way. No one of the race in their tiny village would e'er approach him to offer him food in his starvation, and his nursemaid certainly would not feed him until she had to—and then it would be scraps after dawn of the meals she ate herself.

Putting his dirty fingers to his mouth, he felt the distortion that ran between his upper lip and the base of his nose. The defect had always been thus, and because of it, his mahmen *had sent him out of the birthing room, casting him into the hands of his nursemaid. With no one else to care for him, he tried to do right by the female, tried to make her happy, but nothing he did e'er pleased her—and she seemed to relish telling him, o'er and o'er again, how his birth* mahmen *had banished him from her sight, how he had been a curse unto an otherwise high-bred female of worth.*

His best course was to get out of the nursemaid's way, out of her sight, out of her home. And yet she would not let him run away. He had tried that sometime back and gotten as far as the rim of fields that surrounded their hamlet. As soon as his absence had registered, however, she had come for him and beaten him so badly that he had cowered and cried in the midst of her blows, begging her for forgiveness, for what, he did not know.

That was how he came to be chained.

The metal links ran from the rough collar around his throat to the iron horse hitch at the corner of the cottage. No more wandering for him, and no more shifting position unless he had to relieve himself or keep sheltered. The coarse leather about his neck had worn raw spots in his skin, and as it was never removed, there was no healing of the sores to be had. But he had long learned to endure.

His life, such that he was aware of it, was about enduring.

Bending his knees up to his meager chest, he linked his arms around the bones of his legs and shivered. His vestments were limited to one of his nurse-maid's threadbare wool capes and a set of male's pants that were so large that he could secure them under his armpits with a rope. His feet were bare, but if he kept them under the cloak, they did not freeze.

As the wind gusted through bare trees, the sound it made was like the howl of a wolf, and his eyes widened as he searched the shifting darkness, in the event that what he heard was indeed of lupine nature. He was terrified of wolves. If one, or a pack, came after him, he would be eaten, he was quite sure, as his chain meant he could not seek escape into or up any of the trees, nor could he reach the door to the cottage.

And he did not believe his nursemaid would save him. Sometimes he quite believed she chained him in the hopes he would be consumed, his death from elements or the wild freeing her whilst, if it occurred thusly, not being her exact fault.

To whom she was accountable, though, he did not know. If his mahmen *had disowned him, who paid for his keep? His sire? The male had never been identified unto him and had certainly never shown up—*

As an eerie howling sound wove through the night, he cringed.

It was the wind. It had to be . . . merely the wind.

Seeking something to calm his mind, he stared at the pool of warm yellow light that emanated from the cottage's single window. The flickering illumination played upon the twisted tentacles of the dead raspberry patch that surrounded the cottage, making the thorned bushes move as if they were alive—and he tried not to find anything sinister in the constant shifting. No, instead, he fixed his eyes upon the glow and tried to picture himself before the hearth inside, warming his hands and his feet, his weak muscles uncoiling from their turgor-ous self-protection against the chill.

In his idle dreaming, he imagined his nursemaid smiling at him and holding her arms out, encouraging him to nestle into safety against her. He fantasized of her stroking his hair and not caring that it was filthy, and offering him food that was unspoiled and whole. He would bathe afterward, cleaning his skin and removing the collar from his throat. Ointment would soothe that which pained him, and then she would tell him that she cared not that he was imperfect.

She would forgive him for his existence, and whisper that his mahmen *actually loved him and would come for him soon.*

And then he would finally sleep soundly, the suffering over—

Another howl interrupted his musings, and he rushed back to full awareness, searching once more the brush and the stands of skeletal trees.

It was always thus, this back and forth betwixt him feeling the need to be aware of his surroundings in the event of attack . . . and him seeking shelter in his mind to avoid that from which he could do naught to save himself.

Tucking his head into his shoulder, he squeezed his eyes shut once more.

There was another fantasy he entertained, although not as often. He pretended that his sire, about whom his nursemaid had ne'er spoken, but whom Xcor imagined was a fierce fighter for the race, came upon a steed of war and rescued him away. He imagined the great fighter calling out to him, summoning him forth and putting him high upon the saddle, calling him "son" with pride. Upon a powerful gallop they would set, the mane lashing Xcor's face as they went in search of adventure and glory.

In truth, that was just as unlikely to happen as him being welcomed into the cottage's interior—

Off in the distance, the pounding of horse hooves signaled an approach, and for a moment, his heart leapt. Had he conjured up his mahmen? *His sire? Had the impossible finally occurred—*

No, not horseback. It was an incredible stagecoach, a proper regal one with a gold gilded body and a matched pair of white horses. There were even footmales in back and a uniformed coachman as driver.

It was a member of the glymera, *an aristocrat.*

And yes, as a footmale jumped down and attended the exit of a gowned and ermine'd female, Xcor had ne'er seen someone as beautiful or scented anything even half as fragrant.

Shifting his position such that he could see around the shack's corner, he winced as the rough leather cut anew into his collarbone.

The grand female did not bother knocking, but had the footmale open wide the creaking door. "Hharm mated her upon the birth of the male. It is done. You are free—he shall not hold you unto this any longer."

His nursemaid frowned. "What say you?"

"'Tis true. Father helped with the sizable dowry that he demanded. Our cousin in now his proper shellan *and you are free."*

"Nae, this cannae be . . ."

As the two females backed into the cottage and shut the footmale out, Xcor struggled to his feet, and peered into the window. Through the thick, bubble-

filled glass, he watched as his nursemaid continued to react with shock and disbelief. The other female, however, must have assuaged her contradiction, for there was a pause . . . and then a great transformation presented itself.

Indeed, a joy so pervasive suffused his nursemaid internally that she was like a cold hearth rekindled, no longer the worn wraith of ugliness he was used to, but something else entirely.

Resplendent she became, even in her tattered garb.

Her mouth moved, and even though he could not hear her voice, he understood exactly what she spoke: I am free . . . I am free!

Through the wavy glass, he watched her look around as if in search of sundries of significance.

She was leaving him, he thought with panic.

As if she read his thoughts, his nursemaid paused and looked over at him through the glass, the firelight playing across her flushed and excited face. With their eyes locked, he put his hand to the dirty pane in entreaty.

"Take me with you," he whispered. "Do not leave me thus . . ."

The other female glanced in his direction and her wince suggested the sight of him turned her stomach. She said something to his nursemaid, and the one who had cared for him for his life thus far didnae immediately respond. But then her face hardened and she straightened as if bracing herself against an inclement gale.

He began to bang on the glass. "Do not leave me! Please!"

The two females turned from him and hustled out, and he ran forth to catch them afore they mounted the coach.

"Take me with you!"

As he rushed forth, he reached the end of his chain and was jerked off his feet by his neck, landing hard, the breath knocked from him.

The female in the fine garments paid no mind as she gathered her skirts and ducked her head to enter the coach's interior. And his nursemaid hurried in behind, putting a hand up to her temple to shield her eyes from him.

"Help me!" He clawed at the rope, scraping his flesh. "What shall become of me!"

One of the footmales closed the gilded hatch. And the doggen *hesitated before returning to his post atop the rear.*

"There is an orphanage not far from here," he said roughly. "Break your-self free and proceed fifty lochens unto the north. There you shall find others."

"Help me!" Xcor screamed as the driver cracked the reins and the horses leapt off, the coach rambling down the dirt lane.

He continued to yell as he was left behind, the noises of the departure growing more faint in the distance . . . until they were no more.

As the wind blew upon him, the tracks of the tears on his face turned icy and his heart thundered in his ears, making it impossible to hear aught. From the flush of his anxiety, he grew so hot from his agitation that he cast aside the cloak, and blood seeped from around his throat, coating his bare chest and those huge pants.

Fifty lochens? An orphanage?

Get himself free?

Such simple words, coming forth from a guilty conscience. But of no aid to him a'tall.

No, he thought. He had but himself to rely upon the now.

Even as he wanted to curl into a ball and cry in fear and sorrow, he knew he must shore himself up, for shelter was dearly required. And with that in foremind, he gathered his emotions and gripped the chain with both his hands. Leaning back, he pulled with all his might, trying to get it free of the tether, its links hissing at the movement.

Whilst he strained, he had some notion that the coach could not be that far off. He might still catch them if he could just get free and run . . .

He further told himself that that was not his mahmen who had just de-parted, having lied to him all along. No, that was merely a nursemaid of some uncommon station.

It was unbearable to think of her otherwise.

TWELVE

It seemed appropriate that Qhuinn had to stare through iron bars to see his brothers—not that he wanted to look at them. But, yeah, a separation between him and those other living-and-breath'ings, marked by an ancient, impenetrable gate, seemed like the best course of inaction.

He was not fit for any kind of company.

And clearly, they were not happy with him, either.

As he sat with his ass on the bare stone floor of the cave and his back against a section of the shelves of jars that was still intact, he watched the Brotherhood prowl and snarl on the far side of all that iron, pacing back and forth and running into each other as they yelled at him. The good news—and it was only marginally "good," he supposed—was that the sound on the whole drama had been turned way down, some trick of the universe, or maybe his failing blood pressure, going dimmer-switch on the world around him.

Just as well. He was already an expert in fuck-onomics. There was nothing that even their most creative use of the f-word could teach him about cursing anyone out.

Besides, considering he was the noun in all those sentences? Who needed that right now. He was doing plenty of rounds of self-immolation in his brain already, thank you very much.

Dropping his head, he closed his eyes. Not a great idea. His side was killing him, and with no distractions, the pain took on Jolly Green Giant proportions. He must have broken something in there. Maybe ruptured a liver or a kidney or a . . .

As a wave of nausea inflated his stomach, he popped his lids and looked in the opposite direction from the zoo of condemnation. Talk about trashing the place. The mangled gurney, the broken medical equipment, all the shattered jars and greasy black hearts on the stone floor . . . it was like a hurricane had come through the cave.

Second place he'd trashed. If you counted shooting up Layla's bedroom.

Although this mess, he regretted.

The other one? Yeah, he was sorry about that, too—but he wasn't stepping off from his hard line on her and his kids.

With a groan, he stretched one leg out and then the other. There was blood on his leathers. On his shitkickers. On the knuckles of both of his hands. He was probably going to need medical attention, but he didn't want it—

An abrupt silence got his attention and he glanced back at the gates. Oh great. Fan-fucking-tastic.

The King was right in front of those iron bars, looking like hell's fury standing upright in shitkickers. And apparently, he wanted a one-on-one on the close-up: Vishous had stepped up and was putting the key into the lock on the far side, the tumbler making a clanking noise as it gave up the goods and allowed the gates to be opened.

Wrath was the only one who entered, and then the pair of them were locked in together. Was it to keep the other brothers from attacking Qhuinn? Or to prevent him from running away from whatever the King had planned?

Choices, choices.

As Wrath came forward and then stopped, Qhuinn ducked his stare even though the male was blind. "Is this where you fire me from the Brotherhood?"

Damn those were some big-ass shitkickers, he thought dimly. From his nearly eye-to-boot vantage point, they seemed the size of a pair of Subarus.

"I'm getting really fucking tired of meeting you like this," Wrath snapped.

"Makes two of us."

"You want to tell me what happened?"

"Not particularly."

"Let me rephrase that, motherfucker. You're going to tell me what happened or I'ma keep you locked in here until you starve down to your bones."

"You know, fad diets never work long term."

"They do if you take a lead supplement with 'em."

Qhuinn eyed the gun holstered under Wrath's immense left arm. Even though the King had no usable peepers, it was a good goddamn bet that he could put a bullet wherever he wanted to just by hearing alone.

"Tell you what," Wrath said. "I'll help you out. You can skip explaining why you thought it was a good idea to come down here and attack a prisoner of mine without permission. I can do that math just fucking fine. Why don't you tell me how he managed to lock you inside here."

Qhuinn rubbed his face, but not for long. The motion made his stomach roll even more—hey, he had a headache, too. Maybe it was a concussion?

#BOGO

He cleared his throat. "When Phury left, he gave me the key to lock myself in with Xcor. And I did."

Which was the new protocol. Back when Xcor had first been taken into custody, whoever was on guard duty had been locked in from the outside. Over time, however, they had changed that procedure out of practical considerations, what with all the different coverage shifts and medical checkups and drug dispensing. And yeah, maybe they'd gotten lax after a month of the bastard just lying there on the gurney like a bad piece of modern art.

"And?" Wrath growled.

"I was distracted. So I forgot to take the fucking key out of the lock."

"You were . . . distracted. By what? Plans to trash all of this?" As the King motioned around at the ruined jars like he could see them, it was clear that the stench of *lesser* had reached his nose. Plus, hello, the peanut gallery was bitching about the mess. "What the *fuck*, Qhuinn. Seriously, have you lost your fucking mind?"

"Yeah, I think I have." Short trip. Hah-hah. "Or was that so rhetorical you don't need an answer? Hey, why don't we stop talking about Xcor so you can tell me what you're going to do with that female of his, Layla."

Talk about wanting to throw up.

In the silence that followed, Wrath crossed his arms over his chest, his biceps swelling up so thick he made The Rock look like The Pencil Neck. "Right now, it's not *her* parental rights I'm thinking about cutting off."

Qhuinn glanced up sharply and then had to cough his gag reflex back in place as his head thundered. "Wait, *what*? She commits treason by aiding and abetting an enemy of ours—"

"And you just let an asset of the Brotherhood's go free because you lost your damn mind. So let's drop the treason shit, shall we. It's only going to get your balls squeezed tighter, trust me."

It was kind of hard to argue with the facts, Qhuinn thought. Good thing his emotions didn't give a shit about logic.

"Just tell me you're getting her out of the house," he demanded. "And that my young are staying with me. That's all I care about."

For a split second, Qhuinn thought about Xcor talking nonsense just before the bastard had limped off. Spouting shit about Layla. Love. Not wanting a piece of Wrath anymore.

Yeah, like he was going to believe any of that.

The King glared from behind his wraparounds. "What I do or do not do is none of your goddamn business."

Hold up. Was there even a possibility that—

"Are you serious!" Qhuinn made a move to get up, but that was a no-go. Yet even as he grunted and retched off to one side, he kept talking through the nausea. "She's forfeited her rights! She fed the enemy!"

"If he's such an enemy, why did Xcor leave the key behind?"

"What?"

Wrath jabbed his forefinger in the direction of the gate. "Xcor locked you in, but put the key down. Why did he do that?"

"I don't fucking know!"

"Yeah, and we can't ask him that now, can we," Wrath snapped.

Qhuinn shook his head. "He's still our enemy. He's always going to be our fucking enemy. I don't give a shit what he says."

Wrath's jet-black brows dropped below the rims of his wraparounds again. "So what did he tell you?"

"Nothing. He didn't say shit." Qhuinn bared his fangs. "And don't worry, I'll get him back. I'll hunt that fucker down and—"

"The hell you will. I'm suspending you from active duty effective immediately."

"What!" Now Qhuinn got up, even though he felt like he was going to pea-soup-*Exorcist* all over the King. "That's bullshit!"

"You're off the fucking rails, and I'm not having it. Now be a good little sociopath and shut the fuck up while you get taken in for medical treatment."

In a rush of nuclear anger, that white-hot rage resurfaced, shorting out Qhuinn's brain again—and as his consciousness took a backseat to all his hellfire, he was dimly aware of his mouth moving like he was yelling at the King. But he didn't have a clue what he was saying.

"You know what?" Wrath cut in with a bored tone. "We're done here, you and I."

That was the last thing Qhuinn heard.

The last thing he saw? The King's massive fist flying in the direction of his jaw.

Talk about fireworks, and then it was lights out, no one left at the inn for him, his legs falling from under him, his weight bowling-pin'ing it to the cave floor.

His final thought before he passed out mid-drop?

Two concussions back-to-back were going to do wonders for his mental health. Yup, just the kind of shit he needed at this point.

Up in her bedroom at the Brotherhood mansion, Layla stood over the bassinets, her eyes going back and forth between her two sleeping young. Lyric's and Rhamp's faces were those of angels, all fat cheeks and rosy, smooth skin, their lashes dark and closed, their arching brows like wings. Both were breathing hard as if they were working with great industry in their repose to grow bigger, stronger, smarter.

It was procreation at work, the Scribe Virgin's race keeping itself going. A miracle. Immortality for the mortal.

As she sensed a presence behind her, she said in a rough, low voice, "You better take out your gun."

"Why?"

She looked over her shoulder at Vishous. The Brother was standing just inside her room, looking like a harbinger of doom. Which he was, in fact.

"If you want me to leave them, you're going to have to put me in the Fade."

It was no surprise that Wrath had sent Vishous to take her away. V was like dealing with an iceberg, the warrior cold, intractable, immovable from whatever goal he was set upon. Other males in the household? Particularly those with young, or Phury as the Primale, or Tohr who had lost a mate and a young of his own? Any of those Brothers might have been persuaded to change course and thus allow her to stay or permit her to take her son and daughter with her.

Not Vishous.

And in her case, perhaps not Tohr. He wanted to kill the male she had betrayed the Brotherhood with.

She eyed the handgun that was strapped under V's arm. "Well?"

Vishous just shook his head. "That's not going to be necessary. Come on, let's go."

She turned back to her young. "Did Qhuinn kill him? Xcor? Is he dead?"

"Fritz is out front. We've got a ways to drive. We're leaving now."

"Like I'm a piece of luggage to be transported." There were no tears for her; the horror of what was happening was so great she was numb to her core. "Is Xcor dead?"

When Vishous spoke next, he was right behind her, his voice at the back of her neck, making the hair at her nape stand up in warning. "Be logical about this—"

She wheeled around and narrowed her eyes. "Don't you dare make it sound like I'm being unreasonable in not wanting to leave them."

"Then don't forget the position you're in." He stroked his goatee with his gloved hand. "You could end up with less than no rights to them, irrespective of their birth. But if you come with me now, I will guarantee—*guarantee*—that they will be back with you soon, perhaps even by nightfall tomorrow."

Layla wrapped her arms around herself. "You don't have that kind of power."

His brow, the one with the tattoos beside it, arched. "Maybe not, but they do."

As he stepped aside and motioned toward the door, she covered her mouth with her palm. One by one, the females of the house filed into the room, and even with Vishous as a comparison, they were a fierce group as they lined up in a semi-circle around her. Even Autumn was with them.

Beth, the Queen, spoke up, her voice quiet clearly so she didn't disturb the young. "I'll talk to Wrath. As soon as he's back from the training center. We're going to fix this. I don't give a crap what happened between you and Xcor—mother to mother, I care only about you and the babies. And my husband will see my point of view. Trust me."

Layla all but lunged into the Queen's embrace, and as Beth held her tightly, Bella came forward and stroked Layla's hair.

"We're going to take care of them while you're gone," Z's female said. "All of us. They won't be alone for a second so try not to worry."

Cormia also stepped forward, the fellow Chosen's pale green eyes watery. "I'm going to stay in the room here all day." She pointed to the bed. "I'm not going to leave their sides."

Ehlena, Rehv's *shellan*, nodded. "As a nurse, I've cared for hundreds of young in my line of work. I know babies back and forth. Nothing will happen to them, I promise."

The others murmured agreement, and one of them handed Layla a tissue. Which was how she realized she was crying again.

Pulling back from Beth, she tried to keep her sniffles as soft as she could. She wanted to say something, wanted to express her fear and her gratitude—

The Queen put her hands on Layla's shoulders. "Your parental rights are not going to be terminated. Not going to happen. And I know exactly where you're going. It's a safe house, totally protected—V wired it for security and I did the decorating myself after the Brotherhood bought it a year ago."

"It's secure there," Vishous stated. "Like a bank vault. And I'm spending the day with you as your goddamn roommate."

"So I'm under guard?" Layla frowned. "Am I prisoner?"

The Brother just shrugged. "You're protected. That's all."

The hell that was all, she thought. But there was nothing she could do. This was larger than her, and she knew all too well the reasons for that.

Going back to Lyric and Rhamp, she found that the tears poured down her face faster than she could clear them with the soggy mess the tissue had turned into. Indeed, something about the females of the house showing up and having her back had defrosted the numb lock in the center of her chest, and now her emotions were raw once again.

She wanted to pick up each of her young and smell their sweet skin, hold them to her heart, cradle their heads as she kissed them. But if she did any of that, she wouldn't be able to leave them.

Her hand shook as she had to settle for tugging up their plush blankets closer to their chins.

"My young," she whispered. "*Mahmen* will be back. I'm not . . . leaving you . . ."

There was no going any further with her goodbye. She choked up so badly speech was impossible.

Her journey to have these two precious blessings had started what felt like a lifetime ago, back when she had sensed her needing was upon her, and had begged Qhuinn to service her. And then had come those endless months of the pregnancy, and the emergency births.

There had been so many impossibles along the way, so many challenges she couldn't have foreseen. But this was one that she had never contemplated: Leaving the young in the care of others, no matter how competent and loving those "others" were, was nothing she could have anticipated.

It was just too horrific.

"Let's go," Vishous said with finality. "Before the dawn comes and things get even more complicated."

With a final look at each of her young, Layla gathered the folds of her robe and walked out of the bedroom. In her wake, she felt as though she had left her heart and soul behind.

THIRTEEN

As night fell the following evening, Qhuinn was unaware of the sun's crash and burn on the western horizon. For one, he was deep underground in the training center's clinic—so that giant flaming orb's change of shift in favor of the moon was nothing he could look out a window and see. For another, he was on the kind of drugs that made you forget your own name, much less what time it was. But the main reason he missed the demise of the day?

Even with all the bad stuff going on in his life, he was having the best fucking hallucination. Like, ever.

The conscious part of his brain—which had taken a backseat so far from his steering wheel that the shit might as well have been strapped on his trunk—was well aware that what he thought he was seeing across the hospital room was absolutely, positively not actually happening. But here was the thing. He was so high that, like the pain from the operation they'd done on him six hours ago, the events of the previous evening were temporarily amnesia'd—and that meant he was spectacularly horny.

This was not a surprise. The fact that he was a pig asshole with a tremendous sex drive had been proven over time.

And hey, considering how he'd behaved the night before, he had so many other things to be disappointed in himself with.

So, yeah, as he lay here in this hospital bed, with tubes and wires going in and out of him like he was Xcor's fucking stunt double, he was seeing Blay sitting in that chair over there in the corner, the one that was the color of Cream of Wheat and had rounded arms and a low back.

The male's fly was open, and his cock was out . . . and Blay's fist was wrapped around that thick length, the veins that ran down his muscled forearm swelling up as he stroked himself.

"You want this?" Hypothetical Blay asked in a deep voice.

Qhuinn hissed and bit his lower lip—and what do you know, as he rolled his hips, he could almost not feel the pain from the incision in his side. "Yeah, fuck yeah, I want that shit."

Not Actually Blay shifted down lower in the seat so that he could spread his knees even wider. And as he did, the black jeans he had on stretched tight over his heavy thigh muscles and that fly got pulled open to its limit. And . . . oh, yeah, as the fighter worked himself, his pec on that side flexed and released along with his shoulder while he pumped, nice and slow.

With a rough swallow, Qhuinn's pierced tongue itched for that head, that shaft. He wanted to make up for what had come out of his no-account mouth when he'd been raging, and sex wasn't a bad Band-Aid, it truly wasn't.

And Not Really There Blay was going to let him.

Floating in his little sea of delusion, Qhuinn felt the false relief that came with a forgiveness that didn't exist in RL. Except goddamn it, considering the state of the rest of his life, he was going to go with this. In this little stretch of fantasy, he was going to hop on the Blay train and pray that he could somehow translate the reconnection to the actual male as soon as his drugs wore off.

"What do you want to do to me?" Almost Blay whispered. "Where are you going to go with your tongue?"

Yeah, enough with the talking.

With a sharp surge, Qhuinn went to sit up—because that was what you did when you had big plans: He had every intention of making it across the hospital room, dropping to his knees, and pulling an open-wide until Blay was drained dry. And that was just going to be a prelude to the makeup sex they were going to enjoy for the next twelve to fifteen hours.

So hell yeah, he jacked up to the vertical—but that was as far as he got. His stomach pulled the pin on a grenade he'd been unaware was in its possession and then his gut chucked that bitch right up into his lungs, the pain explosion throwing him into a lie-down-now tailspin that left him retching.

And damn him, the sharpshooter was a terrible clarifier, wiping Hypothetical Blay with his magnificently hard cock right out of the room—

As the sound of someone screaming registered, he put his hand to his mouth to check whether it was him or not. Nope. Lips were closed.

Qhuinn frowned and looked to the closed door.

What was . . . so who was yelling like that? It couldn't be Xcor. If the Brotherhood had somehow managed to recapture him, they would never bring the bastard here.

Whatever. Not his problem.

Glancing to the left, Qhuinn measured the distance between him and the house phone that was on the bedside table. 'Bout two hundred yards. Maybe two fifty.

So if he were a golfer, he'd be out of the irons and into his driver.

With a groan, he initiated the process of heaving himself over and stretching his arm as far as he could. Pretty close to goal. Closer. Annnnd . . . almost.

After a couple of batting passes and some fondling with the tips of his fingers, he finally managed to grab the old-fashioned receiver from its cradle. Even managed to get it over onto his chest without dropping the damn thing.

Getting it up to his ear was a piece of cake, too.

But oh, fuck from the dialing.

He had to remove his IQ—er, IV. Messy, but necessary, the open port on the machine leaking clear shit onto the floor as his blood seeped out of where the tubing had been plugged into the crook of his elbow. Who cared. He'd mop it up . . . when he could stand without hurling.

For a moment, as he stared at the phone's twelve buttons in their neat little square, he couldn't remember the digits. But desperation made his memory far more acute than it had any right to be and he recalled the pattern more than the order of numbers.

One ring. Two ring. Three—

"Hello?" a female voice said.

The light from the sun was, like, ninety-seven percent gone from the sky when Blay opened the door and stepped out onto his parents' new back porch. Cold, really cold, the air so dry his sinuses felt sandblasted.

Man, he hated December. Not just because it could get this frigid, but because it meant that there were, like, four more months to go before the weather eased and you didn't feel like you needed to parka-up every time you went outside.

Putting the cigarette between his lips, he fired up his Van Cleef & Arpels gold lighter—the one from the forties that Saxton had given him when they'd been dating—and cupped his hand around the cheery orange lick of flame. The first inhale was—

Pretty fucking awful.

A coughing fit overcame what was supposed to have been a blissful reunion between two old friends: his lungs and nicotine. But he recovered quickly, and within three puffs, he was back in business, the familiar tingle in his head making him feel lighter on his feet than he actually was, the smoke down the back of his throat like a masseuse's stroke over his esophagus, each exhale something close to chiropractic all the way down his spine.

He'd heard that smoking was a stimulant? And the little buzz in his frontal lobe put paid to that idea. But it was weird how everything about the bad habit calmed him out: The potential for relaxation had started to coalesce the instant he'd found the old, unopened pack of Dunhill Reds in a bedside drawer in his room upstairs, and had culminated in this, his first moment of semi-peace since he'd shown up here twelve hours ago, ostensibly to check on his mother's bad ankle.

He tapped the cigarette over the crystal ashtray he'd balanced carefully on the porch rail, and then it was back between the lips, back with the inhale, back with the exhale.

Focusing on the snow-drifted meadow out behind the house, he felt sorry for his mom. She had had to leave their true family home when *lessers* had attacked the place—an episode that, although he could have lived without it, had proved even accountants like his dad and civilian females like his mom could be ass-kickers if they needed to. But, yeah, no staying there anymore following something like that—and after floating around and bunking in with relatives for a while, his parents had finally purchased this new colonial out where the farms and vacant stretches of land were.

His mother hated the house, even though the appliances were new, the windows opened and closed easily, and none of the floorboards creaked. Then again, maybe all of that was what made her dislike it, but what could you do—and this was not a bad spot. Ten acres with good trees, a great wraparound porch, and, for the first time, central air.

Which you didn't need in upstate New York except for, like, the last week in July and the first week in August.

And during those fourteen or so hot nights, you were really glad you had it.

As he stared at the frozen pond with its whisker-sticks of cattails and s-curve snowdrifts, he let his mind wander to all sorts of non-controversial musings about real estate and HVAC systems and bad habits that weren't actually that bad.

God knew it was a hell of a lot easier than what had kept him up all day.

When he'd arrived the night before, close to dawn, he hadn't had the heart to tell his parents what had happened. The thing was, when Qhuinn had maintained that he, Blay, was not a father to those two kids, the guy had also erased any grandparental rights his mom and dad thought they had, too. So, yeah, no, he wasn't going to explain why he'd—

The creak of the door behind him turned him around. "Hi, *Mah-*

men," he said, tucking the cigarette behind his back. Like he was a fuck-ing pretrans doing something wrong.

Still, good boys liked to make their moms happy, and Blay had always been a good boy.

His *mahmen* smiled, but her eyes flicked to the ashtray, and come on, like she couldn't catch the scent in the air? And it wasn't that she'd ever tell him to stop, except she was like Qhuinn. She wasn't a fan, even though there was no cancer risk to worry about.

"You have a phone call." She nodded over her shoulder. "There's an extension in your father's study if you'd like a little privacy?"

"Who is it?"

He asked this to buy some time, even though it was pretty clear who was calling—but she didn't seem to mind. "It's Qhuinn. He sounds . . . a little off."

"I'll bet he does."

Blay went back to looking out over the pond. Back to the smoking, too, because he was suddenly twitchy.

"I haven't wanted to pry, Blay. But I know there has to be something going on between you two, otherwise, he'd be here, as well. I mean, your Qhuinn never misses a chance to come and eat my food."

"Will you tell him I'm not here?" He tapped the cigarette over the ashtray again even though there wasn't much on the tip. "Tell him I just left. Or something."

"Too late. I said you were right out here on the porch. I'm sorry."

"It's all right." Steadying the ashtray, he stabbed out the Dunhill. "Do you mind if I leave this out here? I'll clean it up before I leave."

"Of course." His *mahmen* stepped aside and then waited with the door held wide. When he didn't come over immediately, she seemed sad. "Whatever it is, you two can work it out. Being new parents can change things, but it's nothing that you won't adjust to."

Well, apparently only one of us is a new parent, so . . .

Blay walked across and kissed her cheek. "The study? You sure Dad doesn't need it?"

"He's up in the attic. I think he's alphabetizing our luggage, as odd as that sounds."

"Nothing is odd when it comes to Dad and organization. Is it by color or make?"

"Make first and then color. Who knew those Samsonite monstrosities from the seventies could live this long?"

"Cockroaches, Twinkies, and Samsonite. That'll be what's left after nuclear war."

It was so much warmer inside, and as he went into his father's work space, his Nikes squeaked over the freshly stained and finished pine floors. Turning on the overhead fixture, he was confronted by a whole lot of in-its-place. The desk, across the way, was nothing fancy, just a nice piece from Office Depot with black legs and a honey-brown top, and on it, there was a phone and an old-school calculator with a humpback of white tape roll. The chair was black and leather and puffy, and the desktop computer was a Mac, not a PC.

Better not tell V, he thought as he closed himself in.

There were a number of windows, all with heavy drapes that were still pulled, evidence that his dad hadn't clocked in yet at the consulting firm he'd started. Telecommuting was a godsend for vampires who wanted to make cake in the human sector, and it was particularly applicable if you were an accountant who ran numbers for a living.

Sitting down behind his father's command central, Blay picked up the receiver and cleared his throat. "Hello?"

There was a click as his mother hung up at the kitchen or in her sitting room or wherever she'd answered the call. And then there was nothing but static coming over the line.

"Hello . . . ?" he repeated.

Qhuinn's voice was so hoarse it barely registered. "Hey."

Long silence. Not a surprise. Blay was usually the one who pressed for communication when there was a rough spot, mostly because he couldn't handle distance between them and Qhuinn always found it tough to open up about "feelings." Inevitably, though, the male would give in, and they'd talk through whatever it was like adults—and then Qhuinn would want to service him sexually for hours, as if the guy wanted to make up for his interpersonal-relating weaknesses.

It was a good MO. Usually worked for them.

But not tonight. Blay wasn't playing that game.

"So I'm sorry," Qhuinn said.

"For what." The pause that followed suggested that Qhuinn was thinking "you know what" in his head. "And yes, I'm going to make you say it."

"I'm sorry for what came out of my mouth when I was upset. About Lyric and Rhamp and you. I'm really sorry . . . I feel like shit. I was just so fucking mad that I wasn't thinking straight."

"I believe that." Blay ran his fingertips over the adding machine's pad with its numbers in the center and its symbols around the edges. "You were really upset."

"I couldn't believe that Layla had put them at risk like that. It made me fucking mental."

Now was Blay's cue to agree, to affirm that yes, anyone would have been upset. And that was not hard to do. "She did risk their lives. It's true."

"I mean, can you imagine life without those two?"

Why, yes. I've spent most of the day doing that.

As a lump formed in his throat, Blay coughed into his fist to clear it. "No, I cannot."

"They're the most important thing in my life. The two of them and you."

"I know."

Qhuinn exhaled like he was relieved. "I'm so glad you understand."

"I do."

"You've always gotten me. Always."

"This is true."

There was another silence. And then Qhuinn said, "When are you coming back? I need to see you."

Blay closed his eyes against that seductive tone of voice. He knew exactly what was going through Qhuinn's mind. Crisis averted, time for sex—and that was not an unpleasant hypothetical in the slightest. But come on, Qhuinn was an orgasm upright in a pair of shitkickers, a dominating, irrepressible force of nature on the horizontal, capable of making a male feel like the single most desirable anything on earth.

"Blay? Wait, is your *mahmen* okay? How's her ankle?"

"Better. She's hobbling along. Doc Jane said just another night or two, and then she can get out of the boot. It's healing well after the fall."

"That's great. Tell her I said I'm glad she's doing well."

"Oh, I will."

"So . . . when are you coming home?"

"I'm not."

Long silence. "Why?"

Blay ran his fingertips over the numbers on that keypad, in proper order—first ascending, from zero to nine, then descending. He didn't press hard enough for anything to show in the light-up section or for the roll of paper to get with its program and start printing.

"Blay, I'm honestly sorry. I feel like shit. I never want to hurt you, ever."

"I believe that."

"I wasn't in my right frame of mind."

"And that's my problem."

"Look, I can't believe I got out a gun and pulled that trigger. I want to throw up every time I think about it. But I've calmed down now and Layla's out of the house. It was the first thing I asked when I came around. She's out and the young are safe so I'm okay."

"Wait, came around from what? Were you hurt after I left?"

"I, ah . . . it's a long story. Come home and I'll tell you in person."

"Did they take Layla's rights away?"

"Not yet. They will, though. Wrath's going to see my side. He's a father, after all."

That lump in Blay's throat came back, but not as bad. No cough needed. "Layla should still be able to see those kids on the regular. They need their *mahmen*, and whether you like it or not, she should be in their lives."

"What are you saying, that she and Xcor take them to McDonald's for fucking fries and a Coke?"

"I'm not going to argue with you. It's not my business to, remember?"

"Blay." Now came the impatience. "What else do you want me to say?"

"Nothing. There's nothing to—"

"I'm back in my right head now. I know that I was wrong to yell at you like that, and—"

"Stop." Blay went for the Dunhill pack, but then put it back into the pocket of his button-down shirt. Not like he was going to light up in the house. "The fact that you've calmed down? Good, maybe it'll help you be more rational when it comes to Layla. But here's the thing, when people are that mad, they speak the truth. You can apologize all you want for being angry and screaming at me and all that shit. What you will never be able to take back, however, is the fact that in that moment, in that split second, when you didn't have the capacity to sugarcoat, or smooth over, or be nice . . . you put out there, for all to hear, what you actually believe. Which is that I'm not a parent to those young."

"You're so wrong. I was just pissed off at Layla. It didn't have anything to do with you."

"Your words had everything to do with me—and listen, it's not like I don't get it. You're those kids' biological father. That's something no one can take away from you or change—that's sacred, a reality that was determined the second Layla became pregnant thanks to you. And that's why the idea that you're going to expect Wrath to pretend from last night onward that Layla shouldn't be in their lives is bullshit. She's in their blood, just like you are—and yes, she made a really bad call when she was pregnant, but the kids came out on the other side fine, and she hasn't left them for a second since she gave birth. You know damn well she's about them, not anyone or anything else, and that includes Xcor. You strip her of her rights? You're just doing it to be cruel because she scared the shit out of you and you want to teach her a lesson and make her suffer. And that's not a good enough reason to take her away from Lyric and Rhamp."

"She consorted with the enemy, Blay."

"And he didn't actually hurt her, did he. Or your kids." Blay cursed. "But that's none of my business—"

"Will you stop throwing that in my fucking face!"

"I'm not saying it to piss you off." Abruptly, his eyes started to water. "I'm saying it because it's my new reality and I'm trying to get used to it."

He hated the roughness in his voice—especially because Qhuinn knew him too well to miss it. And on that note . . . "Listen, I've got to go—"

"Blay. Stop this. Let me come see you—"

"Please don't."

"What's happening here?" Qhuinn's voice got tight. "Blay. What are you doing here?"

As Blay leaned back in his father's office chair, he closed his eyes . . . and the image of Lyric cradled against his chest was like a sword slicing through his heart. God, he could recall every single thing about her: her wide, beautiful, myopic eyes that had yet to settle on a color, her rosy cheeks, her dusting of blond hair.

He could remember smiling down at her, his heart so full of love that his body felt like a glorious balloon, overinflated, but in no danger of bursting.

Everything had seemed more permanent when the kids had come, like Qhuinn and he, already set in concrete, had added steel ropes around each other and pulled the lengths in tight.

He wasn't sure what was worse: losing his place in the young's lives, or no longer feeling that security.

"I've got to go," he said abruptly.

"Blay, come on—"

As he put the receiver down on the cradle, he didn't slam it. Didn't pick up the entire unit and hurl it into the precisely ordered shelves of books on economics and accounting rules.

He wasn't mad.

Getting angry about the truth was just stupid.

It was better to spend your time adapting to it.

Far more logical, even if it made tears come to your eyes.

FOURTEEN

"Seriously. All I'm going to do is take a shower and then stare out the window some more. That's it."

When Vishous didn't say anything, Layla turned around in the chair she'd been in for the last hour. He, too, was where he had last been, in this tidy kitchen with her, leaning up against the granite countertops by the stove, smoking quietly. The safe house they had inhabited overday was a lovely ranch that was small enough to feel cozy, but big enough for a little family. Everything in it was done in variations of pale gray, with carefully chosen accents of buttercup yellow and cheerful blue—so instead of being gloomy, it felt light, airy, and modern.

In other circumstances, she would have loved everything about the home. As things were, it felt like a prison.

"Come on, Vishous. Do you honestly think I'm going to show up at the mansion's front door and demand to be let in? And it's not like I have the key or anything." When he still didn't reply, she rolled her eyes. "Or no, you're worried I'm looking for another opportunity to piss off our King. Because you can see how well that's working for me at the moment."

Vishous shifted his weight from one shitkicker to another. Dressed in black leathers, a muscle shirt, and about fifty pounds of guns and knives, he was like a wraith in the wrong place in this picture-perfect house. Or maybe it was the right place. He'd certainly been a harbinger of doom since last night—and as roommates were, he was about as much fun as her current mood.

Layla nodded at the cell phone in his black gloved hand. "Go to your meeting. That's what that text was, wasn't it."

"It's rude to read people's minds," he muttered.

"I'm not in your skull. Your expression simply makes it obvious that you want to go and feel trapped here with me. I don't need a babysitter. I'm not going anywhere. The King has my young under his roof, and unless I play by his rules, I will never see them again. If you think I'm bucking him in any fashion, you're out of your damn mind."

As she turned back to the window, she was aware that she was cursing, and she didn't give a shit. She was worried about Lyric and Rhamp, and going on no sleep and no food.

"I'll send someone else." There was a tapping sound like Vishous was texting back. "Maybe Lassiter."

"I'd rather be alone." She pivoted around again. "I'm getting tired of crying in front of an audience."

Vishous dropped his arm. Whether it was because he'd sent whatever he'd been composing or was agreeing with her, she didn't know—and she didn't really care.

Learned helplessness, she thought. Wasn't that what it was called? She'd heard Marissa and Mary use the term when referring to the brain freeze that victims of domestic violence sometimes found themselves locked in by.

Although in her case, she wasn't being abused. She'd earned this out-of-her-control honestly.

She went back to staring at the night, shifting herself so she could look out the sliding doors behind the table. There was a porch on the far side of the broad panes of glass, and in the glow of the security lighting, she measured the meager build-up of ice and snow, and tracked the trails of crusty brown leaves break-dancing across the frigid stage. During the day, when she hadn't been sleeping downstairs in the basement, she had turned on the local news at noon. Apparently, there was a freak early blizzard heading Caldwell's way, and sure enough, she could hear the salt trucks rumbling in the distance, laying down tracks of brine on the roads.

Perhaps human children would be off from school when it hit, and this made her check out the houses on the far sides of the backyard fence. She could not see much of the homes, just the glow of lights on the second floors, and she imagined all sorts of human young nestled in beds while their parents caught a bit of TV before they retired for the night.

How she envied them all.

And on that note, God, she hoped V left. She was going to go insane cooped up with his glowering presence—although the idea of Lassiter as substitute was enough to make her suicidal.

"All right," Vishous muttered. "I'll be back when I know something."

"Please don't send that angel."

"Nah. That would make your punishment cruel and unusual."

She released the breath she'd been holding. "Thank you."

The Brother hesitated. "Layla. Listen—"

"At the risk of pissing you off, too, there is nothing you can say to me that will make this better or worse. That's how you know you're in Hell, by the way. No hope and pain is all you can see."

The sound of Vishous's heavy boots on the tile was loud in the quiet little kitchen, and for some reason, she thought of the Brother Tohrment's love of Godzilla movies. Just the other evening, she had come down to stretch her legs and found Tohr kicked back on the sofa in the billiards room, Autumn asleep on top of his body, *Godzilla vs. Mothra* playing on the big screen over the fireplace.

She'd thought things had been complicated then. Now? She wished she could go back to those halcyon nights when all she had had on her mind was guilt and self-blame.

As V stopped in front of her, her shoulders tightened up until she felt an ache at the base of her skull. "Yes," she snapped, "I will set the security system after you leave. And I know how to work the remotes. You showed me that earlier, although I can assure you, I don't even care about *Game of Thrones* at this point."

It was so unlike her to be bitchy, but she was down the proverbial rabbit hole, lost to who and what she normally was.

"Xcor escaped. Last night."

Layla recoiled so sharply she nearly fell off the chair. And before she could ask, the Brother said, "No one was killed in the process. But he ended up locking Qhuinn in the Tomb—which was where we were keeping him. And he left the key behind."

Layla's heart started to pound, but before she could say anything, or really even gather her thoughts, Vishous arched a brow. "Still feel safe on your own?"

She leveled a hard stare at him. "Are you actually worried about that?"

"You remain a member of the family."

"Uh-huh. Right." She crossed her arms over her chest. "Well, he's not going to come for me, if that's what you're concerned about. He's done with me. There is literally nothing that could make that male get anywhere near me—which gives him something in common with Qhuinn, ironically."

Vishous didn't respond. He just loomed over her, his icy eyes tracking every nuance of her body, her affect, her very breathing.

It was kind of like being onstage in front of a hundred million people. With theater lights burning your retinas.

Exactly what she was in the mood for.

"You don't think Xcor would want to know where you are?" The question was posed with such an even tone, it was impossible to guess whether it was an actual inquiry or a rhetorical one.

Either way, she knew the answer. "Nope. Not a chance."

She turned away and refocused on the darkness outside the sliders. Her heart was beating hard in her chest, but she was determined to try to keep that to herself.

"You still love him," V said remotely. "Don't you."

"Does it matter?"

As Vishous lit another hand-rolled, he paced around, going back by the stove where he had been standing. Then over to the door into the basement. And finally returning to the table where she was seated.

In a low voice, he said, "I'm not sure how much you know about Jane and me, but I had to wipe her memories of me once. The circumstances aren't important, and destiny had other ideas, thank fuck . . . but I know what it's like not to be with the one you love. Also know what it's like when nothing about the relationship makes sense to anybody but the two of you. I mean, I fell for a fucking human, and then she died. So now I'm in love with a ghost, and not in a metaphoric sense. This Xcor thing? I know you would have chosen a different path if you could have."

As Layla looked up at the Brother, she could feel her eyes popping. Of all the things Vishous could have said? She would have been less surprised if he'd told her he was buying stock in Apple.

"Wait . . . what?" she blurted.

"Sometimes the heart shit doesn't make sense. And you know, at the end of it all, Xcor didn't hurt you. You saw him for how long? He never terrorized you or those young. I hate the motherfucker, don't get me wrong, and you did consort with the enemy. But damn him to hell, he sure as fuck wasn't acting like one, at least not when it came to you—and he also never attacked us, did he. All that time, he knew where we were, but the Band of Bastards never came on the property. I'm not saying I want to sit down and have a drink with the SOB, or that you weren't in the wrong. But the good thing about being logical is that you can judge both history and the present with clarity—and I'm a very logical male."

Layla's eyes began to water. And then in a broken voice, she whispered, "I hated myself the whole time. But . . . I loved him. And I fear I always will."

Vishous's diamond eyes shifted down so that they seemed to rest on his shitkickers. Then he stretched an arm out and grabbed the mug he'd been using as an ashtray. Tapping his hand-rolled over the thing, he shrugged. "We don't get to pick who we fall for, and trying to talk yourself out of emotions is a recipe for failure. You were not wrong in loving him, true? That part, no one can blame you for, 'cuz it is what it is—and you've suffered enough. Besides, like I said . . . he never hurt you, did he. So there has to be something in him that isn't evil."

"I looked in his eyes." She sniffled and wiped her cheeks with the backs of her hands. "I saw the truth in them and it was that he would never injure me or anyone I loved. And as for why our relationship ended? He didn't want to love me any more than I wanted to love him."

She was ready to talk more, hungry for the unexpected relief that came with someone understanding where she was at. But all at once, V's compassion was gone, the impenetrable mask he usually wore back in place on his face, the door to the discussion closed as if it had never been opened.

"Here." The Brother put his cell phone on the table. "The passcode's ten ten. I don't know how long Wrath is going to take to decide what kind of visitation schedule there's going to be, but you can assume you're going to be in this house for a while. Call me if you need us. My second phone is listed under V two in the contacts list."

Layla reached out and took the cell. It was still warm from him holding it.

"Thank you," she said softly as she held the thing up. "And not just for this."

"Whatever," he muttered. "Funny how curses can come in all kinds of different flavors, true. My mom was creative like that."

Down in the underground tunnel, Qhuinn made his way from the training center's medical clinic to the mansion like a drunk, his stride as uncoordinated as a dice roll, his head spinning, his stomach rolling, the stitches in his side hurting so badly he stopped from time to time to lift up his hospital gown and check that he hadn't *Alien*'d something out of his gut.

All he wanted was a straight shot up to the twins, an unimpeded route from the hidden door under the big house's grand staircase to that bedroom up on the second floor: no concerned looks from *doggen*, no confrontational glares from his brothers, nobody trying to feed him. And please, dear God, nothing at all from Lassiter.

As he emerged out from under the stairs, he paused before he went any further into the foyer and took a listen. First Meal had come and was in the process of being gone, the servants cleaning things up in the dining room, their soft patter of talk and the quiet sound of sterling being cleared from porcelain whispering out from the open archway up ahead.

Nothing from the billiards room.

Nobody on the red-carpeted stairs—

Right on schedule—*not*—a strange pool of light appeared directly in the center of the vast, resplendent space, as if someone had carved a hole in the ceiling and an improbable noonday sun was shining in through the roof.

For a second, all Qhuinn could think of was thank God. The human second coming had arrived just in time to kill all of his suffering on a oner—and actually, a figure did appear in the midst of the shaft of light. But it was not the Christ that Butch prayed to all the time.

It was also not Santa Claus with his streusel gut and his ponies with horns or whatever the fuck they were—which given the Christmas season might have been an option.

Nope, it was the Great Immortal Agitator: Lassiter, the fallen angel, materialized in the midst of the great, source-less illumination, and the sparkling glow faded as he took his form like it was the delivery system that had brought him from wherever he had been.

Okay, the clothes were weird, Qhuinn thought.

And not in the crazy fuck's normal bizarre-drobe of zebra stripes and feather boas. The angel had a flannel shirt tied around his waist. Blue jeans that were one trip through the wash away from losing their structural integrity. And a Nirvana shirt from the Saint Andrew's Hall performance in Detroit on October 11, 1991.

That music wasn't his usual his jam, either. Lassiter was a Fetty Wap fan when he wasn't swooning over Midler.

The good news? The angel just walked off into the billiards room, not even tweaking that Qhuinn was half naked and nauseous at the base of the stairs.

So there was some grace and mercy left in the world, it seemed.

Yeah, except then came Qhuinn's trip up to the second floor. The ascent required the use of the balustrade and a lot of molar grinding, but after several months, if not years, of climbing, Qhuinn made it. At the top, he was relieved to see that the doors to Wrath's study were closed. What wasn't so hot? The fact that there were a lot of voices going back and forth behind those panels.

He could just imagine what the topic was.

Continuing on to the hall of statues, he went down to the bedroom Layla had stayed in, and found himself wanting to knock even though his kids were in there. Manning up, he grabbed the knob of the new door and twisted so hard his wrist felt like it was going to snap off the bottom of his arm.

As he opened things up, he stopped.

Beth had her back to him as she leaned over Lyric's bassinet, the Queen murmuring all kinds of lovely things as she settled the infant into the soft cocoon.

When his presence registered, it was not a surprise that Beth crossed her arms over her chest and squared off at him like he was the enemy.

"Thanks for taking care of them," he said as he limped in.

"You look like hell."

"I feel worse."

"Good." When he cocked an eyebrow at her, the Queen shrugged. "What do you want me to say? That it's okay you kicked Layla out of this house?"

"She did that to herself, not me."

God, his head was thumping, that conversation with Blay going around and around in his brain like a race car stuck on a closed track. So, yeah, talking about that Chosen was really awesome right now.

"Just so you know"—the Queen put her hands on her hips—"I think Layla's rights should stay in place, and I think you and she need to work out a fair visitation schedule where these babies go and stay with their *mahmen* overnight."

"They're not leaving this house. And Layla can't be here. The situation is what it is."

"You're not in charge."

"Yeah, well, neither are you," he said with exhaustion. "So why don't we just drop it at that."

Beth checked on Rhamp, and then came forward. Meeting him directly in the eye, she said, "This is not about your butt hurt, Qhuinn. These two kids need the both of you, and that means you are required to act like an adult even when you don't feel like it. You do not have to see Layla, but they do."

Qhuinn went over to the bed and sat down, because it was either that or he was going to go throw rug on the floor at her feet. "Treason, Beth. Against your mate. This is not a case of a parent forgetting to feed 'em once, or getting 'em off their sleep schedule."

"You don't need to tell me who shot my husband," Beth snapped. "Just like I don't have to tell you that it's up to Wrath—and not anybody else—to forgive or not, punish or don't. This is not fucking about you, Qhuinn. Get your head out of your ass, do what's right for your children, and work on your damn temper."

As she marched out of the room, he was absolutely positive that but for Lyric and Rhamp, she would have slammed that new door hard enough for the sound to echo in the Fade.

Putting his head in his hands, he nearly vomited on his bare feet.

Jesus, he was only in a frickin' hospital gown.

Yeah, 'cuz with all the shit going on, what he was wearing was such a big deal. Then again, when you were surrounded by things that you couldn't control, couldn't make right, and didn't want to deal with, what covered your ass was a welcome vacation for your pea-sized brain.

Dropping his arms, he got to his feet and went over to the bassinets. He picked up Rhamp first, holding his blooded son in his palms and carrying the young over to the huge bed. Placing the infant close to the pillows, he quickly brought Lyric over and stretched out with them both.

Rhamp fussed a little. Lyric was chill.

Before long, both of them were asleep in the crooks of Qhuinn's arms. But there was no rest for him, and not just because his body hurt all over.

Yet the insomnia made no goddamn sense. He'd gotten what he wanted:

Layla was out of the mansion, and no matter what Beth said, Wrath was going to do the right thing and cut the Chosen off from his young. Also, Blay was bound to come around. They'd been through worse things and had always arrived on the far side of the conflict better and stronger together.

Plus he had his young safely with him.

In spite of all that, however, Qhuinn felt like someone had hollowed him out on the inside, nothing left in between his ribs, his pelvis empty of its contents, his skin a useless bag with nothing really to do.

He closed his eyes. Told himself to chill out. Relax.

Within seconds, his lids were open. And as he stared at the ceiling, at the bullet holes he'd put in the corner, he ached in the place where his heart should have been.

Made sense. That vital organ of his was way on the other side of Caldwell, at Blay's parents' new house, the one the male's *mahmen* didn't like because everything in it worked and the floorboards didn't creak when you walked on them.

Without his heart, Qhuinn was an empty vessel. Even with his young beside him.

So, yup, that hurt. He was just surprised by how much.

FIFTEEN

The Caldwell Insurance Company building was some seventy stories high and located in the financial district, serving as a landmark amid the other sleeker but shorter skyscrapers. According to its cornerstone, it had been constructed in 1927, and indeed, compared to its more modern neighbors, it was a glorious grande dame in the company of lesser harlots. With sets of gargoyles marking its three different stages of elevation, and an ornate crown of carvings and Latin phrases at its top, the CIC was a monument to the city's greatness and longevity.

As Zypher formed on its rooftop, the wind whipped his hair straight back from his face, and his eyes watered from the cold rush. Far below, the lights of the city sprawled outward in an earthbound halo that was bisected by the Hudson River.

One by one, the others in the Band of Bastards joined him: Balthazar, the wild one; Syphon, the spy; and Syn, who stayed on the periphery like a source of evil waiting to trip up someone's happy destiny.

Familiar, they all were unto him, these males with whom he had fought side by side for over two hundred years. There was naught that they had not shared: bloodshed, of their own and of the enemy's; females, of the vampire and the human variety; locations, both here and in the Old Country.

"So 'tis the morrow, then," Balthazar commented into the wind.

"Aye." Zypher traced the highway down below with his eyes, noting the white headlights of the oncoming traffic, the red taillights for outgoing. "On the morrow's eve, we leave."

The lot of them had been here in the New World for but a short while, and they had accomplished naught of what they had sought when they had traveled from across the ocean. They had originally come in search of slayers, as the numbers of the enemy back home in the Old Country had shrunk to almost nil and terrorizing humans was fun only to a point. But upon arrival, they had discovered a similarly decimated population here. Ambitions had soon broadened, however. Xcor had wanted to be King, and necessary alliances had been formed with aristocrats in the *glymera* who wanted the Council to take on more power.

The coup had failed.

Even though they had managed to put a bullet in Wrath's throat, the King had not just survived the assassination attempt, he had risen to an even greater height of power—and that had put the Band of Bastards at a critical disadvantage.

And then the fundamentals had changed, at least for Xcor.

Once the Chosen Layla had entered their leader's life, none of anything else seemed to matter to the male—and that had actually been viewed as a benefit to the group at large. Xcor's nature had long been aligned with a cruelty that had inspired fear and thus respect. After that female? The fighter's hard edges had been filed down such that he became far easier with which to deal—and in turn, the Bastards had been more productive, as they were not constantly monitoring what Xcor's mood was.

Except then their leader had been captured or killed.

To this night, they knew not which it was, and ne'er was Xcor to be seen again, evidently. Fates knew they had tried to find him, whether it be the remains or the male himself, and ending the search was difficult.

But with nothing else to go on, and the Brotherhood continuing to hunt them, it was the better choice to return from whence they had come.

Abruptly, an image of Throe came to mind and Zypher frowned.

Alas, there had been one other who had been lost. Throe, their second in command for all intents and purposes, had been kicked out of the group when his ambitions for the throne had proven more enduring than Xcor's. That incompatibility of goal had torn the two of them apart—and thus, the male who shouldn't have been with them anyway had departed, nothing save a footnote in their history. Indeed, Throe, a former aristocrat who had once been ridiculed and conscripted into service as payment for a debt, but who had then proven himself over time, was gone from their ranks, perhaps killed by *lessers* or the others of his station with whom he had conspired. Or mayhap he lived among the blue bloods still, accepted once more unto his fold and scheming anew.

None of them cared about his loss as much as Xcor's, however.

For truth, as Zypher stared out over the city, it would have seemed inconceivable when they arrived on these shores that they would leave without the two who had been partners in all the ways that mattered. But there was one truism that ruled o'er both the quick and the dead: Destiny ran upon its own course, with individual choice and predilection and prediction being, nine times out of ten, naught of consequence.

"Our purpose now is . . ." He let that drift.

Balthazar cursed. "We shall find another, mate. And we shall do it where we belong."

Yes, Zypher thought, so they would. Back in the Old Country, they had a castle that they owned free and clear, and a staff of *doggen* who worked its land, providing sustenance and wares and produce to sell in the surrounding villages. The superstitious humans in the region stayed away from them. There were women and a few females to bed. Mayhap they would find some slayers, after all—

Fates, it sounded too fucking awful. A step backward instead of forward.

Yet they could not stay here. The first rule of conflict was that if you wanted to live, you didn't engage with a more powerful enemy—and the Brotherhood, helmed by the King as they were, had tremendous financial resources, facilities, and armaments. When there had been a possibility of deposing Wrath, it had been a different scenario. But with the Bastards possessing only four fighters, no clear leader, and no agenda?

Nay. It wasnae good.

"On the morrow, then," Balthazar said. "We depart."

"Aye."

Zypher truly wished they were bringing Xcor's body back with them, however. "We will search for him one last time," he announced to the wind. "For this, our final night, we shall endeavor to find our leader."

They would make one more attempt—and even though the outcome was not likely to be different from all the others, the effort would help them make peace with the collective sense that they were deserting their dead.

"Let us off unto the hunt, then," Balthazar said.

One by one, they dematerialized, into the cold darkness.

As soon as Vishous left the safe house, Layla took a deep breath—but the exhale didn't do a damn thing for her.

Staying where she was, at that table in the kitchen, she listened to all the absolutely-nothing for a while, and then she stood up and walked around the first floor, going in and out of the cozy rooms. In the back of her mind, she had a thought that the ranch truly was a perfect little nest, the kind of place a female alone could feel secure in.

Was she even going to get the chance to have the twins come here?

Anxiety made it hard to breathe and she went to the sliding glass door that V had put to use. Pulling it open, she stepped outside, and as her slippers crushed the crunchy top layer of snow on the porch, she tried the whole deep-inhale thing again.

This time, as she let out air, her breath was a cloud that drifted off over her head.

Her cheeks, raw from all the crying and the wiping of tears, burned in the cold, clear air, and she looked up to the heavens above. There was a thick cloud cover blocking out the twinkling stars, and more fresh snow on the lawn, suggesting that the weather had been blustery and marked with flurries during the day.

Wrapping her arms around herself, Layla—

Everything stopped for her. From her heart rate to her breathing to even the thoughts in her messed-up brain, it was like her inner power grid blew its fuse and she became as the inside of the house behind her: utterly still and empty.

Turning to the east, she drew a breath in until her ribs strained from the effort, but she was not attempting to scent anything. She was trying to hold her lungs immobile in her chest—and if she could have paused her heart and the functions of her organs, she would have.

The echo of her own blood was so faint, it was difficult to determine whether or not it was a mistake on her part, a misapprehension of what was actually occurring. But no . . . she was in fact picking up a whisper of her own life source in the direction of the north . . . actually, the northwest.

Now her heart thundered.

"Xcor . . . ?" she whispered.

The signal, such as it was, was not coming from where the Brotherhood's compound was located. It was too far west for that. It was . . .

She looked back at the slider she'd come out of. Hesitated. Except then she thought of Vishous, and everything he'd said.

Unsure of exactly where she was going, she shut her eyes and dematerialized out a short distance, re-forming in a children's park that she had spotted when she had been driven in the night before.

As she stood beside the empty swings and jungle gyms, she stilled herself anew.

Yes . . . there—

Behind her, a metal creak made her wrench around. But it was naught save the wind pushing at one of the swings, its chain links protesting at the disturbance.

Lowering her lids once more, she concentrated on her destination, and tried not to get ahead of herself.

As she flew forth in a scatter of molecules, she heard Vishous's voice in her head.

We don't get to pick who we fall for . . . you were not wrong in loving him, true? That part, no one can blame you for . . . and you've suffered enough.

He never hurt you, did he. There has to be something in him that isn't evil.

This time, when she resumed her form, the beacon she was homing in on was even stronger, and her trajectory was spot-on. So she proceeded another half mile. And then a distance even longer, to the last ring of suburban neighborhoods before the farmland started. After that? She went even farther, penetrating the forested lands that were the beginning of the Adirondack Park.

Her last leg was but three hundred yards, and as she came back unto her corporeal being, it was with a tree branch right in her face.

Pushing the bare limb out of the way, she looked around. The snow was thicker herein, the breeze lesser, the terrain rocky. Shadows were everywhere—or mayhap that was her nervousness making it seem that way.

Close . . . so close by. But where precisely?

Layla turned slowly in a circle. No one was about, and neither were woodland animals moving around.

It seemed unlikely that Xcor would have spent a full day out here and still have survived—although . . . there had been a snowfall and that big storm was on its way. Perhaps there had been sufficient cloud cover? It wasn't a gamble one would have ever taken unless one were out of other, safer options, but if he were incapacitated in some way?

After all, if he were dead, she wouldn't have picked up on anything.

Cranking her head around, she frowned as something atypical in the landscape caught her eye.

There was something . . . over there . . . to the left of an oak so tall and thick it had to be at least a hundred years old.

Yes, it was a mound of sorts that seemed out of place on the forest floor.

Gathering her robing, she took one step . . . and then another . . .

. . . toward whatever it was.

SIXTEEN

alvatore's Restaurant was a staple on not just the Caldwell, but the whole East Coast's, eating scene, a long-standing throwback to Rat Pack days when three-martini lunches, mistresses, and Don Drapers who knew how to dress were the norm. In the modern era, much had changed in the outside world . . . not much had changed under its roof. The red flocked wallpaper of the entrance foyer was still in place, as was the rest of the *Godfather* decor with all the heavy carved wood and the linen tablecloths. Throughout the multiple serving areas and the back bar, the seating arrangements were exactly as they had been opening night way back when, and the waiters and waitresses still wore tuxedoes. On the menu? Only the best authentic Italian food west of Sicilia, the recipes prepared exactly as they should be and always had been.

There had been a few updates, but they were all in the massive kitchen. And two entrées had been added, which had been a thing—at least until the third generation of its clientele had tried the dishes and decided, yeah, that's good.

Well, and there was one other thing that was different.

As iAm sat down behind the desk in his office, he answered the phone and picked up his most recent meat order at the same time.

"Vinnie, how're ya?" he said as he cocked his head to the side to keep the receiver to his ear. "Yeah . . . good. I'm good. Yeah, no, I need more veal than that. Yeah. And I want that other supplier. The quality is—"

His front house manager stuck his head in the door. "She's here. Good experience, nice demeanor. She'll do."

iAm covered the bottom of the receiver. "Send her in."

As the commercial butcher and he continued to go over the order, iAm thought back to right after he'd gotten the place. The humans he dealt with had assumed he was African American, which he wasn't, but as a Shadow, he was used to passing in the human world as a member of that race. And for a black man to take over the historically, and extremely proud, Italian landmark had been a shocker to everyone from the kitchen staff to the front of the house to the patrons and the suppliers.

But the third Salvatore had given him his blessing after iAm had cooked the shit out of some *gato di patate, pasta alla Norma*, and *caponata*— and then presented the old man with the best cannolis the guy had ever had. Not that Sal III had had a choice. Gambling debts to Rehv had meant he'd had to give up what he'd loved, and Rehv had in turn passed the enterprise on to iAm as a reward for good work.

But still, as the new owner, iAm had wanted to keep the continuity going—and also the Italian patrons coming in—and Sal III's support had ensured both. Especially as iAm had let the haters hate, and earned each and every one of the old schoolers back, seducing them with his basil and his fusilli.

The place was thriving, and the respect was flowing, and it was s'all good. He had also found his mate . . . who happened to be the Queen of the s'Hisbe. So his life should have been perfect.

It was not.

The situation with his brother, Trez, was straight up killing him. It was so hard to see a male of worth brought to his knees by fate, the guy's soul bowed under a loss that iAm couldn't even contemplate without wanting to vomit—

"I'm sorry, what?" iAm refocused. "Yeah, sorry, that's good. Thanks, man—wait, say that again? Oh, yeah, I can do that. How much you need? Nah, you don't pay me. If you do, I will be insulted. I bring the *manicot* as a gift to you and your mother. You take it, you enjoy."

iAm was smiling as he hung up the phone. The old-school Italians turned out to be a lot like Shadows: closed off to outsiders, proud of their traditions, suspicious of people they didn't know. But once you were in with them? Once you proved yourself and were accepted? They were so loyal and generous it was almost like they weren't humans at all.

In fact, to him, proper Italians had become a subspecies apart from the other rats without tails on the planet.

That *manicot*? He'd make it for Vinnie's mom, Mrs. Giuffrida, and bring it over in person. And then when his meat order came in? There would be extra chops or some sausage or a choice cut of beef for free. The thing was, he would have made the *manicot* anyway, even if there was nothing coming back toward him—because Mrs. Giuffrida was a love of the first order who came in the first Friday of every month and always ordered the *pasta con le sarde*. And if you were nice to Vinnie's mother? That man would ride or die for you till the end of his days.

It was a great arrangement and—

All at once, iAm went statue, everything about him going stock still. And funny, considering what had come to stand in the office's open doorway, it seemed appropriate that he should try a version of the Arrest on for size.

The female vampire between the jambs was tall and curvy, her body clothed in loose black slacks and a black sweater with a boat neck. Her black wavy hair had been pulled into a clip, and her face was free of makeup—not that she needed any help from the likes of Maybelline. She was stunningly beautiful, with perfect lips and eyes that were almost anime and cheeks that were rosy from her having come in from the cold—or perhaps because she was nervous about interviewing for their waitress position.

The individual components of her and her wardrobe weren't the shocker, however. It was the whole damn thing put together that took his breath away.

iAm rose slowly to his feet, like maybe if he moved too fast, his head would explode.

"Selena?" he whispered. Except this couldn't be real . . . could it?

The female's pretty eyebrows popped. "Um . . . no? My name is Therese? My friends call me Tres?"

All at once, the world spun on its axis and iAm fell back down into his chair.

The female took a step in as if she were worried he needed CPR, but then she stopped like she didn't know what to do. Which made two of them.

"Are you all right?" she asked.

In a voice that sounded absolutely, positively, exactly, like his brother's dead *shellan*.

Instead of heading back to the Brotherhood mansion for the day, Trez had stayed at his club. For one, as a Shadow, he not only could handle sunlight, but he actually liked the stuff—even though there had been none of it to see because of the flurries that had fallen all morning and afternoon. More to the point, though, he hung where he was because sometimes the crush of people at home was too much for his already-done-in head and he had to take a breather and hide, but not hide, here.

One advantage? His chair was so padded it was basically an adjustable hospital bed, just without the rails and the IV bag.

Swiveling around to face the glass wall, he looked down at the dance floor. The house lights were on, and all the scuffs on the black-painted pine boards irritated the fuck out of him. The cleaners did a great job, but there was nothing they could do to fix the damage made by hundreds of drunken feet. It was probably time to strip and restain. Again.

Of course, pulling a re-polish was arguably a waste of time and money because that floor was just going to get ruined once more, and besides, nobody could see the bare spots when the lasers were flashing and the place was dark as the inside of a hat. But he couldn't stand it. He knew the imperfections were there and despised them.

He supposed the floor upkeep was the club equivalent to mowing your lawn: You knew you were just chasing a moving target, but at least for ten minutes, your grass looked like a proper wall-to-wall carpet.

He checked his watch. Seven o'clock.

About two hours ago, around five-ish, he'd taken a shower in his private bathroom, shaved, and put on a fresh version of his work uniform, which was slacks and a silk button-down. Tonight, the top half of him was gray, the bottom half was white, and the shit in the middle was commando.

He took another glance at his watch. And counted the hours since he'd last put food in his mouth.

As if his stomach knew this was its only chance to register an opinion, the frickin' thing roared.

Goddamn Lassiter. Dinner invite. Sal's.

WTF.

The last thing he wanted to do was sit across from that angel and listen to a *Reservoir Dogs* opener about dick symbolism in *Deadpool*. The problem? His brother, iAm, did make the best Bolognese anywhere, and besides, if Trez didn't show? Lassiter was just the flavor of asshole to turn up here in a clown costume and honk his nose until Trez lost his mind.

Short trip lately, granted. But still.

He looked at his watch again. Cursed. Made the decision.

Getting to his feet, he checked that his gun was in place at the small of his back, grabbed his wallet and his cell phone, and pulled on a suit jacket.

Downstairs, Xhex was inventory-ing the liquor at the bar.

"I'll be back," he told his head of security. "You want me to bring you anything from my brother's for dinner?"

She shook her head as she lifted a case of Absolut onto the counter like it weighed nothing. Xhex had shoulders almost as big as a human male's, and the rest of her was just as in shape. With her short hair and her gunmetal-gray eyes, she was the kind of thing that even drunks recognized as a do-not-fuck-with, which made her perfect for her job.

"I'm good. Ate at home." She cocked an eyebrow. "Missed you at First Meal."

That was as far as she would go with the why-didn't-you-come-home-last-night, and he appreciated it. Xhex was like a guy in a lot of respects: short, to the point, and didn't go enmeshment with the sympathy shit.

Frankly, she was one of the few people he could reliably stand to be around. Lately, he had come to detest pitying eyes and long, meaningful sighs and hugs that went on too long. It wasn't that he didn't appreciate the support, but the thing was . . . when you were deep in mourning, it was hard to be around folks who felt bad because you were feeling bad. Seeing the Brotherhood and their mates in pain on his behalf? Well, that hurt him, and then that made him feel even worse and even more exhausted. And around and around again.

"I'll be back at eight." Trez knocked his knuckles twice on the black granite. "I got my cell phone on me."

"Roger that."

Walking over to the main doors, he nodded at the working girls who were just coming in and had yet to change out of their street clothes. As he passed them, he could sense the human women staring at him, wanting him, wondering about him. In fact, they had always been into him, and there had been a time when he'd taken them up on their offers. Not anymore, though, and his abstinence apparently added to his allure.

He'd never told anyone at work the details about Selena. Only Xhex knew, and she would never say anything to anybody.

The good news? After he'd turned down a couple of the prostitutes twice, word had gotten out and they all had stopped coming onto him. Thank God; females and women literally made him sick. The thought of any one of them touching him, or even merely thinking about him sexually?

His stomach turned just on the hypothetical.

Outside, the air was thick and cold—a prodrome for the storm that was coming—and he needed a couple of breaths to tamp down the bile that was in the back of his throat.

Nausea aside, he was utterly content to live out the rest of his nights alone. He couldn't fathom for even a second a reality where anyone else would come into his life and make any impression on him—

From out of nowhere, his Selena came back to him, her voice filling his head. *Can you promise me that you'll let the good things in even after I'm gone . . . even if those things happen because there's another female by your side?*

Trez rubbed his face. "My love. My love . . . that is one fate you and I shall never have to worry over."

Pulling himself together, he glanced in the direction of his BMW. Maybe he should drive, he thought. It would cut the meal by a good twenty minutes, considering he "had" to be back for opening time.

In the end, however, he just dematerialized across town to the far corner of Sal's front parking lot. The broad stretch of pavement had been plowed of what little snow had fallen so far, and the rim of white around the edges was like the piped icing fringe on a sheet cake. A number of cars were lined up, close as they could get to the building, and lights glowed both on top of streetlamps and down the flanks of the restaurant.

Walking over to the main door's awning, he stomped his loafers on the runner and strode down the red carpet to the three steps up to the door.

As he went in, it was a damn shame he was going to have to deal with Lassiter. Otherwise, he might have had half a chance at enjoying what he was going to eat.

"Hey, Mr. Latimer."

"Evenin'."

Trez lifted a hand to the human woman who was at the hostess stand. As her eyes did a quick sweep of him, her smile was the kind that suggested she would have loved to end the night with him. She kept her distance, though.

His reputation for no-ladies had preceded him. Thank you, iAm.

Heading past the gift-shoppy section with its freezers full of entrées and its souvenir shot glasses and decorative spoons—'cuz yes, people traveled just to come to Sal's—he went into the bar area.

"Mr. Latimer, wassup."

The bartender was a good-looking-twenty-something who was almost hot enough to be a cologne ad model for Gucci or Armani: Dark hair, strong chin, bright blue eyes, big shoulders, yada yada yada. He went to shAdoWs on his nights off and did a lot of business there with females of his kind—and you could tell he enjoyed his status as Hot Guy On The Caldie Club scene.

He should enjoy it while it lasted. "Hey, Geo."

Yeah, 'cuz a dude with his prospects couldn't possibly go by his real name. Which was George.

"Your usual?" Geo asked. "You staying for dinner?"

"Yeah on the dinner, nah on the booze. But thanks."

"The boss is in his office."

"Roger that."

Trez pushed his way through the padded flap doors by the mirrored bottle display, and walked into the sunshine-bright kitchen, all of the stainless-steel counters and professional-grade equipment gleaming from regular cleaning. The tile floor was the color of the terra-cotta rooftops in Siena, and chefs in traditional white togs were bent over pots, cutting boards, and bowls. All of the cooks were men, and all of them were Italian, but over time, iAm hoped to change the former—although not the latter.

Dear God, the delicious smell . . . onions, basil, oregano, tomatoes, and sausage sautéing at the burners.

Damn it, he hated to think Lassiter was right about anything. Except shit, he was starving.

iAm's office was in the back-back, and as Trez rounded the corner, the fact that there was a female vampire standing in the doorway with her back to him didn't register as significant in the slightest. iAm regularly hired members of the species, particularly during the winter months when it got dark in upstate New York by four-thirty in the afternoon. And yes, Trez was vaguely aware that her scent was unusual and pleasant, but that was nothing more than he'd notice if he walked by a bouquet of flowers.

Everything started to change as he stepped in behind her and looked over the top of her head at his brother.

iAm was at his desk, his dark face pasty, his eyes wide as satellite dishes, his jaw unhinged.

"You okay there?" Trez said. "What's—"

iAm started shaking his head, his palms rising up in a stop motion as he got to his feet. But then all that was forgotten—along with every single moment of the past, present, and future—as the female turned around.

Trez stumbled back until he slammed into the wall—and then he found himself lifting his arms as if to ward off blows. Through the cross-hatch of his wrists, he took stock of the eyes, the lips, the nose . . . the hair . . . the throat and shoulders . . . the body . . .

Selena . . .

That was the last thing he remembered.

SEVENTEEN

ometime later, having exhausted himself in the wake of his nursemaid's departure, Xcor fell to the cold, hard ground outside of the cottage. There was no more breath in his lungs to yell, no more energy to fight the chain that kept him a prisoner, no further urge to rail against being left behind.

As a numb resignation began to settle into his chest, it brought a cooling of his body. No . . . that was the wind. With an absence of exertion, his temperature was being siphoned by December's frigid bluster, and he knew he had to take shelter or expire.

Gathering his cloak from the ground, he pulled its filthy weight around himself and permitted his body a moment to shiver. Then he got up on his feet and, stretching as far as he could against his tether, he looked around the corner of the thatched abode. The door was still open and he fancied that he could feel heat emanating from within—that was but a lie, however, a function of memory rather than reality, for the fire had long died down.

His eyes went to the horizon. Through spindled trunk and fluffy pine bough, he saw that dawn was arriving soon, its glow coalescing in the east to chase the darkness away. There would be little warmth to be anticipated from the sun's ascendance—but no particular concern, either. As a pretrans, he did not have to be concerned about being consumed by daylight. Starvation and *thirst, however, were worries that needs must be addressed if he were to survive. With no spare fat stores, and a parched throat, he was not going to last long, especially in winter's climate.*

Xcor attempted one last removal of the leather collar at his throat, and had to abort his efforts readily. He had tried so many times to get it free that there was blood flowing from the claw wounds he'd made and further pulling was too painful.

No one from the village was going to help him. No one had before—

A shifting shadow drew his eyes from the gaining light at the east to the thicket of raspberry bushes before him.

Whatever had moved froze as soon as he turned to it. But then there was a second shadow that came in from the other direction.

Wolves.

Dearest Virgin Scribe . . . the wolves had found him.

Heart beating fast, Xcor looked around in panic. He had been waiting for them to come unto him, and perhaps they were zeroing in on him now that he had finally fallen silent.

In vain, he searched for some form of weapon, something he could use to protect himself—

The rock that caught his eye was within reach if he leaned into his chain, but it weighed more than he could handle easily as he sought to lift the thing from the ground. Grunting, straining, using the last of his strength, he got it up—

Growling roiled low and quiet from the brambles, and he had the sense that the wolves were toying with him, giving him notice such that mayhap he would run and provide a bit of fun a'fore he was consumed as a morning meal.

Frantic with fear, he backed away—

A twig snapped under the weight of one of the animals. And then another.

No chance to get in to the door and close himself in, no way to climb upon the roof or . . .

Turning around, he looked up at the dirty window. As the wolves closed in, their chuffing aggression growing louder, Xcor gritted his teeth and hefted

the rock o'er his head. With a surge of power that he did not know he pos-
sessed, he cast the stone as hard as he could at the single pane.

Glass shattered, and he reared back, putting his arm up to ward off the
shards. There was no further time to think. Ignited by the impact, the preda-
tors hunting him lunged forth in attack, all yellow eyes and jagged teeth and
huge, pouncing bodies.

Xcor jumped up as high as he could, grabbed onto the lower part of the
sash, and propelled himself into the cottage—and just as he landed in a bony
heap a mere foot away from his pallet, the wolves hit the outer wall with
thumps and scratches, their snapping jaws gnawing at his escape hatch, their
growls now of frustration.

The door was still wide open.

Pushing himself onto his knees, he scrambled across the bare floor, scatter-
ing dirty bowls and utensils—

His tether reached its end before he reached his goal and he was yanked
back, his feet continuing forth even as the top half of him stopped dead. And
that was when the pack leader appeared in the open jambs. The lupine hunter
was the size of a small horse, and its teeth were like daggers interlocked. With
its jowls curled back, and its frothing drool puddling at its forepaws, it made
the other two seem like young pups.

Smiling. It was smiling at him.

Xcor glanced at the door that was angled into the cottage.

And then he moved so fast that he was unaware of making the decision to
act. He flipped onto his front, punched his bleeding palms into the floor, and
swung his legs in a circle . . . catching the open panels with nary an inch to
spare.

The door slammed shut and the coarse latching mechanism clicked into
place at the very second the massive wolf jumped forward into the air.

The animal hit the wood slats so hard they chattered against the crude
iron bars that affixed them in place. But they held. They held firm.

Trembling in terror, Xcor tucked himself up, holding his knees to his chest.
Bringing his bleeding hands to his head, he covered his ears as he began to cry,
the sound of the wolves echoing loudly in his skull—

And that was when the ghost arrived.

She came unto him through the wall of the cottage, stepping out of that which was solid as readily as one would still air.

Xcor blinked through his tears, regarding the white robing and the long blond hair . . . and the face that was as beautiful as a dream.

In silence, the specter floated over to stand afore him, but he was not afraid. How could anything so lovely hurt him?

And then he realized that the wolves were no more. As if she had sent them away.

I am safe, he thought to himself. With her, and her alone, I am safe . . .

And the motherfucking Oscar goes to . . . ?

As Vishous re-formed in the forest some distance away from Layla, he nearly lit up a hand-rolled. He had stayed downwind of her on each of the legs she had traveled, and she was so distracted that he doubted she'd notice any kind of flare from his lighter or the end of his cigarette . . . but nah.

They'd come this far—and they were so close to finishing this, weren't they.

The Chosen was up ahead a good thirty yards or so, her white robing standing out in the forest like some kind of a beacon. And whaddaya know, something had caught her attention and she was progressing slowly toward whatever it was, her head tilted downward like she was focused on the forest floor.

He smiled to himself. Oldest trick in the book. Take a person you needed something from, get into their emotions through their brain, flip a bunch of levers—and find the motherfucking bastard you're looking for because said female leads you right to him: Xcor escapes and disappears. Layla has her blood in his veins. She is feeling guilty, alone, and afraid, an alienated victim of circumstance. V's job? Lend a supposedly sympathetic ear, offer some understanding in an apparently sincere fashion, and provide her with a blueprint whereby when she stepped onto that porch at the safe house, and caught an echo of herself somewhere out in the world, she followed her impulse to go and help the male she loved.

Had V known for sure that she was going to go and stand in the snow and sniff the air? Nope, but it was a pretty good guess considering how suffocated she'd seemed in that kitchen. Had he given her his phone in hopes that she'd slip it into her pocket and take it with her wherever she went so he could track its GPS on his other cell? Yup. Disappointed that she left it behind? Yup. Made up for it because, as a brother whose own female couldn't feed him, he had taken Layla's vein prior to her pregnancy to survive and he could track her if he concentrated? Yup. Followed her here?

#paid

No, he hadn't been certain that Xcor was even alive. Just like he hadn't been one hundred that the Chosen would actually go out to the guy if she sensed him. But some dice were worth rolling.

And it looked like his had come up double sixes.

Up ahead, Layla stopped. And slowly sank down to her knees.

Bingo.

Vishous dematerialized closer, taking cover behind a thick oak trunk. And as he focused on the female, he tucked his hand into his leather jacket and locked a grip on the butt of his forty.

She was leaning forward to what seemed like nothing but a snowbank— and V did the same at his tree . . . which didn't really help him see any better—

It was not a snowbank. Nope. It fucking moved.

Hey, hey, what do you know: Underneath the frigid cover of snow, there was a barely alive naked male, the drifts having built up around him as the wind had blown against his tucked-in body.

Frowning, V looked up and measured the sky. How in the fuck had Xcor made it through the daylight? Then again, was heavy cloud cover any different from a set of velvet blackout drapes over a window? Any vampire in his right mind would have sought a roof and four walls to shelter through noontime in, but if you were near death already, you no doubt just lay where you landed and prayed to someone, anyone, that you lucked out.

And clearly, Xcor had.

But that Lotto-winning streak was now over, Vishous thought as he dematerialized right up close, ready to bust out and take control of this situation.

And that was when he was able to visualize Xcor's face.

Gray. It was gray. But the fighter's eyes were open and he was staring up at Layla as if she were an apparition . . . a miracle come unto him from the Other Side.

He was crying. Tears were rolling over his sallow skin, and as he reached up to touch her, snow fell from his bare forearm.

Layla captured his hand and brought it to her heart. In a strangled voice, she whispered, "You're alive . . ."

Xcor tried to speak, but only a croak came out.

And that appeared to galvanize her. "I have to save you—"

"No." That was spoken sharply. "Leave me. Go . . ."

"You're going to die here."

"Let me." Layla tried to talk, but Xcor didn't let her, his voice reedy and thin. "I am happy now . . . I shall take your memory with me . . . unto *Dhunhd* . . ."

Layla began to weep over the male, draping herself across his snow-covered form. "No, we can save you, I can save you . . ."

Whatever, V thought. Time to do his job.

What he was staring at now was just emotional bullshit, irrelevant to the true issues at hand—which hadn't changed merely because the pair of them were doing a Kate and Leo after the frickin' boat sank.

Man, thank fuck he was here to make this right, because any other of his brothers might have been swayed by this display. He was of tougher stuff than that, however, and no, it wasn't that he was angry at Layla or feeling vindictive or even particularly hostile toward Xcor.

Hell, in the bastard's current state, that would be like wasting time hating a block of dry ice.

No, he was just fixing Qhuinn's fuckup back at the Tomb when Xcor had somehow overpowered the brother and then locked the fool in: V was going to send Layla back to the safe house, and then he was going to put Xcor down like a dog right here and now.

'Cuz, really, enough with this shit. One bullet through the brain and this waste of energy and focus was going to be over for the Brotherhood. Yeah, sure, they might be able to torture the fucker if they could get him back to viability again by yet another medical miracle. But the Band of Bastards were no dummies. They'd had thirty days to regroup, relocate, and distance themselves from their disappeared leader. Xcor wasn't going to have any intel worth following up on, and as for Tohr and his right to kill the guy? That brother was already on the edge of madness. Taking out Xcor was just going to drive him further down, not elevate him from where he was at.

Besides, the war was heading to a crisis point. The Lessening Society was collapsing, but the Omega wasn't going anywhere, not unless some-one displaced him by force—and that was Butch's job, at least according to the *Dhestroyer* Prophecy: After all these years of fighting, the end was near—and the Brotherhood needed to return to their core function of eliminating the true enemy of the race.

As opposed to getting sidetracked by this also-ran group of vigilantes who had been castrated anyway.

V was making an executive decision on this.

Time to make this all go away, true.

Raising the muzzle of his gun, he stepped out from behind the tree.

EIGHTEEN

As Layla laid herself over Xcor's naked, cold body, she was desperate to make him warm, get him out of the woods, give him food and water. How was he even alive? How had he survived the passage of even an hour in these conditions, much less an entire day? Dearest Virgin Scribe, he was so chilled he was past shivering, his torso, arms, and legs frozen into a statue's intractability, his bearded face contorted with suffering.

"We have to get you out of here," she said urgently. "You can take my vein, and after we're safe, we'll . . . I don't know, we'll have you talk to them or . . ."

Abruptly, she remembered Vishous telling her that Xcor had left the key to the gates behind when he'd escaped the Tomb. Surely that meant something? If he intended harm or retaliation, he would have taken it with him, right? And the Brotherhood had to know that, had to interpret that as a sign of peace . . . right?

"We need to—"

"Layla." Xcor's thin voice was urgent. "Layla, look at me—"

She shook her head as she sat back from him. "There isn't time! You're freezing to death—"

"Shh." His navy blue eyes softened. "I am warm in my soul with you before me. That is all I need."

"Please take my vein? Please—"

"'Tis a fine way to die, in your arms. A better death than I deserve for certain." Against everything that was rational, his gray lips smiled. "And I have something I need to tell you—"

"You're not going to die, I won't let you—"

"I love you."

Layla's breath caught. "What . . . ?"

His dying smile became something close to wistful. Or mayhap worshipful was the better word. *With all of my black and withered heart, I love you, my female. I deserve not the earth beneath your feet, nor the scent of you in my nose, and never the gift of your blood, but I . . . I am e'er grateful for the change that you wrought upon me. You have saved me, and the only thing greater than my love for you is my gratitude.*

He spoke quickly in the Old Language, as if he were aware that he was running out of time.

"I am at peace and I love you, Layla." Xcor reached up, bringing an immobile claw toward her face. When he brushed her cheek, she gasped at how icy his skin was. "And I can go now—"

"No, please, no—"

"I can go."

That smile of his was going to haunt her for the rest of her life: He must have been in excruciating pain, and yet there was peace all over him, emanating from him. On her side? It was the opposite. There was no peace for her. If he lived, they had a terrible fight before them. If he died? He was taking a part of her to the Other Side as well.

"Xcor, *please*—"

"It's better this way."

"No, no, it's not, don't leave me—"

"You will let me go." His tone became stern. "You will walk forth from this moment with your head held high, knowing you have been honored and adored, even if just by the likes of me. You will let me go and live your life with your young and find someone worthy of you."

"Don't say that!" Layla wiped the tears from her cheeks with impatience. "And we can fix this."

"No, we cannot. You must let me go and then go forth out of this forest, clean of the sin I brought unto your life. The fault was, and is, all mine, Layla. You have never done anything wrong, and you must know that you are safer and better off without me."

She leaned forward once more and brushed his matted hair from his forehead. Thinking back to Qhuinn's anger and the issues with their young, it was hard to argue with those words. As much as it was killing her to lose him, it was impossible to contradict the chaos Xcor had wrought in her life.

"Swear to me you will move forward," he demanded. "I cannot be at peace unless you swear it."

She put her hands to her face. "I feel as if I am breaking in half."

"No, no, this is a joyous night. I have wanted to speak my truth for so long, but it was never right. First because I denied it, then because I fought it and sent you away from me. Now that I am departing this mortal coil, though, I am free—but more importantly, so are you. There was no good ending to us, Layla, my love. There will be a good ending for you, however. You shall be forgiven by the Brotherhood, for they are right and just, and they know I am the evil, and you are not. You shall go on and be the *mahmen* you are meant to be, and you shall find a male worthy of you, I promise. I am but an obstacle in your destiny, something to be surmounted and left behind. You will go on, my love, and I will watch over you."

Layla opened her mouth to speak, but then he coughed a little, groaned, and shuddered.

"Xcor?"

He took a deep breath and his lids lowered. "I love you . . ."

As his voice drifted into silence, it was as if all his life force went out of him at once, his corporeal form deflating, his energy spent.

As his head settled back into the snow, she hadn't even realized he'd lifted it. And then there was another of those shuddering breaths, and the light in his eyes dulled even further.

He remained at peace, though. He seemed—

The snap of a twig right in front of her brought her head up and she gasped.

Standing before them, with his boots planted wide and a gun in his hand . . . was the Brother Vishous.

And his face was so emotionless and composed, it was as if he were an executioner wearing a mask.

Xcor felt like he was underwater. His already frail physical state had so degraded from exposure to the cold and the elements that it was as though he had to swim to an unreliable surface against a powerful undertow to hold onto consciousness—and he was not going to last much longer. His message to Layla had been of sufficient import to provide him with extra strength, but once his words had been imparted, he was fading fast.

Her lovely face, though. Oh, her beautiful face.

He was so very glad he had never made love to her. That would have been selfish on his part, a session of passion that would have left her truly sullied for the rest of her life. Better that she should continue on as pristine for the male who would truly claim her as his own.

Although, dearest Virgin Scribe, it killed him to think about that.

But alas, he loved her enough to let her go and wish her all of the best that life had to offer—and his clarity around that was, he supposed, the very highest and kindest thing he had ever done.

Mayhap the only high and kind thing.

"I love you," he whispered.

He'd meant for that to come out more loudly, but he was losing the battle to drag oxygen into his lungs—and thus, to conserve strength and give them a little more time, he stopped trying to speak and contented himself with staring at her. Funny, the way he had merged her arrival here in the forest with that memory of his past, his addled brain inserting her as a rescuer into a terrible recollection.

Then again, whether it be in real life or in the relative fiction of recall, she was his goddess and his miracle—indeed, even his savior, in spite of the fact that he was not going to live through this. And he was so lucky to have—

The instant her eyes shifted from him to something that startled and then frightened her, he was energized with purpose, his body responding as any bonded male's would, his flesh prepared to defend and protect even if whatever it was turned out to be naught but a gentle, scampering deer.

That was the extent of his reaction, however, his instincts seeking to mobilize that which could no longer be moved. He did, however, manage to turn his head ever so slightly and shift his eyes.

Such that he could behold his killer—assuming nature didn't move more swiftly than the Brother Vishous. And given that gun, what were the chances of that.

In Xcor's peripheral vision, he took note as Layla put her palms forth and slowly rose to her feet. "Vishous, please don't—"

Xcor found his voice once more. "Not in front of her. Do not do it in front of her if you have any decency. Send her away and then dispatch me."

Layla crumpled back down beside him, spreading her arms wide to shield him. "He's a good male. Please, I beg of you—"

With supreme effort and pain that nearly made him pass out, Xcor twisted to meet the diamond eyes of the Brother, and as the two stared at each other, Layla continued to plead for a life that was not worth saving.

"Stop, my love," Xcor said to her. "And go now to leave us. I am at peace, and he will do what brings peace to the Brotherhood. I am guilty of treason and this will wipe the stain of me clean from your life and theirs. My death frees you, my love. Embrace the gift that destiny has brought us both."

Layla brushed her cheeks again. "Please, Vishous. You told me you understood. You said—"

"Just not in front of her," Xcor demanded. "A criminal's last request. An opportunity for you to prove yourself as a better male than I."

Vishous's voice was loud as thunder compared to the weakness of Xcor's own. "I already know I'm better than you, asshole." The Brother looked at Layla. "Get out of here. Now."

"Vishous, I beg of you—"

"Layla. I'm not going to ask you again. You know exactly what you stand to lose and I suggest you think of those young of yours. You got enough fucking problems of your own right now."

Xcor closed his eyes in sorrow. "I am so sorry, my love. That I e'er drew you into this."

There had been only two females of significance in his life: his *mahmen*, who had forsaken him at every turn . . . and his Chosen, whom he had hurt on too many levels to count.

He had been a curse to them both, as it turned out.

"Vishous, please," Layla begged. "You told me he wasn't evil. You said—"

"I lied," the Brother muttered. "I fucking lied. So leave. *Now.*"

NINETEEN

rez came back to consciousness to find himself staring up at a flat ceiling that was painted white. Wait . . . weren't all ceilings flat by definition? Not really, he supposed. Not the textured kind people had favored in the seventies, those ones that looked like old-fashioned white boiled icing. And then there were the ceilings of caves, he supposed . . . rather bumpy. Theaters often had descending steps in elevation that helped with acoustics—

Hold up, what was the question?

Blinking, he became aware of a pounding headache in the rear of his skull—

His brother's face, as familiar as his own, came into his line of vision and cut off the ceiling debate.

"How you doin'?" iAm asked.

"What happened? Why did I—" Trez went to sit up—but then stopped that nonsense when the back of his head pounded. "Fuck me this hurts."

Yeah, and then there was the place where his gun had bitten into the lower part of his spine. He should really start holstering that damn thing under his arm. Then again, when was the last time he'd pulled a case of the Victorian vapours?

"Are you okay?" iAm prompted.

"No, I'm not fucking okay." Right, at least he knew the part of his cerebral cortex that supplied f-bombs was still functioning properly. "I don't know what hit me. I came around the corner and—"

Just as he remembered the female in the doorway to iAm's office, he jerked upright and ripped his head around . . . and there she was, standing against the wall of this squat corridor, her arms around her middle, her face all tense.

Selena's face all tense.

"Leave us," Trez said hoarsely.

She bowed a little. "Yes, of course, I—"

"Not you. Him."

iAm put his face in the way so Trez couldn't see her. "Listen, we need to—"

"Get out of here!" As Trez snapped, the female recoiled, and that was probably the only thing that could have chilled him even a little. "Just . . . let me talk to her."

The female . . . his Selena . . . put her palms out. "I really should go, I feel bad enough already."

Trez closed his eyes and swayed. Her voice. That *voice*. It was the one that had been haunting him, night and day, the exact pitch and intonation, the slight huskiness, the—

"Is he going to pass out again?" she asked.

"No," iAm muttered. "Unless, of course, I hit him with a pan. Which is really appealing at the moment."

Trez popped his lids open again because he was suddenly paranoid. "Is this a dream? Am I dreaming?"

The female looked back and forth between him and his brother as if she were praying iAm manned up to answer that one.

"I just want to talk to you," Trez said to her.

"Wait for us in the kitchen for a sec," iAm told the female. And before Trez could get on his high horse again, the guy cut in, "She'll talk to you, but only if she wants to. I'm not going to make her, and whatever the outcome on that, you're going to listen to me first."

The female took a last look at Trez and then nodded and walked off.

"Who is she?" Trez asked in a broken voice. "Where did she come from?"

"It's not Selena." iAm got to his feet and paced around. Which amounted to little more than three short steps one way, a tight turn, and two back toward Trez. "She's *not* your female."

"She's Selena—"

"No, according to her résumé . . ." iAm ducked into his office, leaned over his desk, and picked up a single sheet of paper. "Her name is Therese, and she's just moved to Caldwell. She's looking for a waitress job as she puts down roots here."

As his brother held the thing out to him, Trez stared at the eight-and-a-half-by-eleven and wondered if he could remember how to read.

"I don't understand," he mumbled. "She looks exactly like Selena. And her voice . . ."

He took the résumé and his eyes bounced around, playing paintball with the words, only hitting some. Detroit, Michigan. Thirty-four years old. Had had a number of jobs through the decades, some in IT, some in food service. No mention of her bloodline, but she wouldn't have put that on the thing if she were using it to apply for human jobs as well. Clearly, though, she had to be a civilian as opposed to a member of the *glymera*, because aristocrats didn't let their unmated daughters apply for waitressing jobs.

Oh, God . . . what if she were mated?

"She is *not* Selena." iAm's face was grim. "I don't care who she looks like, this is *not* your dead mate coming back to you."

Therese stood just inside the bustling kitchen and wondered whether or not she should leave.

She had found the job opening on a closed Facebook group for vampires only and had emailed in her résumé. She had also applied for two other positions, one at a human call center on the night shift, and the other for a company that needed data processing, which she could do from home. Out of the three, this waitressing gig had been her first choice, because the call center had no guaranteed income and the data processing was going to be tough because the rooming house she was staying in, which was all she'd been able to afford, didn't have Wi-Fi.

It barely had running water, for godsakes.

Staring down at the floor, she thought about that giant male fainting right in front of her, landing where she'd been standing. Unbelievable. And whereas the drama would ensure she was remembered by the restaurant's owner, it wasn't for any reason that would help her get the job.

Not unless he was looking for people who inspired others to lose consciousness.

With a frown, she pictured the male who'd hit the ground, his face, his eyes . . . his body. He'd been really extraordinary. But a crazy attraction to a guy who couldn't stay upright was not what she had come here for. A job. She needed a job so that her savings, slim as they were, would not get burned out before the end of the month.

There was no going back to where she'd come from. No returning to Michigan—

The owner came around the corner and took a deep breath. "So, listen."

"I don't want to be a problem or anything." Even though she didn't know what she had done exactly. "I can, you know, just go."

The owner looked away, seeming to focus on the lineup of chefs making ambrosia at the stoves. "It's not your fault. My brother . . . he's been through a lot."

"I'm so sorry."

The owner rubbed the top of his head, his nearly shaved hair not realigning itself in the slightest. He was a Shadow, just like his brother—well, duh—with those beautiful Shadow features and that dark skin. But it was the other one she wanted.

Wait. Not that she wanted him.

"Is he going to be all right?" she blurted. "It looks like he might need a doctor."

"We have a private one he can go to."

Therese lifted her brows. "Oh."

"It's just, you look like—"

The male in question entered the kitchen. God, he was so big, with shoulders that were heavy with muscle, and a chest that was padded with strength, and legs that were long and powerful. Handsome? Yup. Like, *really* good looking, with those lips, particularly the lower one, and that face with that deep-colored skin. He was dressed in white slacks, a gray silk shirt, and a black suit coat, and he looked . . . expensive and sexy— jeez, those loafers were so fine they had to have cost more than her room rent.

For, like, half the year.

His eyes, though, his eyes were what truly got her attention. They were dark as night, but hot as fire—and he was staring at her like she was the only thing that existed in the world . . . which didn't make a lot of sense. She wasn't bad looking, but she was no beauty queen, and she wasn't dressed up or anything.

"Can I just . . . speak with you for a sec?" he said.

Not a demand. Not at all. In fact, there was an ache to his voice that suggested he was at her mercy in some way.

"Ah . . . one of your pupils is a different size." Therese pointed to the left one. "I think you need a doctor more than you have to talk to anybody out of a set of scrubs."

"Fine. Will you take me to Havers's?"

"Who is he?"

"Our healer here in Caldwell."

Therese blinked. "I don't have a car."

"We can take his." The male nodded at his brother and put his palm out to the guy. "Gimme the keys."

The restaurant owner rolled his eyes. "No, I'll drive you—"

"That's okay," Therese found herself saying. "I don't have any plans for tonight, and in a weird way, I feel kind of responsible."

Later, she would wonder exactly why she stepped up. After all, the guy could have been a stalker ID-ing his next target, some kind of mentally unstable whack job in a city where she knew no one and had nobody to turn to if she got herself in over her head.

But her instincts told her she was not in danger.

Of course, it turned out that that assumption was wrong, although not because he presented any physical threat to her. No, it was damage of another sort that he eventually brought.

Sometimes, though, for destiny to work, it had to make sure you were blind going into things. Otherwise, you would turn your wheel and hit your brakes . . . and avoid your fate like the plague.

"Perfect," the male said in a low voice. "That's just perfect."

TWENTY

As Vishous stood over Layla and Xcor, he was losing his god-damn patience. Which was kind of like a thief ditching his scruples: not a lot to let go of. But whatever.

"Layla," he commanded, "get the fuck out of here. Right now."

From Xcor's vantage point on the forest floor, the enemy fighter said, "Leave, my love."

"And do it proper, true." V couldn't believe he was backing up that fucker on the ground. "Go all the way back to the safe house. He'll know how far you go, and I will ask him."

"Please spare him," Layla said as she rose to her full height. "Please . . ."

V slashed his gun through the air with impatience. "Worry about your kids, female. Not the likes of him."

In the end, Layla did what was right—because at her core, she was a female of worth: After a last lingering stare at the bastard she loved, she nodded once and closed her eyes. It was a while before she dematerialized, but that was to be expected. Emotions were running high. At least in the two of them.

V? Tight as fuck, thank you very much.

When the Chosen was gone, V focused on the piece of shit at his feet. "She out of here?"

Xcor shut his lids. "Yes, she is away a vast distance. She has honored your request."

"You lie to me, and you're only screwing her."

"Truth is the only currency for me the now."

"Well, ain't you a rich sonofabitch."

As Vishous knelt down, his boots and jacket creaked in the cold.

"I am ready," Xcor mumbled.

V flashed his fangs. "I don't give a fuck how you are, asshole. And I don't need your permission to put a bullet in your head."

"Yes, you are correct." The male met V's stare steadily. "You are in charge here."

With his free hand, V took out a hand-rolled and put it between his front teeth. And he meant to light it. He really did. Yup . . . he was just going to light it and then put a fucking lead slug into Xcor's frontal lobe on the exhale.

Yup. Uh-huh . . .

Yeah.

Some moments later—hell, maybe it was better measured in years—he put his gun away and removed his lead-lined glove, pulling the thing free finger by finger. The glow his curse let out was so bright he got a Mr. DeMille close-up on Xcor, and V's first thought was shiiiiiit, he better hurry up if he wanted to kill the fucker. Bastard made Vincent Price look like the poster child for a tanning franchise.

Bringing up his deadly little friend, V lit the end of the hand-rolled with his middle finger and inhaled.

What the fuck was he doing here?

Or not doing, as was the case.

Hello? he wanted to say to his nut sac. Granted, there was only one ball in there, but usually aggression was not a problem for him.

And yet here he was, completely surrounded by him not shooting Xcor in the skull.

Bad, bad, bad . . . this was bad.

And then things got worse.

Without allowing himself to think about what he was doing, he extended his curse over the naked, dying male, and ordered the energy to flow out of himself and into Xcor. In response, waves of heat pulsated over the almost-corpse, the snow not so much melting from the body as withering away like paper curling back from open flame.

Xcor moaned as his contorted body started to sink into the mud that was created from the heat, the forest floor's layer of frost going springtime.

Now the bastard began to shiver. As his blood started to flow with greater ease, his extremities began to swell and quake, the turgor replaced by a vitality that had to be as painful as getting your skin stripped off with a rusted blade. Hearing the groans and staring down at the slow, twisting movements, V was reminded of flies on windowsills. Not a particularly original analogy, except shit, it was accurate.

"V-v-v-ishous . . ."

"What."

Xcor's eyes were bloodshot and watery as fuck as they looked up at him. "I need you . . . to know . . ."

"What."

It was a while before the bastard spoke again. "It was never her. I accept all responsibility. She was never the instigator, always the victim."

"You're a real fucking gentlemale, true?"

"How else would someone like her be anywhere near a male like me."

"Good point."

"And in the end, I let her go. I cast her from me."

V stabbed his cigarette out in the snow. "So I'll nom you for the Nobel Peace Prize. You happy now?"

"I had to let her go," the male mumbled. "Only way . . . I had to let her go."

Vishous frowned. And then shook his head. But not because he was disagreeing with the miserable piece of shit.

He was trying to get a memory out of his brain. Trying . . . and ultimately failing.

It was back from what felt like a lifetime ago. He and Jane were standing in the kitchen of her condo, him in front of the stove, her leaning on a counter. The recollection was so crystal clear, V could hear the metal-on-metal sound of him slowly stirring a stainless-steel spoon around a stainless-steel pan, the hot chocolate in there growing ever more fragrant as the heat was transferred up from the burner.

When the temperature had gotten to be just right, he had filled a mug and given it to Jane, and he had stared into her eyes as she had held what he had prepared for her. Then he had wiped her short-term memory clean, taking from her all knowledge of them having been together.

Everything was gone. The sex they'd had. Their connection. Their relationship.

Wiped away as surely as if it had never existed.

At least on her side.

On his? Everything had stuck, and he wouldn't have had it any other way. He had been prepared to shoulder all the missing, the years of being without, the separation from the other half that would have diminished him ever after. There had been no other choice for them at that point. She was a human with a life. He was from a species that her kind didn't even know existed and was involved in a war that could only get her killed.

Of course, then, because his mother had been a tough piece of work, and destiny had a sick sense of humor, there had been even harder trials for the two of them to face . . .

Even though he fought against the tide, his mind refused to be denied: All at once, that kitchen scene was replaced by an even worse one.

Jane shot, bleeding out, dying in his arms. And then he saw the aftermath of him lying in his bed curled up, rather like Xcor was right now, wanting to die himself.

Abruptly, Vishous had to look away from the bastard. And he would have walked away if he could have.

Instead, he gritted his molars and reached back into his jacket with the hand that wasn't capable of turning cars into burned-out hunks of modern sculpture. With a herculean effort, he cast out his memories and his emotions, ushering those unwelcome visitors from him with all the affability of a bouncer cleaning house before closing.

Buh-bye.

Emotions had no place in the larger scheme of things. They really didn't.

And neither did recollections of the past.

As Layla stood in the living room of the pretty little ranch, she was in front of a giant clock face that had been mounted on the wall as a decorative element. With curlicue black arms that were as long as her own, and cursive numbers like something out of a Dickens novel, it was both whimsical and elegant—and also functional.

She wasn't crying anymore. Her cheeks were raw and burning, though, the combination of all those tears and the wiping and the cold having stripped off the first layer of her skin. And her throat was sore. And her fingertips, each and every one, had their own heartbeat from having gotten a taste of frostbite.

Vishous had pulled the ultimate trump card, and he had been right, as usual. If she wanted access to Lyric and Rhamp, the last thing that would work in her favor was her stopping Xcor's execution.

Especially if she did something crazy . . . like throw herself in front of a bullet meant for him.

The bottom line, however, was that she would always choose her young over anyone and anybody, even herself—and even Xcor. But oh, the pain of losing that male. It was transformative, really, this agony in her chest, the kind of emotional burden that made her feel like she weighed more and was hindered in her movements—

At first, the sound of a ringing phone barely registered. It was only when the thing fell silent in the kitchen and then promptly started going off again that she frowned and looked around the open archway.

The cell Vishous had left for her went quiet. And immediately began to ring once more.

Maybe it was someone trying to reach him so he could bring her back to see the young?

Rushing across to the table, she checked the screen. It was lit up . . . with Vishous's own name.

He was calling himself? Not possible. He was at this moment putting a bullet into—

As her eyes watered and stung, she put her hands to her face. Would the Brother even treat Xcor's remains with respect? She couldn't bear to think otherwise—

The ringing stopped. And when it didn't readily resume, she turned away. It must be a malfunction, some key or button hit due to a shift in body position or something—

The bell sound piped up a third time. Or was it the fourth?

Pivoting back around, Layla frowned and reached out, picking up the cell. Accepting the call, she said—

"Jesus Christ," Vishous snapped before she could offer anything verbal. "Took you long enough."

Layla recoiled. "I'm . . . I'm sorry?"

"Get out here."

"What?"

"You heard me. Come back to the woods."

Layla began to pant, a combination of terror and sadness choking her. "How can you be so cruel. I cannot see him dead—"

"Then you better get the fuck out here and feed him. We need to get him out of this forest."

"What!"

"You fucking heard me. Now dematerialize back here before I change my fucking mind."

The connection was cut off so abruptly she had to wonder whether he had thrown the phone he'd called her with. Or maybe shot it.

Heart pounding, head spinning, she lowered the cell from her ear and just stared at it. But then she tossed the thing onto the table.

She was out the slider before that phone stopped bouncing across that wood surface.

As she dematerialized and then resumed her form right where she had been standing over Xcor, she found Vishous about five feet away from the other male, smoking with such fervor it was like that hand-rolled between his teeth was his only source of oxygen. Meanwhile, Xcor had been transformed by some source of heat, the snow gone from atop and around him, the ground beneath him puddled and mudded, his flesh no longer gray, but an angry red.

He was alive. And as her presence registered upon him, he moved his head a little and shifted his eyes. "Layla . . . ?"

"What . . . why . . ." she stammered.

Vishous slashed his hand through the air, but when he spoke, it was with exhaustion. "No offense, but shut the fuck up, both of you, okay? No questions. You—just feed him. And you—taking her fucking vein and be quick about it. I'm going to be back in about twenty minutes, and the pair of you better be ready for transport."

With that cheerful little burst of optimism, the Brother ghosted out, disappearing into thin air.

Layla blinked and wondered if this were a dream. And then she jumped into action.

Let us pray Vishous has a lead foot, she thought as she dropped to her knees.

She didn't bother talking to Xcor. She yanked the sleeve of her robe up to expose her wrist, scored her vein with her own fangs, and then put the source of strength and nutrients to Xcor's mouth.

But he refused to part his lips. Even as the life force he so desperately needed wetted his mouth, he denied its entrance.

Mutely, he stared up at her and shook his head from side to side.

It reminded her of that moment when she had first met him under the maple tree in the meadow. He had tried to deny her then, too.

"No offense," she muttered, "but fucking drink."

She had no idea why Vishous had decided to spare the life of his enemy. But she was not about to argue with what seemed to be happening— or take the reprieve for granted. Hell, the Brother might well decide to change his mind again and come back with his gun. Or his dagger. Or reinforcements.

When Xcor as yet still refused her, she reached down with her free hand and pinched his nose hard. "If you love me, you will save yourself the now. Do not so willingly put your death on my conscience."

As he just lay there, seemingly content to suffocate, she started to plot ways of prying his teeth open. Except then he gasped a little—and that was all it took.

A drop or two must have entered his mouth, because he moaned in a different way, his torso arching, his legs sawing as if a great need had struck him.

And then he let out a predatory hiss—

—and bit her so hard she had to hold back a curse.

Now he partook, great swallows draining her so fast she knew she had to be very careful. There was a good chance he could kill her by mistake, his hunger capable of overpowering every other instinct in him, including the one that wanted to protect her.

Dearest Virgin Scribe, she wished she knew what Vishous had planned for them—but sometimes in life, it was best not to look too far ahead. All she had to do right now was feed Xcor and keep him warm whilst Vishous came back with some kind of vehicle.

And after that? She did not know.

Brushing Xcor's hair from his forehead, she met his crazed eyes and was struck by an intense need to pray. Giving into the reflex, she began to recite quatrains she had known since her birth up in the Sanctuary, the ancient, sacred words marching through her head, the rhythm of the Old

Language forming a drumbeat that reverberated down in the center of her chest.

Too bad there was no one up there to hear them anymore. But what did it matter? Vishous was the only savior she and Xcor had—and God knew, she would take what she could get.

TWENTY-ONE

"Oh, I forgot," Trez muttered. "iAm's car is a stick."

As he stood outside the staff exit of Sal's, he frowned at the BMW M6 and tried to think how he was going to keep this take-me-to-Havers thing going—

The female who'd made him faint snatched the key fob out of his hands. "No problem. I'm good with a clutch."

Therese clicked off the security alarm, opened the driver's side, and slid into the leather seat like she owned the sports car. "Well, come on. I can't put you in the passenger seat myself. That's a job you're going to have to do."

Her smile was easy, but not simple. In fact, nothing about her was simple for him, not the way she moved, or the sound of her voice, or the fact that she filled out those black slacks of hers perfectly.

Just like Selena would have.

Oh, and yeah, iAm's warning kept bugging him in his head: *This is not your dead mate coming back to you.*

With a curse, Trez went around the trunk of the sedan. As he got in, he looked over at the female. God, her profile was—

"Um, can you shut your door? This particular model has an anti-rolling mechanism. I won't be able to go anywhere until you do—plus let's face it, it's about the draft. Brrr."

Trez flushed and did the job with the handle. And then he tried to look relaxed as she started the engine, cut the fan down on the heater, and threw them in reverse. With a perfectly executed K-turn, they were off, weeding their way around to the main part of the lot and heading for the four lane road beyond.

"You're going to have to tell me where to go."

As she spoke, she looked so beautiful in the peachy glow of the dash, her straight nose, those full lips, that strong jaw, the stuff that he had been trying to re-create in 3-D from his 2-D memories.

He spoke without meaning to. Without intending to. "I've missed you—"

His voice cracked at the same moment she shot him a look of shock. "I'm sorry? What?"

Shit, what had just come out of his mouth?

"Ah . . . yeah, wow, I'm really not making sense at all over here." He gave her an apologetic smile—that was really fucking sincere. "Maybe I really do need a doctor."

As they came up the parking lot exit, she smiled once more. "Well, the immediate question is, do you want Google Maps? The nav system on this car? Or do you know where we're headed."

Trez got caught up in staring at her face again, and as the sight of her got wavy, he had to wipe his eyes in what he hoped was a quick move she wouldn't notice.

"You really are hurt," she murmured. "Do you need an ambulance?"

And that was when she touched him. It was, once again, a simple thing that was not simple at all: She just placed her warm, soft palm over the back of his hand, the one that was resting on his thigh—and in the process, gave him the chest equivalent of a heart attack.

"I should tell you to go," he said hoarsely.

"Yup, I agree. Left or right?"

Closing his eyes, he told himself to pull his shit together and listen to what his brother had said. This female, whoever she was, was not his

Selena. And it was grossly unfair to her, and to his mourning process, to interject himself into a stranger's orbit simply because of some accident of appearance.

She had a slight Detroit accent, for godsakes, something Selena had obviously never had. And Selena had never worn her hair like that, or had clothes like that—

"What did you say your name was?" the female asked. "Do you want me to get your brother? Hello? Are you . . . have you passed out on me again?"

When he finally spoke, the words came out of him fast and sloppy— exactly the way he fumbled with the door mechanism and jumped out of the car: "I'm sorry. I gotta go. I'm so sorry. I'm sorry . . ."

As he stumbled back from the door, which he'd left open, he managed to catch a slick of ice with his heel—

And go ass-over-idiot for a second time in her presence, landing in a heap.

At least he kept consciousness this time, though.

Whoo-hoo, his ego crooned. Baby steps, you lame motherfucker, baby steps.

The female was out and around to him quicker than a breath, and as she slipped and slid, and then landed right on him, Trez wanted to scream.

He didn't.

Nope. As she fell on top of him . . . he put his arms around her and fucking kissed her.

Therese hadn't expected it. Not at all. As she lost her balance and went down right on the guy's chest, her only thought was how long it was going to take to get back on her feet and run into the restaurant to find his brother.

Because, hello, as a pair of vampires, they were not calling 911. The last thing they needed were human medics showing up and taking him into a human hospital—where he'd get admitted, and knowing their luck, go up in flames when sunlight came through the window by his adjustable bed.

Except that whole get-brother idea didn't happen. As she pushed against his pecs to lift her head, everything came to a crashing halt. Their eyes met, their breath caught—and then he slipped an arm around her waist, a hand onto her nape . . . and pulled her to his mouth.

Soft. His lips were so soft . . . and they trembled against hers, as if he were unsure of what he was doing or maybe affected by something monumental. His body was anything but weak, however. Underneath her, he was big, and he was hard, and she could feel the power emanating from him.

It was only when his tongue came out and licked at her, seeking to get inside, that Therese broke the contact.

She didn't go far, though. She didn't want to.

God . . . his eyes were amazing, and they were no longer black. They were shining an extraordinary peridot green, the light coming from them so bright she had to blink.

"I'm sorry," he whispered. "I should have done that." The male frowned and shook his head. "I mean, I shouldn't have done that."

Therese searched his features, getting lost in the uncoiling that was happening in her gut, her body going hyper-aware and strangely sluggish at the same time.

"Do you have a male?" he asked in a rough voice.

"No." She focused on his lips. "No, I don't."

His lids closed and the relief across those features of his was a surprise. "Thank God."

Therese had to smile. "You are a male of worth, then." Except then she frowned. "Are you with anyone?"

"No, I'm not—"

The honk of a horn brought both of their heads around. A Mercedes had pulled up behind them, and the driver was getting out. "Are you okay?" he asked.

"Just fine," her male said. "Sorry."

Ummm, okay, not that he was hers.

"Yup, we're just fine," she echoed. Seeking to prove what felt like a lie, Therese grabbed his arm and helped the male up to his feet. "We're good. Thank you."

She made a point to escort the male to the passenger side and help him in. Then she strode around, got behind the wheel, and hit the gas, taking a right out of the parking lot because it was easier than cutting through four lanes of traffic.

"I really should go," he said as he stared out the front windshield.

"To the doctor, I know. So where are we headed? I can turn us around."

"Listen, I'll be all right. I always am. Can you please pull over?"

She glanced across at him, and dear God, he was tense, his hands squeezing his thighs, his jaw clenched. He'd been the instigator of the kiss, but he was clearly regretting it.

"Please, pull over," he muttered.

"Okay, sure. But there isn't . . . I don't see anything."

The restaurant was located at the beginning of a strip of some twenty or thirty outlet stores, but her choice of "right" had taken them in the opposite direction from all of that: Accordingly, they were entering a stretch of no-shoulders and a lot of trees, nothing but an on-ramp to some kind of highway, and what seemed to be vacant, unfinished land on either side of the street.

Frowning, she leaned into the wheel. Up ahead, there was something on the horizon, on a rise in the landscape . . . construction cranes, maybe? Or . . . she wasn't sure what it was.

Whatever it was, a parking lot presented itself around the next bend— and talk about an abundance of riches. Pavement opened up on both sides of the road, with enough spaces to accommodate hundreds and hundreds and hundreds of cars. Was it a convention center? She couldn't see any kind of hotel or big facility, though. Just darkness.

As she hit her directional signal, the male stiffened.

"Not here," he said hoarsely. "Oh, God . . . anywhere but here."

"I'm sorry?"

"Keep going."

Hitting the gas again, she passed by what turned out to be—oh, right, an amusement park. Of course. The stuff she had thought were cranes were actually rides like roller coasters and high-elevation spinners, everything currently unlit because it was winter and the enterprise was closed for the season.

She continued on, going by an ice-cream place named Martha's that was marked with a giant rooster. It, too, was shut down for the off-season, but she could imagine the lines at its dozen windows, kids running around with soft-serve cones melting down their arms, parents relaxing even as they kept one eye on the little guys.

That summer fantasy was real for some people. Had been real for her, for a while.

All that was gone now.

"Here," he said, pointing to the rooster. "Turn in here."

"A little farther."

She didn't want the ice-cream place any more than he wanted the amusement park. So maybe they did have something in common. Buzz kills unite.

The souvenir shop they came up to next had lots of windows and lots of little things lined up in the show of glass, all the snow globes, shot glasses, T-shirts, and beer cozies like soldiers waiting to be called to the front lines of family fun. Its parking lot was the baby brother to the big daddies they'd passed, but empty as it was, there was plenty of room.

After Therese stopped the BMW, she put the gearshift in neutral and pulled the parking brake—and what do you know, she agreed with the male sitting next to her. Imperatives for his healthcare aside, it was time for them to part ways. In her current mindset, she was a vacuum looking for a distraction, a hollow mess who only looked put together on the outside. She'd come to Caldwell in search of a fresh start, a new definition of herself . . . an escape from everything that had come before, all the lies and the deceit, the falsity.

Funny how finding out that you weren't who you'd thought you were could make you move over five hundred miles away from your "family."

But the good thing about being on your own?

Unless you lied to yourself, you knew exactly where you stood.

The bad thing, though? You tended to fill the void you had with other stuff—and she didn't need a shrink to tell her it was a bad idea to get lost in whatever was going on with this male. He was sexy, very off, and too much for her to handle with her defenses all down.

"Can you dematerialize home?" he asked.

"Yes, absolutely. I'm still worried about your head, however."

Even as she spoke, though, she was unclipping the seat belt and popping her door. He did the same, and they both got out.

The male came around as she did, and they met in front of the car, right in between the headlights—and as they looked at each other, she frowned, some strange feeling coming over her.

"I'll take care of it," he said. "I feel a lot better."

As she stared up at his greater height, she blinked . . . and tried to remember what he was talking about. Oh, right, his head.

Well, he certainly seemed steady on his feet now, and vampires did heal quickly. There was no slurring of his speech, and those eyes, as they flashed peridot, seemed of equal size now. Besides, he didn't have far to get back to his brother's restaurant. She hadn't gone more than a mile.

"Are you going to be safe?" he asked. "Going home by yourself, I mean."

"Yup." She kicked up her chin and forced a smile. "Perfectly safe."

"I should take you back. Where do you—"

As she thought of that kiss, she put a hand up. "No, I'd rather go by myself. It's better that way."

He inclined his head. "Absolutely."

"So . . ." She put out her palm. "It was weird to meet you."

She tempered the words with an honest smile. Twenty-four hours in Caldwell, and she was making males faint, practicing her interviewing skills, and driving fancy cars. All things considered? It could be a lot worse.

"The pleasure was mine," he said remotely.

She had a feeling he wanted to hug her by the way he left her hand hanging, but she didn't want to go up against that body of his again. She was already in the position of having to forget that kiss. More reasons to have to give herself amnesia was not something she needed.

"Well, good-bye." She stepped back. "Ah . . . have a good life."

On that note, she up and dematerialized. And as she traveled in a scatter, she was amazed at how someone you'd never met before could make such a huge impression on you.

Crazy.

Really just nuts.

TWENTY-TWO

nd yet he didn't kill her.

Somehow, in spite of Xcor's starvation, Layla felt him release her wrist just as she was beginning to feel the effect of his feeding, her blood pressure starting to dip, her head becoming only the slightest bit dizzy.

She could tell the withdrawal cost him dearly. His fangs were fully descended, and he was fighting himself, the muscles up both sides of his neck straining against his skin, his arms and legs churning in the melted, sloppy earth beneath his naked body.

He was also very, totally . . . completely erect.

When it had been a life-and-death situation, his nakedness had been easy to overlook. And on that front, they were still far from out of the woods—natch, as V would say. But in this split second of relief, she became vitally aware of exactly how male he was.

Xcor was *phearsom*, indeed.

There was no dwelling on his thick arousal, though. From behind them, lights began to flash, and then there was the sound of a powerful car engine and the crashing of trees. Layla leapt to her feet and put herself between Xcor and whatever it was—

The Range Rover broke through the forest like a charging bull, stopping just short of plowing her down. And as the driver's side door opened, Layla's heart jumped up into her throat.

It was just Vishous, however.

Well, "just" suggested the Brother was a benign presence, and that couldn't be further from the truth. Vishous looked positively furious, his brows down, his black hair all messed up like he'd been running a hand through it, the tattoos at his temple and that goatee making him seem even more sinister.

"You done?" the Brother demanded.

He refused to look at her so she spoke up as she nodded. "Yes."

"I'll get him into the—"

"No, I'll do it."

"You're not strong enough—"

She bent down, forced one arm under the middle of Xcor's back and the other under his thighs, the mud seeping into her sleeves and sticking to her forearms. She paid that no heed, however—just as she ignored the way he struggled against her, garbled protests leaving his mouth whilst she lifted him from the ground.

"Get the door," she commanded to V.

After an initial shock, the Brother did the deed, clearing the way for her to bring Xcor over. It was a struggle, her slippers sinking into the snow, the tree branches seeming to grab at Xcor out of spite, the mud dripping down the front of her robe—and she wouldn't have made it if he hadn't lost so much weight.

The way she looked at it, though, Xcor was hers and hers alone to help.

Shoving him into the rear seat was an awkward affair, and he aided her by pulling his lower body in and collapsing lengthwise across the back. And she wanted to get in beside him, but even with the wasting, he was still of tremendous length and there was no room for her. She wasn't about to leave him naked, however. Stripping off her robe, she covered him with it, tucking the thing in as best she could before she ran around to the passenger side.

With only leggings and a loose top on now, the cold got to her quick, and she was shivering as she shut herself in.

"Buckle up," V muttered. "This is going to be rough."

No kidding, she thought as she pulled the belt across her chest.

She expected the Brother to move them forward at a brisk pace. She did not anticipate that he'd floor the accelerator and send them careening through the trees, the headlights hitting trunks and boughs just before they did, the SUV taking strike after strike as it bounced and bashed and heaved its way toward what she hoped was the road.

But which could well be the edge of the earth.

Craning around, she checked on Xcor and tried to catch his eye—which was hard because she was going up and down and side to side, although at least Xcor was on the same schedule of movements, his body flopping and slamming about on the rear seat bench. He was doing what he could to anchor himself, one hand gripping the back of her headrest, one foot braced against the door, as everything else made like scrambled eggs in a pan.

When their stares finally met, the question of *Are you okay?* was asked on both sides mutely . . . and answered with a mutual *I have no idea*.

The end of the tooth-rattling trip came as quickly as the start of it all, the Range Rover bursting out of the tree line like it was throwing off a too-heavy cloak, its tires skidding on pavement, the great lurch to right itself in the correct lane the last of them, she hoped.

And for truth, as they made off at even greater speed, things were much quieter, more civilized.

Which only underscored how hard everyone was breathing.

Twisting around again, she tried to see out the back, but with the darkened windows, there wasn't much to go on. She could only imagine the debris they'd dragged into the road in their wake—and meanwhile, Xcor was collapsed into the seats, his body lax, his respiration ragged.

But he was alive and he gave her the thumbs-up sign.

As she refocused on the way ahead, all she got was a whole lot of pavement, a white line on either side, and a double yellow in the middle. Oh, wait . . . there was a leaping deer sign, the unnuanced black form of the animal and its antlers set in a reflective diamond the color of a dandelion head.

No words were spoken.

None were necessary.

At first, she didn't know where they were going—and she wasn't about to ask. But then V made a series of turns that took them back to town. Probably to that ranch once again.

She was right.

About twenty minutes later, he pulled them into the safe house's garage and they all waited in place as the panels trundled back down.

Vishous got out first, and Layla wasn't but a split second behind so she could tend to Xcor. Opening the door by his head, she took his arm and helped as he fought to shuffle himself around and keep the muddy robe in place over his nakedness. When he was on his feet, she snagged the long sleeves, tied them together around his waist, and twisted the white fall so that only his hip and the side of his thigh and lower leg were visible.

"Lean on me," she demanded as she hitched herself up under him and put her hand around his middle.

Vishous had gone into the house already, but he'd left the door open for them, the kick stop in place on the tile floor.

"I'm taking you downstairs," she said. "There are two bedroom suites and a sitting area there."

Xcor leaned on her pretty heavily, especially as they went up the three shallow steps into the house. And as she considered the logistics, she had no idea how they were going to make the descent into the cellar.

"Where are we?" he asked roughly.

"It's a safe house."

"Of the Brotherhood's?"

"Yes."

Vishous was in the kitchen, lounging against the counter and lighting up a hand-rolled, and he didn't spare them a glance as they went by him. He had, however, once again paved the way for them, the door they

needed to get through open wide, the light on so they could make their
way safely underground.

Boy, that stairwell was skinny.

Xcor solved the tight-squeeze problem, however, by breaking away
from her and relying on the railing. When he got to the bottom, he bee-
lined for the stuffed sofa that was opposite the wide-screen TV. As he
collapsed on it, she wasn't sure what let out a bigger exhale, him or the
cushions.

There was a red and black blanket folded over the back of the matching armchair and she snagged it, removing the dirty robe from his lower
body and replacing it with something cleaner.

She took a moment to breathe. And then it was back into action. "I'll
bring you some food."

When he didn't argue with her, just sank further into the couch, she
wondered if the trip into town hadn't done what Mother Nature had
failed, and what V had declined, to do. But no . . . he was still breathing.

Layla took the stairs quickly, and as she came up into the kitchen, she
shut the door quietly. There were things that she and Vishous needed to
say to each other—and yet he didn't seem to want to talk at all. He was
utterly self-contained as he stared at the lit end of his hand-rolled, his
brows down low, his expression so flat it was as if he were a cartoon rep-
resentation of himself.

She went over and put her hand on his arm. "Vishous, thank—"

"Don't touch me!" He jerked away from her. "Do not *fucking* touch
me."

His eyes glowed with anger as he jabbed his cigarette at her. "Don't
get this shit twisted. We are not 'in' this together. We are not cohorts in
Xcor. I'm *not* buying this romantic fantasy you're rocking. What I *am*
doing is leaving you here with a murderer and an open landline. If you're
alive to take the phone call about your fucking kids later, hey, you win
the lottery. If he decides to slaughter you and then call his friends to
come over and party with your corpse? Sorry, not sorry. Either way, I
don't give a fuck. You want him? Now you got him."

V stalked his way to the table and picked up the cell phone he'd left behind.

Then he was gone, heading out through the slider and disappearing into the night.

After a moment, Layla walked across and shifted the lock into place. Then she turned back around and started rifling through the cabinets, looking for cans of soup.

The first thing Trez did when he got back to the restaurant was go into iAm's office and hit the mess on the desk. He didn't have to work very hard to find what he was looking for. The female's résumé was right on the top, and he checked out the header.

Did he dare?

That question was answered as he returned the piece of paper to the pile of bills and orders, and snuck out of the back part of Sal's like a criminal. Dematerializing, he proceeded to a not-so-hot section of town, to a rooming house that made him want to scream. The damn thing was three stories high, a block long, and had at least half a dozen windows that were boarded up. Its paint job had been fresh white back in the 1970s, but had faded to piss yellow, and the couple coming out of its metal double doors looked like they could have been homeless with their dirty clothes and filthy hair.

Had he even gotten the address right?

Shit. Yes, he had.

She shouldn't be here, in this nest of grubby humans. For godsakes, was she staying aboveground with just drapes between her and the sun during the day?

What was she thinking?

As Trez strode across the street, he worried it wasn't a choice.

When he got to the entrance, he looked through the chicken-wire glass panels. It was hard to see clearly because the damn things hadn't been cleaned in a decade or two, but on the far side, there appeared to be a "lobby" of sorts with lights out in the overhead fixtures, a carpet that could have counted as tile for all its nap, and a wall of mailboxes where half the little portals were broken and lolling like the tongues of dead animals.

It was the building equivalent of a colon . . . dank, windowless, with brown sludge staining the walls.

"You need in?"

A human male who smelled like old booze and cigarettes pushed his way past, opening the door with a swipe card and keeping on his merry way.

As Trez contemplated his own entry, he had some thought that it would be better for both him and Therese if he let this shit go. Let her go.

But he went inside anyway.

There were a couple of hardies in the far corner, nodding off like they had recently injected themselves, and their bloodshot eyes passed over him with the marked lack of enthusiasm characteristic of H addiction. No bliss anymore for them. You only got that in the beginning during the rose-colored part of your relationship with opiates.

The elevator was out of service, a half-assed caution tape tied in several places across its closed panels, a handwritten sign taped cockeyed with a Band-Aid to the wall. The sight of it made him think of the Otis in *The Big Bang Theory*—and he was willing to bet this place's bad boy had been broken longer.

There was only one set of stairs and they were cramped and smelled like urine. And as he made his ascent to the third floor, the noises he heard along the way were not any more optimistic and lighthearted than the rest of the dump: yelling, coughing, loud music from bad speakers, thumps like someone was banging their head into the wall repeatedly.

Jesus Christ.

On the top floor, he looked left and right. It went without saying that there wasn't a little plaque telling people which way for which apartments. Oh, yeah . . . of course. Right in front of him, at eye level, there was a bald stain on the cracked wall where one had been ripped off.

'Cuz you could repurpose something like that. For a dinner plate. Or a level to help cut your drugs on.

She stayed in 309, and it turned out to be down on the left.

Goddamn, he hated the number of her apartment. He didn't like threes or nines in sequences. Four-oh-two was a good number. Eight-oh-four. Two-twenty-four.

He was a divisible-by-two guy. He didn't like threes, fives, or nines.

Seven was okay, he thought as he came to stand at her door, but only because two together equaled fourteen.

Thirteen was the bane of his existence.

"You looking for that girl?"

Trez cranked around. Directly across the hall, a guy in a wife-beater and a shitload of tattoos was lounging in the doorway like he owned the place, a real King of the Douche Bags. He had a handlebar mustache, bags under his eyes like canvas sacks, and cologne courtesy of the crack he'd been smoking.

"You her pimp or something?" The human stretched his neck and then scratched over his jugular. "How much is she? She's fresh—"

Trez closed the short distance between them, grabbed the guy by the face, and forced the piece of shit back into his den of self-destruction.

As Trez kicked the door shut behind the two of them, the John-who-wasn't-gonna-get-none started flapping his arms like he was trying to take flight—and hello, roommate on the couch.

Trez used his free hand to pull out his gun and point it to the other guy across the room. "Shut the fuck up."

The junkie over there just put his palms high and shrugged, like people being manhandled and Glocks getting popped were part of his daily life—and he was not about to get involved in anyone else's shit.

Trez shoved the propositioner against the wall, keeping a palm lock on that face. "You don't go near her. If you do, I'm going to take all your drugs and flush them down the toilet in front of you. And then I'm going to kidnap you and drop you off at county hospital downtown where they're going to hold you against your will while the court decides what rehab to mandate you into. Do you hear me? You fuck with her and I'm going to inject your sorry ass into the system—and the next time you see any kind of a hit is ninety miserable fucking days from now."

After all, you didn't threaten someone like this with a gun. They were already dead, for fuck's sake.

Nah, you tortured them with the thought of third-party-enforced sobriety.

And no, Trez didn't feel an obligation to help either of these rats without tails. Killing yourself with chemicals was a God-given right of both species, and he was not interested in interfering in the course of somebody else's addiction. He was, however, more than happy to use any weakness to his advantage.

He glanced over at Couch Man to make sure the sonofabitch was hearing this, too. "I have her apartment rigged. I know where she is every second of the day." He smiled tightly to keep his fangs to himself. "You two or anyone around here get near her, I'm going to know."

Then he refocused on the one he had a hold on, squeezing those features so hard the man's dumb-ass mustache merged with his eyebrows, like a Muppet whose operator was having a hand spasm.

When Trez finally let go, the bastard's face was all Halloween mask, swollen and misshapen, the 'stache off angle like a pair of glasses that had been broken.

Trez looked pointedly at the couch again.

"Yeah. Sure," the guy over there said. "You got it. She no for no one."

TWENTY-THREE

ooner or later, when one stole to survive, one thieved from the wrong sort. And Xcor made that mistake in his twenty-sixth year, in a thicket of woods three hundred and sixty lochens from the cottage that first his nursemaid, and then, after some comings and goings, he himself had abandoned.

It was fate at work, he would later suppose.

What initially drew his attention, as he progressed through the night alone, was the scent of the beef stew. Indeed, he had been long used to searching out sustenance, sticking to shadows with such competence and constancy that he had begun to think of himself as one. It was best that way. Other eyes upon him never went well.

In truth, prior to his transition, he had had a hope that his defect would magically fix itself. That somehow, the change would repair the split in his upper lip, as if his gestation required that last spurt of growth before he was in his proper order. Alas, no. His mouth remained as it was, curled up. Ruined.

Ugly.

So aye, it was wisest to stay in the shadows, and as he currently took cover behind the stout trunk of an oak, he regarded the glow of a fire far off in the forest as a possible meal or source of supplies.

Around the crackling flames, he saw people—males—and they were ca-rousing in the shifting orange light. And there were horses, tied a ways off.

The fire was large. They obviously cared not if they were discovered, which suggested they were fighters, and likely to be heavily armed. They were also of his species. He could catch their scents in the mix of the smoke, the horse flesh, the smell of mead and woman.

As he planned his approach, he was grateful for the heavy cloud cover that kept the moon at bay and deepened the shadows to pitch black. Provided he stayed out of reach of that illumination, he might as well have been wearing a cloak of invisibility.

Closing in, the flames made him think of that cottage he had stayed his first two decades in. He had departed from it after his nursemaid first had left him, finding the orphanage that footmale had spoken off. But he had not been able to stay away for long, thoughts of his sire's possible return making him seek out the structure anew. Over the years, he left again for certain pe-riods, typically the winter months when the wolves were hungry; however, he always went back there.

His sire never did come.

And then the time for his transition had arrived. In the village, there had been a whore who regularly serviced males of the species, but because of his ugliness, he had had to barter the cottage and everything in it in exchange for her vein.

When he had walked away from the site the following evening, with those hateful raspberry brambles and the encroaching forest with its wolves, he had taken a final look over his shoulder. His nursemaid had never returned to check on him, but he had not expected to see her again. And it had been more than time for him to stop pretending his father might seek him out.

With Xcor relinquishing his shelter to another, he became truly adrift in the world.

He took only one thing with him: the collar that had been around his neck until he had used a hatchet to sever its hold upon him. He'd had to work on the leather for hours, his then-young arms lacking the strength to be more efficient. But his nursemaid had left behind only so much water, and very little food, so he'd had to get free.

Fortunately, hunting and killing had been skills that had come naturally to him.

So, too, had stealing.

He had hated it at first. But he had always taken no more than he needed, whether it be food, clothing, or elements of shelter. And it was amazing what one could sacrifice in terms of morals when it came to survival. It was also incredible how one could devise methods for avoiding the sun in a forest of trees, and staying ahead of wild animals . . . and finding ways to pay for the veins of whores.

The forests of the Old Country became his refuge, his home, and he stayed within them, keeping to himself. Which was to say that he steered clear of the lessers *who stalked through the pines and caves, and avoided the vampire fighters who sought them and engaged with them and slaughtered them. He further kept away from the war camp.*

That was no place for anyone. Even he, who tried to avoid all and sundry, had heard snippets of the depravity therein, and the cruelty of the warrior who ran it.

Refocusing, he closed his eyes . . . and dematerialized up into the tree's thick branches. And then he ghosted o'er to the next one, likewise staying far from the ground, like a monkey.

When one was by oneself with no aid e'er coming, one adapted with an eye toward safety, and both vampires and humans alike tended to be far more concerned with what was on their level, rather than what was over them.

Not much farther forth, he did regard the makeshift camp from a vantage point of a mere ten yards away, and ten yards well above. The vampires were indeed fighters, well-armed and thick of shoulder, but they were drunk and passing a human woman around like a tankard of common ownership. The woman was willing, laughing as she made herself available to each in turn, and Xcor tried to imagine participating in such debauchery.

No.

He cared not for sex, at least not that sort. Indeed, he remained a virgin, for the whores had always demanded far more than he could pay for what was betwixt their thighs—and besides, he was not that interested in such well-plowed fields.

Looking toward the stand of horses, he thought, yes, he would invade there. He would not take a steed, no matter how valuable in the open market, as he did not want to be responsible for another living thing. He had enough difficulty keeping himself alive and fed. Weapons, however, he could use. He had three daggers upon him, and one gun that he did not use. Cumbersome, it was, and then there was the inconvenience of keeping it supplied with bullets. The aim was lesser as well: He could throw a knife with better accuracy. Still, it seemed wise to have at least one upon his person.

Mayhap he could lift another good dagger, one sharper than his dullest? Some meat? A bladder of water?

Aye, those would be of benefit.

Xcor dematerialized down to the ground, crouching behind yet another pine. Their steeds were on the edge of the firelight, the heads of the quarter horses lolling in repose, their saddles packed with necessaries and other property.

He made not a sound as he moved through the undergrowth, the second skins of his moccasins cushioning his weight and masking noise.

The horses pricked their ears and craned their thick necks to regard his presence, one making a whinny of inquiry. He was not worried. He was long schooled in scattering himself into the night even in times of duress, and further, the fighters were otherwise occupied.

Xcor was fast and sure as he went through the saddle of a roan that was easily sixteen and a half hands high, flipping up the heavy leather flaps, digging into satchels and sacks. He found clothing, grains, smoked meat. He took the meat, putting it into his cloak, and moved on to the next steed. No weapons, but there was a lady's garments with the scent of blood on them in one burlap sack.

He wondered if the female had survived the rutting. He thought perhaps not—

The fight by the fire exploded without preamble, all well until it was not, two of the males leaping up and going at each other, locking hand to throat, their bodies dancing in circles as they each attempted to muscle the other into submission. And then something was on fire, the portion of an outer coat catching a lick of the open flame and bursting into orange and yellow heat.

The fighter did not care, and neither did his opponent. The horses spooked, however, and as the one that Xcor was attempting to raid balked, his hand got wedged in one of the saddle bags, the torque and pressure rendering him trapped.

Such that as the quarter horse spun around, so, too, did he.

Within sight of them all.

The change in the camp was instantaneous, the woman cast aside in a heap, the argument amongst comrades forgotten, the interloper a target for them all. And as yet Xcor stayed attached to the mincing horse, dancing around sharp hooves, trying to rip his hand free.

The warriors solved that problem for him.

Xcor was tackled upward and that was enough to change the angle of his wrist. His arm was suddenly his own once more and good timing in that. He was pummeled in the face by a fist the size of a boulder, but at least it sent him in a trajectory away from the churning steed.

Unfortunately, he spun directly into the path of another of the fighters, and Xcor knew that he had to establish the upper hand fast or be o'erpowered. There was little hope on that score, however—these males were experts in conflict, punches and kicks flying too quick for him to dodge or counter, his breath knocked from him over and over again.

Indeed, he had experience grappling with fists prior to this. But that had been with humans and civilian vampires. What he faced the now was a different foe altogether.

Blows continued to rain upon his head and his gut, coming quicker than he could parry them, harder than he could withstand, as he was passed around like that woman had been, going from one to the other to the next. Blood flew from his nose and his mouth, and his sight went bad as he whirled around, trying to protect his vital organs and his skull.

"Bloody common thief!"

"Bastard!"

A fist pummeled him in the side and he thought he could feel something burst therein. And it was at that point that his knees went out from under him and he landed into the leaves and dirt.

"Stab him!"

"Not done yet," came a growl.

The boot caught him under the ribs and he went into a flying roll that took him all the way to the fire. He was so stunned that he lay where he stopped on his back, unable to gather his wits sufficiently to cover even his face or curl into a defensive ball.

Dearest Virgin Scribe, he was going to die. And likely in the flames that were already singeing his shoulder, hand, and hip through his clothes.

One of the fighters, who had a heavy beard and smelled like a dead goat, leaned over him and smiled, revealing tremendous fangs. "You thought you could take from us. From us?"

He grabbed the front of Xcor's cloak and jerked his torso up off the ground. "From us!"

The warrior slapped him with an open palm so hard that it was like getting broadsided with a plank of wood. "Do you know what we do with thieves?"

The others had gathered around in a semi-circle, and Xcor thought of the wolves in the forest, back when he had lived with his nursemaid. A pack of deadly predators, these males were. A terrible force by which to be caught and toyed with. A quick route unto the Fade.

"Do you?" The warrior shook him like a rag doll and then dropped him hard. "Allow me to tell you. We cut your hands from you first, and then we . . ."

Xcor didn't dare look away from the face looming above him. But in his peripheral vision, he saw a log that was half in and half out of the flames.

Inching his hand over, he took hold of it and waited for just the moment when the male glanced over at his compatriots with evil mirth.

Quick as lightning, Xcor swung the log hard and caught the warrior in the head, knocking him senseless to the side.

There was a moment of shock from all and sundry, and Xcor knew he had to act with alacrity. Keeping hold of his weapon, he snagged one of the daggers that had been strapped to his victim's chest and then he was up on his feet.

Now he attacked.

There was no bloodcurdling cry from his mouth. No grunting. No growling.

No true memory of what exactly he did. All he knew, all he was aware of, was something unleashing within him. Whate'er it was, he had had hints of *it before, some kind of energy source that was other than anger, other than fear, powering his body and mind. And as it reared within him, all at once, his limbs took o'er his mind, functioning independently, knowing better than his consciousness where to aim, what to do, how to move. His senses likewise parted from his brain, elevating themselves to a higher level of acuity, whether it was hearing to detect someone about to jump him from behind, sight to notice another coming from the left, scent to inform him of a further attack from the right.*

In the midst of all this, his mind was utterly removed. And yet free to extrapolate and thus begin to refine his performance.

He was still going to lose, however. There were too many who were too expert: Even as he put them down on the ground, they never stayed for long, and it was an easy equation that his stamina would be bested by their number.

The solution to the disparity came as unexpectedly as that log.

At first, he knew not what flashed and thus caught his eye. But then he saw that there was some kind of a huge blade on the far side of the fire . . . a weapon larger than he had e'er seen, leaning against a massive stone.

Just as one of the males went to jump upon him, Xcor took a running start and sent his body flying directly over the flames, the somersaulting tuck sparing him the heat, his landing as coordinated as the take-off had been.

Propelling himself toward that massive curved blade, he grabbed for the handle attached to it, and—

It was a scythe. A common field-tilling device, its blade affixed to a wooden superstructure by leather bindings tied tight as bone around marrow. There was little time for an orientation to its attributes. But it turned out he needed none.

Tucking the thing into place and grasping the steering peg, he . . .

Went after each and every one of them.

At first, they laughed and taunted him. But after he cut the first one nearly in half, the tactics changed. Guns were taken out, bullets discharged with great noise and little accuracy, the lead balls flying by him. And then there was a coordination struck among the warriors that brought them into a formation of attack.

It didn't matter. One by one, he killed them, ridding them of arms, or legs, of gut, of groin, blood flying in the dark night, coating him as clothes did.

Until there was a final warrior—which indeed turned out to be the bearded one he had hit in the head with the log. And as soon as the male determined his brethren were deceased or close to dying, he took off through the woods, running as fast as he could go.

Xcor's moccasins made no noise as he tracked the bleeding fighter at quite a pace, he and the injured male crashing through the brush and trees, criss-crossing back and forth as the warrior attempted to get to the horses. Xcor was likewise wounded and leaking, but for some reason, he couldn't feel his deficits. He was both numb and energized.

And then it was over.

The male came up to a rock face that he could not climb, nor could he get around because of a steep cliff.

Xcor knew he had to finish the job.

And it pained him.

"You take what you want," the panting fighter said as he spit to the side. "Just take what you want. I have armaments. Those horses back there are worth much. Leave me and I shall leave you."

Xcor wished that could be the way things ended for the pair of them. He was aware, however, that if he let the fighter live, he would be a marked male. This was a witness who had to be eradicated, lest this fighter find reinforcements and come after the one who had slain his comrades.

"Just take—"

"Forgive me for what I must do."

With that, Xcor sank back on his heels, leapt forth and swung the weapon in a circle, slicing through the arm that the male raised in defense and catching the neck cleanly.

For the rest of his nights, Xcor would remember the sight of the head turning stump over crown through thin air, the spooling blood from the open veins at the throat red like wine.

As the wind kicked up, the body went down like the inanimate object it now was, and abruptly, the scythe became too heavy for Xcor to hold. The farm implement that he had turned into a weapon landed at his feet, its blade dripping.

Xcor tried to get breath into his burning lungs, and as he looked up to the heavens above, his courage and purpose failed him and hot tears escaped the corners of his eyes.

Oh, how the scent of the blood he had spilled mixed with the earthy smell of grass and moss and lichen—

He didn't know what hit him. One moment, he was contemplating the sorrow of what he had wrought. The next, he was flat on his back . . .

. . . pinned in place by the most terrifying vampire he had ever seen.

Huge, so huge were the shoulders, that Xcor could not see the sky any longer. And the face was unspeakably evil, the features twisted into a sly smile that promised suffering first, then death. And the eyes . . . soulless, filled with a cold intelligence and a heated hatred.

This was the leader wolf of the pack, Xcor thought. Just like the one who had come to his open cottage door all those many nights ago.

"Well, well, well," came a voice that was deep as thunder, sharp as a thousand daggers. "And to think they call me the Bloodletter . . ."

With a gasp, Xcor jerked upright on his hips. For a split second, he knew not where he was and looked about in a panic.

Gone were the cave walls, the shelves of jars, the gurney, and his guard of Brothers. In their place . . . an enormous TV screen that was currently black as a hole in the galaxy.

Shaking his head, it all came back to him . . . Vishous's abrupt change of mind, Layla returning unto them in the forest, the Chosen's glorious gift of her vein. Then that horrible ride out of the pines to the slippery road that had taken them into this suburban neighborhood to this suburban house.

Layla was upstairs. He could hear her footsteps o'erhead. And he had the impression of Vishous being gone.

Shifting his legs from the leather cushions, he regarded the dirt trail he'd left down the stairs and across the pale gray rug to where he had all but collapsed. There were pine needles and mud on the sofa as well . . . and also all over Layla's white robing that hung over there on the back of a chair.

The cloth that had adorned her was ruined, stained with blood and debris.

Bit of a theme of his in her life, wasn't it.

Gritting his teeth, he stood up and peered down a shallow hall. There were two open doors, and as he lurched over to them, he assessed the pair of bedroom suites. He chose the one that did not carry Layla's scent, and used the light that streamed in from the corridor's fixture to progress past a king-size bed and into a bathroom that—

Oh . . . heated floor. Heated marble floor.

After so much suffering, first from the head injury and strokes he had had, and then those frigid twenty-four hours in the forest, Xcor faltered as he felt a pleasing warmth emanate up from the bare soles of his feet.

Closing his eyes, he swayed in the darkness, every instinct he had screaming for him to lie down on the marble and rest. Except then he thought of the mess he had tracked into this house, all that mud and filth.

Snapping back to attention, he flipped on the light switch by the bathroom's door—and promptly cursed and shielded his face with his forearm. As his retinas adjusted, he would have preferred not to look at himself in the mirror over the sinks, but that was inevitable as he lowered his arm.

"Dearest Fade," he whispered.

The male staring back at him was nearly unrecognizable. The gaunt, pale, bearded face, the hollowed-out ribs and gut, the loose skin that hung under his jaw, his pecs, his arms. His hair was jagged, having grown out in strange patches, and there seemed to be dirt and blood in every one of his pores, all over his body.

Fates, when one was generally clean, a brisk hand towel applied o'er a sink with plenty of soap could do as a freshen-up. In his current condition? He required a commercial car wash. Mayhap an industrial hose.

The idea of Layla seeing him thus made him cringe and he readily turned away from his reflection, cranking on the shower in its glass partition. The hot water came up quickly, but before he stepped under it, he opened a couple of cabinets and drawers. The toothbrush and toothpaste he found were very much appreciated, as were the soap, shampoo, and conditioner.

He also took a fresh razor and shaving cream into the stall with him.

The simple act of brushing his teeth nearly made him cry. It had been so long since his mouth had tasted fresh. And then the shave . . . ridding himself of the scratchy growth across his cheek, jaws, and chin made him grateful to the company which had made the razor. And then the shampoo. He did that twice, and let the conditioner sit as he scrubbed all of his skin with soap.

There was no reaching his back fully, but he did the best he could.

When he finally stepped out, there was a wool blanket's worth of condensation on the mirror. A benefit, verily, given how he loathed his reflection. Drying off, he wondered where he could find some clothes— and indeed, he found them in the closet in that bedroom: Black nylon pants long enough for his legs, with a pull string that ensured they fit his now-withered waist and hips. A black T-shirt that was wide enough for the bones of his shoulders, but that bagged all over the rest of him. A sweatshirt that had something written across the front.

He didn't find any shoes, but this was more than he could have hoped for.

As he stepped from the bedroom, he expected to have to go upstairs.

The trip was unnecessary. The Chosen Layla was sitting in the padded armchair beside the sofa, a tray with steaming soup, a plate of crackers, and a tumbler of iced tea on the low table in front of the TV.

Her eyes went to his, but didn't stay there. They traveled down him as if she were surprised he had had the strength to shower and get dressed.

"I brought you food," she said softly. "You must be so hungry."

"Aye."

And yet he found himself unable to move. For indeed, he had planned on saying good-bye to her up in the kitchen.

He could not stay here with her. Much as he wanted to.

"Come sit down." She indicated where he had been lying before. And of course, she had tidied up that mess, the dirt that he had left wiped off by some manner of sponge or paper towel. "You have to eat something."

"I must go."

Layla bowed her head, and as she did, the highlights in her blond hair caught the illumination of the fixture overhead. "I know. But . . . before you do."

In his mind, he heard her voice say, *Make love to me*.

"Please eat this," she whispered.

TWENTY-FOUR

ishous was in a nasty fucking mood when he got back to the Brotherhood mansion, and the very biggest part of him just wanted to go to the Pit and crack open a bottle of Grey Goose. Or six. Maybe twelve.

But as he re-formed in the courtyard, and stood in the cold wind by the fountain that had been drained and tarped for winter, he knew that as much as he wanted to escape the situation he'd voluntarily put himself in, he couldn't bail on the mess he'd created.

Striding forward, he hit the stone steps up to the great entrance of the mansion, and checked out the gargoyles perched so high above on the roofline. What he wouldn't give to be one of those inanimate bastards, nothing to do or worry about but sitting up there and occasionally having a pigeon shit on your head.

Actually, that probably sucked.

Whatever.

Yanking the door open, he stepped into the vestibule and shoved his mug into the security camera. When Fritz opened up and did that cheery greeting thing the butler always did, it was all Vishous could do not to snap at the poor *doggen*.

Up the grand staircase. Three at a time.

And then he was in front of the closed double doors to Wrath's study. On the far side of them, he could hear voices, quite a good goddamn volley of talk as it turned out, but sorry, not sorry, what he had to report was paramount to just about anything other than Armageddon.

He knocked loudly and didn't wait for an answer.

Wrath's head snapped up from behind the ancient desk his father had used, and even though those blind eyes weren't visible thanks to the wraparounds, V could feel the glare.

"You need a copy of *Emily Post* shoved down your throat?" the King snapped. "You don't come in here without an invitation, asshole."

Saxton, the royal lawyer and expert on the Old Ways, glanced up from his vantage point at Wrath's elbow. A lot of paperwork was in front of the pair of them. Along with a couple of ancient texts. Sax didn't say anything, but given the way the guy's typically perfect coif was messed up, it was a good extrapolation that they were trying to hammer out custody issues for Qhuinn and Layla.

And yup, the Queen was over on one of the spindly French settees by the fire, her arms crossed on her chest and a frown deep as a ravine in the middle of her forehead.

"I need a minute with you," V said to Wrath in a low voice.

"Then you can come the fuck back when I tell you to."

"This is not going to hold."

Wrath sat back in the massive carved throne that had been his father's and his father's father's before that. "You want to give me a subject matter?"

"I can't. I'm sorry."

There was a period of silence in the elegant pale blue room, and then Wrath cleared his throat and looked in the direction of his *shellan*. "*Leelan?* Will you please excuse us for a moment?"

She got to her feet. "I don't think there's anything further to say. You're going to split the custody equally and Layla gets those kids at sunset tonight. I'm so happy when you and I are in agreement. It really cuts down on the tension."

With that, she walked out of the study with her head held high and her shoulders back—while, over at the desk, the King put his head in his hands like his skull was pounding.

"It's not that I disagree with her," he muttered as the doors were shut with a slam. "I'm just not looking for any more fucking guns to go off in my fucking *house*."

That last word was said with a whole lot of volume.

But then the King dropped his arms and looked across at V. "Can my lawyer stay?"

"No, he cannot."

"Great. Something else to look forward to."

Saxton started packing up his papers and books, but the King stopped him. "Nope. You're coming right back. Wait outside."

"Of course, my Lord."

Saxton bowed even though the King couldn't see him, but that was the way of the guy, always classy, always proper. And as he went by V, even though the interruption's timing sucked, he bowed again.

Good male. Probably still in love with Blay, but what could you do.

On that note, V thought back to his conversation with Layla at the safe house and then all those happy little memories of his own that had swamped him in the forest. Man, he was really fucking tired of romance and true love and all that bullshit.

"So?" Wrath demanded.

V waited until the double doors were closed again.

"I know where Xcor is."

Layla sat in the padded armchair across from Xcor as he ate all of the soup, all of the Carr's water crackers, and then all of the frozen pepperoni pizza she'd slipped into the oven before she'd brought the first load of food down here to the basement.

He didn't speak, and with no talk going on, she found herself staring at him with an absorption so complete, she felt like apologizing for it.

Dearest Virgin Scribe, he had lost so much weight, and yet even though he was starving, he used his silverware with a polite precision—

even cutting the pizza with a knife and fork. He also wiped his lips regularly with his napkin, chewed with his mouth closed, and wasn't sloppy about any of it even though he was consuming the calories at quite a clip.

When he was finally finished, she said, "There is some mint chocolate chip ice cream? A half gallon of it? Upstairs . . . you know, in the refrigerator."

What, like they'd keep it on a bookshelf?

He simply shook his head, folded his napkin, and sat back on the sofa. There was a sizable bulge in his stomach, and he exhaled as if he needed to make room for everything in his torso—and air was a commodity less desirable than the pizza.

"Thank you," he said quietly.

As their eyes met, she was very aware that the two of them were alone . . . and for a moment, she entertained a fantasy that this was their house, and her young were asleep upstairs, and they were about to enjoy some time by themselves.

"I need to go." With that, he stood up and took the tray along with him. "I . . . have to leave."

Layla rose to her feet and wrapped her arms around herself. "All right."

She expected to follow him up the stairs. And then what? Well, perhaps they would share a lingering embrace and then a good-bye that would nearly kill her—

Xcor put the tray back down.

When he came around the table to her and put out his arms, she went to him in a rush. Going up against his body, she held onto him as hard as she could. She hated the feel of his bones, the pads of his muscle having wasted away, but as she turned her head and put her ear to the center of his chest, his heart rate was strong, even. Powerful.

His hands, so big, so gentle, stroked up and down her back.

"It's safer for you," he said into her hair.

She pulled away and looked up at him. "Kiss me. Once before you go."

Xcor closed his eyes as if he were in pain. But then he took her face in his palms and dropped his mouth to hers—almost.

Lingering just a hairsbreadth from her lips, he whispered in the Old Language, "*My heart is ever yours. Where'er I go, it is with you, through the darkness and into the light, from all my waking hours to those in which I sleep. Always . . . with you.*"

The kiss, when it came, was like the fall of snow, silent and soft, but it was warm, so very warm. And as she leaned into him, his arms went around her waist and his hips came up against hers. He was instantly aroused—she could feel his hard erection against her belly—and she had wanted him for so long she teared up.

Dreams. So many dreams she had had, situations she had conjured up in her mind where he had finally come to her, and undressed her, and taken her under himself, his sex going deep into hers. There had been countless fantasies, each more impossible than the last, of them making love out on the grounds of the compound, in bathrooms, in the back of a car, under the tree in their meadow.

Her sex life was non-existent in the real world. In her imagination, however, it had flourished.

But none of that was to be.

Xcor broke the contact, even though she could tell he was fighting his instinct to mark her. Indeed, a scent was emanating from him, the dark spices rich in her nose, turning her on as much as the feel of his arousal, his body, his hands, his mouth.

"I cannot have you," he said in a husky voice. "I've done enough damage to you as it stands."

"This could be our only chance," she heard herself beg. "I know . . . I know you will not come back to me."

He seemed impossibly sad as he shook his head. "It is not to be for us."

"Says who."

Acting on a desperate surge, she grabbed his nape and brought him back to her mouth—and then she kissed him with everything she had, her tongue entering him such that he gasped, her body arching into his, her thighs splitting so that he could get even closer to her core.

"Layla," he groaned. "Dearest Fates . . . this isn't right . . ."

He was perfectly correct, of course. This wasn't right at all, assuming they used the abacus of the rest of the world. But here and now, in this otherwise empty house, it was—

All at once, he set her back from him—and just as she was about to protest, she heard the footsteps overhead. Two sets. Both very, very heavy.

"Vishous," she whispered.

The Brother's disembodied voice came down the stairwell. "Yeah, and I came with a friend."

Layla put herself in front of Xcor, but he was having none of that. He moved her bodily behind him, his protective side clearly refusing to allow her to be before him.

The Brother came down the stairwell first, and he had both his guns out—and at first, she couldn't comprehend who was behind him. But there was only one set of legs that was that long. Only one chest that was that broad. Only one male vampire on the planet who had black hair that fell down to his hips.

The King had come.

And as Wrath took the final step down into the basement, he planted both shitkickers and breathed in deep, his nostrils flaring. Dearest Virgin Scribe, he was an enormous male, and those black wraparound sunglasses, which allowed nothing to show of his eyes, made him seem like a straight-up killer.

Which, she supposed, he was.

"Well, well, well, romance is in the air," he muttered. "Ain't that a bitch."

TWENTY-FIVE

As Xcor stared his previous enemy in the face, he felt no animosity toward the male. No anger, nor greed for the King's position. No aggression toward a target.

"So," Wrath said in a voice suitable for both the aristocrat and the warrior he was, "last time you were able to look me in the eye, I ended up with a bullet in my throat."

Off to the side, the Brother Vishous cursed under his breath and lit up a cigarette. It was obvious that this visitation was not something the fighter supported, but it was not difficult to imagine that if the Blind King made up his mind about something, nothing would disabuse him of his notion.

"Shall I proffer an apology?" Xcor asked. "What is appropriate in situations such as this?"

"Your head on a stick," V muttered. "And your balls in my pocket."

With the way Wrath shook his head at the Brother, one could imagine he was rolling his eyes behind those pitch-black sunglasses. And then the King refocused. "I don't think there's any way of going back from something like a murder attempt."

Xcor nodded. "I believe you are right. And thus we are left exactly where?"

Wrath glanced in Layla's direction. "I'd ask you to leave us, but I have a feeling you won't."

"I would prefer to stay," the Chosen said, "thank you."

"Fine." Wrath's lips thinned to a slash of disapproval, but he didn't force the point. "So, Xcor, leader of the Band of Bastards, traitor, murderer, yada yada yada—hell of a bunch of titles you got going for you, FYI—you mind me inquiring what your plans are?"

"I rather think that is up to you, is it not?"

"What do you know, he's got a brain." Wrath laughed coldly. "And let's wait on that, actually. I'm gonna ask you a couple of questions, if you don't mind? Great. Thanks for being so accommodating."

Xcor nearly smiled a little. The King was his kind of male in so many ways.

"What are your intentions when it comes to my throne?"

As Wrath spoke, his nostrils flared and Xcor gathered the Blind King had some way of sussing out the truth. Fortunately, there was no reason to keep it from the male.

"I have none."

"Do you now. How 'bout your boys?"

"My Band of Bastards served me in all ways. They went where I did, both literally and figuratively. Always."

"Past tense. They kick you out?"

"They think I am dead."

"Can you find them for me?"

Xcor frowned. "And now I shall ask you, what are your intentions?"

Wrath smiled again, revealing descended fangs. "They don't get a pass just because the murder plot they were a part of was your bright idea. Treason is like a head cold. You sneeze on your friends and give the shit to 'em."

"I don't know where they are. And that is the truth."

The King's nostrils flared once again. "But you can find them for me."

"They will not be staying where we once did. They will have moved, perhaps even gone back to the Old Country."

"You're evading my rhetorical. Can you find them for me."

Xcor glanced back at Layla. She was staring at him intently, her green eyes wide. He hated to let her down, he truly did, but he would not give up his fighters. Not even for her.

"No, I will not hunt for them. I will not double-cross my brethren. You can kill me, here and now, if you wish. You can torture me for information that will never come because I do not know of their location. You can put me out for the sun. But I will not lead you unto them so that you may lead them unto their deaths. They are not innocent, 'tis true. They have not attacked you or your fighters, however. Have they."

"Maybe they're not very good at their jobs. They tried to kill me, remember?" The King pounded his heart. "Still kickin'."

"They present you no harm. They are powerful, but the ambition was all mine. They have been content for centuries in the Old Country to fight and to fuck, and I have no reason to believe that status will not be resumed in my absence."

As he realized his candor, he flicked his eyes to Layla—and he wished he hadn't been so crude. She did not seem bothered, however.

After a moment, Wrath mused, "What do you think is going to happen after tonight?"

"I beg your pardon?"

The King shrugged. "Say I decide to let you live and release you—" As Layla gasped, the mighty male shot her a glare. "Don't get ahead of yourself, female. We got miles to go here."

The Chosen lowered her head in submission. But her eyes remained rapt, burning with an optimism that Xcor did not share.

"So say I set you free," Wrath continued. "What are you going to do with yourself?"

Now, Xcor refused to look at his female. "Indeed, I am well aware that the Old Country is favorable this time of year. Far more so than Caldwell. I have property there, and a source of income that is peaceable. I should like to return from whence I came."

Wrath stared at him for the longest time, and Xcor met those wraparounds even though the eyes behind those lenses could not see him.

In the silence, no one moved. He wasn't sure anybody was even breathing.

And the sorrow that rose up from Layla was tangible. Yet she did not argue.

She knew, Xcor thought, exactly how intractable the situation was.

"I've heard that, too," Wrath said finally. "About the Old Country. Nice spot. Especially if you have a defensible position to crash in and the humans leave you alone."

Xcor inclined his head. "Aye. Very much so."

"I am not forgiving or forgetting one goddamn thing here." Wrath shook his head. "That shit's not in my nature. But this female right here"—he pointed to Layla—"has been through more than enough thanks to the likes of you. I don't need to prove my power to anybody, and I'm not going to fuck her head up for the rest of her nights simply to be a vindictive hard-ass. Everything you've said just now has been the truth as you know it, and as long as you get the fuck out of Caldwell, I think both sides can live with that arrangement."

Xcor nodded. "Aye, both sides indeed." He cleared his throat. "And if it helps bring further peace, I would tell you that I do regret my actions against you. I am sorry for them. There was much anger in me, and the effect was corrosive. Things are . . . different . . . the now."

He glanced at the Chosen and then quickly looked away from her.

"I am . . ." Xcor took a deep breath. "I am not as I was."

Wrath nodded. "Love of a good female and all that. Not unfamiliar with it myself."

"So are we done here?" Vishous snapped like he disapproved of pretty much everything.

"No," Wrath said without looking away from Xcor. "Before we kumbaya this shit, you're going to do something for me, right here and now."

The King pointed to the carpet at his feet. "On your knees, bastard."

Of course Xcor was going to have to leave, Layla thought as she tried to keep herself together. He couldn't stay in Caldwell. The other Brothers might accept Wrath's pardoning on the surface, but things happened out in the field in war. There was no way of assuring that in the heat of conflict, one of the King's fighters wouldn't find himself in a frame of mind and a position that was incompatible with this détente.

Especially Qhuinn.

And Tohr.

Except she wasn't going to waste time thinking about all that. As the King pointed to the floor in front of him, her heart jumped into her throat and she nervously looked at Vishous.

Wrath was giving off every indication that this was a meeting of the minds, an agreement to live and let live, by virtue of him proclaiming it as such. But Vishous had well-fooled her before, pulling a double-cross that he'd ultimately relented upon, yet which quite readily could have been adhered to.

Was there a dagger or a saber about to be unleashed upon Xcor's throat? Killing him where he was?

"To what end?" Xcor inquired of the King.

"Get down there and find out."

Xcor glanced at Vishous. Refocused on Wrath. And stayed yet where he was.

Wrath smiled in a gruesome way, like a killer about to strike. "Well? And bear in mind, I'm holding all your cards."

"I bowed my head once and only once to another. It nearly killed me."

"Well, if you don't do it right now, it will be the death of you."

At that, there was a sound of metal on metal, and with a shock of alarm, she found that Vishous had unsheathed one of the black daggers that was strapped, handles down, to his chest.

"Put that thing away," Wrath bit out. "This will be voluntarily or not at all—"

"He doesn't deserve—"

Wrath bared his fangs at the Brother and hissed. "Go upstairs. Get the *fuck* upstairs, right now. That is an order."

The fury in Vishous's face was such that it seemed as though the tattoos at his temple were moving across his skin. But then he did as he was told—which made Layla rethink exactly how much power Wrath had over the Brotherhood. At the end of the day, even the Scribe Virgin's begotten son clearly took orders from the King.

Although Vishous was obviously not pleased: The sound of his boots going up the stairwell was loud as thunder, and when he got to the first floor, he slammed the door so hard she felt the clap in her teeth.

"Did you have fun with morale when you were in charge?" Wrath muttered to Xcor.

"All the time. The stronger the warrior—"

"The harder the head."

"—the harder the head."

As they finished the sentence with the same words, and in an identically exhausted tone, she was surprised. And yet they had faced the same issues, hadn't they, both leaders of groups of males that were highly charged in the best of situations . . . and downright dangerous in bad ones.

While Vishous paced around right above their heads, his footfalls a nonverbal protest that was clearly intended to be logged by those down in the cellar, Xcor closed his eyes for the longest time.

And then . . . he slowly sank onto both knees.

For some reason, seeing him thus brought her to tears. But then witnessing a proud male submit, even under these circumstances, was emotional.

Wrath mutely put out his hand, the one on which the huge black diamond that signified his station rested. In the Old Language, the King proclaimed, "*Swear your fealty unto me, this night and forever more, placing none upon the earth above me and mine.*"

Xcor's own hand trembled as he reached forth. Grasping Wrath's palm, he kissed the ring and then placed it upon his bowed forehead. "*Fore'ermore, I pledge my allegiance unto to you and yours, serving none other.*"

Both males took a deep breath. And then Wrath put his hand on top of Xcor's head, as if in benediction. Looking up, the King sought Layla out with his blind eyes.

"You should be proud of your male. This is no small thing for a warrior."

She brushed at her eyes. "Yes."

Wrath turned his hand over, offering Xcor a palm with which to help himself to his feet. And Xcor . . . after a moment . . . accepted the aid.

When the two fighters were standing eye to eye, Wrath said, "Now, you get each one of your fighters to do that, and you're all free to go back to the Old Country. But I'm going to need that pledge from them all, do you understand."

"What if they've already returned across the ocean?"

"Then you're going to bring them back to me. This is the way it's going to be. The Brotherhood who serve me have to buy in on this, and that is the only path to get them to stop hunting you fuckers down."

Xcor rubbed his face. "Aye. All right, then."

"You will stay here while you're looking for your boys. This will be our meeting site. I will have V leave you a phone to use to get in touch with us. Assuming your fighters are still on this side of the pond, you will call us when you are ready and we will do this one by one, here. Any deviances from our agreement will be regarded as a declaration of aggression and dealt with accordingly. Do you understand this."

"Aye."

"I'm willing to be lenient, but I'm not going to be a pussy. I will eliminate any and all threats against me, do you further understand this."

"Aye."

"Good. We're done." Wrath shook his head ruefully. "And shit, you think you have problems? At least you don't have to go back home with that."

As the King pointed up to the ceiling, Vishous let a particularly hardy step fall—like he knew he was a topic of discussion.

Just as Wrath was turning away, Xcor spoke up. "My Lord—"

The King looked over his shoulder. "You know, I like the sound of that."

"Indeed." Xcor cleared his throat. "With regard to threats against you. I would care to apprise you of a certain individual you would be wise to watch with care."

Wrath cocked an eyebrow over the rim of his wraparound. "Do tell."

TWENTY-SIX

acrifice was also in the eye of the beholder.

Like beauty, it was a personal, subjective assessment, a cost-benefit analysis that had no right answer, only a compass that spun around an individual's variant of true north.

Throe, begotten and then forsaken son of Throe, pulled his fine cashmere coat closer around his lithe body as he strode down a cracked sidewalk. The neighborhood, if one could refer to the grungy walk-ups and shitty little shops with such an otherwise homey word, was more a demilitarized area than anything one would wish to claim for housing.

But for him, the sacrifice of beholding such decay and decrepitness was worth what awaited him.

What *hopefully* awaited him.

In large measure, he could not believe he was on his current quest. It seemed . . . unseemly . . . for a gentlemale of his stature. But life had gone in many directions that he would not have predicted or chosen of his own volition, so he was rather used to such surprises—although he supposed, even under those auspices, this tangent was still rather out there.

Even for an aristocrat who had been conscripted into the Band of Bastards, become a fighter, tried to topple the crown, and then been freed from that group of outlaws to fend with the rich and ambitious on his own . . . only to narrowly survive being burned alive when his lover was killed for keeping a blood slave in her basement.

Craziness, indeed.

And his strange destiny had had much effect upon him. There had been a time when he had been ruled by conventional principles of loyalty and decorum, when he had conducted himself as a male of worth in high society. But then he had had to rely upon Xcor to *ahvenge* a disgrace that, in retrospect, he should have addressed on his own. Once in Xcor's circle of fighters, after he'd risen above his torture in a manner that had surprised not only those bastards but he himself, he had started to learn that one only had oneself to rely upon.

Ambition, once disdained by him as an affect of the nouveau riche, had taken root, and culminated in that coup against the Blind King that had almost worked. Xcor had lost the will to go any further with it, however.

And Throe had discovered that he himself had not.

Wrath may have won a populist vote and castrated the *glymera's* Council, but Throe still believed at his core that there was another ruler far better for the race.

Himself, as it were.

So indeed, he was going to press on alone, finding levers and pulling them to engender the result he wanted.

Or in the case of tonight's endeavor? Creating the lever, as it were.

He stopped and looked around. The promise of heavy snow was thick in the air, the night humid and cold at the same time, the clouds gathering above in such density that the sky ceiling was getting lower and lower to the ground.

The numbers on a street such as this were hard to ascertain as this was hardly a sector of Caldwell where people tended well their real estate. Here, they were more likely to break into their neighbors' and steal than borrow cups of sugar or screwdrivers. Thus, there were few markers, and even the street identifiers had been taken down on some corners.

But his destination must be here somewhere—

Yes. There. Across the street.

Throe narrowed his eyes. And then rolled them.

He couldn't believe there was actually a flashing PSYCHIC sign in the window. Right next to the obligatory open palm sign that was up-lit. In purple.

As he waited for a car to pass, and then had to place his suede loafer into a snowbank to get over the curb, he decided that, yes, the sacrifices he'd had to make were distasteful, but they were necessary, things that he had to endure only for as long as he was forced to. For example, he didn't abide living off of wealthy females the way he'd done since leaving the Band of Bastards. But even with the money he'd managed to scrape together over the last two hundred years, he couldn't possibly keep himself to the standard he deserved. No, that required capital in the millions of dollars, not the hundreds of thousands.

Sacrifices, though. For certain, he'd turned into a bit of a whore, fucking these females in exchange for shelter, lodging, and sartorial necessities worthy of the venerable legacy of his bloodline. But he'd had it with slumming it after his years under Xcor.

If he never saw another cheap sectional sofa with empty pizza boxes on it again, it would be far too soon.

As it stood now, the sex was a small price to pay for all he got in return—and besides, all would be worth it when he was the one on the throne.

Reaching the far side of the road, he jumped the snowbank and stomped his loafers free of slush. "A psychic, though," he muttered. "A human psychic."

Approaching the door, which was painted purple, he nearly turned away. This whole thing was beginning to feel like an ill-conceived practical joke.

How else could his presence here be explained—

The three human males who rounded the corner next to him announced their arrival in three different ways. First, he caught a whiff of the cigarette the one in the middle was smoking. Then there was the cough of the guy on the left. But it was the chap on the right who really sealed the deal.

The guy stopped dead. And then smiled, revealing an incisor made of gold. "You lost?"

"No, thank you." Throe turned back to the door and tried the handle. It was locked.

The three men came closer, and God, had they never heard of after-shave? Cologne? Indeed, it appeared that shampoo might be a foreign concept to the happy little group.

Throe took a step away from the stoop so he could regard the windows above. They were darkened.

He should have called for an appointment, he decided. Rather as one would a barber. Or an accountant—

"You wanna know your future?"

This was spoken quite close to his ear, and as Throe glanced over, he found that the trio had closed in, forming a necklace of sorts around him.

"That why you here?" The one with the gold tooth smiled again. "You superstitious or some shit?"

Throe's eyes flicked over them. The one with the cigarette had put it out, though the thing had been but half smoked. And the COPD candidate wasn't coughing anymore. And he of the 14k incisor had slipped a hand inside his leather coat.

Throe rolled his eyes again. "Do carry on, gents. I am not for you."

The leader who'd been doing all the talking threw his head back and laughed. "Gents? You British or some shit? Hey, he's Brit. You know Hugh Grant? Or that guy who pretends to be American on *House*? What's his name—*asshole*."

On *asshole*, the guy outed what appeared to be a rather nice switchblade.

"Gimme your money. Or I'll cut you."

Throe could not believe it. His favorite suede shoes were ruined, he was being forced to deal with humans, and he was standing in front of a tenement more suited for the consumption of crack than any sort of legitimate business.

Right, this was the last time he took the counsel of a *glymera* sweet-heart who had been drunk at the time. Without that female's rather boozy advocacy for this so-called psychic, he would have been, at this moment, on the right side of the railroad tracks, all the way across town, sipping on a sherry.

"Gentlemen, I shall tell you this but once more. I am not for you. Carry on."

The switchblade got thrust into his face, so close that his nose was in danger of a trim. "Gimme your fucking money and your fucking—"

Oh, humans.

Throe descended his fangs, put up both his hands into claws . . . and roared at them like he intended to rip all three of their throats out.

The retreat was rather delightful to watch, actually, and cheered him a bit: Those three dumb-asses took one look at certain death and decided that their dubious social skills were required elsewhere. In fact, they couldn't have staged a more competent and complete retreat if they had consciously set their minds to such a thing.

Gone, gone, gone, skidding their way back around the corner from whence they came.

When Throe faced the door once more, he frowned.

It was open an inch, as if someone had come down and freed its lock.

Pushing the weight open, he was utterly unsurprised to find a black light overhead and a set of stairs painted purple before him.

"Hello?" he called out.

Footsteps were on the ascent, crossing over the landing above his head.

"Hello," he repeated. Then muttered, "Is this deliberate mystery truly necessary."

Stepping inside, he clapped his feet upon a black mat to once again clear snow from his loafers. Then he proceeded in the wake of whomever was ahead of him, taking the shallow steps two at a time.

"Aaaaaand 'tis purple once again," he said under his breath as he came around that landing and proceeded up to the only door on the second floor.

At least he knew he had reached his destination. A palm motif was upon the panels, the black outline of the fingers and the lifelines done with a casual hand, not anything that was stenciled properly or even done by an artist.

Dearest Fates, this was ridiculous. Why would that drunken female know anything about reaching out to the Omega? Through a human portal, no less.

And yet even as he hesitated, he knew he was going to follow this encounter to its probable dead end. His problem, of course, was that he was looking for a way to power and finding none of particular ease. He did not want to believe that the *glymera* was truly the lost cause it appeared to be. After all, if they were unable to provide him with a platform from whence to assume Wrath's role, where else could he marshal supplies, troops, or things of that nature?

Humans were no great help. And he continued to believe it was best that that other invasive species not know of the existence of vampires. They had subjected all else to their whims and survival, including the very planet that supported their lives. No, they were a beehive not to be stirred.

So what did that leave him with? The Brotherhood was a foregone conclusion. The Band of Bastards was now not an option. And that left him with but one other avenue to explore.

The Omega. The Evil One. The Scribe Virgin's terrible balance—

The door opened with a creak that was right out of a haunted house.

Clearing his throat, he thought, In for a penny, in for a pound. Or, in his case, in for the replacement cost of his Ferragamos, which was about fifteen hundred dollars.

"Hello?" he said.

When there was no response, he leaned in a little.

"Hello? Are you accepting . . ." What was the appropriate term? Clients? Nut jobs? Gullible losers? "Would you be able to chat for a moment?"

He went to put his hand on the panel and immediately frowned, taking it back and shaking the thing out. It had felt as though a slight electrical charge had gone into his palm.

"Hello?" he repeated anew.

With a curse, Throe walked into the dim interior—and presently recoiled at the smell. Patchouli. God, he hated patchouli.

Ah, yes, incense burning over there on a table full of rocks and stones. Lit candles in the corners. Great swaths of cloths in different colors and printed patterns hanging from the ceiling.

And of course, she had herself a little throne with a circular table in front of it . . . and a crystal ball.

This was too much.

"Actually, I think I'm in the wrong place." He turned away. "If you'll excuse me—"

The crash that came from across the space was loud enough to ring in his ears and leave him jumping out of his own skin.

Pivoting back around, he called out, "Madam? Are you all right?"

When there was no reply, he was struck by an overwhelming feeling of paranoia. Glancing around, he thought . . . *leave*. Now. Take thee from this place.

All was not well here.

At that very moment, the door he had come through slammed shut and appeared to lock itself.

Throe rushed over, grabbed the knob, and tried to twist it back and forth. It did not move, and neither would the panels give when he attempted to wrest them from their jamb. He pounded his fist until it hurt—

Throe froze, the short hairs on the back of his neck prickling.

Glancing over his shoulder, he was prepared for he knew not what. But something was in the room with him . . . and it was not of this world.

TWENTY-SEVEN

ver at shAdoWs, as Trez stood on the edge of the dance floor, his eyes were supposedly on the crowd in front of him. In reality, he was seeing nothing. Not the purple shooting laser beams or the clouds of smoke from the machines. Certainly not the humans who were packed in against each other like spoons stacked in a silverware drawer.

The decision to leave, when it came to him, followed the pattern of the night: It arrived from out of nowhere and he was powerless against the imperative.

Heading around to the bar, he found Xhex with her arms crossed and her eyes narrowed on a couple of meatheads who were demanding another round even though they were well over the legal limit—and probably high as well.

"Good timing," she muttered over the din of music and sex. "You know how much you like watching me sweep the floor with humans."

"Actually, I gotta go. I may not be back tonight, is that okay?"

"Hell, yeah. I've been telling you to take a break for how long."

"Call me if you need me?"

"Always."

Uncharacteristically, Trez put a hand on her shoulder and gave her a little squeeze—and if the gesture surprised her, Xhex hid it well. Then, turning away, he—

His head of security caught his wrist and stopped him. "You want someone to go with you?"

"I'm sorry?"

Her gunmetal gray eyes went over his face, and the focus in them made him feel like she could see down into his soul. Fucking *symphaths*. They made intuition a bad thing, at least when it came to guessing other people's moods.

"Your grid's off the charts, Trez. Come on."

"What?"

Next thing he knew, she had hitched ahold of his arm and was marching him into the back, where the working girls changed and the deliveries were accepted.

"Honest, I'm fine."

Even as he protested, she all but shoved him out the rear door of the club, and then her phone was in her hand and she was texting.

Trez threw up his arms as he did the math. "Don't bother iAm— Xhex, seriously, you don't need to—"

His brother literally dematerialized only a second after Xhex lowered her phone, dressed in his chef's whites and his toque, a dish towel in his hand.

"Okay, this is ridiculous." Trez cleared his throat so his voice sounded more convincing. "I'm perfectly capable of getting myself where I need to go."

"And where is that?" iAm demanded. "A rooming house across town? Maybe to the third floor? What was that apartment number—and don't tell me you didn't look at that fucking résumé."

"You wanna clue me in on what the hell you're talking about, boys?" Xhex glanced back and forth between them. "And maybe explain to me why a male who's been half dead from mourning these last months is suddenly carrying his own bonding scent?"

"Nope," Trez interjected. "We don't feel the need to explain that at all."

A quick glare in his brother's direction—and Trez wondered whether or not he was going to have to throw down out here. But iAm just shook his head.

"Long story," the good chef muttered. "Come on, Trez, let's get you home."

"I can dematerialize."

"But will you, that's the question."

"You don't have time for this," Trez said as the guy made like he was going over to Trez's BMW.

Which, yes, was the same model and year as his brother's. They'd gotten a deal on the dual bitches, so sue them.

And oh, snap, iAm had somehow managed to remember to bring the damn key. Like he'd planned this, maybe even with Xhex.

Mental note: Get that fob back from the guy. And if he couldn't, buy a new fucking car.

"Come on," iAm said. "Let's go."

As the pair of them stared at him like he'd grown a horn in the middle of his forehead, Trez considered dematerializing off on his own, leaving iAm with no one to chauffeur and Xhex by herself with her mental-health theories about his "grid," whatever that was. But something in the back of his mind happened to agree with them. Much as he hated to admit it.

So yeah, like the good little idiot he was, he got in shotgun, and even did up his seat belt—and iAm didn't waste any gears as he got them on the Northway and headed out of town at a dead run.

"You went over to her apartment, didn't you."

Even though Trez's head had started to pound, he turned on SiriusXM. Kid Ink was talkin' "Nasty," and Trez closed his eyes—and thought of that kiss. Had he lost his fucking mind? His *shellan* hadn't been dead for three months and he was making out with some stranger?

And see, this was what had been bothering him, the reason he'd had to leave the club. Being around all those humans sucking face in front of him and fucking in the private bathrooms that he'd built for expressly that purpose had made what he'd done with Therese loud as a Vegas billboard—and the guilt that had curled into his gut was like having food poisoning.

He was totally nauseous and bloated, light-headed and weak.

iAm canned the radio. "Did you?"

Turning his head away, Trez measured the cars in the slow lane—that he and his brother were passing like the damn things were parked on the shoulder. "Yeah. I did. She lives in a dump. It's not safe. You are going to hire her, right?"

"No, I'm not fucking hiring her."

Trez shifted his focus from the other midnight traffic to the apartment buildings that were nestled in tight to the highway as the city made its transition from urban to suburban. In countless windows, he saw people walking from room to room, or sitting on sofas or reading in bed.

Right now, he would have traded places with any one of them, even though they were humans.

"Don't ding her an opportunity on account of me." Trez rubbed his eyes and blinked to clear the spots in his vision. Damn night driving always fucked him up. "That's not fair."

God, he couldn't believe he'd kissed another female. When he'd been with Therese, when she had been up against his body and staring into his eyes, it had been easy to convince himself she was Selena reincarnated. But with distance and time came logic: She was just a stranger who looked like the female he'd lost.

Shit. He'd put his mouth on another female's.

Trez looked over at his brother in an attempt to quit thinking about what he'd done. "I mean it, iAm. If she's qualified, then give her the job. She needs to get out of that horrible place she's staying in—and I won't bother her. I'm not going back there."

"Well, I don't want you not coming to the restaurant because of her, either."

Trez refocused on the road ahead, but the headlights from the opposite side of the highway made his head swim. Rubbing his eyes again, he felt his stomach roll.

"Hey, do me a favor?"

iAm glanced over. "Yeah, anything. What do you need?"

"Pull over."

"What—"

"Like right fucking now."

iAm wrenched the wheel and hit the shoulder, and before the car even came to a stop, Trez was popping his door—which triggered the anti-roll mechanism and ensured the wheels completely locked up.

Just like that female had said.

Leaning out as far as he could, Trez vomited what little there was in his stomach, which was actually nothing but bile. And as he retched and gagged, and then felt another wave coming on, he cursed as he realized the spots in his vision were getting organized into an aura.

Migraine. Stupid, fucking migraine.

"Headache?" iAm said as a semi rumbled past them.

This wasn't safe, Trez thought as the cold licked into the BMW's interior. They should have gotten off at an exit—

He answered his brother's question by throwing up some more, and then he collapsed back in the seat. For no apparent reason, he looked down at his white slacks and noted there were scuff marks from where he'd passed out and hit the ground.

This was why you didn't go *blanco*.

"What can I do?" iAm asked.

"Nothing." He shut the door. "Let's keep going. I'll try and hold it— but can we turn down the heater?"

He didn't remember much about the trip back to the mansion, his time spent monitoring the aura's evolution from a tight collection of sparkles at the center of his vision to its spreading its wings and flying off the periphery of his sight. But the next thing he knew, his brother was helping him out of his seat and escorting him like an invalid up to the mansion's grand entrance. Once they were inside, the foyer, with all its colored columns, gold leafing, and goddamn crystal sconces, was enough to make him nauseous again.

"I think I'm going to be—"

Fritz, the *doggen* butler, presented him with a barf bag at exactly the right moment. A barf bag. A hospital-grade, bright-green barf bag.

As Trez bent double and held the circular opening to his mouth, he thought a couple of things: 1) who the fuck went around with barf bags on the ready; 2) what the hell else was the male carrying in that penguin suit of his; and 3) why did it have to be bilious green?

If you were going to make something for people to throw up in, why did you have to make the damn thing the color of pea soup?

A cheery yellow, perhaps. A nice, tidy white.

Although considering the shape his pants were in . . .

When Trez finally straightened, that telltale anvil-sitting-on-one-half-of-his-head had started to kick in, and his thought patterns had begun to take on the convoluted weirdness that came along with his migraines.

"Help me upstairs?" he mumbled to no one in particular.

It was not a surprise that iAm took charge and got him to the new room he'd been staying in since Rhage, Mary, and Bitty had taken over the suites on the third floor.

Across the way. Onto the bed. Flat on his back.

As usual, getting off his feet offered only a slight reprieve, a brief moment where his stomach settled and his head took a breather—and then things came back a hundredfold worse.

At least iAm knew exactly what he needed. One by one, Trez's loafers were removed, but his brother knew that the socks had to stay on because Trez's extremities lost circulation and got cold during the headaches. Then the belt and the slacks were pulled off and the duvet taco'd around him. Suit jacket stayed on and so did the shirt. Taking those from his body would have required too much shifting around and likely triggered more throwing up.

Which was exactly what you didn't need when your head was pounding to begin with.

Then came the drawing of the curtains, even though there was no moon out tonight. The placement of the wastepaper basket right by the side of the bed. And the inevitable depression of the mattress as iAm took a load off next to him.

God, they had done this so many times.

"Promise me," Trez said into the darkness of his closed lids, "that you'll give her the job. I'm not going to go after her, I swear. I don't want to ever see her again, actually."

He was too liable to do something stupid again—

As the taste of her came back on his tongue, he moaned as his heart ached.

"I wish you'd take medication for these things." iAm cursed softly. "I hate to see you suffer like this."

"It'll pass. It always does. Hire the female, iAm. And I won't bother her."

He waited for something to come back at him from his brother, some kind of reply or argument, and when he didn't get anything, he popped open his eyes—only to wince and recoil. Even though the only illumination in the room was coming from the mostly shut door to the hallway, the shit was too much for his hypersensitive eyes.

"I know she's not Selena," he muttered. "Trust me. I know *exactly* how much she is not my female."

Hell, the implications of that kiss were the reason he'd gotten this fucking migraine. His regret had literally blown the top of his head off: guilt as a vascular event.

Doc Jane should write his ass up in a medical journal.

"Don't punish her for a mistake that's on me."

At least, that was what he'd meant to say. He wasn't exactly sure what came out of his mouth.

"Just rest," iAm said. "I'm going to get Manny to come up and check on you."

"Don't bother him." Or something to that effect. "But you could do something for me."

"What's that?"

Trez forced those lids of his to open and he lifted his head even though the world spun. "Get me Lassiter. Bring that fallen angel here."

· · ·

"Now if you don't mind, I'm going to have a word with the Chosen upstairs."

As Wrath spoke, Layla wasn't fooled. His tone made it clear he was hardly asking Xcor for permission to talk to one of his own subjects.

If the King's voice had been any drier, it would have left dust all over the furniture.

But indeed, she wanted to speak with him in private as well, and as Wrath indicated the steps, she nodded. With a quick glance at Xcor, she hurried up the stairwell, opening the door at the top and bracing herself to meet Vishous in the eye.

She shouldn't have worried.

The Brother refused to look over at her from where he was standing by the table. He merely picked up the mug he was using as an ashtray and went out the sliding glass door.

The King came up more slowly, and she felt bad for not aiding him.

"My Lord," she said, "there is a table off to the right about fifteen feet—"

"Good." Wrath shut the cellar door. "You're going to want to sit down. Vishous outside? I can smell the fresh air."

"Ah . . ." Layla swallowed hard. "Yes, he's on the porch. Do you . . . shall I summon him for you?"

"No. This is between you and me."

"But of course." She bowed even though he couldn't see her. "And yes, I do believe I will sit down."

"Good call."

The King stayed exactly where he was, just over a bit from the door he'd shut—and for a moment, she tried to imagine what it would be like to go through life with no visual orientation at all. There could have been an open pit before him, or a scatter of thumbtacks over the floor, or . . . heaven only knew what.

Yet as she measured the set of his jaw, he certainly appeared capable of withstanding all and sundry. And how she envied him that.

"So sit, why don'tcha."

How did he know? she wondered as she hustled over and settled into one of the four chairs.

"Yes, my Lord?"

Wrath proceeded to speak in a calm, even voice, laying out a number of sentences filled with words that, under other circumstances, she would have readily comprehended.

In this case, however, nothing much after "Your young are . . ." sunk in.

"—every other night and day, tracking his rotation schedule. It's fair and equitable, and I believe balances everyone's interests. Fritz will be responsible for escorting you to—"

"I'm so sorry," she choked out. "Could you . . . please, could you repeat what you just said?"

The King's face seemed to soften. "I want you to have your kids every other night and day. Okay? You and Qhuinn will split physical custody fifty-fifty, and you will be jointly responsible for making all decisions pertaining to their welfare."

Layla blinked fast, aware that every part of her body was shaking. "So I am not cut off."

"No, you are not."

"Oh, my Lord, thank you." She covered her mouth with her palm. And then spoke around her hand. "I couldn't have gone on without them."

"I know. I get it, trust me. And the Sanctuary will ensure safety."

Layla recoiled. "I'm sorry, what?"

"You'll transport them to the Sanctuary and stay with them in the Scribe Virgin's private quarters—shit knows she's not using them anymore. It's the safest place for the three of you because it's not even on the planet, and Phury and Cormia have assured me that you'll be able to easily travel in the way of a Chosen up and back with the kids—all you have to do is hold them to you and off you go." Wrath shook his head. "Qhuinn is going to hit the fucking roof when I lay this on him, but there is no way he can argue about their welfare if they're up there. And when they're not with you . . . you're free to go wherever you want, be with whoever you want, and you can use this place as your home base."

There was a pause, and Layla flushed.

Because Wrath knew exactly what she was going to want to do and with whom. At least until Xcor departed for the Old Country.

"Yes," she said slowly. "Yes, yes, indeed."

"One caveat—you have to bring them back down when it's time for Qhuinn to have them. Just like he's going to have to give them to you when it's your night. The schedule has to be honored by the both of you."

"Absolutely. They need their father. He's very important in their lives. I don't want to do anything to hamper that."

And Wrath was right. Now that she had been essentially pardoned of her treason charges, Qhuinn's main argument against her having contact with the young was going to be that she couldn't be in the Brotherhood house with them, and there was nowhere else, no safe house, no refuge, no structure, even if it was wired for security by a hundred thousand Vishouses, that was going to come close to the protection offered at that mansion.

The solution? Off the planet.

After all, there had been but one raid on the Sanctuary, some twenty-five years before. And that had been a coup staged by malcontents in the *glymera* who were no longer living.

She and Lyric and Rhamp would be well and happy there, too. All the flowers and the green grass, the marble fountain, the temples. There would be much to explore as they grew older and more mobile.

"It's perfect," she said. "My Lord, it's perfect."

"I'll head home and talk to Qhuinn now. I'm going to put him on rotation at nightfall tomorrow. You come to the mansion then and get the kids."

Layla lowered her head. "That's . . . so long to wait."

"It's the way it's going to be. Qhuinn is highly unstable and I don't want you there when we present him with the visitation schedule or when you come to take the kids. So the timing is what we've got. But I'll have Beth send you some more pics."

"Pictures?"

"Yeah, you haven't been getting them on your phone?"

"I didn't bring my cell with me . . . has she been taking photographs?"

"They all have. There's a loop and you're on it—or so I've been told. The females wanted to make sure you didn't feel like you were missing out."

"They are so . . ." Layla took a bracing breath. "That is very kind of them."

"They know what you're going through. Or have enough of a sense of it that they're fucking horrified."

Layla put her hands to her face. Like that was somehow going to help her hold herself together.

"Come here."

As the King motioned for her to approach him, she burst out of her chair and ran over. Embracing Wrath was like throwing her arms around a grand piano, everything hard and too big to accommodate.

But the King held her in return, patting her back. "Do me a favor?"

She sniffled and looked up at the hard jut of his chin. "Anything."

"Be careful with Xcor. Even if he doesn't kill you physically, he can still ruin you for life."

Layla could only shake her head. "He already has, my Lord. The damage, I fear, is already done."

TWENTY-EIGHT

s Throe searched the psychic's fabric-draped, candlelit office or room or whatever one would call it, he could hear nothing but the drumming beat of his own heart. It seemed as though he was alone, but every instinct in him was telling him otherwise. Tucking his hand into his coat, he palmed the butt of his gun and thought of the trio of humans he'd scared off down on the street.

He rather wished he was facing nothing more exotic than three thugs and a switch.

Swinging his eyes around, he searched for a source of that noise he'd heard, a trigger for his warning instincts, a—

Dearest Fates, what was this?

Nothing was moving in the space. Nothing . . . at all.

By some trick . . . or he knew not what . . . the flames on the candles were utterly stationary, as if they were in a photograph, no wax melting, no unseen drafts teasing at their gold licks of fire, no gentle fingers of smoke rising into the air.

With a feeling of utter dread, he lifted up his arm, pulled his sleeve back, and regarded his Audemars Piguet watch.

The hands, which had been oh-so-functional when he'd left his current abode, were likewise no longer circling their dial.

Falling into ambulation—just to prove to himself he could, he marched across to a window, pulled back the drapery, and looked down at the street. There were no cars coming or going. But then none were to be seen—

Across the way, in the walk-up directly opposite the one he occupied, there were a pair of humans sitting in ratty armchairs watching TV. Their heads were facing each other, and one was in the process of bringing a beer bottle to his mouth.

They were not moving.

Nor was the ad for KFC on the screen.

"Dearest Virgin Scribe . . ." He closed his eyes and rolled back against the wall. "What manner of insanity is this?"

He thought back to what the female who had sent him here had told him. A psychic downtown. A witch. A human witch who had portals to the other side.

The conversation had started around a dining table beset with high-society females, all nattering on about their "problems" and the solutions to such terrible issues as floors that were stained too light, too dark, too inconsistently, and Birkins that were showing wear on their bottom corners, and oh, what else . . . lovers who were inconsiderate and *hellrens* who could not understand the moral imperative that came with Chanel's new spring/summer collection.

At some point, one of the females had brought up psychics and tarot card readers, and how she'd been helped by this woman herein. How it had been spooky what the human witch had ascertained. How the female had eventually stopped going because "something hadn't seemed right."

Who knew that that had been a correct assumption.

Probably the only one the dear girl had of late.

Steeling himself for some sort of attack, Throe waited for some ghostly apparition to materialize out of a darkened corner, or a bat to fly around his head, or a zombie to drag-a-leg out of the back. And would that it be those last two as they were things his gun might be effective against.

When nothing happened, he began to feel foolish. At least until he regarded those candles across the way.

"You will release me," he said into the still air. "I shall go about my business, bothering you no more."

He had no idea to whom he spoke. And when there was no answer, he motivated himself, stepping forward toward the circular table. Closing in upon it, he resisted looking into the crystal ball, and checked over his shoulder—

A scratching sound, like a set of nails going across bare wood, drew his eyes to the left.

There was something on the floor.

He was cautious on his approach, and kept his gun up—and it wasn't until he was nearly upon the object that he recognized the contours for what they were.

A book. There was a book upon the floor, one that appeared to be of great age with a battered leather cover and thick pages that had rough edges.

Kneeling down, he frowned. A scorch pattern surrounded the thing, as if its presence contained heat sufficient to burn the wood fibers beneath its weight.

Was this the noise he'd heard? he wondered. Had its arrival on this plane of existence been announced with that loud slamming sound?

Reaching out, he touched the patterned cover—

With a hiss, he retracted his hand and, as he had done at the door when he had sought to enter, he shook his palm, trying to rid himself of an unpleasant tingling sensation—

The cover threw itself open without notice and Throe shoved himself back, landing on his arse.

As a puff of dust emanated from the parchment pages, he narrowed his eyes. The ink pattern was horizontal and filled with characters, but it was no language he could discern.

He leaned in . . . only to gasp.

What'er had been written was mutating, the hashes and tags of the ink shifting themselves around until . . . the text became the Old Language.

Yes, it was the Mother tongue.

And the passages appeared to be about . . .

Throe lifted his eyes. Looked around. Then, acting on an impulse that suddenly seemed as strong as that of survival itself, he closed the front cover and picked up the tome.

The tingling sensation was no longer unpleasant. Indeed, the volume seemed to be alive in his hand and approving of its holder, rather like a cat might curve and purr itself around an owner's arm.

And that was when it happened.

All at once, a distant siren sounded out, and as he glanced toward the windows, the candle flames in the corners of the room began to move in the drafts once more.

The door he had entered through let out a creak.

That which had been locked . . . was now open.

Throe held the book to his chest and bolted for the exit, running as if his life depended upon it. And he did not stop until he was once more down on the street, in the slush and the cold. For a moment, fear dogged him like a predator, but that did not last for long.

Buoyed by the book against his heart, he found that he was smiling when he dematerialized out of the neighborhood.

TWENTY-NINE

fter the King departed, Layla went back down into the ranch's cellar, and she was not surprised to find Xcor up on his feet and pacing as he waited for her to return.

"So are they gone?" he asked.

"Yes. They are."

"Is there a security system herein? And are there any weapons in this house?"

"The security system control pad is up in the kitchen, and V told me how to engage it."

"Did you do so?"

It wasn't that he was being demanding, but he was incredibly intense, as if the only thing that separated them from . . . wolves, or something . . . was his ability to lock them down and gather armaments in the event of an attack.

"I did not."

Xcor smiled as if he wanted to make an effort not to seem unpleasant, but his eyes were anything but relaxed. "How do you activate the alarm?"

"I, ah, I'll show you."

She had a feeling that he was not going to be satisfied until he understood the way the thing worked and operated it himself. And she was right. He insisted on running through the code and pushing the buttons.

Then, evidently, it was time to check every single door and window in the place.

Layla followed him as he went, one by one, through all the rooms and bathrooms, inspecting the locks on the windows and the stops that were on the sashes so that they couldn't be lifted more than an inch or two. Then it was the dead-bolt review. And he even checked out the garage doors, though he insisted she stay inside for that because it was cold.

Reentering the kitchen, he nodded as he set the alarm. "This house is well secured."

"Vishous takes care of these things."

"He does a fit job."

Xcor went across by the stove and began pulling open the drawers. "These will have to do."

One by one, he laid out all the knives he could find: a cleaver, a serrated blade, two little paring types, and a carving one. Putting them on a dish towel, he rolled them up in a bundle and then held his hand out to her.

"We go downstairs."

Layla approached him and shivered as their palms connected. And as the two of them descended, her body loosened.

When they got to the bottom of the steps, he stopped and stared at her.

She gave him a moment to speak. When he didn't, she whispered, "Yes, please."

He closed his eyes and swayed. Then he dropped his head. "Are you certain?"

"Never more than anything in my life."

His lids lifted. "I shall be gentle with you."

It was on the tip of her tongue to tell him not to restrain himself: In truth, the last thing she wanted from him was to hold anything back because this could very well be the one and only time they were together.

But then her mind stopped functioning.

Because Xcor was drawing her against his body. With his free hand, the one that didn't have all those knives in it, he stroked her cheek and then brushed her lower lip with his thumb.

The next thing she knew, his lips were on hers, stroking, pressing in, caressing.

The kiss was as soft as a breath, and that was frustrating. She wanted more—and yet as she strained to get it, he moved back subtly, keeping control.

When he finally broke the contact, he smoothed his palm down her hair. "May I enter your bedroom, female?"

His eyes were so beautiful, shining and hot, the deep navy blue nearly black from the lust he had for her. And to her, his face was handsome, everything that was strong and masculine and powerful, the defect in his upper lip not anything she noticed or dwelled on. In fact, it was the whole of him that appealed to her, his power and his vulnerability, his savage nature and the polite effort he was making, the warrior in him and the protector who came out for her.

"Yes," she whispered.

"I would carry you, but I am not that strong, the now."

He took her hand and together they walked into the bedroom she had tried to sleep in during the day. And what do you know, in spite of the lack of rest, she felt vitally awake, almost painfully aware.

Xcor willed on the lamp at the bureau and shut the door. Then he led her over to the bed, bending to tuck the roll of knives right under the box spring.

As they sat down, she felt herself blushing.

He smiled. "Your shyness is my undoing, female. Regard my hands."

As he held them out to her, the fine tremor was at odds with the heavy veins that ran down his forearms and into his wrists.

"I have dreamed of touching you," he murmured. "So many times I have . . ."

"So touch me now."

When he seemed frozen, she was the one who grabbed his shoulders and brought his mouth to hers—and oh, dearest Virgin Scribe, when she held nothing back, neither did he. Xcor tasted of sex and desperation, and it wasn't long before his hands became rough and his growling permeated the quiet, dim bedroom. Indeed, he was no longer careful with her as he mounted her, his body pushing hers back into the pillows, his knee jutting between her legs and forcing them wide—

He stopped instantly, and yanked back. "Layla . . . my love, I'm on the edge of—"

"Take me. Hurry, oh, just have me . . . I've waited too long already."

Xcor bared his fangs and hissed, his eyes flashing with a purpose that might have been unholy but, in her frame of mind, was exactly what she needed from him.

"Let me see you, I have to see your body," he groaned as he swept a hand down to her waist.

Layla arched as he took the bottom of her casual shirt and began to pull it up her stomach to her—

Xcor gasped as her breasts were exposed. "Oh, sweetest female."

Frozen as he became at the sight of her tight nipples, she finished the job, getting what had covered her torso over her head and pitching it she cared not where. As she resettled on the pillows, Xcor sat up into a kneeling position, straddling her hips with his bent legs.

His hands really shook now as he ran his fingertips over her collarbone and down onto her breasts. "You are more astounding than even my daydreams."

As his rapt, reverent eyes passed over her bare skin, Layla realized that feeling beautiful had nothing to do with actual looks. It was a state of mind—and nothing put a female there faster than the male she wanted staring at her the way Xcor was now.

"Thank you," she whispered.

"'Tis I who should thank you for the gift of your flesh."

Looming above her, Xcor seemed enormous even with the weight loss, his shoulders so broad, his arms so heavy in that sweatshirt. And as he bent down to put his mouth to the side of her throat, the seams of what he wore strained, a subtle tear happening somewhere.

Heart pounding, heat roaring through her veins, Layla arched again as he moved his lips back and forth, brushing at her skin. Meanwhile, his hands, those incredible hands, cupped the outsides of her breasts—and then he was at her nipples, kissing them, drawing first one and then the other into his mouth.

In response, her body ceded to him to the point of bonelessness, her first wave of urgency easing up a little as she became enthralled by sensation.

As he worshipped her breasts, she had a dim thought that, in a way, she had come full circle. Trained as an *ehros*, as a Chosen whose sole purpose was to pleasure the Primale and bear him young, she had arrived at her maturity and entered into service at a time when there was, in fact, no one to service: The previous Primale had suffered a tragic end and the new one had yet to be appointed. And so she had waited . . . until Phury had been elevated to the position. He, however, had taken but one mate, and would lie with no other. And so she had waited some more, life taking on different contours as Phury had freed her and her sisters from the Sanctuary, permitting the Chosen to come down to earth with an autonomy unparalleled.

But there had been no love for her. No sex, either.

Just a brief infatuation with Qhuinn that she had realized was a fiction compared to what that male shared with his true mate, Blay.

And yet the two males had not been together, had seemed doomed to lead separate lives. So, when she had gone into her needing, she had asked Qhuinn to ease her in her fertility, not because he loved her, but because he was, at that time, as lost as she was: During those horrible hours of her suffering, they had lain together only for the sake of conception and it had worked.

She had little memory of the acts themselves, nor did she want to recall them.

Especially given the way things were between her and Qhuinn the now.

Thus, in spite of having given birth, she was all but a virgin, unfamiliar with a loving touch, a caring touch . . . from a sexual partner she loved who loved her in return.

"I'm so glad it is you," she said as she watched his tongue circle her nipple.

Xcor's eyes flashed up to hers, and as they darkened with self-loathing, she wished she could spare him the emotion.

"No." She placed her fingertips on his lips, silencing him when he went to speak. "That is for me to decide, not for you to judge. And please . . . don't stop."

Xcor shook his head. But then he moved down to the waistband of her leggings, his lips brushing low as he hooked his fingers into the elastic.

"Are you sure?" he said in a husky voice. "There is no going back after I remove these."

"Don't stop. Ever."

He bit his lower lip with his fangs. "My female . . ."

And then he pulled the leggings off along with her panties, stripping her bare to his hot stare.

Oh, how his eyes went everywhere, all over her legs and her hairless sex, her lower belly . . . back up to her breasts again.

His bonding scent became so intense it was all she could smell.

Xcor was careful now as he stretched out on top of her, easing his weight down gently, going slowly with his movements. And the feel of the hard ridge behind those thick sweatpants made her pivot her hips and rub her core on him.

When he kissed her again, and his tongue entered her mouth to meet her own, she scored his back with her nails. She couldn't take a moment longer, her sex aching for him, her body straining at being so close and yet not joined with his.

"Now," she begged. *"Please . . ."*

One of his hands disappeared between them, and she cried out as he slid his warm palm down the inside of her thigh. And then he was touching her at the center of her heat.

She was so ready for him, and still the release that came over her was both unexpected and a surprise, the pleasure ricocheting through the inside of her, making her float up from the bed even as she stayed where she was.

He helped her ride out the waves of sensation, and then his lower body lifted from hers. There were a series of movements down at his hips and she grew excited to feel his skin on her own, know his sex without any impediments.

Except when his pelvis came back down to hers, he still had his sweat-pants on.

His arousal had been freed, however. And her eyes fluttered shut as his blunt head brushed against her.

"I'm trying to go slowly," he said through gritted teeth.

"You don't have to."

With that, she shoved her hands down, found his thick, hard length, and brought it to her in just the right place. Digging a heel into the duvet, she moved herself up—

He slid into her and the fit was perfection. It was home and it was the whole galaxy at once, and she was so overwhelmed, tears speared into her eyes—because she knew he was equally affected: Xcor orgasmed the second he was fully inside of her, his warrior's body beginning to empty into her—and yet he recoiled, his head jerking back, alarm marking his face even as his body continued to release.

"Have I hurt you?" he said in horror.

"What?"

"You cry!"

"What—oh, no, no, no . . ." She took his face in her hands and kissed him. "No . . . not from pain. Never that."

She kissed him again and tried to get a rhythm started between their bodies.

But he would have none of it.

"Why do you cry?" he demanded, holding himself back from her.

Layla brushed impatiently at her eyes. "Because . . . I never thought I would ever get to have you like this. I didn't think . . . I didn't think it would happen for us and I'm just so very grateful. It has been so long, this waiting, this aching."

Xcor propped himself upon his elbows. "It was the same for me," he whispered. "In the course of my life, I have learned that dreams are not what come true. 'Tis only the nightmares that find you in real life. I had no real hope for this."

As a haunted light entered his eyes, she wondered what horrors he had seen throughout his hard life. What horrors had been done to him. His ruined lip would not have been an easy defect to bear.

Seeking to finish what they had started properly, Layla forced herself to cast aside such sad thoughts and refocused by going for the bottom hem of his sweatshirt.

But when she sought to pull it up, he prevented her, removing her hand.

"Will you not join me?" she said.

Mutely, he shook his head, and before she could question him, he began to kiss her again, his hips moving against her, his arousal stroking up and down inside her. As sensations overtook her once more, subsuming her in heat and wonder, she allowed herself to be lost.

It was a place she wished they could stay together forever.

She knew better than to aspire to that, however.

Destiny had seen fit to give them this one respite, this short period of time before he had to return from whence he had come—and although she wanted to be grateful for it, she was at her heart just greedy for more.

Love was like life itself, she supposed.

No matter how much of it you were blessed with, when the end came, it never felt like enough.

THIRTY

s V arrived back at the mansion with the King, he'd really just plain fucking had it with everyone. And that included himself.

But as the pair of them rematerialized side by side next to the fountain, he was well aware that his job as personal guard wasn't done until he got Big, Bad, and Really Fucking Bossy through the vestibule and into the foyer. Then, and only then, would he be free to abandon ship and go get hammered.

With any luck, those two bottles of Grey Goose that Fritz had brought over were still where they'd been dropped off, namely under the counter in the Pit's galley kitchen.

After a night like tonight, he wasn't even going to need ice.

Or a glass.

"Congratulations," Wrath said.

V grabbed hold of the arm that was nearly the size of his own thigh and started walking them forward. "What for?"

"You have another opportunity to be reasonable tonight."

"I'm always reasonable."

"In your own mind, I'm sure that's true."

"Step up," V muttered as they came to the stone stairs. "And now what are we doing. It better be good, by the way. I have a date with a vodka bottle."

When the King hit the ascent but kept quiet, V wanted to bare his fangs and hiss. Instead, he demanded, "Tell me."

As they arrived at the vestibule's outer door, the King stopped and looked over at him. "I'm ready to talk to Qhuinn. Your opportunity is to get shot at because you're coming with me to speak to him."

"That's not a chance to be reasonable. That's called being a target."

"Tomato, tomahto. Whatever."

"I swear, I keep winning the lottery around you." V yanked open the way into the vestibule. "Every frickin' night, true?"

Wrath did the duty at the security camera, finding the lens with his hand and then putting his face in its camera. "You're a lucky mother-fucker, for sure."

Fritz opened things wide, and the light from the glorious foyer was enough to leave V blinking as his retinas adjusted.

"My Lord!" the *doggen* exclaimed. "Sire! Oh, it is good that you have arrived home before the storm! May I get you a libation?"

Fritz's smile was like that of a basset hound's, all wrinkles and enthusiasm, and the butler had a dog's lack of time conception, his joy as if the pair of them had been gone for five years, not an hour.

"How 'bout a couple of bulletproof vests," V said under his breath.

"But of course! Would you care for the Point Blank Alpha Elites, or is this more of a bomb-detonation occasion requiring the Paraclete tactical vests?"

As if the choice were nothing more than having to pick white tie and tails over your standard-issue tuxedo.

You had to love the guy, V thought grudgingly.

"It was a joke, my man." Vishous put a hand-rolled between his lips and talked around it as he got out his lighter. "At least I hope it was."

"Anything for you both! Oh, and my Lord, I took the liberty of allowing George to relieve himself about fifteen minutes ago."

"Thanks, Fritz. Did you—"

"And I fed him, as well. I gave him the tenderloin left over from last night, but I warmed it up and served it with fresh whole carrots, pump-kin mash, and green beans. Everything was organic, of course."

"You love that dog, don't you."

The *doggen* bowed so low it was a wonder his bushy gray eyebrows didn't Swiffer the mosaic floor. "I do. Oh, I do."

"Good male, you're a good male."

Wrath seemed like he wanted to clap the butler on the shoulder, or maybe offer his palm for a high five, but he didn't follow through. Even though he was King, there were some things you didn't do, and that was make contact with an old-school servant like Fritz.

The poor guy was liable to mushroom cloud out of embarrassment.

Instead, Wrath strode forward like he owned the place, and V fell in line.

"Three feet," V said when it was time.

The Blind King stepped up onto the bottom of the great staircase with the coordination of a tap dancer, hitting the mark perfectly, and he knew when he got to the top, as well. First stop was his study, where he opened the double doors and got attacked by George, who had clearly never expected to see his master again.

"Come on, boy, back to work. Lead."

George trotted off to the desk and came back with his halter, which Wrath put on so quick, you'd swear he could see what he was doing. And then dog and master were reunited and heading in the direction of the hall of statues.

With V pulling up the rear. No doubt looking like the bad guy in a Disney movie.

Hell, even he didn't want to be anywhere near this black mood he was sporting. But of course, everywhere you went, there you were, and all that bullshit.

When they got to the room that the young were in, Wrath knocked once and then opened things up. In the glow of a night-light that was in the shape of the moon and the stars, it was easy to pick out Qhuinn on the bed, his two kids tucked in tight and sound asleep on either side of him.

But the brother wasn't at rest.

"Hey," he said softly.

"Time to talk," the King announced as George parked it in a sit at his side.

"You mind if we go out in the hall?"

"Nope."

Qhuinn nodded and slowly sat up. Then he looked back and forth between the two sleeping babies . . . like he couldn't decide which one to take to the bassinets first.

"V, can you give me a hand?"

For a moment, Vishous couldn't comprehend who the guy was talking to, even though his name was in the mix. But then Wrath's head turned in his direction, like the King was waiting for an answer, too.

Okay, why couldn't he just be drinking right now? Still, bassinet jockeying one of these pooping machines had to be better than dodging bullets.

Right?

V glanced at the matched set of milk addicts. Fine, maybe the goo-goo, gaga/Glock assessment was more of a fifty-fifty.

"V?" Qhuinn prompted.

"Yeah. Sure." *I'd fucking looooooove to manhandle your DNA. And maybe afterward, we can take turns doing each other's hair.* "What do I do?"

Qhuinn's brows popped as V approached the bed. "You pick Rhamp up and carry him over here."

The head. Support the head—

"You need to support the head," Qhuinn tacked on.

See? V told himself. This was going to be fine.

Except then Vishous realized that he had a lit cigarette in his hand.

"Gimme your hand-rolled," Wrath announced in a bored tone. "What the hell, V—you can't bring that around a young."

As Qhuinn got to his feet with Lyric, V gave the cig over like it was his last heartbeat. And then he was extending his good hand, as well as the one wrapped in black leather, to the brother's son. Man . . . outside of a medical situation, it felt all wrong to pick up anything more precious than a bag of dog food with his curse, but he knew intellectually nothing was going to happen to the kid.

Hell, it wasn't like the heat source was going to turn Rhamp into the infant equivalent of a pig-in-a-blanket or something. No, really. True?

Fuck—

Small. Warm. Strong.

That was what it felt like. And it was utterly bizarre to realize . . . that he was picking up a young outside of a clinical setting for the first time in his life. It wasn't that he had avoided them; he'd just never been interested in the stinky, whiny little bastards.

In the slightest—

Without warning, Rhamp opened his lids just as V was settling him down in the crib-thing next to his sister.

V recoiled. Okay, wow, those eyes were really fucking intense, very direct, and slightly hostile—like the kid knew this happy little transfer was waaaaaaaaaaaaay above Vishous's pay grade and not something that should have been sanctioned by any kind of self-respecting parental unit.

"Chill, my man," V murmured as he checked on what Pops was doing over at the other bassinet—and then V followed suit, pulling up the blanket just like Qhuinn was. "S'all good. You good, true?"

Qhuinn looked over. "He's a fighter, all right. You can already tell."

V sat back on his heels, crossed his arms, and continued to look down at the little bag of vampire. And what do you know. That infant sonofabitch glared right back at him.

Vishous started to smile. He couldn't help it. You had to admire that kind of strength—and it obviously came from breeding. How else could you explain why something that was barely more than a month old was ready to take on a grown-ass male who was heavily armed and really fucking cranky.

"My man," V said as he put his good hand out. "Gimme five."

Rhamp didn't know from high-fiving anything, but he did grab onto what was right in front of his face, and oh, how he squeezed.

V laughed deep in his throat. "Yeah, you can fight with me in the field when you're grown. And soon as you're big enough to hold a dagger . . . I'll make one for you. Forge it myself. You're gonna be just like your dad, one helluva a fighter. Just like him . . ."

As Vishous seemed to find a partner in surly crime with Rhamp, Qhuinn found himself staring at the brother. For a lot of reasons.

One, the fact that V seemed to be falling all kinds of enchanted over Rhamp was . . . well, a person was more likely to see God up close and in person before a male like V was ever going to ohhh and ahhh over a kid. Second, Rhamp was starting to warm up in return, the little guy's initially hostile response easing, his body relaxing its tension, his expression and those myopic baby-eyes assuming a kind of fondness.

Sort of like if one tiger met another in the wilderness and the pair decided to hang out instead of try to eat each other in a bid for dominance.

But the main reason Qhuinn couldn't look away?

Shifting his head, he glanced up to the far corner. To those bullet holes in the ceiling.

You're gonna be just like your dad.

Just like him.

With a wince, Qhuinn rubbed his temples. "We ready?"

Wrath and George turned themselves around. "Door."

As they left, Qhuinn wondered whether V was going to stay behind and hang with the kids. You know, maybe read some *Goodnight Moon.* Chill with a little *Pat the Bunny.*

That kind of shit.

But Vishous came along, so that the three of them and the King's golden gathered together in the hall.

Right before anyone said anything, Zsadist came out of his door down at the end of the corridor. The brother took one look at them, shook his head, and went riiiiight back into his suite.

Yeah, everyone knew what this was about.

"So here's the way it's going to be," Wrath said without preamble.

"Half and half. And she takes 'em to the Sanctuary for her time. Starts tomorrow after sundown when you leave to go out in the field. This is not subject to negotiation, nor is it up for your consideration. This is royal edict and I expect you to behave like a male and not a mental patient about it."

Qhuinn put his palms back on the sides of his noggin. Like maybe the extra padding would help his brain work. Or something.

"The Sanctuary?" he asked.

"She can travel as a Chosen does and so can they." Wrath handed V's cigarette back to the brother. "The Scribe Virgin is not using her quarters anymore, so there's a place there they can sleep when they need to."

"I just took some more songbirds up there," V mused as he took an inhale. "And I betcha those kids would like them. Those chirpy little fuckers are colorful and they sound nice. You know, sensory processing benefits have been shown as a result of—"

The brother recoiled and then looked annoyed as both Qhuinn and Wrath stared at him like he'd changed out of his leathers into a pink dress and bedroom slippers.

"What? I'm just sayin'." V rolled his eyes. "I don't care, you know. Not at all."

"Back to the visitation," Wrath continued. "I'm assuming your biggest concern about Layla taking them out of here is safety, and there's no better place for her to be with them—because she can't be here."

Qhuinn crossed his arms and stared at the carpet. Then he paced up and down, passing by the marble statuary that had been carved by humans known as Greeks and Romans. The male forms were powerful and positioned in various poses, their empty hands gripping spears that had been lost over the course of centuries—and the accoutrements of conflict weren't the only things that were missing. A few had limbs that stopped at the elbow or the knee, some accident or another stripping them of that which had been necessary to complete them. One was even headless.

Naturally, he thought of that essential part of him which he had recently lost.

His Blay.

And now . . . his young?

As Qhuinn turned around and came back slowly, V put out his hand-rolled on the sole of his shitkicker and tucked the half-smoked end into the ass pocket of his leathers. Then the brother surreptitiously slipped his un-gloved palm onto the butt of a forty holstered under his arm.

Good move, Qhuinn thought, 'cuz he was getting angry. In fact, even the hypothetical of that Chosen taking his kids anywhere was making that white rage start to vibrate at the base of his skull.

Except then he heard V's voice in his head.

You're gonna be just like your dad.

As the words rebounded around and around his cranial blank space, he felt like he was caught between being where he was . . . and behaving as he should.

In the end, the memory of those bullet holes tipped the scale.

Looking over at Vishous, he said roughly, "You can keep your weapon where it is."

"Turning over a new leaf?" V drawled without lowering his hand. "And in such a short time, too. So you're either exhausted or waiting for a better opportunity."

Qhuinn focused his eyes on the closed door of his young's suite, seeing through the panels to the room beyond. He pictured the sweet moments like that night-light, and the bassinets with their ribbons, and the little cursive *R* above Rhamp's bed and the *L* over Lyric's.

"Neither," he heard himself say after a while. Although he was tired to the point of zombie.

"So you accept my terms," Wrath prompted.

"I don't want to have to see Layla." Qhuinn shook his head. "Ever again. We're done, she and I. And I want to speak personally with the Amalya, the Directrix. I want to make absolutely sure they can get up and back okay. Also, if Layla tries to hoard them there—"

"She won't."

"How do you know that," Qhuinn said bitterly.

"She told me how important it is for you to see them."

"And you believed her?"

Wrath touched the side of his nose. "You think I wouldn't know if she were lying? And gimme a fucking break. She's not the source of all evil in the world."

"That would be the Omega," V chimed in dryly. "In case you forgot."

"So it's done." Qhuinn didn't bother voicing his disagreement on the subject of the Chosen with them. "Do we have to sign anything?"

The King shook his head. "Not unless you insist. We all know how it's going to be."

"Yeah. Guess we do."

After Wrath, George, and V went off, Qhuinn stayed where he was, staring at the statues. He was of half a mind to go down to Z's door and let the brother know that the coast was clear. But in the end, he just went back inside the bedroom.

A quick check of the clock, and he knew that it was going to be bottle time in about an hour. Fritz and the *doggen* took great pride in delivering the milk promptly on schedule and at the perfect temperature. Feeding two at a time was going to be a thing, but he'd figure it out.

God . . . Blay loved doing the bottle thing. Loved diapers, even the ones that made your eyes water.

Qhuinn went back over to the bassinets and thought about Layla taking the two infants anywhere. He literally couldn't imagine it—and every bone in his body, every fatherly instinct he had, screamed for him to stop the madness. He didn't care that she had birthed them. Didn't give a shit what the King said. And completely disagreed with the general consensus that that traitor in a white robe had any right to be even in the same zip code as his young.

Much less take them away from him.

Looking down at Lyric, he frowned. There was so much of Layla in the little girl, from the shape of the face, to the hands . . .

The hands were really freaky. A miniature carbon copy.

As his emotions churned, he turned away from her. And focused on Rhamp.

THIRTY-ONE

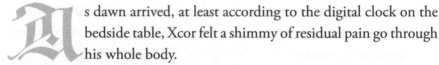s dawn arrived, at least according to the digital clock on the bedside table, Xcor felt a shimmy of residual pain go through his whole body.

To think where he had been a mere twenty-four hours ago.

If some angel had come unto him and told him that, in the mere shift of a single day and night cycle, he would go from being on death's door to lying beside his love in a safe house owned by the Brotherhood? He would have called impossibility on any such destiny.

Even if it had been uttered by the Scribe Virgin herself.

He glanced at Layla. His female was collapsed on his chest, sprawled upon him like the very best throw blanket anyone had ever had. And part of what he loved so much about this moment? Aside from the fact that he was utterly satiated sexually and so was she?

She slept soundly. The Chosen Layla was complete in her repose, her body loose and languid, her breathing even, her eyelids down hard as if it had been a very, very long time since she had had a proper rest.

Indeed, the quality of her sleep mattered to him for a lot of reasons, most important of which was that she could not possibly have been so at peace if she didn't have faith that he would take care of her. Keep her safe. Protect her against any and all threats.

As a bonded male, his female's safety was his ultimate source of purpose, her trust in him his biggest point of pride, her well-being that which was put before anything and everything else.

Serving her was the highest and best use of his life, and it was with great sorrow that he recognized this was a job that he would not enjoy for long.

Wrath was right to get the Band of Bastards to swear upon that black diamond of his before they all were banished by royal decree to the Old Country. Xcor's fighters were a principled lot of thieves and renegades—and if he, Xcor, commanded them to shift their allegiance unto the Blind King? They would do so, and they would keep to their word, although not because of what they had sworn to Wrath. But because of their loyalty to Xcor.

For him alone would they give their lives.

The Brotherhood, however, would not buy into all of that. No, they would only be persuaded by an oath to their liege—and even then, the brokered peace would be tenuous.

Again, the Band of Bastards had to leave the New World.

But how was he going to find them? Caldwell was a big city if you wanted to cross paths with someone who had no objection to being located. Trying to discover the whereabouts of a group of males who defined their nights and days by being hidden and staying that way?

Next to impossible. And that was assuming they hadn't already decided to return across the ocean.

With a soft sigh, Layla stirred against him, repositioning her head on his arm. Seeking to soothe her further, he rubbed her back slowly with his palm.

He knew he should close his eyes and follow her example, but there was no chance of the latter. Fortunately, he was used to operating on no sleep.

Lying there in the dark with his love, Xcor marveled anew at how she had transformed him. And then he went back into his past.

It was hard not to wonder what would have happened if he had decided not to rob that group of fighters in that particular wood on that specific night. Harder still not to regret that single decision that had led to so much else.

Because an evil had found him . . .

The Bloodletter.

Dearest Virgin Scribe, Xcor had thought as he had stared up at the tremendous male vampire who had appeared in the wood from out of nowhere and thrown him onto the ground. Indeed, it seemed as though Xcor had sought to rob, but then had to kill . . . a squadron of the Bloodletter's males.

He was going to die for this.

"Have you nothing to say," the great warrior demanded as he stood over Xcor. "No apology, for what you have taken from me?"

In the now-brisk wind, the Bloodletter stepped from Xcor and went over to pick up the severed head by the hair, dangling it such that blood dripped from the open neck.

"Do you have any idea how long it takes to train one of these?" The tone was more annoyed than anything else. "Years. You have, in one night—in but one fight—robbed me of a vast investment of my fucking time and energies."

With that, he cast the cranium aside and Xcor shuddered as the head bounced through the undergrowth.

"You," the Bloodletter pointed at him, "shall make amends unto me."

"No."

For a moment, the Bloodletter seemed taken aback. But then he smiled with all his teeth. "What say you?"

"There will be no amends." Xcor got to his feet. "None."

The Bloodletter threw his head back and laughed, the sound traveling through the night and flushing out an owl overhead and a deer elsewhere.

"Are you mad, then? Is it insanity that gave you such strength?"

Xcor slowly eased to the side and retrieved the scythe once again. His palms were sweating and the grip was slippery, but he held onto the weapon with all the strength he could.

"I know who you are," Xcor said softly.

"Aye. Do tell." More with that hideous, bloodthirsty grin, as the gusts

picked up long, braided hair. "I rather like to hear my accomplishments come out of the mouths of others—before I kill them and fuck their corpse. Tell me, is that what you've heard of me?" The Bloodletter took a step forth. "Is it? Is that what horrifies you so? I can promise you, you won't feel a thing. Unless I decide I want you whilst you still breathe. Then . . . then you will know the pain of possession, I promise you that."

It was as if Xcor were being confronted by pure evil, a demon given unto flesh and placed upon the earth to torment and torture souls who were otherwise more pure.

"You and your males are thieves yourselves." Xcor tracked every twitch in that body, from the curl of the hands to the shift of weight from one foot to another. "You are defilers of females and law unto yourselves, serving not the one, true King."

"You think Wrath is coming for you the now? Truly?" The Bloodletter made a show of looking around the vacant forest. "You think your benevolent ruler is going to turn up here and intercede upon your behalf and save you from me? Your loyalty is commendable, I suppose—but it is not a shield against this."

The sound of metal upon metal was like a scream in the night, the blade the Bloodletter outed nearly as long as that of the scythe.

"Still pledging allegiance, are you?" the Bloodletter drawled. "Are you aware, I wonder, that the King is nowhere to be found? That after the slaughter of his parents, he hath disappeared? So no, I think you shall not be saved by the likes of him." A pumping growl started up. "Or anybody else."

"I shall save myself."

At that moment, the clouds lost their battle with the wind elements, the heavy cover breaking apart and providing an oculus through which brilliant moonlight shone down from the night sky, bright as the daylight Xcor hadn't seen since before his transition.

The Bloodletter recoiled. And then angled his head to one side.

There was a long moment of silence, during which naught stirred save for the pine boughs and the underbrush.

And then the Bloodletter . . . reholstered his dagger.

Xcor did not put down his weapon. He knew not what was transpiring, but he was very aware one should not trust one's enemy—and he had put himself against this feared warrior through his actions in self-defense.

"Come with me then."

At first, Xcor did not comprehend the words. And even when he did, he did not understand.

He shook his head. "I shall go to my grave a'fore I go anywhere with you. 'Tis one and the same, at any rate."

"No, you shall come with me. And I shall teach you the ways of war and you shall serve beside me."

"Why would I e'er do that—"

"It is your destiny."

"You do not know me."

"I know exactly who you are." The Bloodletter nodded at the decapitated body. "And it makes this much more understandable."

Xcor frowned, a sudden quickening that was not about fear vibrating in his veins. "What lies do you speak."

"Your face is the giveaway. I thought you were but a rumor, a slice of gossip. But no, not with your dagger hand and that lip. You come with me and I shall train you and put you to work against the Lessening Society—"

"I am . . . a common thief. Not a warrior."

"I know of no thief who could do what you just did. And you realize this as well. Deny it all you like, but you have been bred for this outcome, lost into the world, now found."

Xcor shook his head. "I shall not go with you, no . . . no, I shall not—"

"You are my son."

Now Xcor lowered his scythe. Tears came to his eyes, and he blinked them away, determined to show no weakness.

"You shall come with me," the Bloodletter repeated. "And I shall teach you proper the ways of war. I shall harden you as steel tempered by fire, and you shall not disappoint me."

"Do you know my mahmen still?" Xcor asked weakly. "Where is she?"

"She doesn't want you. She never did."

This was true, Xcor thought. This was what the nursemaid had told him.

"So you will come with me now, and I will pave the way for your destiny. You shall succeed me . . . if the training does not kill you."

Xcor returned to the present by opening lids he was unaware of having closed. The Bloodletter had been right about some things, wrong about others.

The training in the war camp had been so much worse than Xcor could ever have imagined, the fighters therein battling each other for scarce food and water and also when they were pitted one against the next for sport and contest. It had been a brutal existence that had, night after night, week after week, month in and out . . . throughout the course of those five years . . . done exactly what the Bloodletter had promised.

Xcor had been hardened into living steel, his compassion and emotions stripped free of him as if they had never existed, the cruelty upon cruelty layered upon him until his nature had been suppressed by all that he had at first seen, and then later done.

Sadism could be trained into a person. He was living proof of that.

And it was also viral, such that he had done to Throe what the Bloodletter had done to himself, subjecting the former aristocrat to a barrage of indignities and challenges and insults. The effect had been similar as well: Throe, too, had risen to the tests, but also been soured by them.

As it was, so it had turned out to be. Although unlike Xcor, Throe seemed not to be mediated by any blessed force, his ambition as yet unchecked.

Or at least it had been prior to Xcor's abduction—and there was little to suggest any change in the male's proclivities or ambitions might have happened in the passage of time.

Which was why Xcor had taken pains to warn Wrath about the male.

Xcor caressed Layla's shoulder and marveled again at her effect on him, her ability to cut through the armor of his aggression and hostility and reach the male beneath, the real one.

The one he had lost touch with long ago.

She was his reset, the mechanism of reverse that took him back to who he had been before his destiny had crossed paths with the Bloodletter's.

An image of that horrible warrior came to his mind as clearly as if he had seen the male the night before, everything from that heavy brow to those penetrating eyes, the jutting jaw and thick neck, the girth and breadth of that massive body. He had been a mesomorph among the huge, a force of nature to shame both the hot fury of summer's thunderstorms and the explosive, frigid nature of winter's blizzards.

He had also been a liar.

Whoever Xcor's sire was, it had not been he. The Bloodletter's actual progeny had told him that.

Xcor shook his head back and forth on the soft pillow to try to clear his thoughts.

For so long, he had wanted to know who his parents were, something that he supposed was true for most orphans in the world: Even if he was unwanted by them, even if he were to have no relationship with them, he still had a desire to learn their identities.

It was difficult to explain, but he had always felt he was subject to a certain lack of gravity as he moved about the earth, his body possessing an essential weightlessness that, in retrospect, had predisposed him to falling into the Bloodletter's ideology of destruction, chaos, and death.

When you had no compass of your own, anyone's would do.

And in his case, the most debased, evil one any could imagine had been that which he had fallen into and embraced.

God, did he have regrets.

The Bloodletter had spoken of training for war, but it had become amply clear that he served his own bloodlust rather than any defense of the species—and still Xcor had gone along with it all: Once he had had a taste of fatherly pride, however perverted it had manifested itself, the approval had become the drug he needed, the antidote to the hole inside of himself.

Except the paternalism had been naught but a chimera, as it turned out. A lie that had taken an unexpected truth to uncover.

With the male's loss, Xcor had felt as though he had been abandoned a third time: The first had been at his birth. The second had been when the female who had been his nursemaid . . . or someone else to him . . . had left. And then the third had been as the Bloodletter's falsity, undoubtedly constructed to ensure Xcor went with him to his war camp, had fallen away, the news delivered from a source that was undeniable.

V's blooded sister, Payne, had killed their true father, the Bloodletter. Killed the lie, too.

But it was all right, Xcor thought. In finding his love? All his questing had ended. He was through pursuing a family that didn't exist because it had never wanted him. He was over searching for outside sources to fill his inner cistern. He was done assuming any value system other than his own.

And in no longer trying to find that which did not exist? He had discovered the destination he'd always sought within himself, and it felt . . . good.

It was good to be whole.

It was good to offer himself without reservation or hesitation to a female of worth whom he loved with all that he had in him.

Xcor frowned. But fates, how he was going to leave his Layla? Destiny was what it was, however, and as much as he had improved himself, as fine a track as he was now on . . . it couldn't erase his past or the dues he had to pay for all he had done. Nothing could do that.

In truth, he would be e'er unworthy of her. Even if the great Blind King had not mandated him into deportation, he would have volunteered for it willingly.

They just had to make what little time they had left together count.

For a lifetime.

THIRTY-TWO

The following evening, as night came over Caldwell, Blay tried to get out onto the back porch for his first smoke after he'd woken up. The setup was perfect. He had his YETI mug full of Dunkin' Donuts coffee, made by his *mahmen* from the little bricks you could order online, and his pack of Dunhills—which he was having to ration because he had only six left, and was sporting a Patagonia parka that had more down feathers in it than all the pillows in the house.

Yup, it was a good plan. Caffeine and nicotine were mission critical when you hadn't slept for more than fifteen minutes at a stretch all day and you didn't want to bite the heads off of everyone around you.

The problem? When he attempted to open the porch door, he had to put his shoulder into the effort.

And then he got a face full of driving snow.

Recoiling, he cursed and shut things back up. "Holy crap, it's bad out there—"

The crash from the kitchen was loud and involved something that sounded like a stainless-steel pan or maybe a baking sheet, at least going by the cymbal-like nature of the *claaaaaaaaaaaaaaaaang*.

"Mom?" he called out.

Forgetting all about his chemical start-up, he hustled for the other room—

—and found his *mahmen* down on the tile in front of the stove, her ankle twisted at an unnatural angle, the pecan roll she'd been putting in the oven on the floor, the pan it had been on three feet away from her.

Blay ditched the coffee and pack of cigs on the counter and rushed to kneel beside her. "*Mahmen?* Did you hit your head? What happened?"

Lyric sat up with a grimace, bracing her body with her elbows. "I just wanted to get this in before your father came down for First Meal."

"Your head, did you hit your head?" As he pushed her hair out of the way, he prayed he wasn't going to find all kinds of blood. "How many fingers am I holding up?"

She shoved his hand out of the way. "Blay, I'm fine. For goodness' sake, I didn't hit my head."

He sat back. The female was in her standard mom-jeans, her cheery red sweater and bright white turtleneck making her look like a cross between Santa Claus's wife and Mrs. Taylor from *Home Improvement*. And she did seem okay, her eyes tracking him, her coloring good, her affect one of embarrassment, not trauma.

"Blay, I just slipped on the throw rug. I'm all right."

"Good, because that means I can yell at you. Where the hell is your boot? Why isn't it on your foot?"

Abruptly, his *mahmen* feigned light-headedness, fluttering her lashes and throwing out her hands like she couldn't see. "Is it ten fingers? Twelve?"

When he glared at her, she winced sheepishly. "That boot thing is just so ungainly, and this is such a cramped space. I was going to put it on as soon as I made the eggs."

"Did you slip—or did your ankle give out?"

When she didn't say, Blay guessed it was the latter and moved down to her foot. The instant he attempted to even touch the slipper she had on, she hissed and went white as a sheet.

"It's fine," she said tightly.

He focused on her thin lips and the way her hands trembled. "I think you've dislocated your ankle again. And maybe you've broken something, I don't know."

"It'll be fine."

"You know, those are my three least favorite words. Qhuinn always says them whenever—" He cut that off, and pointedly ignored the way his mom looked at him. "Can you dematerialize? Because I am very sure Doc Jane needs to take a look at this. No, Manny. He's the bones guy."

"Oh, that's not necessary."

"Why don't we have Dad decide." As her eyes flared, he drawled, "Or you could be reasonable and go with me without complaint."

Lyric's expression became annoyed, but he knew he had her. Ever since the raids, his father had been a little overprotective of his mate. He seemed to get hysterical at the most ridiculous things—paper cuts, hang-nails, a stubbed toe—which meant when Lyric had slipped on the front stoop when going to get the newspaper a couple of nights before, the poor guy had just about lost his damn mind.

And this injury was worse than the first.

"Can you dematerialize?" Blay asked.

"Do you really think it is necessary?"

"You can answer that yourself. How'd you like to try and stand up?"

His mother glared down at her foot. "I wish I'd put that damn boot on."

"Me, too."

She frowned. "How do I get to the training center clinic? Even if I can dematerialize, I don't know where its true location is."

"We can get close and have them pick us up." Blay stood and looked to the ceiling. Up above, he could hear his father moving around, getting dressed. "Do you think it'll be better or worse if we go without him knowing?"

"We can text him? Tell him we're going to be right back. Tell him . . . we went to the grocery."

His mother hated lying, but she hated upsetting her *hellren* more. And Blay had to back her up in this rare instance. His father was going to be a thing about this.

"Let's go." Blay took out his phone and started to text Doc Jane. "Do you know that vegetable stand out on Route 9? The one that is housed in the barn?"

Except even as he spoke, he thought of trying to open the porch door and wondered what the hell he was thinking. His mother needed to dematerialize somewhere warm and dry with her ankle. That barn was unheated and probably locked up. It was better than the fucking forest, but really?

What was he thinking?

He lowered the phone with the text halfway done and regarded his *mahmen*. She had closed her eyes and laid her head back on the tile—and the hand that was on her stomach had contracted into a claw.

The other one was shaking on the floor beside her, her trimmed nails tap-dancing.

"You can't dematerialize," he said numbly. "No way."

"Sure I can."

But the denial was weak.

And then his father came into the kitchen, a tie half-knotted around his throat, his hair still wet and combed into something Barbie's Ken would rock, each individual strand well ordered and seemingly frozen in place.

"—video conference with my clients and—Lyric! Oh, my God, Lyric!"

As his father ran to his mom's side, Blay looked toward the door that opened into the garage. His parents started to argue, but he cut right through all that.

"Dad, make my night and tell me your car is four-wheel drive."

Back at the Brotherhood's mansion, Qhuinn was doing something that was inconceivable: He was stuffing a black duffel bag full of bottles, formula, and distilled water. Diapers. Wipes. Desitin. Rattles and pacis.

Of course, the whole filling-up-a-bag routine wasn't a big deal. Usually, though, his gear was more of the Smith & Wesson or Glock and Beretta variety, the kind of thing that came with bullets and laser sights, not Pampers and Evenflo.

The other reason it was strange was because he couldn't believe he was packing up for his kids to frickin' leave the house. Without him.

They were so little. And he really didn't want them around that female at all.

He refused to refer to Layla as *mahmen* anymore, even if it was just in his head.

But it was what it was. He'd gone up to the Sanctuary with Amalya, the Chosen's Directrix, and she'd walked him through the bucolic landscape, showing him the reflecting pool and the temples, the dormitory, the Scribe Virgin's private quarters.

Where Layla would be with his kids.

It had been impossible to argue with the setup. The shit was even safer than what was doing at the mansion, for fuck's sake, and Amalya had assured him that his children would be able to enter and return without a problem.

And when pressed, she had personally guaranteed him she'd bring back his young. If Layla caused a problem.

A soft knock on the bedroom door brought his head up from the bag. "Yeah."

Beth came in and she was a lot more toned down. Then again, she'd gotten what she'd wanted. "Looks like you've got everything ready."

He glanced back down at what he'd packed. "Yeah."

There was a long pause.

"It's going to be all right, Qhuinn. I'm proud of you for—"

"No offense, but you get to be with your kid twenty-four hours a day—because the person you had the thing with isn't a liar and a traitor. So you gotta excuse me if your version of 'all right' and mine are slightly different." He stepped back from the foot of the bed. "I'm not allowed to have my 'all right'—which would be my children staying here in this room while I go out to fight. My 'all right' is not being out in the field, defending the race, with half my mind on whether or not Layla is going to give them back to me when she's supposed to. And my 'all right' sure as shit doesn't involve that female having any contact with them ever again. I don't need you to be proud of me and I don't want your fake-ass concern. All I require from you is to baby-sit the two of them while I get the fuck out of this house."

Beth crossed her arms over her chest and slowly shook her head. "What's happened to you?"

The words were spoken so quietly, it was clear she was posing them to herself.

"Really. You're seriously asking that."

Qhuinn turned away from her and went to the bassinets. He glanced at Lyric and then focused properly on Rhamp, putting his pacifier back in his mouth.

"You be brave up there, my man." Qhuinn stroked back the thatch of dark hair. "I'll see you in twenty-four hours. Piece of cake, right?"

Wrong.

It was so fucking hard to turn away. His chest was on fire with a pain that went down into his DNA . . . especially as his eyes passed over Lyric one last time. He wanted to go to her, but he just couldn't look at that face.

Couldn't see it right now.

As he walked by Beth, he kept his eyes straight ahead. He didn't trust himself to open his mouth for even a good-bye. No doubt he'd end up going off on the Queen, and that wasn't going to help anyone.

Grabbing his weapons and his leather jacket from a chair, he stepped out and closed the door quietly behind himself. He didn't know exactly when Layla was going to come—after sunset, sure, but that had been a while ago. She was probably due to arrive at any minute—

"You ready for the meeting?"

He looked over his shoulder. Z was coming out of his suite of rooms, and the brother was strapped up and ready to fight, all kinds of metal hanging off him, his yellow eyes narrow and shrewd.

That scar on his face, the one that ran down his cheek and distorted his upper lip, made Qhuinn think of Xcor's fucked-up mug.

"We got a meeting?" Qhuinn asked as he fished his cell from his leather jacket.

He'd been checking the damn thing solely to see if Blay reached out with a call or a text. A picture. A fucking emoji.

Nothing. And he hadn't paid attention to anything else.

Well. What do you know. Group text calling the Brotherhood to Wrath's study. At precisely this hour.

"Guess we do," he muttered as he put the thing back in the jacket and followed Z.

There wasn't any conversation between them on the way to the study, and that was just fine with Qhuinn. And as he walked into the meeting, he kept his head down and went over into the corner farthest away from the fire. The last thing he needed was a re-live of the colossal goat fuck that the night before last had been about. Everyone knew the facts, and shit knew they'd all given him a piece of their minds when he'd been locked in the Tomb.

No reason they couldn't collectively chalk that up to a great time had by all.

Still, the whole him-discharging-a-weapon-in-the-house had some ground left to cover on it. There could always be a rehash on that.

Or maybe there was a door number three, something that had, bless-edly, nothing to do with him.

Wrath was seated behind his ornate desk, in the throne that had been his father's for so many years. And Vishous was right beside him, a hand-rolled lit in his gloved hand, his icy eyes traveling over the assembled. Butch was on the sofa with Rhage, that flimsy French antique looking like it was well over its weight capacity. Z had taken up res next to Phury by the bookshelves. And Rehv was there.

When John Matthew came in, the guy glanced around, and as he saw Qhuinn, he came over. He didn't sign anything, just eased back against the wall and put his hands into the pockets of his leathers.

Qhuinn glanced at his friend. "You and I are supposed to be paired up tonight."

John nodded and took his hands back out. *I don't think we're going anywhere.*

"They won't let me out into the field?"

No, the snowstorm. Record fall. Unheard of for this time of year.

Qhuinn let his head fall back so it hit the plaster behind him. Just his frickin' luck. There was no way he could stay all night in this house while his kids were with that female, Blay was not speaking to him, and his brothers were still pissed off over the whole Xcor-escaping-the-Tomb thing.

Fuck this shit, he thought. He wasn't in a prison. He didn't have to—

Wrath spoke up from the throne. "So let's get this over with."

Qhuinn crossed his arms over his chest and got ready for another round of how horrible he was.

"We know where Xcor is," the King announced. "And he is going to bring the Bastards to me."

Instantly, the room exploded with talk and cursing, the brothers stamping their shitkickers, everybody on their feet—and Qhuinn did some shocked-to-the-balls of his own. Was the male back in custody? Surely, someone would have told him—

He thought of the mess he'd made in the Tomb and decided . . . nah, the Brotherhood was pretty much done with him and Xcor for right now.

"He is mine!" Tohr yelled over the din. "He is mine to kill!"

That is fucking debatable, Qhuinn thought—but he kept it to himself. Finders, killers, and all that shit.

If he got to that sonofabitch first, he was going to slaughter him and to hell with—

"No, he's not," Wrath ground out. "He isn't anyone's to kill."

As the King's words sank in, everybody shut up, and V stepped in behind Tohr like he was prepared to put a choke hold on the brother.

Wait . . . say what? Qhuinn thought.

"Do you understand me," the King ordered. "No one is killing him."

And then, as if to drive the command home, Wrath looked first at Tohr . . . and then directly at Qhuinn himself.

THIRTY-THREE

In the Brotherhood's safe house, Xcor was in the shower, his face turned to the rush of water, his body regaining further strength by the minute. As soon as night had fallen, he had left Layla asleep in the bed they had shared and gone up to the kitchen, where he had located all manner of calories and set about consuming them. It mattered not to him that the combinations were unappetizing: He had orange juice with mint chocolate chip ice cream, chili out of a can without bothering to warm it, a loaf of bread with a stick of butter, both whole, all of the cold cuts and sliced cheese, and both of the pizzas from the freezer.

Which he had had to cook in the oven because he couldn't bite into them when they were frozen.

He was going to need to replenish the supplies, although he knew not how. He had never handled his group's money and thus had no access to any bank accounts or financial resources. And he was not a thief any longer.

Throe had always controlled their funds. He had been among them the best face to put forward when contact with the human world was required—

Xcor sensed Layla's presence the moment she appeared in the open doorway of the bath, and as he shifted to look at her, he nearly fell to his knees. She was gloriously naked, her high, pink-tipped breasts and her lovely hips, her long legs and perfectly made sex, bared for him, and him alone, to see.

His cock hardened instantly.

But he shielded it from her. Even though they had made love throughout the day, he folded the length up onto his belly and held it there with both hands.

She padded silently over the marble floor, opening the glass door and joining him.

Her eyes flicked down to where his palms were. "Why do you not show me yourself?"

Indeed, he had kept his clothes on all night, pulling the sweats down when he entered her, returning them unto his hips when he cradled her against him afterward.

"Xcor?" she whispered as the steam billowed around her and her skin sparkled from drops of moisture. "Why do you not want me to see you?"

Shaking his head, he preferred not to speak. It was just too difficult to put into words how hard it was to have her sight upon his flesh. She had never seemed bothered by his defect, never appeared to notice it or judge him the lesser because of it—still, clothes were a mask that he preferred to wear in her presence. It had been different when he'd wanted to repel her from him, when he had sought to challenge her with his ugliness in hopes that she would turn away and stop the torture for them both. But now . . .

He had been rejected all his life. None of that would matter in the slightest, however, if she turned away from him—

Layla sank down on her knees with the grace of moonlight falling from the heavens. And his first instinct was to help her back up, as he didn't like the idea of her on the hard tile. Yet when he went to bend unto her, she stopped him.

Leaned in toward his palms.

Extended her tongue . . .

. . . and slowly licked up the middle finger of his right hand.

Her tongue was slick, slick as the water, and soft, soft as velvet. And he collapsed back against the shower's wall.

Layla's eyes stared up his body as she repeated the movement—and then sucked his finger into her mouth. Swirling tongue, hotter now, just like the inside of her . . .

"Layla," he begged.

One by one, she sucked at his fingers, loosening his hold on his erection, making him so weak that his hands fell away from his sex not because he willed them as such, but because he lacked the strength in his arms to do aught else.

Freed from constraint, his cock jutted straight out from his hips, the water from the shower making the proud length glisten. Fates, he wanted her to do what she was about to, craved the feel of her lips on his head, his shaft, wanted the suction and the—

"Fuck," he groaned as her mouth captured him.

She didn't take all of what he had to offer. She concentrated on his tip, teasing him, backing off, then taking him in a little again—and just as he thought he was going to lose his ever-loving mind, she extended her tongue and ran it around his head, slowly, oh, so slowly. And the entire time, her green eyes looked up at him, and the water fell on her, too, dripping off her nipples, falling down her stomach, disappearing between her split thighs.

Xcor had to grab onto whatever he could find to stay on his feet, his palms squeaking down the glass, but finding a home of sorts on the marble wall.

"Oh, God, Layla . . ." He had to close his lids. "Too much . . ."

She didn't stop, though. She finally sucked him in whole, taking all of him even though he had to be down her throat.

He had to look. And the second he saw her lips stretched wide around his girth, he started to come.

"I'm . . . oh, *fuck* . . ."

Even though he tried to push her back, just in case she didn't know what was happening, she wouldn't let him. She found a rhythm with the sucking and accepted his orgasm into her mouth, her hands going between his legs and cupping his balls.

Xcor ended up on his ass. Literally.

His thigh muscles gave out, and it was all he could do not to fall in a heap and crush her as he went down. And still she pleasured him as she repositioned with him, making him find another release right after the first, his legs cranked wide to accommodate her, his hands going to her wet hair, his head and neck getting squeezed in the corner of the shower.

When she was finally finished, she lifted herself up and licked her lips. Meanwhile, all he could do was just catch his breath and stare at her, his skull lolling on his spine, his arms flopped loose, the shower spraying him with warm rain like he was a rock in the forest.

"I want to do the same to you," he said in a guttural voice.

She sat back on her heels and smiled at him. "Do you?"

He nodded his head. Like a dumb-ass.

"You look a little tired, warrior," she murmured. "Have I worn you out?"

Xcor was about to deny it when she eased back, fitting her shoulders into the far corner, mirroring his pose. As her lids dropped low, she brought her knees up . . . and then spread them, giving him a stunning sight.

"What would you do to me?" she drawled. "Would you kiss me here?"

She drew her elegant hand down the side of her throat. And as he nodded like a planker, she smiled. "Here . . . ?"

Now her fingertips were at her collarbone, and he nodded again.

"How about . . . right here?"

As she brushed one of her nipples, he ground his molars so hard his jaw let out a crack.

"Right here, warrior? You would kiss me here?"

She teased her own nipple, pinching it so that she hissed and then rubbing it as if she were soothing the sensation. And then her other hand drifted over her stomach.

"How about . . . here?" she whispered as she stroked down to the very top of her cleft.

A pumping growl left him, and Xcor said in a low burst, "Yes. Right there."

"What would you do with your mouth?" One fingertip traced the outside of her sex. "Or . . . no, you would use your tongue, wouldn't you, warrior. Your tongue . . ."

She gasped as she touched herself, her eyes sticking with his as she had to tilt her head to the side, the sensations clearly beginning to get the best of her.

"You would put your tongue here—"

Xcor lunged at her, moving so fast he wasn't aware of making the decision to get on her. And he was rough, shoving her hand out of the way and sealing his mouth on her sex, taking what he wanted, what she had teased him with.

Now she was the one throwing hands out, looking to keep herself in some semblance of physical order. But he was having none of that. He yanked her down flat on the tile, slapped his palms on the inside of her thighs, and butterflied her open, going in deep with his tongue, consuming her.

She came hard against his face, her hands spearing into his damp hair, pulling at it until it hurt. Not that he gave a shit. All he cared about was getting into her, making her say his name, marking her with his lips and tongue.

That wasn't enough.

Even as a release claimed her and she jacked up off the tile, her shoulders jutting back, her breasts surging up, the water on her skin making her flesh gleam in the low light, he wasn't getting enough.

Xcor mounted her and pushed his cock in deep, his fingers biting into her hip bones and holding her as he started to pound. Now her breasts were kicking this way and that, and her lower teeth clapped into her upper ones, and her arms flapped. But her eyes were like fire as the animal in him subjugated the animal in her.

He pulled out at the last minute, rising above her, his shoulders blocking the spray of the shower. Grabbing his erection, he was even more brutal with himself than he had been with her, yanking at his sex, making himself come.

So that he covered her.

It was the marking of a bonded male, a practice done so that any other male in her presence would be fully warned that if he approached her, he had best beware.

She was another's.

Not as property. But as something far too precious for others to toy with.

By the time Xcor was finishing with her, the spray falling from the shower had started to lose its heat—not that Layla cared. She had her warrior between her legs, and he was doing what a male did when he claimed a female, an ancient instinct bred into the species to ensure its survival. It was raw and it was beautiful, it was primordial and yet very much welcome in the modern world.

At least her modern world.

When he finally collapsed on top of her, she wrapped her arms around slick shoulders and closed her eyes with a smile.

"I weigh too much," he mumbled into her neck.

Before she could stop him and tell him that she didn't care that her tailbone was aching or that she suspected she had a couple of black-and-blues in her future, he was picking her up and getting to his feet, holding her in his arms as if she were cut glass.

Outside of the shower, he took a fluffy white towel and wrapped her up in it. Then he took a second one and patted her face dry before moving behind her. With gentle squeezes, he drew the terry cloth down the long length of her hair, rolling up the ends, getting most of the water out.

The whole time, she watched him in the mirror, memorizing the details of his expression, his body, his still-wet hair, and his coiled power. His face was especially dear to her: The fierce planes and angles had softened—and she had a sense that he wouldn't have liked her seeing the vulnerability in him.

"Will you be safe tonight?" he said in a low voice. "As you go to that house? And then to the Sanctuary?"

"Yes. I promise you. They will not hurt me."

"And no one else is welcome up there, correct? No one can get at you?"

"No, others outside of the Chosen have to be granted access. I'm not sure how it works, but it has always been thus. Only my sisters and the Primale are permitted to come and go as we please."

"Good. This is good."

"Where are you going to go?"

As she waited for his reply, her heart beat faster because she hated the idea of him out there in Caldwell, alone—and also because she dreaded the passage of the night. The sooner he found his males, the sooner he would be gone from her.

When Xcor didn't answer, the silence between them was a palpable weight.

"So I'm staying up there during the day, too." She said this even though she'd already told him what the plan was. "But upon the nightfall I shall return to this house."

"And I will be here to greet you."

As she exhaled in relief, Xcor put the towel aside and picked up a brush. Starting with the very tips, he continued to tend to her hair, carefully removing the knots.

"I'm going to miss you," she whispered to his bent head.

It seemed utterly incongruous that a male as hardened by war as he could wait upon her like this, that brush so small in his hands, his shoulders so big behind her, his harsh face wearing that impossibly kind expression.

"'Tis only a day and night." He moved to the crown of her head, seemingly enthralled with the way the black bristles went through her golden hair. "We shall be back together before we know it."

Layla nodded only because she sensed her emotional equilibrium was of vital importance to him—and she wanted to pretend she was all right for his benefit. But their twenty-four-hour separation was not what was on her mind. The one that was going to last for the rest of their lives was.

Closing her eyes, she tried not to think about it. Her heart had just been eased. There was no reason to rush a return of sadness.

"I love you," she said.

Xcor stopped, his eyes flipping to hers in the glass. "What?"

She turned around and looked up at him. Dearest Virgin Scribe, she was never going to get tired of that face of his, his scent, his body.

Rising on to her tiptoes, she put her arms around his neck, and as her breasts came up against his chest, she felt a now-familiar heat curl in between her thighs.

"I love you," she repeated.

His lids closed and he seemed to sway.

But then he unclasped her hands and lowered her arms. "Shh . . ." He kissed her once, and then again. "I have to go, and so do you."

THIRTY-FOUR

ohr told himself, as he stood in Wrath's French study and listened to a big bucket of piss about Xcor, that he was going to keep tight. He was just going to slap all kinds of no-problem-boss on his face, and nod at the right times, and maybe shrug once or twice.

As if Wrath letting a known criminal walk free just because the motherfucker had kissed a ring that meant nothing to him was no BFD. Happened on the reg. NP.

Oh, and of course, yeah, sure, bringing the Band of Bastards in to do the same was a perfectly sane idea. Yeah, one by one, that'll really cut down on the risk.

'Cuz it wasn't like Xcor and his boys would think about coordinating an attack.

Nah. Why would they do that?

"—everybody, and I mean, *everybody*"—Wrath turned his head in Tohr's direction again and then swung those sunglasses of his around to Qhuinn—"to be on board with this. After the oaths, they're leaving for the Old Country and we are done with them."

Actually, Tohr thought, maybe he should just eat the business end of a shotgun now. More efficient than waiting for his brain to explode in this solution that had STOOPID IDEA stamped all over it.

As Wrath fell silent, there was a whole lot of quiet in the room—which indicated there were a number of people sitting hard on their opinions—and Tohr glanced over at Qhuinn. The brother's eyes were lowered to the floor like he was inspecting the structural integrity of the laces on his shitkickers.

Tohr looked back in Wrath's direction. The King was dead fucking serious with this dumb-ass plan of his, his jaw set, his affect all kinds of don't-mess.

And yeah, even though the rest of the brothers didn't like it, they would go along with shit, not because they were weak, but because they knew that Wrath wasn't going to budge—and they took very seriously their roles as private guard.

So they were going to do their damnedest to keep the male alive.

Even as he went to some safe house and expected the Band of Bastards to get on one knee like a bunch of human future bridegrooms.

The trouble was, oaths given by males with no honor were nothing but a waste of syllables.

"Good," Wrath muttered. "I'm glad you're all behind me on this."

A couple of brothers coughed, and there was some feet-shuffling. Vishous lit up again, and Butch took out that huge Jesus piece he wore, rubbing the symbol of his faith back and forth between his thumb and forefinger. Like he was praying in his head.

Smart guy.

And then, like everything was copacetic, Wrath moved on to regular business, chatting up shit like the rotation schedule, when the next order of guns was going to be placed, and what was doing with the training program.

"Now about this storm." Wrath shook his head. "It's ripe nasty out there. I'm calling off tonight. It's a fucking snow day, assholes."

There was a murmur of agreement. And then it was dismissal time.

Tohr wanted to be the first free of the room, his anger choking the shit out of him, but he held back, filing into the center of the pack, lingering in the way he usually did. He didn't talk because he didn't trust himself to crack his pie hole, though he did try to make it seem like he gave a shit about whatever the others were planning.

Pool tourney. Poker. Drinks. MYO sundae bar.

That last one was Rhage.

Tohr waited . . . until finally what he was looking for presented itself.

Qhuinn came out of the study last and he was looking like he was a pro wrestler in search of a ring. As he stepped by, Tohr placed himself in the guy's path so their shoulders bumped.

When Qhuinn glanced over, Tohr stared hard into those mismatched eyes. And then in a soft voice, he said, "Garage. Ten minutes."

Qhuinn seemed surprised, his brows flaring. But he recovered fast.

The brother's nod was nearly imperceptible.

After which they went their separate ways.

Down the hall from all the happy-happy, joy-joy in the study, Trez woke up in his room and knew better than to move quick or get excited over the fact that his stomach seemed to finally be a calm sea. The true test was going to come when he tried to sit up, and after having spent a good twelve hours flat on his ass feeling like a semi's road kill, he was not in a big hurry to tempt fate and be about the vertical.

But he couldn't stay like this forever.

As he slowly lifted his upper body off the mattress, he tried not to hyper-focus on every little nook and cranny of his body and his head. Reading tea leaves into how this was going to go was—

"What the fuck!"

Trez recoiled so fast and so hard he slammed his skull into the headboard and promptly got a flashback to what the day had been like.

There was someone sitting in his room, over on that chair—

"Are you kidding me?" He exhaled a curse and rubbed the back of his brain. "Really? Are you fucking kidding me?"

Across the way, like some fucked-up scarecrow, a pair of blue jeans, that Nirvana concert T-shirt of the angel's, the flannel bullshit, and a set of Nikes had been stuffed with God only knew what. The head of the "Lassiter" was made out of a nylon bag that had had potatoes in it, and the black and yellow hair was a collection of knee-high business socks— probably Butch's—and Swiffer cleaning rags that had been safety pinned in place.

Around its neck? A handwritten sign that read: THE BOSS WAS HERE.

"Mother*fucker*."

Shifting his legs off the side of the bed, Trez gave his heart rate a chance to get under two hundred BPM, and then it was bathroom time. The good news was that the migraine seemed to be solidly in his rearview, the anvil that had been on the right side of his head gone, his stomach growling for food.

After a shower, and a shave, and a fresh set of clothes, he was ready to do what he should, which was head to shAdoWs and see what was doing.

Instead, he got his cell phone and dialed his brother. iAm answered on the first ring.

"How you feeling?" the guy asked.

"I'm alive."

"This is good."

"Well?"

"Well what?" When Trez didn't fill in the obvious, iAm started muttering things that began with the f-word. "Trez, seriously, leave it, would you?"

"Not gonna. Will you please hire that female?"

There was a long period of silence—which Trez inferred was all about iAm hoping against hope that he was going to see the light. But Trez didn't give a shit. He was going to wait it out, and he was going to get his way, and Therese was going to get the job at Sal's.

"Fine," iAm bitched. "I'll give her the job. Are you happy now?"

No, not even close. "Yeah. Thanks, man. You're doing the right thing."

"Am I? I'm not sure how giving you contact with that female is going to help either one of us."

Trez closed his eyes and remembered the feel of Therese's lips, her taste, the scent of her traveling across the cold air into his nose . . . his soul.

A spike of nausea cleared all of that out of his mind. "It's going to be fine. I'm not going to bother her."

"Yeah. Right."

After Trez hung up, he shot a glare over at the angel effigy in the corner. "Lassiter," he said out loud. "Come on, I know you're here somewhere."

He waited, expecting the angel to come through the door. Break free of the walk-in closet. Slither out from under the bed. The guy was always around, whether you wanted him or not.

But he should have known better. Ten minutes, and absolutely-no-angel later, it seemed kind of fitting that the one time he wanted the bastard to show up, the fucker played ghost.

Pulling on a fresh suit jacket, Trez left his room and took out his phone again as he headed for the grand staircase. He texted Xhex as he went on the descent, and was surprised when he got a ping right back. Usually she'd be checking the liquor in—

Oh. Got it. Snowstorm, club closed, no one going anywhere in the city.

As he hit the foyer, he crossed over the mosaic depiction of an apple tree in full bloom and zeroed in on the billiards room—where, like, three quarters of the Brotherhood were milling around with pool cues and booze in their hands.

Butch came over to him, the former human cop looking sharp as hell, as usual. "You going to join us? You want a drink?"

Before he could answer, Xhex came around from behind the bar. "Yeah, I made the call about closing. The bouncers were phoning me, saying they couldn't get across town, the bartenders, too. No working girls. The only thing that showed up was the liquor delivery and the DJ, although the latter was only on the premises because he got too wasted last night and had to crash in the back."

Trez gave Butch a no-thanks and turned to Xhex. "I don't think we've ever been closed on a Thursday night."

"Firsts come when you least expect them."

"Is the snow really that bad?"

"See for yourself."

As she nodded to one of the eight paned floor-to-ceiling windows, Trez used that as an excuse to break away from the conversation and begin his graceful exit from the room and the household at large. It wasn't that he didn't love the Brothers. It was just, in this post-migraine tenderzone, all the talk and the laughter, the smacking of pool balls, the J. Cole and Kendrick Lamar, were over his limit.

Picking a window that was closest to the archway back into the foyer, he moved the curtain aside and looked out into the courtyard—or what little he could visualize of it. The snow was coming down so hard he could barely see two feet past the mansion, and clearly it had been falling for a while like this. In the security lights, it was as if a heavy white tarp had been thrown over everything, the contours of the rooftop of the Pit, the great pines of the mountain, the cars parked on the far side of the fountain, filed down by a foot of what had come from the sky—

At first, the figure didn't register, its white robe and hood indistinguishable from the white-out landscape. But then he recognized a hole in the pattern of snow gusts, the swirling cascade moving around a figure.

Who was staring at him.

In a cold rush, all the blood left his head.

"Selena?" he whispered. "Is that—"

"It's the wrong time of year for this kind of storm," Xhex murmured by his side.

Trez jumped so high, he nearly hit the ceiling. And immediately, he looked back out through the glass.

The figure was gone.

"Trez?"

At that moment, the bell at the vestibule rang. Trez turned and ran out of the billiards room, hitting the heavy door, cranking it open—

The Chosen Layla reared back, the white hood she'd pulled over her head falling off her blond hair, her white robing dropping all kinds of snow at her feet.

"I'm allowed to be here," she said as she put her palms out like he was going to point a gun at her. "I'm permitted. Ask the King."

Trez sagged in his own skin and closed his eyes for a second. "No, yeah, no . . . of course. C'mon in."

As he stepped aside, he didn't know why she'd be so defensive—or why she'd be out on a night like tonight. But he didn't dwell on any of that.

He was a little too distracted copping to the fact that when he'd seen her out there . . . he'd immediately assumed that it was his Selena, come to see him, back from the dead.

Which was crazy. Really fucking nuts.

I'm not sure how giving you contact with that female is going to help either one of us.

"Oh, shut up—" he muttered.

"I beg your pardon?" the Chosen Layla asked.

"Shit, sorry." He scrubbed his face. "I'm talking to myself."

Yeah, because he wasn't going insane or anything. Not at all. Nah.

For the love of God, he needed to pull himself together before he crazied himself right off the planet.

THIRTY-FIVE

As Layla entered the mansion and looked around the foyer, she marveled at how fast what had been home now felt unfamiliar: After all the time she'd spent at the Brotherhood's estate, she knew its rooms and elevations, its people and rhythms, as well as she did those of the Sanctuary. Now, however, as Trez left her and she regarded the resplendent foyer with its multi-colored columns and crackling fire and twinkling crystal sconces, it seemed to her as though she were standing in a museum or a palace she had never visited before.

Then again, home implied you were welcome. And she really wasn't anymore.

"Yay! You're here!"

As Beth came across from the dining room and gave her a big hug, Layla was so happy to see a smiling face.

"Did you get my pictures?" the Queen asked.

"I didn't have my phone, but I can't wait to see them."

What Layla really wanted to say was that she couldn't wait to see her young. She didn't care about photos, she wanted the real thing and *now*—except she didn't want to be rude, and she certainly wasn't going up to the second floor without an invitation. God only knew where Qhuinn was—

Right on cue, as if the universe were determined to put them in the same space, Qhuinn appeared at the head of the grand staircase. And dearest Virgin Scribe, he was dressed for war, his body wrapped in black leather, his weapons strapped on his chest and his hips, his lean face a study in aggression.

Instantly, he looked at her, and his eyes narrowed like he was assessing a target. And then he came down the red carpeted steps like he was on a mission.

Beth immediately stiffened, and Layla moved back, in case he was going on the attack, her back bumping into the carved wood of the vestibule's inside door. But instead of rushing at her, Qhuinn just kept going, stalking into the dining room, his shitkickers punching into the floor.

Even after he had departed, it was like he'd left flaming footprints in his wake, his fury lingering like a bad smell.

This was not good for the young, Layla thought as she brought a trembling hand to her hair. The two of them had to do something about this breakdown in their relationship, but she feared that although she'd like to imagine Qhuinn softening with time, she had a feeling he wasn't going to.

"Come on," Beth said quietly. "Let's go upstairs."

Layla nodded and fell in behind the Queen. The fact that she was being escorted to the second floor was not lost on her, but with each step up, her heart leapt with anticipation that she was going see Rhamp and Lyric. It also sank with sadness, however. As a sense of alienation dogged her, she reflected that another era of her life had ended almost before it had begun: She had not realized that, even in the midst of her guilt and anxiety over Xcor, she had had a happiness here with the young—as well as expectations of raising them with Nalla, L.W., and Bitty.

All that was over now.

But, she reminded herself, what was left to hang onto was the fact that she could at least see her own young. That had not been a foregone conclusion before Wrath's decision.

When they reached the top, Layla lost her stride at the sight of the closed doors to Wrath's study, and she had to gather herself so she could proceed onward to the hall of statues. Halfway down that corridor, she hesitated again, but this time, it was for Beth to open the door to the room that Layla had once thought of as her own—and in the split second that took, she dimly noted that down on the floor there was a folded, paint-spotted drop cloth next to some paint cans, a drywall bucket, and some brushes. Her stomach clenched as she guessed what they were for.

The bullet holes in the wall.

But then the way was clear and she was running across to the bassinets.

"My loves! My loves!" Eyes full of tears, she didn't know who to focus on first, her head going back and forth and back and forth. "*Mahmen* is here!"

Some paranoid part of her worried that they would have forgotten her already, or perhaps become angry, even in their infant states, that she might have deserted them of her free will—which she had certainly not. She needn't have worried, however. At the sound of her voice, both sets of eyes opened and arms started to pinwheel. Bending down, she took the hold from her hair and let its weight cascade around Lyric first, and then Rhamp.

As her young cooed and reacted to her scent and voice, she felt a joy race through her, her chest swelling with love, all of her worries briefly ceding to a happiness that was undimmed by anything worldly.

"They are so happy to see their *mahmen*."

Layla looked over her shoulder at the female voice. "Cormia!"

She was indeed very well pleased to see the other Chosen, and the two embraced tightly. Then they stepped apart and Beth spoke up.

"We have everything ready up in the Sanctuary."

Cormia nodded. "I have just returned from taking supplies to the private quarters and I believe you'll find everything you need. I was wondering if you'd like me to help you get one of them up there so you don't have to make two trips?"

"Oh, that would be wonderful. Thank you." Layla gave into a compulsion to smooth her white robing, her reliance on the kindness of the other females making her teary. "I . . . ah, I am very grateful for your help. Perhaps you will take Rhamp?"

"Absolutely!"

As Cormia gathered her son, Layla picked up Lyric and held the warm, vital young to her heart. "Shall we?"

Right before she dematerialized with the other Chosen, she glanced into the far corner of the room . . . to those bullet holes up so close to the ceiling. She was willing to bet they were going to be gone by the time she returned twenty-four hours from now.

They would not be forgotten, however.

Closing her eyes, she tried to remember the last time she had gone up to the Sanctuary. Oh, indeed.

It had been a month ago . . . when she had found out who Xcor's father was.

Annnnnd she had his scent on her, too.

As Qhuinn marched through the dining room, he was furious, but at the same time, not at all surprised: Wrath had given Xcor a free pass, and Layla had been in the outside world for twenty minutes, so yes, of course, the pair of them had met up. Probably banged all day.

Meanwhile, her kids were here without their mother.

"Hope you had a great frickin' time, sweetheart," he muttered as he stormed along.

The door to the garage was in the way back of the house, on the far side of even the mudroom, and he had to go *doggen* dodging through the kitchen to get there. He was halfway to goal when, hey, hey, what do you know, Tohr came in from the staff stairs.

Neither of them made eye contact. They both just continued onward, falling into line and entering the shallow room that was full of spare coats, snow boots, hats, and gloves. On the far side, Tohr opened the way into the unheated, barn-y garage beyond and then shut them in together.

The air was cold and dry and smelled vaguely of fertilizer and gasoline. And as the motion-activated lights came on, there was a whole lot of perfectly tidy and concrete going on, drums of birdseed and rock salt all lined up, the riding mowers parked in a row, Weed Eaters, hoes, and shovels hanging on racks. High above, the rafters were made of old wood, and sturdy as the mountain the house had been built on, and across the way, sixteen coffins were stacked one upon the next, as if they were nothing but moving boxes from U-Haul.

The fact that Tohr strode over and stood right by them seemed apt.

When the brother spoke, his voice was quiet, but deep as the lowest point in Hell. "I have no intention of letting this go."

No reason to define *this,* was there.

Qhuinn shook his head slowly. "Me, either."

"I don't know when Wrath turned into a fucking Millennial." Tohr started pacing around. "But maybe he should get off the throne and start sharing Snapchats about how everyone needs to forgive and get along. Throw a fucking bunny face on himself and do a guided meditation on unity. This is *insane.*"

The brother stopped and put his hand on one of the coffins, his jaw grinding hard and hollowing out his cheek.

Tohr shook his head. "Sometimes you have to take care of the King even if he doesn't want you to."

"I agree."

"Sometimes matters have to be taken into different hands."

"I totally fucking agree."

Tohr's navy blue eyes looked over. "The field is a very dangerous place."

Qhuinn flexed his hands into fists. "People get hurt out there all the time."

"*Lessers.* Humans. They can do a lot of damage even to trained fighters."

As Qhuinn nodded, he recognized that while they were coming at it from two completely different perspectives, they'd certainly arrived at the same damn place. Xcor was going to die out there while he was supposedly looking for his boys. Whether it was Qhuinn's bullet or Tohr's, the fucker was going down.

"Is this a race, though," Qhuinn interjected. "Like, the first to catch the bastard wins the prize of slaughtering him?"

"No. We work together and keep this between us. Whoever gets him presents him like a meal to be communally consumed."

As Tohr put his palm out, Qhuinn grasped it without hesitation. "Deal."

The other brother nodded as they released their palms and dropped their arms. "Let's go, then," Tohr said. "He'll be searching for his fighters even though it's snowing badly because he's going to want to gather his troops ASAP. We'll find him somewhere in the field tonight."

With the plan in place, the pair of them headed back for the mudroom and geared up with white-on-white parkas. Then they exited the mansion through a side door that led out into the rear garden. Or tried to. The second they opened the panels, they were both slammed in the face with the kind of sleet and snow that made lesser mortals seek fireplaces and hot toddies. But fuck comfort.

They were going to take care of this situation, and keep the solution to themselves.

No one had to know one goddamn thing about this.

THIRTY-SIX

cor waited until he sensed Layla had fully dematerialized away from the ranch, and then he went on a search mission of the little house, quickly moving through all the closets and drawers and possible hiding places in the bedrooms. His assumption was that if the Brothers ever stayed here, they would keep weapons where they slept—but ultimately, he found nothing.

Frustrating.

He did locate adequate outerwear for himself, however. There was a coat closet on the way to the door out into the garage, and therein he found a parka and snow pants that were big enough to fit him, as well as a pair of ski gloves and a skullcap. Unfortunately, they were all black, and in the snow, they were going to make him stand out like a sparkler in the pitch dark—but beggars, choosers, and all that.

There was, however, something else in there that made up for the potentially dangerous eye-catch of it all.

After gearing up, he headed out into the garage, to the Range Rover in which they had evac'd from the forest the night before. The SUV looked as if it had been through a salt bath, great white streaks all down its sides and up its front grille and hood. No keys, and he wasn't surprised. Vishous would have taken them with him.

The vehicle was unlocked, however, and what he was hoping to find turned out to be in its back compartment: From an emergency box, he took three red flares, and tucked them into the parka, securing them by zipping up the front of the puffy jacket.

And then he went back inside, engaged the security system, and quickly departed through the slider in the kitchen. He didn't expect Layla to come back during the night, but in the event that she did return, he wanted her in a house that had been at least nominally secured. Further, he had no way to lock up the place behind himself, assuming he wanted to reenter and spend the day here.

Which he wasn't sure would be the case.

Out on the porch, the weather conspired a great assault against him, the snow falling in heavy bands that came with blustery winds, as if there were storms within the storm. Visibility was poor, and he was willing to bet there would be few humans out. This would work in his favor.

Closing his eyes, he dematerialized . . .

. . . and re-formed in a neighborhood about fifteen miles to the southwest.

As he came into his corporeal body once more, he was in a cul-de-sac of two-story colonials, the houses at a more expensive price point than the ranch, but very far from mansion status. All around, there were lots of lights on, whether it was in living rooms or bedrooms, on garage corners or in trees, but with the thickly descending flakes, the illuminations were isolated, carrying not far at all.

Leaning into the wind, he walked the rest of the way, his heavy boots shuffling powdery snow out of his path, his hearing going in and out of acuity depending on the direction of the gusts. The specific property he was after was in the back, and like the others, it too had lights on inside. Stopping out in front, he watched through the windows as a lanky human male, of some fifteen or sixteen years, strode into the sitting room and said something to a middle-aged human female who was sitting before a lit hearth and talking on a cell phone.

Xcor went up the pathway that was no pathway at all, the snow falling with such density that no one was attempting to plow or shovel prior to the storm's cessation. When he got to the front door, on which an ever-green wreath had been affixed, he reached out and tried the brass handle.

It was unlocked, so he opened things up and walked right in.

Everything went in slow motion in the sitting room. The young male looked over his shoulder, and then leapt back in alarm. The older female jumped to her feet, whatever hot beverage she had been consuming from a mug going flying.

Xcor shut the door as the son took cover behind the mother.

Coward.

And yet he felt a stab of some emotion he did not wish to entertain as the mother shoved the boy further to the rear of her, even though he was taller than her and probably a little stronger.

"Wh-what . . . what do you want?" she asked.

As a strand of brown hair flopped in her face, she blew it out of her eyes; her hands were too busy holding her son in relative safety.

"There's—" Her voice squeaked. "My purse is in the kitchen on the counter. Take what you want, there's . . . I have jewelry, upstairs. Just please . . . don't hurt us."

Xcor regarded the high color in her cheeks and her trembling form from what felt like a vast distance. Then he glanced around. The furniture had changed since he and his bastards had stayed under this roof, the sectional sofa gone along with the perpetual layers of pizza boxes and duffel bags, weapons and ammunition, boots and knives.

"I have not come for your money," Xcor said in a low voice.

She closed her eyes briefly, her face abruptly going white.

"Nor have I come for you." Xcor held up his palm because he knew they would both focus on it. "I am not a defiler of females or young."

As the eyes of the humans locked on what he had raised, he went into their brains and froze everything about them, such that all they did was blink and breathe. Meanwhile, down on the floor, the cell phone, which the mother had dropped, was still engaged, a panicked voice coming out of a tiny little speaker and demanding someone answer.

'Twas a good guess that talking to a vampire would not assuage who-ever it was of their fear.

Leaving the human who was getting worked up to their exercise for the evening, Xcor stomped both of his boots on the mat to get most of the snow off of them, then took the stairs two at a time. Up at the top, he went into the master suite, which had been nicely redecorated in an elegant white and blue scheme.

No more hideous ruffles and frills. And gone, too, were the rosebuds that had peppered the pink bathroom.

However offensive to the eye it had all once been, he spent no time appreciating the improvements in decor. He proceeded directly to the tall, narrow closet beside the shower where the towels would have been kept had he had any when he had stayed here—

Oh, of course, now the shelves were filled with precisely folded, bright white terry-cloth stacks.

Dropping down on his knees, he pulled out cleaning supplies at the bottom, exposing the tile floor that, blessedly, the homeowner had left as was. The panel he had previously created was one foot by one foot and all the way in the back, and he had to strip off his gloves to locate the lip and free the thing with his fingertips. Then he stretched his arm out and dipped his hand into the hidden space.

The pair of semiautomatic forties were exactly where he had left them.

So, too, the box of ammunition.

Xcor replaced the top of the secret compartment only because it made the amount of mental shit he had to tidy up in those humans downstairs a little less.

Leaving the bathroom, he strode by the bed, and then paused in the doorway. Glancing back, he thought of the time he and his males had spent in the house.

And was surprised by how much he wanted to see them again.

The descent took no time at all, and then he was back on the first floor with the mother and son. They were still standing together, the female shielding what she loved and sought to protect with the very body she had brought it forth unto this world with.

He delved into their minds once again. "You heard a noise. You went outside to check. It was nothing. When you returned, your wet boots left water on this mat. Odd night. Probably the wind. Good thing it was nothing."

Xcor dematerialized outside, and he stood for a moment to watch them reawaken, the pair of them looking at each other like they couldn't figure out why their hands were clutched together. And then the mother reached up to her temple and rubbed at it as if her head hurt, and the young male glanced around and cracked his neck.

They both looked toward the door.

As the female bent over and picked up the phone, Xcor took himself on his way once more.

The Sanctuary was indeed a sacred place of peace and tranquility, and as Layla sat out by the Scribe Virgin's fountain with both of her young, she took a deep breath. The three of them were arranged on a soft, thick blanket, and the temperature was perfect, the air as gentle and warm as bath water. Overhead, the milky white sky was bright, but not glaring, and the white marble of the courtyard glowed as if from within.

Lyric and Rhamp had made the trip like champs, and Cormia, as if sensing that Layla wanted some private time with them, had departed readily once the twins were settled out here by the sparkling water and the blooming tree that was full of new songbirds.

Tucking her feet under her, she dangled a yellow tulip over one young and then the other . . . and then she brought it back to the first.

"Isn't this beautiful? Tulip . . . this is a tulip."

Indeed, the petals were as the green grass and the blue water were: resplendent and mysteriously jewel-like in their coloring. It was something about the light here, the way it came from nowhere and fell with no particular angle—or mayhap there was some sort of sacred magic at work.

And it was funny. She could tell that her precious ones were gathering strength from the energy herein, their cheeks growing pink, their eyes shining with an extra healthy brightness, their movements more coordinated.

Yes, she thought. They had her blood in them for sure. Even Rhamp, who looked so much like Qhuinn it was eerie, was very obviously her son. Members of the Chosen always did better when they came here to recharge.

So maybe this was a good thing—

A strange sense that she was being watched made her twist around. But there was no one in the colonnade, and nobody in the open archway into what had been the Scribe Virgin's private quarters. No one anywhere, as it were.

She remembered when things had been so very different, when Chosen had borne and raised the next generations of Chosen and Brothers here and had served the Scribe Virgin, adhering to her schedule of worship and rest and celebration. There had been joy and happiness, purpose and fulfillment—although there had been such sacrifices.

And no color. Anywhere.

Layla reached out and stroked Lyric's soft cheek. Much as she still revered the Scribe Virgin and the traditions that had been so valued and respected, she was glad that her daughter would not be forced into a role that had no way out and was solely in service of others.

Yes, as much as she missed the old days and the old ways, and as sad as she was to have this marvelous place so empty and lifeless, she had no regrets.

She was of the generation who knew both servitude and liberation, and the latter was certainly not without its difficulties and tragedies. But at least now she had a sense of who she was as an individual, and she had desires that were her own and unlegislated by anyone else. She also had two young who were going to be free to choose who they wanted to be and where they wanted to go in life.

It was always better to follow a bumpy course of one's own than a smooth but intractable trail set by another.

The former was harder, yet far more vital. The latter was like a living death . . . except you didn't know you were dying because you were in a coma.

THIRTY-SEVEN

As Vishous pounded down the underground tunnel away from the training center, he approached the door that led up into the mansion . . . and kept right on going. The Pit, which was the aptly named carriage house where he and Butch stayed with their *shellans*, was another two hundred yards up, its subterranean entrance exactly the same as the big house's, all kinds of codes and locks preventing people who weren't supposed to be getting in or out from getting in or out.

After punching in the correct sequence on a keypad, the deadbolt sprang loose, and then it was home sweet home.

The layout was a not-much, just a living room in front with a galley kitchen off to the side, and a short hallway that led to two bedrooms lined up back to back. He and Jane had the first one, Butch, Marissa, and the cop's wardrobe had the second—although there wasn't enough room for all those goddamn clothes. In the cramped corridor, there were rolling stands full of suits and shirts on hangers. Also a row of shoes on the floorboards that, as far as V could tell, were the same fucking loafer, just in different leathers and skins with different hardware.

Motherfucker was in a serious rut with the footwear. Then again, how much could you really do with a men's shoe?

As V shut the door behind him, he stalled out by the racks of Canali and Tom Ford. Everything was quiet, Marissa at Safe Place, Butch playing pool back at the big house, and Jane . . .

With a curse, V headed for the kitchen. The Grey Goose bottles were right where he liked them, under the counter next to the deep drawer where Butch kept the Fritos, the Parmesan Goldfish, and the Milanos.

Those were the only snacks the guy ever ate.

Funny, it hadn't dawned on V before now, but Butch was a rut kind of guy. He liked what he liked, and wasn't interested in innovation.

SOB would probably faint if you offered him a bagel chip. And forget about multi-grain crackers or foofy melba toast.

Old school, the cop was, and even though V would never say it, it was part of why he loved his best friend. When you were a couple of centuries old, you learned that the more things changed, the more they stayed the same. So yeah, sure, you could waste a lot of time and taste buds trying to re-create a new version of what was already working, but that was grossly inefficient: There was, quite literally, a maximum amount of happiness that could come from a snack cracker or finger food. Wading through a bunch of shit that didn't quite make it, just so you could go back to what you'd liked in the first place, was a human move.

Shit, you could see it all over their culture, from "fashion," which was simply a reactive, fifteen-minutes-of-fame carousel of ugliness from season to season, to entertainment where you ended up with great swaths of the same, to technology and all its planned obsolescences and needless innovation.

Which culminated in Apple saying it was "courageous" for doing away with a headphone jack. In its dumb-ass cell phone.

Yeah, real Purple Heart stuff there, boys. Presidential Medal of Freedom. Maybe they were going to put themselves on a stamp, once they bought the American government.

Opening a cabinet, V took out a tumbler, filled it full of ice . . . and then went to the top rim with vodka.

You want courage? he thought. How about you do away with yourselves, humans. There was a plan.

Not that he was bitter or anything.

Nah.

Over at his desk, he sat down in front of his bank of PCs, eased back in his ass palace, and one by one, signed into all his computers.

It had been a long time since he'd had a night off to himself, and as he checked in with his security cameras, and monitored the Brotherhood's various properties in and around Caldwell, he was reminded of why.

The last thing in the world he wanted to do was sit here like a fucking loser with his Lenovos and his Goose, all alone while everybody else was doing their thing.

But his brain was still scrambled from all the Xcor shit. He was also bone-tired—but didn't want to sleep. He needed to feed—and had no interest in taking a vein. He had to eat—and wasn't hungry. He wanted to get drunk—and that wasn't happening fast enough.

Pushing back in the chair, he focused on getting the alcohol into his bloodstream, taking big swallows that singed his throat and swirled in his gut.

As he started to make progress on his goal, he thought about Jane just now in her clinic. How when he'd gone to see her, she'd been knee-deep in crisis, Assail screaming in that room of his, Manny asking her questions about something, Ehlena coming to her with a drug order issue.

V had stood on the periphery and admired his mate's purpose. And commitment. And passion.

God, Assail.

Those screams were something else, a reminder that addiction was nothing to fuck around with. Sure, you started down a chemical highway just so you could keep yourself in your life. But the next thing you knew, you were in a rubber room—literally—in restraints because you had tried to tear your own face off with your fingernails.

By the way, pass the vodka.

Reaching across his desk, he grabbed his bottle and pulled a refill. The ice was getting low in his glass, but after this load, he wasn't going to care that the shit was room temperature.

At least Assail had his Jane on the job, and she sure as hell was trying to give him the best treatment in his withdrawal she could. The question was whether the psychosis would ever lift. It had been a month since the male had last shoved white powder up his nose, so he might just be a wasteland in the aftermath. Sometimes that happened with vampires and the coke.

'Course, the former dealer probably hadn't known that when he'd started doing so much of the shit. But there were a lot of times in life when you were dancing with the devil and had no idea evil was your partner. And you didn't find out until it was too late.

That was how destiny worked. Curses, too.

As V took another slug of numb-in-a-bottle, he found himself thinking about that hot chocolate again, the stuff he'd served Jane way back in the beginning. Or rather . . . way back in the first of their endings.

He'd always assumed that the last finale they had would come when he died. But as he sat here in an empty house, and tried to recall the last time they'd spent any meaningful group of hours together . . . he had to wonder.

Payback was a whiner, he supposed. When he and his brothers were out in the field, fighting for the race, they weren't thinking about all the mates and females who were holding down the fort back at home. They were just trying to do their job and stay alive.

The same was true down in that clinic. Jane wasn't thinking about him right now. She was working with Manny to salvage what was left of Assail's brain. She was helping Qhuinn's brother Luchas regain mobility and mental health after horrible abuse at the hands of the Lessening Society. Every night, she handled all manner of injuries, from the chronic to the acute, from the Band-Aid to the life threatening, with tireless focus and devotion to her patients.

So it wasn't that he didn't get it.

And it wasn't that he didn't love her. Shit, she was smart. She was tough. She was . . . probably the only female he had ever met that he would consider his equal—and no, that wasn't a misogynistic statement. He didn't think any males were his equal, either.

Which was what happened when you were the son of a deity, he supposed.

He absolutely could not see himself with anyone else but his Jane. The trouble was, he was devoted to the war. She was devoted to her job. And in the beginning, when everything was new and fresh and the impetus to be with each other had been an itch that had to be scratched or they would go mad, they had made the time.

Now?

Not so much.

But it was fine, he thought as he sat forward and refocused on the lineup of monitors. Neither one of them was going anywhere.

It was just . . . he was beginning to worry the same was true of their relationship.

A sudden image of Layla putting her body in front of Xcor and shielding his dying flesh with everything she had, popped into his head and wouldn't leave. Jesus, in that moment, she would have taken a bullet for the motherfucker. A dumb move, sure, and one she would have regretted the instant she thought about her young . . . but in that split second, she had been motivated by love.

And Xcor, in turn, had meant what he'd said when he'd begged for her to be sent away before he was killed. That bastard had been dead fucking serious . . . and really fucking in love.

V frowned as he realized that that sonofabitch and he had something in common, didn't they. They'd both been through the Bloodletter's war camp.

Dollars to nut sacs, they'd lost their virginity in the same way.

So, yeah, maybe they should get a set of bestie tattoos or some shit.

"For fuck's sake . . ."

More with the Grey Goose . . . until he needed a second refill. And he forced himself to get out of his head and focus on the images on the screens in front of him, all those interior and exterior shots of various rooms, whether it was the Audience House, that little ranch Layla and Xcor were love-shacking in, the other three homes they owned in Caldie, Sal's Restaurant, or the mansion and its grounds.

Only the mansion was showing signs of life. The other places were shut down because of "Snowmageddon," as the reporters were calling it.

As he watched his brothers play pool and laugh, he noticed that the vast majority of them had their *shellans* by their sides. The females of the household all had their separate, independent existences, but on a night like tonight, when their males were off the clock of the war, they made spending time with their loves a priority.

"Yeah, and I'm here with the Goose," he muttered as he took another drink. "Not half bad . . ."

Unfortunately, his mind remained stubbornly, unacceptably, clear. And that meant he was being triggered by too much, his emotions getting a disproportionate amount of airtime.

Which was to say they were on his radar screen at all.

He hated feeling anything, true?

Trying to engage his gray matter in something, anything else, he fired up the Internet and decided to monitor some of the human news outlets. That was always worth a laugh. The shit those motherfuckers could get themselves worked up over was just incredible—and then inevitably they ended up yelling at each other through their computers.

Truth was nuanced. Hysteria anything but.

After idling through CNN.com, Fox News, and TMZ.com, he ended up on YouTube watching McKamey Manor videos, which was one of his absolutely favorite things to do, and which did, as usual, cheer him up a little. And it was after about a half hour of that when a notification flared on the bottom of the screen, indicating an email had come through to him.

With a frown, he went over to Outlook and opened the thing up.

Well, well, well, good ol' Damn Stoker had posted something new.

V smiled and swallowed another healthy load of Goose as he hopped on the blog that he'd been following for the last month. It was new on the paranormal scene, written by a guy who seemed to be a cross between an investigative reporter and a fang fucker.

I.e., a human who was determined to prove the existence of vampires.

They were so amusing to watch as they twisted and turned at the end of their lexicon of falsities, repeating all kinds of lies and bullshit that humans had been using to mythologize that which actually existed in their midst.

Good times, good times.

Talk about YouTube vids. There were only about a hundred thousand snippets, sound bites, and soliloquies on that Internet platform purporting to show actual vampires vampiring in their vampware. Driving Vamps-wagons—

Okay, it was possible the alcohol was kicking in.

But Damn Stoker was different, and that was why V had tagged the motherfucker's not-so-rambling ramblings.

He actually had the goods.

Somehow, the guy had gotten video of the showdown out at the Brownswick School for Girls, the one where the Lessening Society and the Brotherhood had met and danced in the moonlight, so to speak. It was your typical, jumpy-jerky iCrap-shot footage, but there was enough to suggest that something big and otherworldly might have happened on the abandoned campus.

Fortunately, the Omega had done a stellar clean-up job after the fighting, and what the recording showed was nothing that couldn't arguably have been generated on someone's computer. *Lesser* blood on the ground, after all, looked like shadows thrown on grass or black paint or old motor oil.

Good thing it wasn't Smell-O-Vision or bitch would have been making people sick.

And of course, the fact that there was nothing presently on the grounds was a big invalidator, that little storage house Rhage's beast had eaten having been ready to collapse anyway, just like a lot of the facilities there.

Still, this guy who was hiding behind a not-so-clever alias was on V's radar. He'd posted a lot of links to other content on YouTube, mostly blah-blah-blahs of other humans who swore up and down that they had had contact with "real" vampires or, again, more of those bumpy, night footage clips of fights or figures moving in and out of doorways wearing capes. But again, it was the shit from that abandoned school campus that was a marker—and also the fact that the guy's grammar was good, he didn't overuse caps or do this !!!!!!!!!!!!! at the end of his sentences, and there was a general professionalism to it all.

None of which was the kind of thing the race needed.

Ridic humans with artificial incisors and walking sticks with skulls on them? Fine. Give V a hundred million of those. A canny, more-Scully-than-Mulder type who seemed to be systematically scouring the Internet and debunking the bunk while isolating those few instances when something had actually happened?

Not good news for a species that wanted to keep hiding in plain sight.

"Another video . . ." V murmured as he scanned the new post. "What do we have tonight, Damn? Wrong season for Halloween."

V bypassed the write-up that gave context to whatever was on the link, and just fired the thing up.

At first, he wasn't sure what he was looking at—oh, okay, black-and-white security cam footage of a parking lot at night. Car entering and turning around . . . parking, but not turning its engine off going by the subtle puffs of condensation out the back.

V took another draw off his glass and patted around his desk for a hand-rolled. No luck. He needed to—

"Oh . . . hello there, Mr. Latimer."

As both doors opened, he recognized the male who emerged from the passenger side. It was Trez. And well, well, well . . . a female got out from behind the wheel, one with dark hair and civilian clothes. Impossible to see the face as she was looking down like she was trying not to slip on the ice, but the body was good.

Maybe the poor SOB was drowning his sorrows the old-fashioned way.

Trez walked around the car, and met her in front. The two of them talked for a minute—

"*Shit.*"

V shook his head and then squeezed the bridge of his nose. Then he hit *pause*, went back a little, and replayed things.

The female just up and disappeared, dematerializing into thin air. And then Trez got behind the wheel and drove off like nothing had happened.

V scrolled up and read the bumph that Damn had posted: local souvenir shop across from the Storytown—which was, if memory served, a mere half mile down from Sal's Restaurant. The footage was the property of the shop, of course, but the owner had forwarded it to Damn with permission to post. No authorities had been contacted, and there was a statement from the owner, in full quotes like this was a newspaper article, that "Nothing has been altered on the recording."

Vishous watched the clip two or three more times, and told himself to chill. What the hell was someone going to do with this? Go to the local CBS station and get them to air it as an exposé? It didn't really prove anything—other than the fact that sex was an effective, short-term painkiller when it came to the grieving process.

No one was going to believe the vid hadn't been spliced.

It was fine.

But Damn was starting to be a pain in the ass: Twice in one month, some human managed to post videos that actually showed shit going down?

Sometimes, yes, conspiracy theorists got it right.

And when they did that too many times in a row, they had to be contained, true?

THIRTY-EIGHT

The next location Xcor dematerialized to was not inhabited. Indeed, the little cottage and larger farmhouse beyond was a property that was well outside of Caldwell, and as he reformed in the blowing snow, he was not surprised that there were no lights on, no fires burning, no figures in any windows in either abode.

As he plodded forth, he passed by the cottage and entered the tree line, which, blessedly, offered him some relief from the driving wind. He had purchased both structures and the plot of land upon which they had been built for Layla and him. Indeed, he had had some fantasy—one that he had ne'er vocalized nor even much acknowledged unto himself— that the pair of them could shelter in the little cottage with its charm and its coziness whilst his males bunked down in the farmhouse across the way.

Indeed, she had visited him here a couple of times, back when she had been heavy with her young and so resplendently beautiful, and he had found it nearly impossible not to express things that he had had no business feeling much less speaking of. And then she had called him on exactly where his emotions had evolved to, providing him with a crushingly accurate picture of the weakness he possessed in her favor.

He had sent her away at that point. Said cruel things he had not meant because it had been the only manner by which to get her to leave him alone. Some warrior he had been. A coward for her was more like it. But he had not been able to see any future for them, and he had begun to worry about her safety being so pregnant . . . and more than both of those, he had been terrified that she read him so well.

Terrified at the power she held over him.

Thus she had left. And then he had been captured.

And now they had this little eye of the hurricane, this tiny peaceful stretch that was going to end as soon as he found what he was seeking.

The farmhouse was boarded up on the first floor, all of the glass covered with plywood that had been tacked into place with nails his bastards had cheerfully struck. The front door was unlocked, however, and as he pushed it wide, the creak was so loud it drowned out even the storm's relentless growl.

They had deliberately left the hinges un-oiled, the cheapest alarm system there was.

His eyes adjusted to the darkness. The rooms had nothing in them except bare floorboards and cobwebs, but then his fighters had never cared for the trappings of civilization. Once one had survived the Bloodletter's war camp, one did not require even a roof over one's head. The lack of a dagger at your throat was sufficient.

Taking out one of the flares from inside his jacket, he removed its cap and struck it, the hissing red light illuminating a fat circle around him.

Xcor went through the downstairs rooms, his footfalls echoing in the empty, cold house. As he progressed, he held the flare out, inspecting all manner of walls and jambs and stretches of the floor.

It took him three trips, three circuits of parlor to study to dining room to 1940s kitchen and bath, before he saw it.

And he had to smile a little as he crouched down in the far corner of the parlor.

What had eventually caught his eye was a scrape across the floorboards, something easily missed—indeed, he had almost ignored it himself. But upon close examination, it clearly pointed in the direction of this eastern juncture of walls and a buildup of dust, sticks, and leaves.

So unassuming this collection of litter—as if someone had taken a broom and sought to tidy things up, only to lose interest prior to a dust-pan being found.

Angling the flare down to the floor, he brushed aside the debris and regarded the message that had been left for him.

"Good male," he murmured as he stared at the markings that had been carved in the wood.

To the unknown eye, it was naught but a random series of whittles and stabs. To him . . . it was a map of Caldwell that was built on both a previously agreed-upon compass orientation that was not based on true north, and an assortment of symbols that would not be recognized by anyone but the Band of Bastards.

Xcor had never learned to read. It was not a skill that served him in the Old Country nor in the war, and he was hard-pressed to think himself diminished because of its lacking. But he was stellar with directions, and he also had a photographic memory, something that had developed as a result of him needing to make sure he could recall as many details as he could whenever he was shown or described something.

He didn't bother to search for weapons. He had never planted any and they would have taken all they had with them.

Departing through the creaking door, he extinguished the flare by shoving it headfirst into the snow and then he closed his eyes, dematerialized . . .

. . . and re-formed in a wind tunnel.

The gusts were so brutal he had to turn away from them, and even with his back to the source, it was too much for him to withstand. But that was what you got when you were nearly a hundred floors up from street level in downtown Caldwell, at the top of the Caldwell Insurance Company building.

Proceeding with alacrity, he took shelter behind some HVAC blowers that were the size of ambulances, and from there, he was able to gather his orientation, which had to be from the east in order for him to interpret the directions appropriately.

Except there was a problem that quickly became evident. With so much snow falling, he couldn't see the grid pattern of streets well enough to find the location: Although there were some illuminated landmarks that gave him an idea of the city's layout, he was not going to be able to pinpoint anything from up here.

His only chance was to get down on ground level and work it out from there. The good news? His fighters would stay in on a night like tonight.

Like humans, even the slayers would not venture out into this mess. And his bastards had never cared much for the cold.

If they were still in Caldwell, he would find them this evening.

THIRTY-NINE

"What is in that book?"

The female voice that came over Throe's shoulder was that of a petulant child, even though it emerged from the luscious lips of a thirty-six-year-old vampire who had natural DD breasts, a stomach so flat he could have used it as a dinner plate, and a set of legs that were long enough to wrap twice around his waist.

Ordinarily, he would have enjoyed an interruption from the likes of her.

"Throe! I will *not* be ignored."

Not tonight.

As he straightened from the ancient tome he'd brought home from that psychic's, his back cracked, and he was annoyed to find that his neck was so stiff he couldn't look over his shoulder. Instead, he had to turn his entire torso to make eye contact.

"I am studying," he heard himself say.

Odd, he thought. It didn't feel as though he'd had a conscious thought to speak those particular words.

They were correct, however. He had indeed been studying what was written upon the parchment all day long and into the—was it night already? He felt as though he had just sat down.

"Forgive me." He cleared his throat. "But what time is it?"

"Nine o'clock! You promised me we would go out."

Yes, he recalled that. He had done so to get her off his back and into her *hellren's* bed at dawn in order that he should have privacy with the book.

Or The Book, as he had begun to think of it.

And she clearly had taken him at his word, her outfit one that was both revealing and expensive. Roberto Cavalli, given the animal print. And she had on enough gold Bulgari jewelry to make the eighties file a police report.

"Well?" she demanded. "When are you getting ready?"

Throe looked down at himself, an odd disassociation taking root as he noted that he had on pants, a shirt, and shoes. "I am dressed."

"In the same clothes you were wearing last night!"

"Indeed."

Throe shook his head a little and looked around. The guest room he recognized, and that was a bit of a relief. Yes, this was where he had been staying since that fire that had destroyed his previous mistress's *hellren's* mansion. A month he had spent in this navy blue and mahogany suite, with its grand canopied bed, its paintings of hunting scenes, and its high-boy and writing desk.

He had moved in here and promptly assumed a sexual relationship with this under-fucked female, much in the way he had done with his previous mistress: This one was, likewise, mated unto an older male who was incapable of servicing her in bed—and thus Throe, as a "gentlemale of fine bloodline," had been welcomed unto the household, held in esteem and sheltered without any end date.

Clearly, they knew not the gossip of where he had ended up with the Band of Bastards. Or they were aware of it and had low standards. In any event, it was unwritten that provided he took care of the *shellan*, he could expect his room, board, and wardrobe needs to be met nicely, and in this case—which had not been true in the previous one—he rather suspected that her mate knew and approved.

Perhaps the older male was aware that she would stray, and was afraid she would leave him entirely.

In the *glymera*, that would be an embarrassment one would not like to endure right before one's grave.

"Are you unwell?" she asked with a frown.

He turned back around slowly. He was seated at the writing desk, the one in between the two long windows with their regal drapes and their bubbly old glass. The mansion was large and rambling, filled with antiques and furnishings far, far too old and distinguished for the likes of its current chatelaine. And one could rather suspect that she would have preferred to be down at the Commodore, in a penthouse overlooking the river that was filled with white leather couches and Mapplethorpe reproductions.

She rather liked sex. And she was good at it—

"Throe. Seriously, like, what is the problem here?"

What had she asked him previously? Oh . . . right. And he had pivoted in this direction to regard himself in the mirrored upper doors of the desk.

Though the old glass's mercury backing was pitted and scratched, there was enough of a reflection to verify that, yes, he did look the same as he had before he'd gone unto that psychic's lair. Still with the thick, blond hair, and the classically handsome jaw, and the heavily lashed eyes that he used with quite a lot of success on the females.

He didn't feel the same, however.

Something had changed.

As a ripple of anxiety went through him, he put his palm on the open book, and instantly he was calmed, sure as if the tome were a drug. Like red smoke, perhaps. Or mayhap quite a lot of fine port.

What had they been discussing—

"Whatever, I'm going out without you." She pirouetted away in disapproval, her stilettos cursing their way over the carpet as she headed back for the exit. "If you're going to be basic, I'm not going to—"

Throe blinked and rubbed his eyes. Glancing around, he got to his feet, and then fell back down as his leg muscles cramped. On the second try, he managed to sustain both verticality and ambulation, although the latter was with a herky-jerky step as he went across the fine Oriental carpet to the door his lover had just walked through.

Opening the way out for himself, he wasn't quite sure what he was going to say to her, but there was no sense in propagating an argument. He was quite in need of her the now, this roof over his head and the sustenance in his belly necessary for him to be free to pursue his true ambitions.

Hooking a grip on the ornate jamb of his suite, he leaned into the finely appointed corridor and looked left and right. There was no sign of her, so he went down four doors and knocked softly. When there was no reply, he checked again to make sure there was no one else around, and then he entered her peach and cream boudoir.

There were several lights on. A couple of outfits strewn on the bed. A lingering whiff of her perfume.

"Corra?" he said. "Corra, my darling, I apologize."

He went into her huge white and cream bath. Over at the hair and makeup chair, there was all manner of Chanel compacts, tubes, pots, and brushes on the counter. But no Corra.

Throe left things as he had found them and returned to his room. Just as he was shutting his own door, his eyes happened to pass over the clock on the bureau—and he froze.

Ten o'clock. Actually, a little after.

Throe frowned and went across to the ormolu masterpiece. But proximity did not change the fact that the hands proclaimed the time to be ten.

Corra had just told him it was nine, however. Hadn't she?

Throe glanced over at The Book.

In the recesses of his mind, he noted that it was odd that although he had been reading for how many hours now—Fates, had it really been almost twenty-four?—he nonetheless hadn't made it past the first page he'd turned—

Throe felt a tricking sense of vertigo tease his mind with the impression that the world was spinning around him.

Stumbling over to the desk, he sat down in the hard chair again, his knees pressed together, his head bent, his eyes on the open tome.

Funny, he was unaware that he had made any conscious instruction unto his body to resume his position here—

Wait, what had he been—

Why was he—

Thoughts went in and out of his mind, moving as clouds across a vacant sky, nothing staying with him nor finding any traction at all. He had some consideration that he was hollowing out, that parts of him were being drained, but he was hard-pressed to say what exactly had departed from him or where it had gone.

For a moment, fear struck him and he looked away from The Book.

Rubbing his eyes so hard he made them water, he realized that he had no idea what he had read. All of those hours spent sitting before the open book . . . and he had no clue what had been printed on any of the pages.

He needed to close the cover and burn the thing.

Yes, that was what he would do. He would keep his eyes averted, not regard the pages, and slam the cover shut. After which, he would pick up the evil volume and carry it downstairs. There was a hearth constantly lit in the library and he would . . .

Throe's eyes returned to the parchment and the ink, a pair of dogs summoned by their master, coming to a heel.

And he focused on the symbols, on the text.

He opened his mouth. Closed it. Attempted to remember why he had gone looking for that psychic in the first place.

As his fear sharpened anew, he tried to force himself to concentrate on getting free—and indeed, he was reminded of those dreams one had from time to time, where one was awake, but stuck in a body that was frozen, a sense of rising panic causing one to struggle to wake up.

Moving a hand or a foot was often enough to pull oneself from the brink, and he sensed that now, if only he could have one solid, claiming conception, he could rescue himself from a peril he would otherwise ne'er escape.

Why had he gone to that psychic . . . what had been the impetus . . . what had he been after . . .

And then it came to him.

In a voice that didn't sound like his own, he said aloud, "I need an army. I need an army with which to defeat the King."

Something like a lightning bolt snapped o'erhead, and yes, an electrical current burst through him, bringing with it a clarity and a purpose that wiped away all of his previous confusion.

"I seek to defeat the King and assume power o'er both my race and the race of all the humans. I desire to be lord and master o'er all the earth and its inhabitants."

All at once, pages started flipping, the dry, dusty smell entering his nose and threatening to make him sneeze.

When the mad dash to whate'er stopped, he felt himself bending down, sure as if there were a hand on the back of his neck that was pushing his torso thus.

Abruptly . . . the words made sense.

And Throe began to smile.

FORTY

huinn moved through the falling snow as if he were one with the storm, his fury to rival the howling wind, his white-on-white dress camouflaging him in the drifts that were forming in the alleys of downtown. Beside him, Tohr was the same, a predator to match the landscape that seemed no longer urban, but arctic.

Gusts of flakes thick as smoke bombs swirled around them and hindered their progress down yet another block that was vacant of pedestrians and moving cars. It was so cold that the snow was light and fluffy, but the volume was tremendous, inches and inches adding up to feet on the ground. And still the shit came down.

He prayed to see a Bastard, any Bastard.

But especially the one they sought.

This was their best chance to catch Xcor in a solitary environment where they could make the assassination look like an ambush by the enemy . . . where they could take care of things properly. And the motherfucker was definitely out here, looking for his boys in spite of the storm.

As Qhuinn trudged along, his thigh muscles burned, and his front teeth hummed from the cold, and the heat his body was generating made him want to open the white parka. In the back of his mind, he was aware that he was pressing on with this treasonous plot not just because of a rightful revenge on the Bastard, but also because of everything he was escaping back home: Blay gone, Layla with the kids, Wrath and him at odds.

Staying out here all night on the hunt was a far better option than being stuck in the house—especially given that he had all day locked up under that roof to look forward to. Shit, he was going to go fucking insane with—

Up ahead, through the fog-like vista of snow, a black figure the size of a vampire warrior was revealed and then obscured as a squall rolled across an intersection they were about twenty yards away from.

Whatever it was, it was big, and it didn't belong.

And it stopped as soon as it noticed them, the wind battering at his and Tohr's backs clearly bringing their scent down to it.

At that moment, as if things were preordained, the gusts obligingly shifted . . . and carried the figure's olfactory Hello, My Name Is down to them.

"Xcor," Qhuinn whispered as he put his hand into all his Gore-Tex and locked a grip onto the butt of his forty.

"Good timing." Tohr likewise outed his weapon. "Perfect timing. Over before it begins."

Xcor gave them time to approach, and Qhuinn was damn sure the Bastard knew who it was.

Closer . . . closer range . . .

Qhuinn's heart started to pound, an excitement boiling up and frothing his emotions but not his head or his body: His arm remained steady and down by his side.

Closer . . .

Just as he lifted his gun, his phone went off against his chest, the vibration getting his attention—but not diverting him.

He and Tohr pulled their triggers at the same time—just as Xcor, being no fucking idiot, hit the ground.

With the storm raging, it was a chicken-and-egg situation, difficult to know what had come first, the duck or the impact of a bullet.

With his phone continuing to ring, Qhuinn and Tohr broke into a run, both pumping off rounds at where the Bastard had been standing as well as where he had fallen or landed while they charged forward through the driving snow.

"Sonofabitch," Qhuinn spat as they reached where Xcor had been.

The fucker had disappeared. And no scent of blood.

Had they missed entirely?

He and Tohr looked around, and then the brother said, "Rooftop."

The pair of them ghosted up out of the alley, to the top of the ten-story office building that was right in front of where the shooting had gone down. Nada. The visibility was so poor they couldn't even see down to the street below, and Xcor wasn't anywhere to be scented.

With the wind roaring in his ears even through the skullcap he'd pulled down tight, and his eyes watering from the cold, Qhuinn felt a frustration that went all the way to his marrow.

"He couldn't have gone far!" he yelled over the din.

"Fan out. I'll go—"

"Motherfucker!" Qhuinn felt his phone go off a second time. "Who the *fuck* is calling me!"

He jerked the zipper of his parka down and shoved his hand inside. Taking the fucking piece of shit out, he—

Immediately accepted the call. "Blay? Blay . . . ?"

He couldn't hear a thing and pointed to the alley below. As Tohr nodded, Qhuinn tried to focus—and a second later, dematerialized back to where they'd been.

Cupping his opposite hand over his free ear, he said, "Blay?"

His mate's voice was thin over the crackling connection. ". . . help."

"What?"

". . . the Northway? Exit . . ."

"Wait, what?"

". . . twenty-six . . ."

"Blay?"

And then one word came across loud and clear: "Accident."

"I'm coming!" Qhuinn looked at Tohr. "Right now!"

He wanted to keep the connection open, but there was a risk that the snow was going to cause his phone to malfunction and he might need it.

Tohr spoke up. "Let's fan out, I'll take the north—"

"No, no, Blay's in trouble. I have to go!"

There was a split second where they stared at each other. For Qhuinn, though, there was no question. Love versus vengeance.

And he would choose love.

Shit, he felt awful that Blay had been in an accident . . . but at least the male had called him: Blay had reached out when it counted, and fuck yeah, Qhuinn was going to go to where his heart was. Even if Xcor were bleeding from a chest wound and required only one last slug to put him in the Fade? Qhuinn was out of here.

Tohr, though, was another story.

Xcor could see the two Brothers from his vantage point on the rooftop across from where Qhuinn and Tohr were standing: Even with those white parkas, the gusts and snowfall shifted around their bodies, marking their outlines.

There had been a number of times during the course of Xcor's life when he could have sworn some outside force was determined to keep him alive.

Tonight had been another one of them.

Both of those guns had been pointed at him, and they had discharged at the same time, as if those Brothers shared a brain—or at least a set of trigger fingers. And yet somehow, he hadn't even needed the bulletproof vest that he'd strapped on before he'd shrugged into the black parka back at that ranch.

He blamed the wind.

Or credited, was more like it.

Even with him wearing the perfect target for clothes, and them being no more than fifteen yards away, those bullets had gone elsewhere.

And he hadn't wasted a heartbeat dematerializing away.

Thank Fates he tended to get more focused instead of less so when it was crunch time, and he'd also guessed right, thinking that their move would be to go up on exactly the rooftop they had. Which was why he'd proceeded to the shorter building behind where they'd tried to gun him down. His advantage wasn't going to last, however. They were going to fan out to find him so they could finish the job.

And this assassination attempt meant one of two things. The pair of them were either going rogue from the King . . . or Wrath had lied about his own intentions and all of the Brotherhood was out here looking for him.

The male had seemed sincere, but who could tell?

And who could argue with those forties—

As Tohr and Qhuinn dematerialized, Xcor crouched down and ghosted out himself, on the theory that a moving target was harder to hit.

He re-formed three blocks to the west on a tenement. And as he resumed his corporeal body, he triangulated his location vis-à-vis that map on those floorboards at the farmhouse. He was close, so close, to the location that had been illustrated.

And there was no better place to be than with his fighters if he were being hunted.

Traveling from rooftop to rooftop, he was reminded of his time in the trees, way back before the Bloodletter had come unto him in that forest. Indeed, he might well have to fall once more upon his thieving skills, depending on how all this went over time.

He had little ammunition and no money—and that was a problem requiring a solution. But he was getting ahead of himself.

On that note, he transitioned down to an alleyway that was narrow and dark as the inside of his skull. The wind could not reach into this crevice created between the brick buildings, and snow had built up in great drifts at both ends with a lagging in the middle. He stuck to one side, crouching and shuffling quickly past inset doorways and the occasional Dumpster.

He knew he had the right entrance when he saw three deep stab marks in the upper right-hand corner of the doorjamb—and when he tried the battered old knob, he didn't expect it to turn. It did.

Glancing left and right, and then checking up above, he pushed his shoulders into the panels and shifted his body indoors.

As he shut himself in, he didn't say a word. His scent would announce his presence—just as the scents that greeted his nose told him that his males had been here very recently. Within hours.

This was where they were staying.

With boarded-up windows and that door closed, he decided to take a chance and light the second of the flares. As that red, fluttering light exploded from the tip, he moved the stick around slowly.

It was an abandoned restaurant kitchen, all kinds of utensils and old pans, crates, and plastic buckets covered with a thick dust. There were signs of his males' inhabitation, however, vacant places against the walls where large bodies had stretched out for rest.

The Domino's boxes made him smile. They always liked their pizza.

After he had gone through the entire kitchen, and then proceeded out to the restaurant in front, finding the latter similarly boarded up, disordered, and empty, he returned to the door he had entered through.

And slipped back out into the storm.

FORTY-ONE

t had been a good plan.

And as with all good plans that eventually went into the crap-
per, things had started out okay: Blay had taken the wheel of his
pop's new Volvo sedan, with his dad riding shotgun and his mom in the
back sitting against the door with her bad foot across the seat. Yeah, sure,
they'd had a little fun getting out of the driveway, but they'd made it to
the main road and even onto the Northway with no trouble.

Now, naturally, the highway was closed, but as it was New York State,
people had fucked that off and created a set of parallel tracks that ran
right down the center of the two lanes heading north. All you had to do
was bump your way into them and hold a steady pace as the windshield
in front of you turned into what Han Solo saw every time the Millennium Falcon went into hyperdrive.

So yup, all good in the beginning. They'd listened to old-school Gar-
rison Keillor, and sang along with his version of "Tell Me Why," and were
almost able to forget the fact that they were heading toward the long
exits, the ones where there was no way to get off for ten or fifteen or even
twenty miles at a stretch.

The turn for the worse came without preamble or a courtesy an-
nouncement that maybe they needed to call Houston with a problem.

They were going a modest thirty-five, sticking in the tracks, descending a rise . . . when the Volvo hit a stretch of ice that didn't agree with any of its tires, traction control, or four-wheel drive.

One minute they were going quite the thing, and the next, in slow motion, they were in a pirouette . . . and landing in a ditch.

Like, literally, a frickin' ditch.

Facing backward.

The good news, Blay supposed, was that he had been able to slow them down enough so the air bags had not gone off and pillowed him and his dad in the face. The bad news? The "ditch" was more like a giant ravine capable of swallowing Swedish cars whole.

The first thing Blay did was check on his mom, who had had to remain unrestrained. "How're we in the back?"

He was trying to remain casual, and he didn't take a breath until his mom flashed him the thumbs-up. "Well, that was exciting. And I'm just fine."

As his dad and *mahmen* started to chat nervously, he looked up, up, up to where the highway was. Then he turned off the engine. There was a good chance the tailpipe was impacted with snow, and if the heater kept running, they'd wake up dead way before they were incinerated in the morning by the sun.

"Any chance you can dematerialize?" he asked his *mahmen*.

"Oh, sure, absolutely. Not a problem."

Ten minutes of eyes closing and concentration on her part later, it was clear that was a lost cause—and it went without saying that neither he nor his father were leaving the car without her.

Annnnnd that was how he'd ended up calling Qhuinn.

Now, that decision had taken some time.

And with that male coming for help at a dead run, Blay sat with his hands on the wheel in spite of the fact that they were going nowhere, and wondered if he shouldn't have called John Matthew instead.

Or maybe the Sugar-Plum-fucking-Fairy.

"This all will be fine," his *mahmen* said from the back. "Qhuinn will be here soon."

As Blay glanced in the rearview, he noted the way she zipped up her parka. "Yeah."

Damn it, he should have had Jane come out to his parents' house. But he'd been thinking about Assail and anyone else who was really injured. It had felt selfish to take either of the docs or Ehlena away from the clinic.

Besides, Manny, as a human, couldn't dematerialize.

No, and it had been best that he call Qhuinn. Especially given that he was trying to keep his parents calm about the fact that he'd spent one, and now two, nights at home—and hadn't mentioned the twins at all. He was well aware that he wasn't fooling either of them, but he was so not ready to talk about the situation: *Oh, yeah, remember those kids you'd liked so much? Yeah, Mom, including the one that was named after you? Well, they're not going to be—*

From out of the blowing snow, a ghost emerged. A big-ass ghost that was sporting a skullcap.

"Oh, here he is," his mom said from the rear.

And her relief was the kind of thing that Blay couldn't afford to acknowledge feeling himself. Except yes, he was glad the Brother was here. Come on, it was his *mahmen*. He needed to get her to the mansion—and he'd known that even a blizzard wasn't going to keep Qhuinn from coming to get them all.

Yeah, apparently the line was not drawn at gale-force winds or blinding snow.

Diaper duty was the divide.

"Stay here," Blay announced as he went to open his door.

He'd meant to emerge triumphantly, an equal to an equal who had been only temporarily bested by a failure of his Bridgestone radials. But the door was fucking stuck.

He ended up dematerializing out of a two-inch crack in the window.

Damn it was cold, he thought as the wind started smacking his face around.

"She's injured!" he shouted into the gale.

Qhuinn just stared at him, those eyes reaching across the space that separated them, questioning, begging. But then the guy shook himself out of it. "Because of this accident?"

"No, before! She slipped and hurt that ankle again. She wasn't wearing her boot. I was trying to drive them to the training center."

"You should have called me before—I would have—"

From out of the storm, another figure arrived. Tohr. And as Qhuinn tweaked to the presence, he turned around and seemed surprised. Then relieved.

"Can she dematerialize?" Qhuinn yelled as he refocused.

"No! And we're not leaving her!"

Qhuinn nodded. "I need to go and get the Hummer!"

They were yelling back and forth, cupping their hands, bracing their bodies—and oddly, Blay thought that it was a lot like communicating through the events that had happened around Layla and the kids. That whole storm had blown in between them, rocking them both, creating an emotional blizzard that made the landscape of their relationship impenetrable—and the bad weather had yet to move on.

In fact, he feared it never would.

"I'll stay with them!" Blay said.

Tohr spoke up. "I'm going home and getting blankets! And then I'll be back to help guard!"

Blay had to turn his head away and get the snow out of his eyes. "Thank you!"

When he felt Qhuinn's hand on his shoulder, he jumped, but didn't step out of reach.

"I'm coming right back, okay?" the Brother said. "Don't worry about anything."

For a split second, Blay just stared into those mismatched eyes. Something about the sight of them, so concerned and intense, made the pain in the center of his chest feel fresh as the moment it had first been created.

But that wasn't all he felt.

His body still wanted the guy. His body was still ready . . . for more of Qhuinn. Goddamn it.

Without another word, Qhuinn got gone and so did Tohr.

Blay stood there in the storm for a heartbeat or two longer, pivoting around so he could look up to the highway. Oh, check it. They'd managed to break through the side rail.

Before he got back inside the car, he went around to the front hood, got down on his knees, and took out his Swiss Army knife. His hands had no gloves so he worked fast, brushing the snow away, removing the two screws that held the license plate to its holder and snagging the tag. Then he fought his way through the wind to the back and did the same thing to the rear plate, tucking them both into the inside of his jacket.

Dematerializing into the car, he smiled at his parents. "They're coming right back. Won't be a problem."

His *mahmen* nodded and smiled. "They are just the best."

"Uh-huh." He pointed to the glove compartment. "Say, Dad, would you mind—"

"Already did."

His old man gave him the registration and insurance cards, both of which V had faked, and Blay put them inside his parka as well. The VIN numbers had been scrubbed as soon as they'd gotten the thing for just this occasion—when you were a vampire in a human world, and your ride wrecked, a lot of times you just up and left it because the hassle wasn't worth the retrieval.

FFS, it was going to be a day or two before anyone could even get to the sedan, maybe longer, so it was best to simply write the whole thing off.

As he stared out the side window, Blay felt a curling anxiety that had nothing to do with his mom's appendage or the blizzard.

You can't go back, he told himself. Only forward.

"I'm really going to miss this car," his mom murmured. "I was just getting used to it."

"We'll get another one, honey," his pops said. "And you can pick it out."

Yeah, too bad you couldn't just go to a RelationshipMax lot and buy a new version of whatever you'd crashed, one that maybe had some technology upgrades and better suspension on your partner.

But life didn't work like that.

FORTY-TWO

Behind the wheel of his Hummer, Qhuinn felt like it took a month to get back to where that Volvo had deep-sixed itself off the side of the highway. He supposed, though, as the mile marker that he'd waited forever for finally presented itself, that he should be grateful he could get out here at all. His second new SUV was tight like that, though, its claw-treaded tires fortified with a set of King Kong chains, its wide wheelbase, and mile-high clearance exactly what you needed on a night like tonight.

When you were rescuing the love of your life and his parents out in the middle of the blizzard.

Even with the vehicle's kick-assness, though, visibility was for shit, and he'd had to turn the headlights off in favor of parking lights as soon as he'd picked up speed on the Northway: With his keen eyes, the illumination was still plenty and this addressed the issue he'd had with the whiteout created by those Xenon motherfuckers hitting all the flakes.

As he passed the marker, he steered the Hummer off the center track and onto the shoulder. Squinting, even though it didn't improve his visual acuity, he tried to make out exactly where they'd gone off the road on the opposite, northbound bunch of lanes.

He'd gone about three feet with that act before he decided, fuck it.

Wrenching the wheel to the left, he broke off onto the median, crossed into oncoming traffic—which was nonexistent, at least at the moment—and headed down the Northway going the wrong way. Flipping on the side-mounted spotlight, he used its handle to flash the powerful beam off to the side.

He found the Volvo about three hundred and fifty yards up, and something about seeing the station wagon off the highway at an angle, some six feet down from that busted side rail, made him want to throw up. Instead of going that bad-goiter route, however, he hit the brakes, threw the engine in park, and opened his door.

The Volvo had lost traction at the base of a hill, its grille going head-first into the snow in such a way that the driver's door couldn't be opened. Blay and his family had taken advantage of the other side, though, his father and himself out and helping his *mahmen* from the backseat. Lyric was grimacing in pain as they manhandled her, but she wasn't complaining. She was trying to smile.

"Hello, Qhuinn," she shouted into the storm as he came down the incline to them.

That was as far as she got with the talking. The jostling was obviously killing her, and Qhuinn wished he could help.

Meanwhile, Tohr was standing by as well, with the blanket he'd brought and a thermos in his hands. Qhuinn had been shocked that the brother had shown up on the scene, and man, had it been good to know that he was holding things down while the Hummer had been brought out here.

"I'll take her up," Blay's dad announced, as any bonded male would.

And out of deference to him, everyone stood back as the guy got his mate up into his arms. Blay then fell in behind his father, pushing his parents up the incline to the Hummer as Tohr scanned the storm for the enemy and Qhuinn ran ahead, turned the SUV around, and opened the rear door.

God, please let no human come by. Especially not in a CPD or state police car.

It was another case of things taking forever before Lyric was safely in the back of the vehicle, and Qhuinn took a deep breath.

But they still had to get to the mansion in one piece.

As Blay got in beside him in front and the male's dad went around and sat with Lyric, Tohr came over.

Qhuinn put his window down. "Thank you . . . thank you so much."

The brother passed him the blanket and the thermos. "This is hot chocolate. Fritz apparently has it at the ready on nights like tonight."

"Are you going back downtown?"

Tohr looked off into the blowing snow. "We go together, it's what we agreed on."

Qhuinn put his palm out. "Amen, brother."

After they shook, Tohr stepped back. "I'll follow you home."

"You don't have to. But I'm glad you are."

Tohr nodded once and then fist-bumped the hood. "Drive safe."

Qhuinn put up his window and hit the gas—gingerly. The Hummer was kitted out for all kinds of terrain, including Fuckloads of Fucking Snow, but he wasn't going to take chances with his precious cargo—and then there was the fact that Blay's mom hissed as the SUV bumped over into the snow track.

As they commenced the trip, Blay's mom and dad talked quietly in the back, support being offered and accepted, the murmurs warm and intimate.

You know, basically the opposite of what was doing in the front of the vehicle.

Qhuinn glanced at Blay. The male was staring straight out the windshield, his face impassive.

"So I'm going to take us right into the training center," Qhuinn said.

This was a dumb-ass statement, of course. Like he was going to Santa them down the chimney or something?

"That'd be great." Blay cleared his throat and then unzipped his parka. "So the Brotherhood was out in the field tonight?"

"What?"

"Wrath still sent everyone out in this storm?" When Qhuinn continued to look confused, Blay said, "You and Tohr were talking about being in the field?"

"Oh, yeah. No. Everybody's off."

"So what were you guys doing downtown?"

"Oh, nothing."

Blay refocused out the windshield. "Private Brotherhood business, huh. Well, I can smell the gunpowder on you."

When the Hummer arrived at the training center, stopping in front of the reinforced door at the base of the parking garage, Blay was the first out of the SUV. The ride into the compound had been marked by a series of awkward conversational stops and starts between him and Qhuinn, to the point where it was a toss-up whether strained silence was better than all the throat clearing. And meanwhile, in the back, his parents were listening to everything, even as they pretended to chat among themselves.

Nothing like baring your relationship's low point in front of Mommy and Daddy.

It was almost as much fun as a broken ankle.

Just as Blay was opening his mother's door, Dr. Manello came out with a gurney, the human male smiling pleasantly, but also doing that eagle-eye thing all physicians and surgeons did when confronting a patient.

"How are we, folks?" the guy said as Lyric struggled free of the Hummer's backseat. "Glad you made it in in one piece."

Blay's *mahmen* tilted her head and smiled over at the healer as she leaned on her *hellren*. "Oh, I was stupid."

"You didn't boot up."

"No, I didn't." She rolled her eyes. "I was just trying to make First Meal. And here you have it."

Dr. Manello shook palms with Blay's dad and then put his hand on Lyric's shoulder. "Well, not to worry, I'm going to take really good care of you."

For some reason, that simple statement, coupled with the complete confidence the guy wore like an aura granted from God Himself, made Blay have to look away and blink quick.

"You all right?" Qhuinn asked quietly.

Blay pulled it together and ignored the comment as his mom was carefully put onto the stretcher and Dr. Manello did a fast examination like he couldn't help himself.

"When are you coming home?" Qhuinn whispered.

When Blay didn't answer, the male pressed, "Please . . . come back."

Blay stepped over to the gurney. "*Mahmen*, do you need a blanket over you? No? Okay, I'll get the door."

With purpose, he held things open and stood off to the side as everyone fell into a line and entered the training center. After he was sure he had closed things properly behind them, he joined the march down the long concrete corridor, going past the classrooms and the break room that the new trainee class used.

Like everything else in Caldwell, things were shut down tonight, no students around, everyone hunkered down.

Just as well, the screams . . . dearest Virgin no-longer Scribe from the screams.

"What is that?" Blay's mom asked. "Is someone dying?"

Dr. Manello just shook his head. Although vampire healthcare had no HIPAA rules, the doctor never talked about his patients, even when the information was Brother to Brother—and Blay had always admired that about the man. About Doc Jane, too. Hell, in the mansion, everybody tended to know everybody else's business. And when things were going okay? That was fine. When they weren't?

The household's loving, caring, swearing peanut gallery could get to be a bit much.

"So when can we see those young?" Blay's dad asked as he glanced over his shoulder at Qhuinn. "I haven't held my grandbabies in ten nights. It's been too long. And I know their *grandmahmen* could use some cheering up, right, my love?"

As Blay sucked in a curse, he made sure he didn't look in Qhuinn's direction. But at least he knew he could rely on the guy to bow out of the—

"Absolutely. Can we wait until tomorrow night, though? Because I'd love to bring them out to your house and have a proper visit in your home."

Excuse me, Blay thought. Are you *fucking* kidding me?

As he shot the male a glare, Blay's mother filled the silence with a gasping happiness.

Twisting around on the gurney, she looked up at Qhuinn. "Truly?"

The Brother blithely ignored Blay as they all went into an exam room. "Yup. I know you've wanted us to come see you and I think now would be a great time."

Unbelievable. Un-*frickin'*-believable.

But he had to give the guy credit for a well-played card. Lyric had wanted to fuss and bake and take pictures of the kids in her own home for quite a while, although she had certainly never said anything overt about it because she hadn't wanted to be pushy. Her campaign had been far more subtle, nothing more than dropped hints here and there about the possibility of sleepovers, when they were much, much older, and visits during the festivals, when they were much, much older, and movie nights, when they were much, much older.

The yearning had always been in her voice, though.

As Blay's mom reached out and squeezed Qhuinn's forearm, Assail picked that moment to scream again—which, what do you know, was exactly what Blay was doing in his own head.

"Okay, let's see what we've got here."

As Dr. Manello spoke up, Blay wondered what the hell the doctor was going on about—and then remembered, oh, right, they were in an exam room. After they'd gone off the highway. In the middle of the worst early December snowstorm ever recorded.

FFS, he really just wanted to hit Qhuinn with something. A cabinet full of medical supplies, or maybe that desk over there.

"We're going to need to get an X-ray. And then we'll . . ."

As the physician started talking, Blay's dad got all serious and focused, and Blay wanted to as well. Instead, he waited for Qhuinn to glance over.

And then he mouthed, *Out in the hall. Right now.*

Message delivered, Blay glanced across at his parents. "We're just going to chat for a sec, be right back."

He hated the way his mom looked at him approvingly, like she expected whatever was wrong to blow over in time for the family to Norman Rockwell it up at nightfall tomorrow.

That was one gift he was not going to be getting her for Christmas.

The second Qhuinn joined him out in the corridor, Blay reached across and pulled the door shut behind them. And after checking to make sure there was nobody else around, he got his lawn mower out.

"Are you *fucking* kidding me," he said in a hush. "You are *not* coming there tomorrow night."

Qhuinn just shrugged. "Your parents want to see—"

"Yeah, those two young you made sure I knew weren't my kids. So no, you're not bringing your son and daughter out to my parents' house, just as an excuse to see me. I'm not going to let you do that."

"Blay, you're taking this too far—"

"Said the asshole who wanted to put a bullet in the mother of his children's head. As she stood over their bassinets." He threw up his hands. "Qhuinn, you can't possibly be this critically self-involved."

The male leaned forward on his hips. "I don't know how many times I can say I'm sorry."

"Neither do I, but apologies won't make this better."

There was a break of silence, and then Qhuinn eased back, a remote expression coming down over his features.

"So that's it, then," he said. "You're throwing our whole relationship away over one comment."

"It wasn't a comment. It was a revelation."

And one that had pretty much killed him where he stood. Hell, he'd have had a better chance of survival being the one Qhuinn had shot at.

Qhuinn crossed his arms over his chest, in a way that made his biceps get so big they strained even the loose sleeves of that white parka.

"Do you remember . . ." The male cleared his throat. "Do you re-member back, like a million years ago, when you came over to my house after my dad—you know, after he went off on me?"

Blay looked down at the concrete floor between them. "There were a lot of nights like that. Which one?"

"Fair enough. But you were always there for me, you know. You'd sneak over, we'd hit PlayStation and chill. You were my salvation. You're the only reason I'm alive right now. Why those kids even exist."

Blay started to shake his head. "Don't do this. Don't use the past to try and make me feel guilty."

"You always told me that my father was wrong for hating me. You said you couldn't understand why he—"

"Look, I paid my dues with you," Blay snapped. "Okay? I fucking paid my dues. I was your kiss-ass, your Band-Aid, your safety blanket. And you want to know why? It wasn't because you were so special. It was because you were a slut I couldn't have and I took your promiscuity as my not being enough—and that made me want to prove myself to you over and over again. And I'm not doing that anymore. You pushed me away for all that time, when you were fucking other people, but I'll give you a pass on that because I didn't have the balls to come out and tell you how I felt back then. But when you pushed me away up in that bedroom? You knew how much I love you. I'm not coming back from that—"

"What I was *going* to say," Qhuinn barked, "was that you always told me you were sorry he couldn't forgive me for something I couldn't change—"

"That's right—your DNA is not your fault. What the hell does that have to do with anything between us? Are you saying you're not respon-sible for what comes out of your mouth?" Blay shook his head and paced around. "Or even better, that it's not your fault you cut me out of those kids' lives?"

"I just invited myself and those kids over to your parents' house to-morrow night, remember. So I'm clearly not cutting you out." Qhuinn's chin lifted. "And my point is that I don't get how someone who pros-elytized the importance of forgiveness is refusing to accept my apology."

Without thinking about it, Blay reached into his coat and took out the pack of Dunhills. And as he lit one up, he muttered, "Yes, I'm smoking again. No, it has nothing to do with you. And when I was talking about your father, it was about eye color, for godsakes. I wasn't asking you to step off from what you thought were your goddamn children. That was my life, Qhuinn. Those children . . . were my future, what was going to be left of me when I'm dead and gone. They were going to be . . ." As his voice cracked, he took a long drag. "They were going to carry my parents' traditions forward. They were milestones and happiness and a wholeness that even you can't give me. That's *nothing* compared to a genetic accident that resulted in your having one blue eye and one green one."

"Whatever, Blay," Qhuinn said darkly as he circled his face. "This defect was my whole life, and you know it. My defect in my parents' house was my *whole* fucking life. I was cut out of everything—"

"So fine, you know how I feel."

As their stares clashed, Qhuinn shook his head. "You're as bad as my father was, you know that? You really are."

Blay jabbed his lit cigarette at the guy. "Fuck you. For that. Seriously."

Qhuinn stared across the tense air for a moment. Then he said, "What's going on here. I mean, really, do you just want to blow us up? You want to go back to Saxton or maybe fuck someone else? You want to play it like the way I used to be? Is that why you're doing this?"

"Why I'm doing—wait, like I'm taking this stance as an exit strategy? You think maybe this is a soapbox to make an arbitrary point? You honestly believe I'm playing here?" He shook his head as disbelief made him dizzy. "And no, I don't want to be like you. You and I aren't the same and we never have been."

"Which is why we work." Abruptly, Qhuinn's voice grew reedy. "You're my home, Blay. You always have been. Even with Lyric and Rhamp in my life, I'm lost without you, and yeah, I can get pissed off in the middle of a conversation like this, but I'm still man enough to admit that I'm nothing if you're not with me." He cleared his throat. "And FYI, I'm going to fight for you, for us, so I'll ask you again. What's it going to take? Blood? Because whatever I need to do to get you back, I'm going to do it."

As Assail let out another scream, Blay closed his eyes, exhaustion coming over him like a death shroud. "Yeah, sure, fine," he muttered. "Blood. It's going to take blood. Now, if you'll excuse me, I'm going to go look after my mother."

"I'm showing up with the young tomorrow night at your parents'."

"I won't be there."

"That's your decision. And I'll respect it. But I mean what I say. No matter what it takes, I'm going to prove that I love you and I need you and I want you—and that those kids are yours."

With that, the Brother turned away and strode off down the concrete corridor, his head high, his shoulders back, his step even—

"Son?"

Blay jumped and turned around to his dad. "How is she? The X-ray done yet?"

"She's asking for you. Dr. Manello says they might have to operate."

Shit. "Of course." He put his arm around his father's shoulders. "Come on, let's figure this out together—"

"Are you and Qhuinn okay?"

"Peachy. Just peachy jim-dandy," he said as he pushed the exam room door open. "Nothing to worry about. Let's just focus on Mom, okay?"

FORTY-THREE

Throe had long heard that one could make a bomb out of common household materials. That one could quite readily produce a highly explosive unit with naught more than items found in most kitchens.

Yet, although this was true, as he proceeded down the formal stairs of his lover's *hellren's* mansion, he was almost disappointed at the ubiquitous nature of what he was seeking. However, with his book under his arm, and a welcomed clarity of purpose in his mind, he told himself his faith would be rewarded, his purpose served, his goal achieved.

Even if this seemed a bit anticlimactic.

And again, at least he was focused now.

Such strange business that previous confusion had been, he thought as he came down to the first floor's foyer, the crackling fire in the marble hearth offering warmth and light, the crystal chandelier overhead twinkling as if real diamonds had been strung from the ceiling. Pausing, he looked into the sitting room beyond and approved of the silk sofas and the candelabra, the textiles that hung around the long, narrow windows, the jewel-like colors that had been chosen by someone with a very good eye and a very deep pocket.

On the opposite side of the grand open space, as was tradition, the study of the house's first male gleamed of power and distinction, the wood paneling and leather-bound books, the broad desk with its leather blotter and matching chair, the stained glass windows, lending such an impression of aristocratic entrenchment that a sense of nostalgia warmed the center of his chest. There had been so many years since he had lived like this, so many hovels in between. And further, there had also been crassness and vulgarity, death and blood, sex of the most base kind.

It had not been the life he had once seen for himself, and indeed, as much as he had once felt tied to the Band of Bastards and their leader, now he believed that his time with them had been naught but a bad dream, a fated storm that had passed through his destiny on its way to wreak havoc on some other poor sod's existence.

This was where he belonged.

In fact, of all the places he had been in in the New World, this mansion suited him best. It was not the largest of his female friends', but it was appointed with the very best accoutrements, at a standard he himself would have chosen for his abode—

What he would soon *choose* for his abode, he corrected himself, when he o'ertook the race—

"You will not last with her."

Throe pivoted on his heel. The *hellren* of the house, an elderly vampire of some eight hundred years, came creeping out of the formal bathroom that was off the library, the sound of a flushing toilet announcing his presence more than his dwindling scent or thinning voice.

"I beg your pardon," Throe murmured, even though he had heard perfectly well.

"She will not last with you any longer than she has with the others. You will be back out on the streets by the New Year."

Throe smiled, particularly as he noted the cane that the male required in order to ambulate. For a moment, he entertained the notion that the thing slipped out from under the grip of that arthritic hand, and the male lurched off balance, falling to the hard marble floor.

"I think you vastly underestimate my appeal, old male." Throe shifted his hold on The Book, bringing it unto his chest. Funny, it seemed to tingle against his heart. "But that is not a topic for polite conversation, is it."

Gray hair, bushy eyebrows, tufts of whiskers growing out of ears . . . oh, the indignities of age, Throe thought. And the inevitable erectile and sexual dysfunction. After all, Viagra could help only so much. Even if the cock could harden thanks to pharmaceuticals, if the rest of the body was as toothsome as a rotten deer carcass, what else could a young female do other than take a more palatable lover?

"She is out, you know," the male said in his wobbly voice.

Why didn't they have the walking cane equivalent for speech, Throe wondered idly. A little speaker to project things better? Perhaps with a knob to add bass along with volume.

"She is, yes," Throe intoned with a smile. "I sent her out to find another female so she and I could play with a toy. We've done this before— and she will come back and bring me what I want."

When the male stuttered as though shocked, Throe leaned in and dropped his words to a whisper, as if he and her *hellren* were in on a secret together. "I believe you will find that happening with some regularity from now on. You must realize, kind sir, that I am not like the others she has entertained in the past. I tell her what to do and she does it. Which rather differentiates you and I, as well, does it not?"

The old male recovered his composure and wagged that cane. "You'll see. She's done this before. I am the one she can't live without because I can support her. You, as a drifter, a con artist, and a fallen aristocrat, most certainly cannot."

Well, Throe mused, perhaps one has mis-guessed the phlegmatic nature of this particular mate. No matter, however.

Throe inclined his head. "Believe what you will. It never changes reality, does it. Good evening."

As he headed off toward the butler's pantry, the *hellren* said with some volume, "Using the servants' door, are you. Quite appropriate. You used to be a member of the *glymera*, but that is no longer true—and hasn't been since your blooded family removed you from their estate and their lines of ancestry. Such a pity. Unless you look at it from their point of view. Disgraces must be excised or they threaten the entirety."

Throe stopped. And slowly turned back around.

Narrowing his eyes, he felt a familiar anger curl around his gut, a viper that liked to strike out. "Be of care, old male. I shall tell you once more, but never again—I am not like the others."

"You are a gigolo. You trade your body for food and shelter like any common whore. A fine suit does not change the stink of the flesh upon which it rests."

Dimly, Throe was aware of The Book becoming hot against his sternum. And he felt a temptation to give in to his rage like never before.

But then he remembered what he had come downstairs for. And what he would do up in his bedroom when he had assembled what he required.

Now he smiled again. "You are lucky I need you."

"You better remember that. And so should she."

"We shall, I promise. Especially, while your *shellan* comes for me."

Throe continued on, leaving the *hellren* to whate'er he would do for the rest of the night—and what a party that would be. Due to his mobility problems, he spent most evenings in the rear library that led into the solarium, propped up like a statue whose base was broken.

So when it was time . . . he would be easy to find.

Meanwhile, one needs must go unto the pantry and gather ingredients.

Locating the dry-storage room with its multitudinous shelves and its rows of cans and boxes and jars was simple enough. Finding precisely what he needed, however, was going to take some time and concentration: As he measured the breadth of what had been purchased for the household's consumption, he was a bit overwhelmed.

But something told him not to ask any of the staff to help.

The Book, he would later think. Yes, The Book was communicating to him without words, rather as an animal with whom one had great familiarity might "speak" through a series of eye and muzzle movements, intangibles that meant little to all save the two involved.

Opening the tome upon the center butcher block, Throe smiled as its pages flipped themselves to the correct passages. And then he sought to collect what was listed.

'Twas a nasty stew, indeed.

Angostura bitters. Red wine vinegar. Ginger. Licorice, black. Arugula. Saffron. Sesame seeds.

And then he needed black candle wax. And . . . motor oil? From a car?

For a moment, he chafed at the effort that gathering it all was going to require, his old way of being waited on hand and foot rearing its privileged head. Except then The Book fluffed its pages, as if in disapproval.

"Aye," he told it. "Follow through I shall."

Picking up a basket from a stack by the entrance, as if this indeed were a shop of sorts, he set about taking from the shelves what was indicated.

Oh, and a copper pot. He was going to find one of those in the kitchen, he hoped.

Yes, this was quite the stew. Yet hardly the sort of thing you'd think you could make an army out of, and mayhap this would not work—

The Book flurried its pages, like a dog well miffed.

Throe smiled back at it. "Don't be so touchy. I have my faith, and my faith has me."

Odd way of putting things, but the refrain set up shop in his brain and came out of his mouth on a murmur.

"I have my faith, my faith has me, I-have-my-faith, my-faith-has-me, myfaithhasmemyfaithhasme . . ."

FORTY-FOUR

3ypher led the Band of Bastards back unto where they had been seeking shelter well before dawn approached. The blizzard was so bad, and had raged for so long, that not only had their travel plans to the New World been curtailed—along with so many humans'— but the city of Caldwell and its surrounding neighborhoods had likewise turned into snowy ghost towns, no cars upon the impassible roads, no pedestrians upon the impassible sidewalks.

They had tried the night before to locate Xcor, for what they had assumed would be the final time. But when they had become stuck on the East Coast, their return flight across the Atlantic delayed, they had endeavored, once again, and for what surely would be the final, final time, to find their leader.

And, as had been the case before, they had discovered naught. Whether that was because of the storm or . . .

Oh, who was he kidding, Zypher thought as he turned the corner on an alley that had become quite familiar. Xcor was well and verily gone, most likely unto his grave. They truly needed to give this up, especially as they were all now not just frustrated, but freezing cold. Rest was best, for on the fall of darkness on the morrow, they were going to have to begin the battle to find a different flight, or perhaps even a different path to return home.

One thing he was looking forward to? Resuming their castle accommodations.

The abandoned restaurant they had been staying in was better than some places they had had to camp out in over the centuries, but it held not a candle to their well-hearthed stone pile back in the Old Country. They had, however, made the best of what they had taken residence of, tunneling into the building next door to provide an additional escape, and monitoring the other empty businesses in the event that humans made a resurgence into the degraded neighborhood.

Aye, he would be glad to depart, even as he mourned the one they had had to leave behind.

Zypher reached the door first, and as was protocol, he stood to one side and guarded his fellow fighters as they opened things up and filed into the interior—not that there was aught to protect against.

Would that storms such as this happened with constancy, he thought, so that humans were driven into their shelters every evening.

Syn was the last through the open portal, and then Zypher checked once again the snowed-in alley and the vacated, wilted buildings across the way. Then he, too, disappeared into the interior, which was no warmer, but considerably less breezy, than the streets.

It was a relief not to have snow flying into one's eyes and muffling one's hearing.

The sound of the group of them stomping snow from their cleats and shaking off hats and gloves reminded him of a trampling herd, accompanied by birds. Not that he had actually e'er seen such a thing, but he imagined it would—

"Something smells wrong."

"Someone has been herein."

As an intruder's presence registered on all of them at once, they went on the defensive, crouching into their legs, taking out their weapons. But it was not . . .

"Gunpowder?" one of them said.

"A flare mayhap—"

At that moment, the door opened right behind him—

And the scent that came in with the cold stopped everything. The scent . . . and the size of the male who filed the doorjambs . . . and the aura of power that accompanied him . . .

The panels were closed slowly. And still no one moved.

That voice, the one that Zypher had given up on ever hearing again, spoke clearly. "No greeting for your leader? Have I been gone that long?"

Zypher took a step forward in the darkness. And another.

Then with a shaking hand, he took out of his coat and turned on a battery-powered torch.

It was Xcor. A thinner, rather older looking version of Xcor, but the fighter nonetheless.

Zypher reached out and touched the heavy shoulder. Then, yes, he touched the face. "You live," he breathed.

"Aye," Xcor whispered back. "Barely. But aye."

He did not know who reached out first, whether it was him or his leader. But arms were wrapped, and chest to chest they came together, the present realigning itself with a past that had always included the male who miraculously stood before him.

"My brother, I thought this night would not come." Zypher closed his eyes. "I had lost my hope."

"And I, too," Xcor said roughly. "I as well."

When Zypher stepped back, Balthazar came up and so did the others.

One by one, embraces were exchanged, hard pounds being shared upon shoulders. If tears formed in eyes, they were not shed, but no voices were capable of any sort of speech—even Syn entered into a brief clutch, the worst of all of them affected yet and still.

Their missions to try to find Xcor alive had decayed into an unspoken resolve that perhaps if only they could discover what had happened, or perhaps locate some remains to dispose of properly, mayhap they could live in peace with that. But they had long lost the conception that this reunion could be the fate of them all, this vital return a gift they had not dared aspire to.

"Was it the Brotherhood?" Balthazar demanded. "Did they take you?"

"Aye."

Instantly, the growls that pumped through the cold, still air were a pack of wolves come to life, a promise of pain in exchange for the wrong that had been done unto one among them.

"No," Xcor said. "It is more complicated than that."

Xcor had been across the street in hiding, watching the entrance of the abandoned restaurant, waiting to see if any of his males came unto the vacated space prior to dawn. He had preferred to pass the night thus, as opposed to within the dingy interior, given that Qhuinn and Tohr, and possibly others, were on the hunt: He was afraid of getting trapped and slaughtered.

So he had hunkered down in a walk-up that had offered visibility and plenty of plain glass to dematerialize out of if he heard even a whistle of the wind that he didn't like. And as the time had passed, his thoughts had strayed frequently to Layla, which had been of benefit as the images in his mind of her naked had warmed his body and kept him alert through unaccustomed fatigue. With the dawn coming closer and closer, he had had no solid plan of what to do upon its arrival, his only conclusion that he would not be returning to that ranch house.

At least with the rise of the sun, he wouldn't have to be worried about the Brothers still searching for him.

The issues with noontime light affected them equally.

Except then his males had arrived, materializing out of the storm like wraiths coming in for a landing in a cemetery, their great bodies appearing in the midst of the falling snow one by one. So happy he had been to see them that he had opened his mouth to call out from his perch at the window. Years of training in war, however, had silenced him before he had emitted a syllable of greeting.

It had taken everything he had in him to wait for a time, just to make sure they had not been followed.

And as he had entered their lair, he had been unsure of his welcome, worried that the power structure that he had once created and enforced so brutally had caused an irreversible mutiny.

Instead, he had been welcomed as a brother. One whose assumed demise had been sorely mourned.

Oh, how he wished they could stay a little longer in this mood of camaraderie, this emotional reunion. But he had little time, and the longer he was with them, the less safe they were.

"So you escaped from the Brotherhood," someone chuffed with pride. "How many of them did you kill?"

He thought of Qhuinn trying to claw his way through those gates in that cave. "I killed none of them. And I am not free."

"Whate'er does that mean?" Zypher asked.

In the steady glow of the male's electric torch, Xcor crossed his arms over his chest and looked each one of his bastards in the eye. "I have given my vow unto the Blind King. I have sworn my allegiance to the throne."

The silence that came after his pronouncement was expected.

"You were coerced, then?" Zypher said. "For the price of your freedom, you granted Wrath your pledge?"

"No, I granted it to him after I got free."

Balthazar shook his head. "The Chosen, then."

"No, the King, then." Xcor spoke slowly and clearly, relying on their long years of surviving in the field of battle together to give his words the weight of his full conviction. "I have come unto Wrath, son of Wrath, of my own free will, irrespective of the Chosen Layla, and not in the manner of making amends for my previous actions."

"You have subjugated yourself?" Zypher asked.

"Aye. And I say unto you all, the King seeks your oaths as well."

"Is that an order from you?" Zypher inquired.

"No." Xcor once again met the eyes of his fighters. "He seeks it in return for your freedom from a death sentence. He shall release each and every one of you of your treason, and entertain a safe return for you to the Old Country, if you come unto him and swear your loyalty."

"But you are not commanding us to do so?"

"I shall fight side by side with any of you until the night I die. But I will never force you to bow your heads before a leader. I respect you too much for the likes of that, and besides, I suspect that Wrath would know it. For all of his blindness . . . he sees things with a great clarity."

There were murmurs among the group. And then a deep voice said, "What did they do to you."

It was Syn, and it was not a question.

"They kept me alive."

"A traitor unto them," the bastard said as he stepped forward. "A traitor unto their King and they kept you alive?"

"I was injured in the field. They took me in and kept me alive."

Zypher shook his head. "Wrath is not known for his weakness any more than you are. That does not make sense."

"It is the truth." Xcor offered both his hands unto the heavens, raising them up. "I offer you naught but what happened. I was injured in the field, they took me in, and they ensured that I survived." So that they could torture him, true. But if he wanted peace between the Brotherhood and the Bastards, he was going to redact that. "I escaped and now I have come unto you."

"This makes no sense," Syn echoed in his low, evil voice. "You escaped, but then how did you make an oath to Wrath? Were you held by a faction of the Brotherhood, unknown to the King?"

"The details are unimportant."

"The hell they are. And I do not understand this oath. It is not your nature to be under another."

Xcor smiled coldly. "I do not believe I have heard you speak this much in a very long time, our Syn."

"If there is ever cause for conversation, this would be it. And so I say unto you again, this makes no sense and I do not comprehend the bowing of your head to another."

"My thinking has evolved."

"Or your cock has."

Before Xcor could think twice, he flashed up in Syn's face even though the other fighter had considerable weight on him.

Baring his fangs, Xcor said, "Do not o'erstep. I am in an egalitarian mood, but that only goes so far."

The two of them stayed eye to eye, chest to chest, for quite some time, the others backing away in the event that the conflict exploded.

"Over a female, then," Syn drawled.

"Over the love of my life. And well you remember that, bastard."

As Xcor spoke, his bonding scent flared, and that got the other male's attention, Syn's brows popping high, his recoil subtle but well noticeable to one who knew him to the marrow—which Xcor did.

After a moment, Syn's incline of the head was slight, but unassailable. "Apologies."

"Accepted. And she has nothing to do with this." The group took a collective deep breath as the aggression dissipated, but Xcor did not give them time to relax. "As I said, in exchange for your vows, Wrath will release you all from punishment, but you must return to the Old Country. As must I."

Zypher laughed a little. "Indeed, that is where we had plans to be the now. We were in the process of departing, but then this snowfall? It prevented us surely as if this reunion were preordained by the Scribe Virgin."

"Fortuitous, indeed."

The assembled fell quiet, and Xcor permitted them ample time to study him and think upon what he'd said. But he could not tarry among them for much longer.

He'd already been shot at once tonight. He didn't want to bring the Brothers unto them.

"So that is what is upon the table," he said. "And I shall leave you to your considerations. If you choose not to comply, there is a reasonable chance that should you return unto the Motherland, you will be safe for some time. But it will be an existence I personally am well tired of. You shall never not look over your shoulder, and make no mistake, Wrath shall come for you. It will take a while, as there are other priorities that capture his attention the now. In the end, however, his vengeance will find you. He is a male of peace, but not of castration."

"Wait," Balthazar interjected. "If you are with the King, why is it not safe for us to be around you? I presume that is why you are departing."

Xcor hesitated, and then concluded certain information was their due. "There are some among the Brotherhood who are not accepting of my oath."

"The father of the Chosen's young, then," one of his fighters said.

Xcor let that stand, as it was both a logical conclusion and nobody's business. He had never denied the Chosen Layla was with young, but nor had he ever commented upon it—and he was certainly not about to discuss his private life now or ever with anyone.

Xcor went back over to the exit. "I shall leave you presently. There is much for you to ponder among yourselves. I will find you twenty-four hours from now, at our meeting place. You shall give me your answer then."

He suspected that they all knew what they were going to do already. But he needed time to ensure that if he brought them to Wrath, his males would be safe.

"Where will you go?" Zypher asked.

"I will see you at four a.m. tomorrow night." Xcor turned away. And then before he opened the way out, he looked over his shoulder. "I never thought I would see you again."

The fact that his voice cracked was nothing he could change. And it was also evidence of how much *he* had changed.

And it wasn't that he was a new male, he reflected as he steeled himself and re-entered the cold and the snow.

No, it was more that he had resumed who he had originally been, the transformation a comeback to the male that ambition and cruelty had eclipsed. And he found the return was as welcome as the sight of those fighters who were the only family he had ever known, the only ones who had accepted him when all others, both of blood and of stranger, had turned him away.

As snow lashed at his face and wind cut through the outerwear he had borrowed, he prayed that he could broker a true peace with the King he had sought to overthrow such that his soldiers could be safe.

If he could not be with the female who had his heart and soul? At least he could take care of the fighters who had served him so well for so long.

He had much to make up for.

FORTY-FIVE

The following evening, Layla woke up and immediately reached for her young—but there was no need for concern. Rhamp and Lyric were right beside her on the bedding platform in the Scribe Virgin's private quarters, their precious lashes down, their deep breathing and expressions of concentration evidence of the effort it took to grow big and strong.

As she rolled over onto her back, she had a sense that night was arriving down below on earth. It was always thus, some transmutation of the shift there from light to dark, season to season, reverberating up to the Sanctuary.

Moving carefully so as not to disturb her young, she got to her feet and took a lingering look at those sweet faces. It had been a lovely time, this private interlude, every moment savored, each touch and smile, every cuddle and stroke, something that she filled her heart with.

How was she going to leave them?

It was going to be so hard, a ripping off of what had healed during these quiet, poignant hours.

To save herself from tears, she pivoted away and padded over the white marble floor. The thought that she had slept in the Scribe Virgin's personal space with her young was nearly too bizarre to comprehend, but then she couldn't have imagined a night when the mother of the race was gone and there was a visitation schedule in place for her and Qhuinn.

Alas, however, change came unto you when it did, and sometimes all you could do was yield and make the best of it.

And besides, the quarters had been most accommodating, the bedding so soft, the white marble floors, walls, and cabinetry, soothing, the—

Layla frowned. Across the way, one of the closet doors was open ever so slightly. Odd. The banks of marble panels with their nearly invisible pulls had been fully flush when she had come in here to rest.

Going over, she was nervous for no good reason. It wasn't as if the Scribe Virgin was in there hiding or something.

Hooking a finger into the pull, she opened things up, not knowing what to expect—

"Oh . . . my."

Zebra print leggings. A black leather jacket. Boots as big as your head, a pink feather boa, blue jeans, Hanes T-shirts in white and black—

"I tried not to wake you."

Layla wheeled around at the male voice and slapped her hand over her mouth so she didn't rouse the young. When she saw who it was, however, she dropped her arm and frowned in confusion . . . and then downright shock.

No, it couldn't be . . .

Lassiter, the Fallen Angel, smiled and came across to her, his blond and black hair swinging down to his hips, his gold piercings and chains making him glow.

Or mayhap he glowed now for another reason.

Layla cleared her throat as the implications piled one upon another upon another. "Are you . . . is she . . . did she . . . what is . . ."

"I know you're stammering because you're just so excited," he said, "that you're rendered speechless."

Layla shook her head—then quickly nodded so she didn't offend. "It's just . . . I mean . . . *you?*"

"Yup, me. The Scribe Virgin picked me, me, me." He made a show of skipping around like a six-year-old with a sucker and tap shoes. Except then he cut the act and got dead serious, staring into her eyes with a hard expression. "I haven't told anyone yet, and neither can you. I just figured if you're going to be staying here with the kidlets, you'd find out sooner or later because I'm moving in."

She looked to the bed in alarm, but he put up his palms. "Oh, I won't be here when you are. I know you want your privacy and I respect that. I also want to help you out. You've been through a thing, haven't you."

Lassiter's compassion and understanding was so unexpected that she teared up. "Oh, dearest Virgin Scribe, I am so—" She stopped herself as she realized that particular incantation no longer applied. "Um . . ."

"Yeah, I'm not a virgin and I hate writing. So you're going to have to use different verbiage. I was thinking of going with Grand Exalted Pooh-Bah, but I believe the humans already have one, damn it."

"Ah . . ." As she faltered, she was just so shocked, she couldn't think of anything to say. "Well, I'm sure you'll come up with something."

Goodness only knew what it would be, though.

"And as for these quarters," she said, "I don't want to inconvenience you. I'll move us to the dormitory—"

"Nah, I don't sleep here. I just put some clothes in there to see how it felt, is all. The promotion's been an adjustment for me, too—you know, trying to find out what powers I have." He leaned in conspiratorially. "I.e., how much I can get away with. Hey! Did you know I can make snow?"

"What?"

"Snow." He made a show of something falling by wiggling his fingertips. "I can make a shitload of snow. And you know what is going to be even more fun? Watching the human scientists try to figure out why that storm down there happened. They're going to start talking all about climate change and weather patterns, but I had to help your boy out."

"Xcor? I'm sorry . . . I don't understand."

"Long story. Anyway, how you doing? How're the kids?"

You know, like there was nothing else going on. "Forgive me, ah, um . . ."

"Let's try Your Excellency."

Layla blinked. "All right. Forgive me, Your Excellency, but how did you help Xcor?"

"Needed to keep his fighters on the northern seaboard. So hellllllllooo nooooooor'easter."

"So he found them!"

"You know, it turns out destiny is a lot of work for someone like me." He shrugged. "Who knew it took this much effort to give people a chance to exercise free will. It's like the world is a chessboard for each and every person I'm in charge of. So I'm, like, playing a hundred thousand different games all at once."

"Wowwww."

"I know, right? Thank God for ADHD!" He grinned—and then frowned. "Actually, I guess that's more thank me for it."

Layla had to smile. "You will certainly be a change, Your Excellency."

Lassiter squirmed his shoulders. "No, that's weird. Let's try *Eminence*. I've got to get something I'm comfortable with here."

"All right, Your Eminence."

He cracked his neck. "Nope. Also not it. We're going to have to work on this title thing—oh!" The Fallen Angel—er, head of everything . . . um . . . jumped like he'd been poked in the side. "Okay, so I've got to go. You take care, and you know what you've got to do next."

"I do?"

"Yup. You have a card to play, a piece to move, as it were. You know what it is. And remember"—he put his forefinger to his lips—"shhhhhhh. My new job is our little secret until further notice."

"Oh, but of course—"

"Toodles!"

With that, Lassiter up and disappeared, a fall of shimming sparkles hitting the floor—just as, at that very moment, Cormia appeared in the open doorway to the private quarters.

"How did everyone get on?" the female asked.

Ah, he'd left so he wasn't seen, Layla thought.

With a shake, she pulled herself together. "Oh, ah, very well. Very well indeed, thank you."

The other Chosen walked over to the young. "Hi, guys. Are you waking up? Well, hello, there."

Surreptitiously, Layla went over and shut the closet door so the zebra print wouldn't show—and then she tried to smile as if she didn't know what she did, hadn't heard what she had. "They have done so well. I kept them to schedule, of course. Let me just gather our trash and we'll head back down."

She went over to the duffel she'd stashed the used diapers in and slung the thing up on her shoulder. Then she approached the bed.

"I'm sure Qhuinn will be excited to see them. I know I was when I . . . anyway, I'm glad you came to help with the transport again. Thank you."

Cormia's eyes were sad, but her voice steady and deliberately cheerful. "Of course! Which one would you like to take?"

"Rhamp, as I had Lyric on the way up." Shuffling the duffel so it hung behind her, she addressed her son. "Have to split my time. Fair is fair, after all."

She glanced over as Cormia picked up Lyric. She couldn't help it. It wasn't that she didn't think the Chosen knew what she was doing . . . but it was a *mahmen* thing.

A mom thing, as Beth would have termed it.

"Did anything exciting happen?" Cormia asked as she took Lyric into her arms. "Hmm? Any news flashes of note?"

"No," Layla murmured. "Not at all."

"I got the job, I goooot the jooooooob . . ."

Therese continued to talk to herself in the mirror as she threw on a little eye makeup and hit her hair with the straightener. She was going to pull the stuff back so it was out of her face and looked tidy, but if she didn't calm things down a little first, she always felt like she had a tutu shooting out the back of her head.

Funny, she'd always assumed she got all those waves from her mom.

Turned out that was a big, fat nope.

Unplugging the wand, she double-checked she hadn't overdone it with the foundation and blusher. Then nodded at herself. "You got this."

Just as she went to turn off the light, a cockroach scurried by in front of the stained tub, and she had to catch herself so she didn't stomp it flat—she didn't have shoes on yet. That woulda been hella nasty.

"I cannot *wait* to get out of this dump."

Walking into the bedroom/living room/kitchen area, which sounded so much better than the dingy reality of it all, she grabbed her coat, her cell phone, and her purse, and on impulse, a scarf. At the door, she took a moment to lower her head and say a prayer to the Scribe Virgin for protection.

Which wasn't about the job or traveling to the job. It was about getting down the stairwell to the front door and out onto the street in one piece.

Pretty sad to know you were safer in the dark in a bad part of town than in your own building.

But at least she had a best practices plan: In the week and a half since she'd moved in with her suitcase, her backpack, and her seven hundred dollars in cash, she'd created a procedure for departure. First? Ear to the door.

Closing her eyes, she concentrated on what was doing out in the hall. Nothing unusual it seemed. Just your normal everyday shouting, loud music, and muffled slamming.

"Great! Now let's go on to step two."

She shifted the safety chain free, unlatched the bar lock that ran vertically across from jamb to jamb, and threw back the deadbolt. Then she flashed out and shut things up quick. It was a toss-up whether she was in greater danger walking in the corridor or getting forced back into her room. Sure, as a female vampire, she was far stronger than most human males. But the thing she always worried about was what would happen if one of them came at her with a gun. A knife she could probably handle by overpowering them, but a bullet was—

Perfect. Frickin'. Timing.

As if he had been waiting for her, the creep across the way came out just as she did. Compared to her, he was a lot more blasé about his exit, taking his time because, for one, he was probably high as a kite, and for two, she had the sense, in her limited interaction with him, that he kind of was in charge of the place.

He'd certainly always looked at her like she was a meal to be consumed.

Creep.

Bracing herself for the kind of smarm he'd been throwing at her, she—

"Oh, fuck!" he muttered as he saw her.

Then he whipped back around and started fumbling with his doorknob. Like he was trying to get back into his apartment.

Therese looked up and down the corridor. Nobody else was around. Maybe he was having a paranoid delusion or something? Whatever, she sure as hell wasn't going to ask him if he was okay—or argue with the fact that he suddenly seemed to want to avoid her.

Hurrying off, she took to the stairs, flying down them. She knew she should probably just dematerialize, but all of the windows in the whole building were covered with chicken wire made of steel and none of them opened. And although it was a fair guess that the concrete or the brick or whatever the heck the walls were made of probably wasn't fortified with anything, she couldn't run that risk. She'd heard the horror stories of what happened when vampires guessed wrong on what they tried to ghost through.

As she was out in the world all alone, it was yet another risk she couldn't afford to take.

Therese was halfway down the stairs and making a turn, when two men who were coming up hit the landing at the same time she did.

Recognizing them from the lobby, she dropped her eyes and shoved her hands into her coat to bring her purse closer to her body—

Both of them jumped back and knocked into each other, before flattening against the stairwell wall so she could go by them.

When something similar happened as she was leaving the main exit, another human she had seen around the building pointedly getting out of her path, she decided that maybe she had a communicable disease that only that other species could sense?

Then again . . . shoot, maybe they had all found out she was a vampire? She had no idea what she might have done to give it away, but why else would these guys be treating her like she was a lit stick of dynamite?

'Cuz, come on, sure, they were all on drugs, but a common psychosis against women with dark hair was unlikely.

Still, why argue with it if it kept her safe? Unless, of course, it was about her species identity, in which case she could be in real trouble. Then again, what kind of credibility could people like that have? Drug addicts frequently had delusions, right?

Outside, she had to pause for a moment.

Okay, wow. Snow. Everywhere . . . snow. There had to have been at least three feet of it dropped all over the place, and the wind that had kept her up late during the day had pushed the stuff around into drifts.

As she headed off, she was not surprised that the front walkway, such as it was, had not been cleared. What she was bummed about was the fact that her Merrells, which were waterproof and comfortable, only came up to her ankles. Wet socks were going to be in fashion tonight, she feared.

When she got out to the sidewalk, she found that, of course, the concrete had likewise not been shoveled. Looking left and right, she debated on whether to just f'-it and dematerialize in plain view, but no. The sun was down, but it was only dark-ish, the ambient glow of the city reflecting and being magnified thanks to all the white powder.

She was bound to be noticed, so she needed to find a more hidden spot.

Going down two blocks, she hunkered into her coat and really didn't enjoy the feeling of her ears burning from cold. At least her neck was warm and her hands toasty in the deep, padded pockets. Hanging a left, she entered an alley that was far dimmer than the street beyond, and closing her eyes, she . . .

. . . dematerialized to the back of Sal's Restaurant.

As she re-formed, she saw a couple of cars coming in and parking by the service entrance. A human man and then two human women got out of their vehicles, not really saying much as they rushed to the staff door as if they were either late or cold. Maybe both.

Therese followed their example, catching the heavy panel before it closed fully and then stamping her snowy shoes on the textured rubber mat inside.

"Hey."

When she looked up, it was into the stare of a surprisingly attractive human male. He had dark blond hair, eyes that were blue as a Magic Marker, and a jaw that was pretty darned square.

"Are you the new hire?" he asked.

"Yes, I am."

A rather large hand extended toward her. "I'm Emile."

"Therese. Tres."

"And you have an accent. Like myself. Well, not French, as I have."

She smiled. "No, I'm not from France."

Wasn't there an old *SNL* skit that went something like this? she thought. Maybe she was a vampire and he was an alien.

"Come, we'll go to the staff room?" He indicated the way forward. "Yes?"

She nodded and fell in with him, unwrapping her scarf and undoing the buttons on her coat. "I've waitressed before. I'm still nervous, though."

"Enzo, the front house manager? You interviewed with him? He is very nice. Very good. He will give you a fair chance."

"I got a copy of the menu. I spent all day memorizing it."

As they entered the kitchen, there was an anteroom with lockers where people could put their things, and she glanced around at the humans who were milling about in it. The men and women seemed to be in their early to mid twenties, clearly scraping by to get their start in life and become independent from their families—which was exactly what she was trying to do. And a couple of them looked over at her, but everyone was mostly just focused on getting prepared for the dinner service.

The head of the front house, Enzo Angelini, came in and addressed her and then the others. "Good, you're here. Everybody, this is Therese. Therese, you'll learn names on the go. Come with me to sign your paperwork, and I have your tux ready."

There was something comforting about falling into a routine and a set of procedures. After having left home, everything had been free of restrictions, but also way too light and kind of wilderness-without-a-map feeling.

This was going to be a good thing.

The only not-so-hot that was happening? She couldn't seem to get the thoughts about that male from the night before last out of her mind. Images of him were like a hangover without her having done any drinking, her head thumping, her stomach flipping when she remembered that kiss.

He'd been determined to leave her be.

And that still seemed like a good plan.

It was weird, though, to miss someone you didn't know, someone who was a complete stranger. But her heart ached a little at the idea that she'd never see him again.

Whatever, though. It was probably just her hormones. Or maybe the sadness over everything that had gone down as she'd left Michigan was bleeding into other areas of her life.

Yup, that was it.

Because how was it possible to mourn someone you hadn't known for more than twenty minutes?

FORTY-SIX

As soon as Qhuinn walked into the twins' bedroom, he was all set to be alone with his young and get them ready to go to Blay's parents' house . . . but Cormia was over by their bassinets, settling them in. The good news? At least Layla wasn't around, although he caught her scent in the air—and that insult got worse as he went over to the bassinets and smelled her on the kids themselves.

Ignoring Phury's *shellan*, he immediately marched into the bathroom, put the two blue tubs into the pair of deep sinks, and got the hot water running.

When he came back out, Cormia looked at him with a directness he didn't appreciate. "Would you like help with their baths?" she asked.

As if he couldn't do it himself. "Thanks, but no."

The Chosen hesitated, still standing right between the bassinets. "Listen, I know this is really hard right now."

Actually, you really don't, he thought.

"But," the female continued, "Layla loved being with them, and you can see that they fared well."

His children were still breathing, at any rate. This much was true.

"I really think that you—"

Qhuinn put his hand up. "Thank you so much for all your help and concern. I mean, really, you're just great. I can't tell you how grateful I am."

He gently, but firmly, took her elbow and led her over to the door. "I mean, really, just terrific."

As soon as she stepped out into the hall of statues, he shut the door and locked it—and then he was all about those baths, making sure that the water was the right temperature, doing Rhamp first, because his son was easier to handle on so many levels, and then quickly soap-and-rinsing Lyric.

When he got the pair of them back in the bassinets, all rosy and toasty, he thought, fuck, he was going to have to dress them for their exciting trip out of the mansion.

He went into the walk-in closet, where a pair of bureaus had been set up side by side. And as he pulled open drawers, he marveled at all the little clothes, the onesies and the tiny shirts, the "pants" and "skirts." For a second, he wondered how long it took to wash all of this stuff, fold it, and make sure it was in the right place, everything pink on one side, and camo and navy blue on the other.

Layla liked to dress up Lyric in pretty things.

So he put his daughter in a pair of itty-bitty blue jeans and a red polo shirt of her brother's. Then he jacked Rhamp into the smallest suit and bow-tie combo anyone had seen this side of a Ken doll.

He checked the clock, thinking he could shower himself—but holy shit from the time elapse. He'd had an idea of being at Blay's parents' well before First Meal was put on the table. At the rate this was going? He'd be lucky to get those two kids over there before they were driving. And this was before he had to tackle the little booties and then the tiny coats—and fuck him back and forth a couple of hundred times from getting the pair of them into the goddamn carriers.

When he finally had both kids freshly diapered, fully clothed, parka'd, mitten'd, and hat'd—and had strapped the suckers in like they were in danger of break-dancing out of those padded buckets? He actually looked at the bed and thought maybe he needed a nap.

And come on, his night job was fighting *lessers*. Who were trying to kill him.

It wasn't like his basis for comparison was a frickin' desk job.

"Okay," he said to those two faces staring up at him. "You ready? Let's do this—"

At that very instant, a stench that was a cross between a stink bomb, a dead lizard, and some kind of rotting fruit rind wafted up and slapped the shit out of his sinuses.

Jesus H. Christ. It was the kind of thing that made your eyes water and your nose threaten to pack its bags and leave you with nothing but a pair of black holes in the middle of your face.

"Are you even kidding me?"

For a split second, he debated just going with it. After all, he could pop the windows in his Hummer, crank up the heat, and with supplemental oxygen, he might just make it across town.

But he couldn't present Blay's mom with this kind of thing. She already had a broken ankle. One whiff of that green cloud of death and she was liable to get blown off her good foot through a wall.

Leaning down, it became amply clear that Rhamp had deployed the hot bomb. And Qhuinn had to admit, as he undid the buckle and got the kid back out, that he kind of respected the effort, man to man.

Yeah, no pussy loads for his son. The boy dropped that shit like he owned it.

Um . . . literally. Yeah.

Back at the dressing table. Once again with the button and the zipper on the miniature pants that made Qhuinn's hands cramp. And then . . .

"Oh . . . wow," Qhuinn muttered as he had to turn his head away for some fresh air.

Who knew you could see God without leaving the planet?

And clean-up was going to require a backhoe and a hazmat suit.

Meanwhile, Rhamp just lay there, looking up at him with little fists pumping like he was expecting a high five or something.

Given that unaffected focus and coordination, one could only deduce that, while vampire young matured much quicker in their beginning stages than human babies did, clearly their sense of smell didn't kick in until later. Otherwise, the kid wouldn't be smiling.

As Qhuinn got to work on the tabs of the diaper, he had to shake his head. "You're a real pisser, you know that—"

A knock on the door provided an excuse to turn his head away again and breathe deep. "Yeah?"

Saxton, the King's solicitor and Qhuinn's own cousin, put his perfect blond head in. "I have those documents that you—"

The recoil would have been comical if Qhuinn hadn't been up to his elbows in baby poop.

The attorney let out a cough. Or maybe that was a gagging noise. "Dearest Virgin Scribe, whatever are you feeding them?"

"Enfamil formula."

"And this is legal?"

"For the most part, yes. Although depending on the digestive tract it goes into, clearly there are military applications."

"Indeed." The male shook his head as if he were trying to reprioritize his brain away from his respiratory requirements. "Ah, I have what you requested."

"Great. Thanks. Will you put it in Rhamp's carrier? No, wait—actually, the diaper bag. As you can see, I've got my hands full over here."

"Yes, I believe no one in this house would wish your attention be diverted. Make that the eastern seaboard."

As Qhuinn tucked the dirty diaper under his son's butt and started pulling out wipes from the warmer like he was going to make a parachute out of them, he wondered what he was going to do with that Pampers. Maybe burn it in the backyard?

Probably would flame green. Hell on that theory, he should shut off the lights and see if it glowed in the dark.

"Qhuinn."

"Yeah, man?"

When the guy didn't say any further, Qhuinn glanced over his shoulder at the precisely dressed, bow-tied solicitor. "What?"

"Are you certain? About this?"

"Yes, I am absolutely positive that this diaper needs to be changed. And thanks, you've been so helpful. I mean, great. Just really great."

Guess that was his new good-bye. Praise that he honestly felt and meant, but that was designed to end conversation and move people along and away from him.

And yet again, it worked.

Saxton didn't linger much longer, and then Qhuinn was restrapping his son in the carrier, throwing the duffel over his shoulder, and picking up the matched set of baby-delivery devices.

Immediately, he set them back down. Opened the door Saxton had shut behind himself. And then tried again with the whole cash-and-carry out of the room.

'Cuz it was kind of hard to work a frickin' doorknob when you didn't have a free palm.

As he walked past all the marble statues, he felt an abiding exhaustion and figured it could be one of a number of things. He hadn't slept all day long, his mind consumed with thoughts about Blay, anger at Layla, and anxiety over what the hell Rhamp and Lyric were doing. Plus the Xcor thing. And then there had been the infant Olympics of getting the kids ready to go out just now.

Hell, maybe he also had anticipatory depression over the prospect of having to get the damn carriers into the bases he'd strapped in the back of the Hummer. He'd done a dry run right at nightfall and had nearly lost his IQ trying to get the plastic pieces of shit aligned with where they had to click into—and that had been without actually having Rhamp and Lyric in their bucket seats.

Why the idiot humans who had made the things couldn't construct them so the two parts fit was a Sherlock Holmes problem. You'd figure if those rats without tails could put a motherfucker in a space suit on the moon, they could make it so parents didn't have to fight with car seats.

It was really just that simple.

As he hit the grand staircase, he let his mind continue on its various rants, giving his gray matter all kinds of leeway to bitch about kid accoutrements.

It was better than worrying about whether Blay was going to be at his parents' or not. Or whether they were going to make it through this. Or not.

Much better.

As Layla re-formed on the back porch of the ranch, she triggered the motion detectors, lights coming on and illuminating her. That was fine, though. None of the humans would have seen her arriving from out of nowhere because she'd materialized into a deep pocket of shadows by the fence.

Heading for the sliding glass door, she crunched through the thick snow, the sadness of leaving her young behind and her worry that Qhuinn might do something crazy like kidnap them being replaced with anxiety about whether or not Xcor would be waiting for her. Her mind was so scattered, she had barely been able to dematerialize, and she couldn't seem to sense him on the premises.

On the keypad by the handle, she entered a code, heard the lock disengage, and pulled open the door.

Warmth greeted her, and so did silence.

She'd left the light on over the stove, and also one in the living room by the front door. Everything seemed in order—no, wait, the trash had been emptied.

"Xcor?"

She closed the glass door and listened. Breathed in deep.

A piercing disappointment stung her sternum as she got no reply and did not scent him. Curious about who had emptied the kitchen bin, she went across and checked the refrigerator. It had been completely restocked . . . and she was willing to bet that the bedroom downstairs had been refreshed as well.

Clearly, the *doggen* staff had been in to clean up after Xcor had left for the night. And further, the male obviously hadn't spent the day under this roof.

Sitting down at the circular table, she put her hands on the polished top and spread her fingers wide. Then she closed them. And spread them wide once again.

She had assumed that he would be here when she returned. Hadn't they made that plan? Perhaps it had only been on her side. She could not remember.

Oh, God, what if he had been killed during the previous night or day. But no, that was paranoia talking . . . right? Or . . . had he found his males? Had they taken their vows to Wrath already and left without Xcor saying good-bye?

As she listened to the silence in the house, the quiet broken by nothing save the sounds of warm air whistling out of the vents and the occasional tumble of ice falling inside the freezer, her heart pounded from both sorrow and fear.

And then, as time passed, she was struck by the fact that, like the ranch, so, too, was her life so very, very empty. Without the young to attend to, without Xcor to enjoy, what did she have?

Considering that he would be leaving very soon—assuming he hadn't already—and also that there was little chance she was going to go back to live at the mansion ever again, she realized it was time to find something for herself, something that wasn't tied to being a *mahmen* or a mate. When she had functioned as a Chosen, she had had plenty to occupy her mind and her time, all sorts of duties to perform. Here, in the outside world, though? In the post–Scribe Virgin era?

With freedom came the obligation of self-discovery, she supposed.

After all, how could you exercise choice if you didn't have a clue who you were? Labels weren't going to do it, titles like "*mahmen*" or "*shellan*" weren't really going to help you. You needed to dig into yourself and find out how to fill your hours with pursuits that were meaningful to you and for you, as a person, an individual.

Too bad that what should have been viewed as an adventure of exploration and enlightenment struck her as a burden.

As her stomach let out a growl, she glanced over at the refrigerator door. There had been all kinds of things in there, but little that interested her enough to have her even cross the floor, much less get out pots and pans. And takeout? She had heard of it, but she had no cash, no credit cards, and no interest in tangling with humans—

Knock knock knock—

Layla jumped and twisted around to the slider. And then she smiled. Smiled big.

Smiled huge.

Leaping from the chair, she sprang the lock on the glass door and looked up, way up, at the face that had been in her mind for the past twenty-four hours.

"You came back," she breathed as Xcor stepped inside and shut them in together.

His eyes narrowed on her mouth. "Where'er else would I go?"

Layla was tempted to make him swear that he wouldn't leave for the Old Country without a proper good-bye, but now that he was in front of her, she didn't want to mar even a second of their together-time with thoughts of the split that was coming.

Rising on her tiptoes, she leaned forward until she went off balance, sure that he would catch her—and he did, his arms solid and strong around her.

"Tell me," he said before he kissed her, "are the young well? Are they all right? Are you?"

For a moment, she closed her eyes. The idea that he would ask about the offspring of a male who had paid him no honor was such a kind and generous thing to do.

"Layla?" He pulled back. "Is all well?"

She blinked quickly. "Yes, yes, very well. We had a lovely night and day. They are a wondrous sight to behold. A true blessing."

For a moment, she entertained a fantasy about him meeting Lyric and Rhamp, of him holding them and getting to know them. But that was never going to happen, and not just because Xcor would be returning to the Old Country.

"And you?" she said. "Are you well?"

"I am now."

His lips found hers, his arms went back around her, and he picked her up, holding her flush against his powerful body. Melding their mouths, he moved her against the wall and pinned her with her feet dangling from the ground.

With a groan, she put her legs around his waist, tilted her head to one side . . . and kissed the ever-living crap out of him. All of her worry, all of her concern and anxiety over him, the young, Qhuinn . . . her stress just went out the window as the taste and scent of him became the only thing she knew.

All too soon, Xcor eased back, his hot eyes raking over her hair, her shoulders. He was seeing her naked, she thought as he stared at her. He was remembering exactly what she looked like with nothing but bare skin and passion to clothe her—

"When did you eat last?" he asked.

Okaaaaay, so maybe he was thinking about other things.

"I don't know." She moved her hands from his shoulders to the nape of his neck. "Kiss me again . . . oh, kiss me—"

"We are going to feed you now."

With that, he set her in a chair like she weighed no more than a doll. And just as she was going to point out that there would be time after making love to bother with the whole caloric thing, he undid the black parka he was wearing.

Which was a movement in the right direction—

"Is that a bulletproof vest?" she demanded.

He looked down at his chest. "Yes."

She closed her eyes for a moment and not just from relief that he had one on. It was also because she wished that the war didn't exist. That no one from his camp had tried to shoot Wrath. That there was no reason for him to have to worry about guns or knives or any other kind of weapon coming at him.

"What would you care for?" he inquired as he set the parka aside and started working on the straps of the vest. "And bear in mind, I am no great chef. I wish I could provide you with fare of great sophistication, however."

Princeps or a pauper, chef or not, she thought, I do not care.

Especially if you keep taking off your—

"Wait, are you hurt?" she said as she stood up.

"What?"

"You're hurt."

As he pulled the vest off of himself, she pointed to the dried blood on his side. And before he could minimize it, she got right in there, yanking the T-shirt up—and gasping at the wound.

"You were shot." After all, what else could make that kind of stripe? Not a knife, certainly. "What happened?"

He shrugged. "I didn't feel it."

She pushed his hands away as he tried to cover himself up. "Down to the bathroom. Right now. Come on."

When he didn't seem inclined to obey the order, she took his hand and pulled him along with her, forcing him to descend to the cellar and enter the bedroom they'd shared. In the bathroom, she ran warm water in the sink, got out the soap and a washcloth, and then started to remove the shirt.

"Layla—"

"Xcor," she muttered, mimicking his bored tone. "And yes, I know better than to ask you to go see Havers or let me get Doc Jane. So in return for my sensible nature, you are going to let me clean the wound."

"It's healed up."

"Has it?" She wet the washcloth and put some soap on it. "Is that why it's bleeding anew now that you've taken the vest off? Now remove that shirt or I'm getting a pair of scissors."

Xcor started to grumble, but at least he did as he was told—and then hissed as she started to gently rub the streak of inflamed and torn flesh. When she could see things better, it appeared that the bullet had just grazed him, catching his torso at the side panels of the vest that didn't have the protective inserts in them, maybe because he had been jumping or running at the time. The vest had then shifted back into place and sealed the wound, binding it until the thing had been removed.

Or at least that was her rather inexpert conclusion.

"So what happened?" she asked as she rinsed the washcloth and started blotting to get the soap off. "Well?"

When she glanced up from her work, she got a heck of a view of Xcor's iron jaw, and the way his molars were clenched. Likewise, he had crossed his arms over his chest, a veritable picture of disapproval.

"Did you find your males?" she prompted.

"No," he clipped out. "I did not."

Well, at least it hadn't been one of them, angry at him for his vow unto the King.

"Was it *lessers*?"

After a long moment, when she was beginning to wonder whether she was going to have to drag the explanation out of him with a grappling hook, he reluctantly nodded.

Layla closed her eyes. "I hate this war. I really do."

Dearest Virgin—um, Dearest Most-Definitely-Not-a-Virgin Lassiter, she hated to think what would have happened out there in that storm if he'd been shot somewhere else, like the head—

"I'm all right," he said gently.

Focusing on him, she found that he'd dropped his arms and was staring at her with softness in his eyes.

"Don't cry, my love."

"Am I?" she whispered.

"Aye." With care, he brushed her cheeks with his thumbs. "Never cry for me."

He urged her to straighten and come up against his body. "Besides, I am well enough. Witness me here and now."

With that, he kissed her long and slow, his lips teasing and taking, his tongue licking and stroking at her, and soon she melted, all thoughts of nursing his wound leaving her head. Which was undoubtedly his plan—and yet she couldn't help but give in to him.

"You are the great eraser," she said against his mouth.

"I'm sorry?"

Shaking her head, she leaned into him even more—and then let out a curse as he moved back and out of reach.

"Food," he announced. "Now."

When she started to protest, he cocked an eyebrow. "I let you take care of me. So I am going to take care of you."

With that, he snagged her hand and led her back toward the stairs. As they passed by the bed, she muttered, "You realize that's a mattress right there. Riiiiight there."

"And it shall be waiting for us when we finish feeding you, my female."

FORTY-SEVEN

As Qhuinn pulled the Hummer into Blay's parents' driveway, he checked out all the windows in the house. There were a lot of them that were lit up, and he searched for one specific big body moving around, one large, beautifully built—

The front door was thrown open, and sure enough, the male in question's *mahmen* came out with her crutches and her cast, looking for all intents and purposes like she was going to come down the walkway even though it was slick with ice and snow.

In a panic, Qhuinn reached for his door handle, prepared to dematerialize in her path to stop her, but then Blay's dad ran out and said something.

For a moment, Qhuinn just watched their expressions as they argued, the fondness and the love they had for each other turning the conflict into a negotiation between reasonable parties.

Something to work for, he thought.

"You ready, guys?" he asked as he glanced into the review mirror. "Time to go see *Grandmahmen* and Grandfather."

Shutting the engine down and getting out, he waved toward the porch. "Evening all!"

"I'm so excited!" Lyric called out.

"She's been cooking," Blay's dad said with a shake of the head. "She's been cooking even though she's on doctor's orders to stay off her feet and those two young are on formula."

"But I have our Qhuinn to feed!" Lyric was positively bubbling over with enthusiasm, bouncing up and down in her own skin. "And besides, the house will smell good for the young. They'll appreciate the cinnamon and spice in the air."

Or maybe not, Qhuinn thought as he went around to get Rhamp out first. It was quite possible his son's sniffer was broken.

After wrestling with the car seat, he got the carrier free and then combat-booted himself and his boy up the walkway. "Care for a kid?" he said to Blay's dad.

"Oh, you have no idea," the male replied as he accepted the transfer.

As Qhuinn was about to turn away, he got a load of their expressions as they looked down at the young—and he nearly teared up. The two older vampires were rapt with love, their stares glowing, their eyes blinking, their faces flushing.

It made him think about what Blay had said about not torturing them with kids that were not their own.

Well, he'd fixed that.

Trying to be surreptitious, he leaned to one side and looked into the front hall. No Blay. And no Blay coming down the stairs, either. Or emerging from the back of the house. And Qhuinn was far too scattered to be able to sense the guy.

Hmm, how to put it into words—

"Is Blay here?"

As his mouth opened and the syllables came out, the male's parents froze.

Blay's father frowned and glanced at Big Lyric. "He's just on the back porch. Where else would he be?"

Lyric, on the other hand, clearly knew what was up. "Why don't you go get him?" Then she looked at her *hellren*. "Honey, grab Lyric out of that enormous carbon-footprinted nightmare, will you?"

As Blay's dad hopped on that duty, Qhuinn felt like hugging the female. So he did—and the fact that she accepted his embrace so readily gave him hope.

"Go on, now," she whispered in his ear. "You two work out whatever this is. We'll watch the young."

When Qhuinn straightened, something of what he was feeling must have shown in his expression, because she reached up and stroked his face.

"I love you, even if your choice of automobile appalls me. That gets, what, maybe two miles per gallon? On the highway?"

Blay's dad piped in as he came back with Little Lyric: "It did get us safely to the training center last night. Your Prius? That thing wouldn't have made it out of the driveway."

Like the male knew he'd pushed it as far as he could, Rocke winked at Qhuinn, smiled with love at his *shellan*, and beat feet into the house with both carriers like he was being chased with a rolled-up copy of *Mother Jones*.

"You two take your time," Blay's mom said. "I'm going to quote some climate change articles to your young. Maybe make them watch Bill Gates's *Innovating to zero!* TED talk."

Qhuinn helped her back into the house, even though she tried to resist the hand on her elbow, and she was right: The cinnamon and spices did smell terrific, and the warmth from the fire in the family room was perfect on a cold night, and everything seemed to glow with love.

Bracing himself, he passed by the kitchen and went to the porch door in the back. Before he opened things up, he checked to make sure the collar on his button-down was where it needed to be and that his wool coat was, like, properly whatever'd. Also did a quick Desitin review in case he had the stuff on anything.

And then . . .

Through the glass panes in the upper part of the door, he saw Blay standing in the cold, nothing but a sweater on, staring out over the snowy landscape to a frozen pond. As the male took a drag on his cigarette, the end flared orange, and then a cloud of smoke drifted off over his red head.

He looked regal in his reserve, his shoulders back, his eyes narrowed on some distant point, his feet planted on the otherwise empty porch.

Something told Qhuinn to knock before he went out.

When he did, Blay didn't turn around. He just shrugged a little.

Beggars couldn't be choosers, Qhuinn thought as he opened the door and stepped into the early winter's night.

And shit knew he was more than willing to beg.

"More toast?"

As Xcor made the inquiry from across the table, Layla shook her head, wiped her mouth with a paper towel, and sat back.

"You know, I think I'm quite satisfied, thank you." Translation: I've sucked back two pieces of toast, two eggs, and a mug of Earl Grey. Can we be done now and go downstairs to make love?

"I'll just get you one more slice. How about more tea?"

Whilst he got up from the table, she could tell by the set of his shoulders and the disapproval on his face that he somehow knew she had lied about being full—and he had no intention of being diverted from the goal of feeding her properly.

"Yes, please."

Her tone was closer to "screw that" than "thank you for your further Earl Greying on my behalf," but that was what sexual frustration would do for a female.

"How about we take it and go downstairs?" she suggested, thinking that way, they'd be closer to the bed they were going to mess the heck up. "In fact, I'll just head down now."

Over at the toaster, Xcor put in another two slices of Pepperidge Farm white and pushed down the lever. "I shall bring you everything. Go and put your feet up—leave your mug for me."

Heading for the cellar door, she paused and glanced over her shoulder. The gray and white kitchen was small, and Xcor's heft dwarfed the space sure as if a German shepherd had wandered into a dollhouse. And it was so incongruous that this warrior was bending down over the toaster to carefully monitor its toasting process.

Not too light, not too dark.

Then there was the buttering. He approached the dispensation of sweet butter over a crispy bread surface with the seriousness and attention span of a heart surgeon.

It was exactly how she had always wished the male she loved would treat her—and that wasn't about whether it was First Meal or Last Meal, day or night outside, winter or summer. Xcor's focus and concern simply showed that she mattered to him. That he cared about her.

That he *saw* her.

After a lifetime of being one of many to somebody divine, it was a rare gift to be the only one to someone mortal.

But damn it, why couldn't they be having sex right now?

Down in the cellar, she lowered the lights and turned on the TV, hoping to find one of the romantic movies Beth and Marissa liked to watch on cable. News. News. Commercial. Commercial—

What was taking him so long, she thought as she glanced to the stairs. Commercial. Commercial—

Oh, this was good. *While You Were Sleeping.*

Where was Xcor, though?

Finally, after what seemed like a hundred years, she heard him coming down the stairs. "I turned the security system on," he said.

She muted the volume on Sandra Bullock trying to pull a Christmas tree into her apartment through an open window and then attempted to arrange her and her robing in a suitably come-hither fashion on the sofa. The robe was frustrating. When the *doggen* had refreshed the house, they had delivered several of the Chosen uniforms for her, not knowing she didn't wear them anymore. Too bad it hadn't been lingerie. With the loose folds swallowing the contours of her body, she was hardly beauty queen material.

Although her male did seem to prefer her naked.

When he wasn't stuffing her with food, that was—

"Oh," she said as she took a gander at the tray he'd brought with him.

Xcor might as well have lugged the kitchen table down to the cellar. He'd toasted the rest of the loaf, scrambled more eggs, and made a teapot full of hot stuff. He'd also included the cream, even though she hadn't used it, and the honey pot, which she had.

"Well, that's . . . just lovely," she said as he set it all down on the low coffee table.

Sitting himself next to her, he took a piece of toast off the stack and began the buttering process.

"I can do that," she muttered.

"I should like to serve you."

Then drop your pants, she thought as she eyed the huge thighs that strained the seams of the black nylon sweats he was wearing. And then there was the way the bottom of the sleeve of his T-shirt struggled to hold the thick circumference of his bicep. And the shadow of beard growth that darkened his jaw.

Sinking her nails into her knees, she looked at his mouth. "Xcor."

"Hmm?" he asked as he moved a mathematically precise layer of butter over the toast with a knife.

"Enough with the food."

"I'm almost finished here."

And I'm totally finished over here, she thought.

Sitting forward, Layla tried to distract herself with pouring some tea, but it was a lost cause. She did, however, note the way the lapels of her robing loosened.

Take it, run with it.

Bringing her hands to the tie at her waist, she released the knot and pulled the two halves apart, exposing the translucent sheath that was the traditional undergarment of the Chosen. Okay, that had to go, too—and what do you know, as she slipped the tiny seed-pearl buttons free of their eyelets, they followed the prompting with an ease that suggested they were determined to be of aid in her endeavor.

Taking her cue from them, she then slipped herself out of all that covered her and lay back into the nest of the robing.

Yet him still with the frickin' toast.

As he sat back a little and contemplated the buttering job he'd done, she had a thought that although the bonded-male-feeding-his-female thing clearly had its evolutionary advantages, this was ridiculous.

What was he going to do next? Get a ruler to check the verticality?

"You know what would be good on toast?" he said as he went in again with the knife tip.

Yup, 'cuz there was a millimeter on that left upper edge that was underserved.

"What?"

"Honey," he murmured. "I think it would be rather good indeed."

Layla looked at the honey pot.

"I believe you're right." Reaching forward, she picked the thing up and arched her back. "Honey is good on a lot of things."

Swirling the dipper, she took the thing out and held it over her breast, and as the honey spooled and fell, her nipple caught the sweetness. The tickle made her bite her lip, and then more of the amber glow dripped onto her skin, a river of it easing down to her abdomen.

"Xcor . . . ?"

"Yes—"

When he glanced over at her, he did a double take—and dropped the toast on the tray. Which was a relief because, really, if she couldn't win a competition with carbohydrates for his attention she was seriously in trouble.

His navy blue eyes were instantly hot and very, very locked on the way the honey slowly, tantalizingly hit her breast drop by drop and meandered down, down . . . down.

"I wonder," she said in a husky voice, "whether honey is sweeter than me?"

With that, she cocked one knee up and flashed her core at him.

Her male shoved that tray away so fast it was like the plate on it had said something bad about his fighters.

The pumping growl coming out of him was more like it, and so was the sight of the tips of his fangs descending in a rush. And then he was rearing up over her, great arms bowing out above her body, his tremendous strength barely in check as his tongue extended just under her nipple . . . to catch a drop.

With a moan, his warm, slick lips captured and sucked, licked and kissed. Layla's head fell back, but she turned it to the side so she could watch her enormous male. The sensations were so erotic she could feel an orgasm coming on, but she didn't want this over with. Having been impatient to be with him, she now wanted to savor every second they were together.

"Xcor . . . look at me."

As his eyes flipped to hers, she held the wand over her mouth and let the last of the honey land on her tongue. And then she did some swirling of her own before sucking the bud in and pulling it out . . . sucking it in and pulling it out . . .

"You'll be the death of me yet, female," Xcor cursed.

With a deft move, he took the dipper from her and returned it to the pot, just as her body became what she had poured on herself, her bones melting away, her muscles going lax. As her legs fell even further open, he took her mouth hard, their lips clinging from the stickiness, his arousal pressing into her core through his pants.

That didn't last.

With rough hands, he freed his sex and then he was inside of her, pumping while he kissed her, their bodies finding a rhythm that was so rough the sofa itself rocked and banged against the wall.

Harder, faster, deeper, until they couldn't keep their mouths together anymore. Reaching up, she held onto his surging shoulders, the muscles under his smooth skin like an ocean that was storming—

Pleasure broke like a lightning strike, but also made her whole—and then he found his own release, pouring himself into her.

And Xcor didn't stop.

Or slow down.

FORTY-EIGHT

B lay's heart tap danced as that porch door opened behind him and the scent of his one-and-only preceded the guy coming over to the railing.

One good thing about smoking was that it gave you something to do with your hands. One bad thing about smoking was that when you decided to tap your ash as busywork, if you had a tremor going on, it showed.

"Hi."

Blay coughed a little. "Hey."

"I'm glad you're here." Pause. "I didn't think you were going to be."

For a moment, Blay just wanted to yell, *Neither did I, motherfucker!* But that seemed like an omission best kept to himself if he wanted to look strong, be strong . . . stay strong.

God, why did Qhuinn have to smell good?

"I brought Rhamp," Qhuinn murmured.

"That was your plan." Except he frowned. "Where's Lyric—"

"Oh, she's here, too. Yeah."

As a soft breeze came in from the south, Blay thought of a ballet dancer spinning with controlled turns over the blue-tinted snowy landscape. There were no more leaves to pirouette with her, everything covered with that white blanket, but on the edges of the property, evergreen boughs that were bent under the weight of what had landed on them got some relief as snow swirls jetted off of their burden.

In his peripheral vision, through the windows behind Qhuinn, he could see his parents moving around in the yellow, homey light of the kitchen. His *mahmen* had insisted on cooking for six hours straight, her excitement and happiness reinvigorating her after a trying night and day. So great was her joy, it was hard to remember that they'd had to put her under and reset that bone. That there were stitches under her cast. That she was going to have to go back in the night after tomorrow to have Dr. Manello check everything.

At least Fritz had been able to take them back here in the blackout van, even though it had been daylight by the time Lyric had been released from the clinic. His parents had really wanted to get home after the ordeal, and Blay sure as hell hadn't been into arguing with that—

"I have something for you," Qhuinn said.

As the male reached into his coat, Blay shook his head and stabbed out his half-smoked cigarette. "Let's go inside? I'm cold."

He didn't wait for any acknowledgment, and wasn't interested in whatever it was.

Stepping back into the house, he was hit with a warm wall of scents that reminded him of family, and made him want to vomit. Especially as Qhuinn followed him into the kitchen, the male's presence undiminished even though he wasn't in Blay's line of sight.

Maybe even magnified.

"How can I help?" Blay asked as he smiled at his mom.

The elder Lyric was sitting on a stool in front of the gas stove, frying up bacon and eggs and French toast.

"You can say hello to your kids," she tossed over her shoulder. "And set the table."

Swallowing a burst of pain in his chest, like someone had kicked him in the sternum, Blay put his Dunhills by the house phone, went to wash his hands—and tried to prepare himself for seeing the young.

Nope, he thought as he dried off what he had scrubbed. He couldn't look in those carriers yet. He needed to get ahold of himself somehow first or he was liable to break down.

Busywork at the drawer where the silverware was kept. Busywork gathering red-and-white napkins. Busywork getting out four plates.

At the island that ran down the entire middle of the kitchen, Qhuinn and his father were talking about the war, about human politics, about the NCAA football playoffs and the start of NCAA conference play in basketball.

Qhuinn's eyes were on Blay the whole time.

And the male was smart. He knew if he said one thing about Blay going over to the young, who had fallen asleep in their carriers on the table, it was going to backfire.

Damn it, Blay thought finally. He couldn't keep avoiding the kids.

Bracing himself, he made a pile of napkins and forks and knives and other stuff and walked over.

He tried not to look. Failed.

And the instant his eyes drifted over the young, he was stripped of his self-protection: All those lectures about how he needed to remain a dis-interested third party to them so he didn't get hurt ever again went out the window.

As if sensing his presence, the pair woke up, looked at him, and in-stantly did that pinwheeling thing with their arms and legs, their cheru-bic little faces becoming animated, soft clicking noises coming out of their mouths. They clearly recognized him.

Maybe even had missed him.

Slowly lowering whatever the hell he was carrying—it could have stuff to eat with and on, or maybe a toaster oven, a snow shovel, or a television—he leaned down.

He opened his mouth to speak, but nothing came out. His throat had closed up.

So he was going to have to rely on touch to communicate. Which was fine. They couldn't talk, either.

He went to Lyric first, stroking her cheek, tickling her soft neck. And he could have sworn she giggled.

"How's my girl?" he whispered in a broken rush.

But then he realized the pronoun he'd used—and squeezed his eyes shut. *Not* my children, he corrected himself. These are *not* my kids.

Yeah, sure, Qhuinn was back on the family train. Except how long was it going to last? When was he going to get triggered by the Layla thing again and go off the rails? The smart thing to do was take the hit once, heal the wound up tight so the pain never had to happen again—and never look back.

On that note, he focused on Rhamp. Such a chunk, such a little tough guy. Blay strongly believed that the traditional sex-role thing was bullshit, and that if Lyric wanted to be an ass-kicker like Payne or Xhex, he was on board with that. And likewise, if Rhamp decided to be a doctor or lawyer and stay off the field, that was fine, too. But man, they were so obviously different—although it was critical that that not define them. He believed it was vitally important that kids be free to—

Shit. He was doing it again. Forgetting where the boundaries were.

The sound of forks and knives knocking into each other brought his head up. Qhuinn had taken over the plate-setting thing, making nice with the napkins and the silverware, his head bowed, his face somber.

Blay cleared his throat. "I can do that."

"It's okay. I got it."

At that moment, Rhamp let out a stink bomb that was enough to make a grown male's eyes water.

"Oh . . . *wow*."

"Yeah," Qhuinn said. "You should have smelled him right before I came over here. It's why I was late. Would you do me a favor and check him? Maybe we've lucked out and it's just gas."

Blay locked his molars. It was on the tip of his tongue to tell the guy to do it himself, but that seemed churlish. Besides, in his heart, he wanted to hold the young, and his parents were over there, watching while trying not to watch.

As everything seemed to freeze in place, he abruptly felt as though his whole life and his concept of family boiled down to this moment—and it was weird how life came at you like that. You went along, building ties or breaking them, moving forward or backward in relationships, riding out the sea of your emotions and the emotions of others—but for the most part, it was a trees-for-the-forest kind of thing, a piecemeal one-step/two-step dance of choices and decisions more trail than marker, more random direction than compass.

Except then, suddenly, the camera aperture opened so fast you got existential whiplash, and you were forced to look at everything and go, okay, wow, so I'm *here*.

All over a kid that had taken a crap in his pants and who was going to deal with it.

Qhuinn came around and set a place right in front of Blay. In a voice that didn't carry, the male said, "I miss you. They miss you."

"I'm an uncle," Blay heard himself say. "Okay? Just an uncle."

With hands that shook, he released the straps and scooped up Rhamp. Holding that baby butt high, he put his nose right in there and breathed in deep.

"We're clear, Houston," he said roughly. "Repeat, that was a gaseous cloud. There has been no breach of the force field."

Transferring Qhuinn's son into the crook of his arm, Blay took a seat and played the fingertips-in-front-of-the-eyeballs game.

"Who's hungry?" his mother said cheerfully. Like she'd decided all would be well just because he was holding a kid.

"Look at those reflexes," his dad remarked as Rhamp's hands moved from side to side and grabbed with astonishing accuracy. "Qhuinn, that is your kid, isn't he."

"Yes," Blay chimed in. "He really is."

Layla lost count of how many times they made love. Twice on the sofa. Then in the shower. Three more times in the bed?

As she lay side by side with her male, stroking his heavy shoulder, feeling him breathe into her neck, she smiled in the darkness. Insatiability was an asset when it came to having a lover in your life.

And Xcor was a very, very hungry male.

The insides of her thighs ached. Her core had a hum in it from all the friction. And his scent was all over her, inside and out.

She wouldn't have changed a thing.

Well, maybe one thing—

"What ails you?" he asked as his head popped up.

"I'm sorry?"

"What is wrong?"

She shouldn't have been surprised that he could read her mood even half asleep and in total blackness. He was amazingly in tune with her, and not just sexually.

"Layla," he prompted.

"I just don't want you to go," she whispered. "I can't bear the idea of not . . ."

As she let her voice drift, his head lowered back into position and he kissed the side of her throat. When he didn't say anything, she wasn't surprised. What words were there? She had her young, and as much as she loved Xcor, she was not going to take them to the Old Country. They needed their father.

And Qhuinn would never allow that, either.

"Do not think of it, my female."

He was so right. She had the rest of her life to miss him. Why start now when he was still with her?

"I know so little about you," she murmured. "How you grew up. Where you have traveled. How you came to be here."

"There is naught to tell."

"Or is it that you don't want me to know."

His silence answered that question. But it wasn't as if she couldn't extrapolate from what she had read of him up in the Sanctuary. Indeed, her sadness at the cruelty shown to him was an ache that went right through to her soul—especially as she thought of Rhamp. The idea that a parent could decide to turn away an innocent young simply because they had a defect not of their own doing?

It didn't bear thinking about, and yet she couldn't stop.

"We don't have much time left," she said softly—even though she had just promised herself not to dwell on the parting. "As soon as you find your males, you will bring them unto Wrath and they will swear their oaths . . . and then you will go. I need to live a lifetime in these nights we have."

"You will go on."

"And so will you," she countered. "Just not together. So please let me in. While we have this time . . . spare nothing of both the goodness and the evil so that I know the whole of you."

"If you don't want to waste time, let us not talk."

Except as he tried to kiss her, she held him back. "I am not afraid of your past."

His voice dropped. "You should be."

"You have never been hurtful to me."

"That is not true and you know it."

As she remembered how he had sent her away, he sat up, turned the light on, and swung his feet out from between the sheets. He didn't leave, though.

She wanted to touch him, smooth her hand down his spine, ease him as he put his head in his hands. She knew better, however.

"I can feel your regrets," she whispered.

Xcor was quiet for a long time, and then he said, "One can be influenced in directions that . . ." Abruptly, he shook his head. "No, I did what I did. No one forced me into any of it. I followed an evil male and behaved in evil ways, and I hold myself the now accountable for it all."

"Tell me," she prompted.

"No."

"I will love you anyway."

Xcor stiffened, and then slowly turned to her. His face was marked by harsh shadows—that were nothing compared to the ones in his eyes. "You know not what you say."

"I love you." She put her hand on his arm and held his stare steadily, challenging him to deny what she felt. "Do you hear me? *I love you.*"

He shook his head and looked away. "You do not know me."

"So help me to do that."

"And run the risk of you throwing me out? You say you want to spend the time we have together. I will guarantee that won't happen if you know me any better than you do the now."

"I would never throw you out."

"My *mahmen* already did. Why would you be any different?" He shook his head again. "Mayhap she knew what course I would take. Mayhap . . . it wasn't because of the lip."

Layla was well aware that she had to tread carefully. "Your mother eschewed you?"

"I was placed with a nursemaid . . . someone . . . until she left me, too."

"What of your father?" she asked tightly. Even though she knew some of that.

"I thought he was the Bloodletter. That male told me he was my sire, but later I learned that was not the case."

"Have you never . . . attempted to discover who your father is?"

Xcor flexed his hands then curled them tight. "I have come to believe that biology is less indicative of family than choice. My males, my soldiers, they chose me. They chose to follow me. They are my family. Two individuals who brought about my conception and birth and then deserted me when I was incapable of surviving on my own? I need not learn of their identities nor their whereabouts."

Pure fear sliced through Layla's heart as she imagined him first as a young newly born, and then as a little boy incapable of defending himself, and finally a pretrans going through the change unattended.

"However did you survive?" she breathed.

"I did what I had to. And I fought. I have always been good at fighting. That is the only legacy my parents gave me that has been of value."

"How did your transition . . . how did you make it through the change?" This was an honest question, as it had not been included in his scribed volume.

"I gave the whore who serviced me the cottage I stayed in. I had to pay her or she would not have allowed me to take her vein. It seemed like a fair trade, my life for my shelter. I figured I could find another place to live, and I did."

Layla sat up and pulled the sheets to her chin. "I couldn't do that to a young. I just couldn't."

"And that is why you are a female of worth." He shrugged. "Besides, I was a failed conception. I'm quite sure that both of them would have rather I had died in the womb or the birthing canal—probably even if it killed my *mahmen*. Better to have a young passed on than to bring the likes of me into existence."

"That is wrong."

"That is life, and well you know it."

"And then you went into the war camp."

Xcor glanced over at her, his expression hard. "You are determined to get this out of me, aren't you."

"You do not have to hide with me."

"Do you want to know how I lost my virginity, then?" he snapped. "Do you?"

She closed her eyes briefly. "Yes."

"Oh, wait. Perhaps I should be more specific. Would you like to know when I fucked a female for the first time—or is it when I had sex for the first time? Because they are not one in the same. The former cost me ten times the going rate with a prostitute in the Old Country, and the first thing she did afterward was run for the river and bathe me off of her. I actually wondered whether she was going to drown herself, she hit that water so hard."

Layla blinked back tears. "And . . . the other."

His face grew dark with rage. "I was fucked by a solider. In front of the war camp. Because I lost to him in a fight. I bled for hours afterward."

Closing her eyes, she found herself mouthing a prayer.

"Still want me now?" he drawled.

"Yes." She opened her lids and looked at him. "You are not unclean to me. And you are not any less of a male."

The smile on his face scared her, for it was so cold and distant. "I did it to others, by the way. When I beat them."

The sorrow she felt was so deep and abiding, it was beyond tears.

And she knew exactly what he was doing. He was pushing her away again, challenging her to leave so she wouldn't tell him to go. He had done it before, and what else could you expect from a male who had been shunned his entire life.

"Still want this? Still think you love this?" When she didn't respond, he indicated his face and then his body as if they belonged to someone else. "Well, female, what do you say?"

FORTY-NINE

ishous left the Brotherhood mansion alone and told nobody where he was going. It wasn't that he was hiding anything, it was just that Butch was out in the field with Rhage, John Matthew and Tohr, Wrath was at the Audience House with Phury and Z, and yada, yada, yada.

Oh, and Jane was down in the clinic.

Which was fine.

So yeah, he had no one to tell and nobody whose radar was trained on his whereabouts. S'all good.

The snowstorm of the night before had left a cleanup problem in its wake, and as V dematerialized to the outer rim of Caldwell's urban downtown, he saw all kinds of what he expected: some removal progress, but really, still a shitload of white stuff covering all manner of parked cars and apartment buildings, the main roads down to two lanes, the alleyways impassible, the sidewalks uncleared.

The address he re-formed in front of was a three-story Victorian that had been cut up into a trio of flats. Lights were on in each of the levels, and the humans inside were chilling, winding down from work.

Or . . . in the case of the apartment he was interested in, getting stoned.

Shifting his position up to the roof of the building across the street, he lit a hand-rolled and watched. And waited. The particular human he was waiting for was not yet home, and he knew this because he'd done some research on good ol' Damn Stoker.

Turned out "he" was a woman. A Ms. Jo Early, who happened to work at the *Caldwell Courier Journal.*

The fact that she was female had kind of impressed him, actually. He'd assumed the clarity of voice and non-emotional presentation of facts in that blog meant a male set of fingers were doing the walking, but come on. As if his *shellan* wasn't the same?

Jane was as tough as they came, and more clear thinking than he was.

Like, for example, he was quite sure Jane wasn't in a funk over the status of their mating. No, she was working at her job saving lives. He was the one doing the Dr. Phil bullshit—

Okaaaaaaaaaay, let's try and not make everything about ourselves, shall we, he thought.

As he smoked and tried to get his brain off his relationship, his gray matter did indeed take him in another direction. Too bad it wasn't much of an improvement. Assuming he wanted a little peace.

As he had been sitting at his desk during the day and checking YouTube videos and Facebook pages and Insta accounts for vampire sightings by humans, he had been tempted by an old email addy of his, one that he'd abandoned as soon as Doc Jane had come into his life.

Well, actually, he'd stopped using it pretty much after he'd met Butch.

The handle, which was a pseudonym, and its associated Gmail account, was one he had registered on websites where subs went begging for Doms, both inside the species and out.

There had always been volunteers for him, back in the day. Females and males, men and women, all of whom were looking for a certain kind of experience—and V had had a routine that he followed with them. First, he'd meet them out at clubs or through references and screen them, picking and choosing the most attractive ones—or the ones who he thought would put on a good show. Then he'd take them to his penthouse at the top of the Commodore and play around with them until he got bored. Whenever he was done, he'd kick them out.

A few he saw more than once. The vast majority had been one and dones.

There had been only three regulars.

Back then, it had been all about burning off his edge, tempering his dark side, turning the dimmer switch down on his drives.

He signed into the account today.

Around noon.

Right after he'd gotten a text from Jane telling him that Blay's mom had come through the operation just fine, but wanted to go home—so Jane had to stay at the clinic and try to talk the female out of leaving. The quick missive had come through about two hours after she'd told him she was done in the OR and on her way to the Pit—all she had to do was make sure the older Lyric came out of anesthesia. Which had been pre-ceded two hours prior to that with a text talking about Assail.

There had been almost two hundred emails in the account.

And he had read through every single one of them. Some were short, nothing but vital stats with maybe a picture as an attachment. Others were long and rambling, streams of consciousness about what they wanted to have done to them. There were also two-paragraphers that begged for him to reconsider, reconnect, resume. And introductory sen-tences with phone numbers. And angry tirades that he couldn't just for-get them, no, no he could not, they weren't going to have it, they were going to find him and make him realize how they were the right one for him . . .

It was like an archaeological dig in the relics of a city he had once constructed, assumed residence in, and lorded over.

Down below, on the cramped, snow-choked street, a Honda pulled up to the apartment building. Whoever was in it talked for a minute, and then the passenger-side door opened and a slender, red-haired human female got out.

"We'll talk tomorrow, then?" she said into the car. "Okay. Yup, I'm on it—yeah, I'll get it posted on the *CCJ* website tomorrow first thing. Dick can go pound sand."

With a final wave, she shut the door and scooted around the blunt hood of the car. Putting her arms out to balance, she stepped through a snowbank in the predetermined footprints many people had used, then she skated up the walkway and checked the mailbox beside the right of the two doors.

A few moments later, he saw her walk through the second story's front room and talk to the guys who were passing a bong back and forth as they sat on the sofa in front of the TV.

She looked pissed, V thought, as she put one hand on her hip and shook a stack of what looked like bills in their direction.

Then she marched off into the front bedroom and closed the door.

He looked away when she started to undress, but he didn't need to bother. As it turned out, she just took off her outer coat and finished the rest in a bathroom that had a frosted window.

She ended up at her desk, in front of her POS Apple product, hitting the Internet.

As V lit another hand-rolled, he debated just putting a bullet in her head, but then decided he was only being cranky. Apart from the videos and shit that she posted, a cursory check of her background hadn't yielded any red flags. She was the adopted kid of some rich folks. Meh job working at the *CCJ* on Internet content. Previously had been a receptionist at a real estate company. Pretty fancy school résumé, but like a lot of young kids, hadn't done shit with that.

Unless you counted using proper grammar while talking about vampires.

So yeah, all he needed to do was erase her and he could go back to the Pit.

Taking a drag, he released the smoke and watched it float away on the mostly still air.

Off in the distance, he heard a siren.

Ambulance, he thought. That was an ambulance.

Overhead, in the crystal clear, velvet blue sky, only the brightest stars twinkled because of downtown's sweating of illumination, but the planes showed up well enough, their flight patterns around the Caldwell International Airport concentric, invisible rings.

Like maybe God was using a highlighter to circle the city for some kind of follow-up.

After a while of staring at the human female, he wondered again why he wasn't getting on with what he'd come out here to do. Hacking into her site and taking control of it, and then erasing content off YouTube, he could do back home.

Had to do, that was.

The Internet, after all, was kind of like a petri dish in a lab. If you wanted to a grow a certain culture, you just created the right conditions and let time do its thing: Enough chatter and talk about vampires, backed up by enough footage, and sooner or later it was going to catch on, because humans loved spooky shit, particularly if they thought it was sexy.

Yawn.

Conversely, if you had to kill an idea? You just made it disappear, and soon enough, the white noise of human drama replaced it with something else.

Humans' ability to be distracted was, aside from their relatively easily extinguished mortality, their best feature.

'Cuz, really, when it came to vampires, who the fuck needed Ellen interviewing the Omega about his favorite holiday traditions or a posthumous book on Lash hitting the *New York Times* bestseller list, true?

Or worse, and all jests aside, the motherfuckers going on a hunt for the race.

Those rats without tails couldn't get along with each other. They suddenly find themselves coexisting with another species on the level that vampires were shoulder-to-shoulder'ing them?

You could wipe the *co-* and *-exist* thing right outta your vocab.

So yeah, he was going to have to tidy up this little mess out on the Net, as well as have a "talk" with Ms. Jo Early, too: Assuming she'd been a vampire lover all her life, that kind of cognition was not going to be reversible, but he could certainly tinker around in her gray matter and redirect her from her blog.

Yup, he thought. It was time to ghost into her bedroom, find out what was doing in that skull of hers, and then head back to get his virtual Swiffer rocking on the Internet.

Uh-huh.

Yeaaaaah.

And yet V stayed where he was, ashing on the snow-covered roof, shifting his weight back and forth whenever his legs got tired, stretching his back from time to time.

The reason he didn't leave had nothing to do with that woman.

No, he stayed for the same reason he had gone out.

When you were contemplating cheating on your mate, it was not easy on the conscience. And not something you wanted to do in the home you shared with her.

FIFTY

s Xcor waited for Layla to tell him that she wanted him to leave, his blood was raging in his veins and his head was frothing with memories. He had never talked to anyone about what had been done to him or what he had done in the war camp. For one, nobody had ever asked. His fighters had all either done that themselves or had it done to them, and it was hardly a topic of conversation among the group, something one reminisced about because it elicited warm and happy feelings. And outside of his fighters, Xcor had never run into anyone who had wanted to get to know him.

"Well," he demanded. "What say you, female."

It was not a question. For he knew what she was going to—

Layla looked him straight in the eye, and as she spoke, her voice was utterly level. "I say that survival is a gruesome, sometimes tragic, endeavor. And if you expect me to feel anything but sadness and regret on your behalf, you've got a long wait coming."

Xcor was the one who broke eye contact. And as silence stretched out between them, he had no idea what he was feeling.

It seemed, however, as he regarded his hands from a great distance, that he was shaking.

"Have you never wondered what became of your parents?" she asked. "Wanted to find a brother or a sister, perhaps?"

At least, that was what he thought she said. His mind wasn't processing things all that well.

"I'm sorry," he muffled, "what?"

The bed moved as she shuffled over and sat beside him, her feet dangling, whereas his reached the floor because his legs were longer than hers. After a moment, he felt something drape over his bare shoulders. A blanket. She had covered him with the blanket that had been folded at the base of the duvet.

It smelled like her.

It was warm, like her.

"Xcor?"

When he didn't respond, she turned his face to hers. As he looked at her, he wanted to shut his eyes. She was too lovely for him and his past. She was all that was good, and he had already cost her so much: her home, her peace with her young, her—

"Love is a matter between souls," she said as she put her hand on the center of his chest. "Our love is between my soul and yours. Nothing is going to change that, not your past, our present . . . or whatever futures we may find apart. At least not on my side."

He took a deep breath. "I want to believe you."

"I'm not the one to believe or disbelieve. It is a law of the universe. Debate such at your leisure—or you could just accept the blessing for what it is."

"What if she was right, though?"

"Who? What if who was right?"

Xcor looked away, focusing on their bare feet. "My nursemaid always told me I was cursed. I was evil. When she would—" He stopped there, not wanting to go into the beatings. "She told me I was rotten. That my face was only what showed of the rot inside of me. That the real festering was within."

Layla shook her head. "She was talking about herself, then. She was revealing the truth of herself. To say those things to an innocent young?

To warp his mind and terrorize him like that? If there is another definition of evil and rottenness, I don't know what it is."

"You see too much of the good in me."

"That's what you've shown me, though. You've always been good to
me."

Her hand took his from where he had clamped it on his knee, and as
she squeezed his palm with her own, he struggled to process her loyalty
and kindness. Indeed, she would never understand the extent of his
atrocities, and perhaps that was just as well. It would save her from feeling bad at her misjudgment of him.

"I need to tell you something."

As he heard the tension in her voice, he glanced over. "What."

Now, he thought, now she would tell him to go.

"I owe you an apology." Releasing the hold she had taken on him, she
locked her own hands and seemed to have difficulty finding words. "I did
something that maybe I shouldn't have done—and that I definitely
should have told you about before now. And my conscience is killing
me."

"Whate'er is it?"

When her distress appeared to intensify, it was both easy and a relief
to switch gears and focus on whate'er bothered her.

"Layla, there is naught that you could do to upset me."

She rushed through her words, speaking the syllables quickly, but
clearly. "Up in the Sanctuary, where the Chosen dwell, there is a great
library of lives. And in those stacks, in those volumes, the details of all
the males and females of the species are kept, the passages written by the
sacred scribes after they witnessed in the seeing bowls all the events, good
and bad, that have e'er transpired down upon the earth. It is an entire
chronicle of the race, the battles and the celebrations, the feasts and the
famines, the sadness and the joy . . . the deaths and the births."

As she paused, he was aware that his heart started beating faster. "Go
on."

Layla took a deep breath. "I was seeking to know more. About you."

"You looked at my record."

"I did."

Xcor cast aside the blanket she had draped upon him and stood, pacing forward and back. "Why did you bother to ask me about my past, then? Why force me to say—"

"Not everything is in it."

"You just said it was."

"Not feelings. Not your thoughts. And I didn't know about . . ." She cleared her throat. "I knew you had gone into the war camp, but what precisely transpired there had not been recorded."

He stopped and turned toward her. She was blissfully naked, her spectacular body bare to his eye in the warm bedroom, only her long, lovely blond hair covering her. She was nervous, but not cowering, and once again, he wondered why in the hell someone like her would have anything to do with a male like him.

What was wrong with her, he wondered.

"So what did you read about me?" he demanded.

"I know who your father—"

"Stop." As he put his palm forward, sweat broke out on his upper lip and across his brow. "You must stop there."

"I'm so sorry," she said as she reached for the discarded blanket and pulled it around herself. "I should have told you. I've just—"

"I'm not angry."

"You aren't?"

He shook his head and meant it. "No."

After a moment, he went over to the pants he'd had to borrow and pulled them on. Then he did the same with the T-shirt he'd been wearing when he'd been shot. Moving the hem around, he inspected the hole in the fabric where the bullet had grazed him and then he checked his skin. Healed up.

The result of Layla's Chosen blood.

"I know what you're going to ask," he said remotely.

"Well, do you want to know?"

His bare feet started walking again, taking him from one end of the room to the other and back once more. "You know, I had this fantasy . . . when I was a young lad. Well, I had several of them. I used to conjure them up when the nursemaid kept me chained outside the cottage during the night—"

"Chained?" Layla said weakly.

"—to pass the time. One of my favorites was imagining who my father was. I pictured that he was a great warrior on a fierce steed, and that one evening, he came out of the woods and took me away on the back of his saddle. In my idle dreaming, he was strong and proud of me, and we were of like kind, seeking nothing but honor and goodness for the species. Great fighters, side by side."

He could feel her eyes boring into him, and he didn't like it. He felt vulnerable enough. But as with removing a bullet lodged in skin, one had to finish the job.

"It kept me going. To the point that, even after I turned myself in at various orphanages, I never could stay in them because I always worried he might come to that cottage and find that I wasn't there. Later, when my path crossed with the Bloodletter's and he told me that lie to get me to join him? That he was my sire? I was so desperate that I recast myself to fit that evil male and made one of the biggest mistakes of my life." He shook his head. "And when I discovered the falsity? I felt betrayed, but it was also a return to where I had been as a child. I've lived with the rejection of my parents all my life. They have had a century or two to rethink what they did and try to find me, but they have chosen not to. To discover now what either of their names are, or what happened to them, or where they live? It will change nothing, for them or me."

Layla's beautiful eyes were shining with tears, and he could tell she was trying to be strong for him.

He wished he had not once again put her in that position.

"I'm not mad at you," he said as he went over and kneeled before her. "Never."

He put his hands on her thighs and forced a smile. He wanted to reassure her, ease her conscience and her mind, but his own emotions were in a great upheaval. Indeed, talking with her had opened up a Pandora's box of the past, and all manner of images were flashing through his brain, memories from childhood, and then the war camp, and still afterward with his fighters, crowding like invaders at a gate, threatening to overtake everything about him.

This was why the past must stay buried, he decided, and why truths long left unrevealed must remain as such. To bring them forth solved nothing and only created a dust storm that would take much time to settle.

The good news? He'd told his males he would meet them at four a.m., and that gave him an excuse to firmly end this conversation. So what if it was only just after two. He was going to need some time alone to compose himself.

"I must go."

"To find your fighters."

"Yes."

She seemed to take a bracing breath. "Will you put your bulletproof vest back on? In case of more slayers?"

As Xcor stood back up, he made a dismissive motion with his hand so as to reassure her. "Yes, but do not worry. They're almost non-existent the now. I can't remember the last time I saw one."

First Meal with Blay's parents was, at least on the surface, a picture-perfect breakfast scene: You had a couple in love, two beautiful kids, and a pair of grandparents in a kitchen that was out of an old-fashioned ladies' magazine.

The reality, however, was not even close to perfection.

As Qhuinn sat back in his chair, he took his coffee mug with him and set it on his stomach. Not a good idea, given what was doing in his guts. To make the elder Lyric happy, and pay respect to all her hard work, he'd sucked down four eggs, six pieces of French toast, three cups of coffee, and an orange juice. Oh, and three frozen After Eights.

Which had been ingested on the Monty Python Thin Mint Theory. So yes, it was entirely possible that he was going to explode all over this beautiful kitchen, with its maple paneling and its wooden floor and the copper pans that hung as decoration over that island.

"More French toast?" Lyric asked him with a smile.

When she held the platter out to him, his gag reflex hit the playback button and he nearly refunded all that nice food she'd cooked right onto the leftovers.

"I think I'll take a breather before seconds."

Or was that more like eighths?

"You certainly packed it away, son," Blay's dad said as he, too, sat back. "Been a while since you had a good meal? What's Fritz feeding you guys over there, kale and tofu?"

"Oh, you know." Actually, it's been a little hard to eat given that my mate has essentially moved out. "Busy, busy."

"You work too hard," Lyric said as she repositioned her namesake in her arms. "Doesn't he? Your father works way too hard."

Little Lyric let out a coo that was timed perfectly—if the kid's aim was to melt her grandmother.

"She looks so much like Layla." Lyric glanced at her *hellren*. "Doesn't she? She's going to be so beautiful when she grows up."

Rocke nodded and toasted both Qhuinn and Blay with his mug. "Good thing you boys know your way around a gun."

Blay spoke up. "She's going to learn her own self-defense. So she can take care of herself and—"

As he stopped abruptly and looked out the windows, Qhuinn murmured, "That's right. And you're going to teach her. Aren't you, Blay?"

When the male didn't reply, Lyric looked at Qhuinn. "I'm hogging your daughter, aren't I? You haven't held her all night."

The female went to turn the young around, and as Qhuinn saw those features that were a spitting image of her *mahmen*, he recoiled—and recovered fast.

"Actually, I'm good. But thanks."

He made a show of leaning away and talking to Rhamp, who was in Blay's dad's arms. "And we're going to teach you to fight, too. Ain't that right, big guy?"

"Are you really going to put him into the war?" Lyric said. "I mean, perhaps he could find another way in this world—"

"He's the son of a Brother," Blay cut in as he stood up. "So he's going to be what his father is."

The male picked up his plate and his *mahmen's* and headed for the sink.

"Oh, here, Qhuinn take her," the female said.

Qhuinn shook his head. "Would you mind putting her into her carrier? I'm going to help with the dishes."

"And you," Blay's dad murmured to his mom, "need to get off that foot. Up to bed. Come on."

"I need to tidy up."

"No," Blay said firmly. "You cook, I clean, remember?"

"Listen to your son, Lyric."

As another of the couple's genteel, respectful arguments started, Qhuinn set about desperately trying to catch Blay's stare while they moved platters and plates, pitchers and mugs over to the island.

Blay was having none of it. In fact, the guy seemed livid for some reason—though he hid it well as his parents got ready to pair off and get Lyric settled in bed.

As Blay's mom gave Qhuinn a hug, he more than returned the favor. "I'll come again soon."

"You better. And bring my grandbabies, thank you very much."

Blay's dad swept her up into his arms. "I'll be down to help in a minute, boys."

"Or," Lyric said, "you can watch a little television with your mate."

"This mess needs to—"

"They're grown males. They'll take care of it just fine. Come on, there's a show on the next mass extinction I've wanted to watch with you."

"Just what I've been looking for," Blay's dad said with dry affection.

As the two went off for the stairs, Qhuinn could have sworn Lyric gave him the nod of, *I've got this. You take your time*—

"You want to tell me what the hell is going on here?"

Qhuinn recoiled and stopped in the process of heading back to the table to pick up the napkins. "I'm sorry?"

Blay leaned against the sink and crossed his arms over his chest. "You haven't looked at her all night. You won't touch her. What the hell is going on?"

Shaking his head, Qhuinn said, "I'm sorry, I'm not following—"

Blay jabbed his finger at the carriers. "Lyric."

"I don't know what you're talking about."

"Bullshit."

As Blay glared at him, Qhuinn felt his exhaustion return tenfold. "Look, I'm not—"

"I know I'm not her parent, but—"

"Oh, God, not that again." He let his head fall back on his spine and stared at the paneled ceiling. "Please, not again—"

"—I'm not going to stand here and let you ignore her just because she looks like Layla and you can't stand the Chosen. I'm not going to have it, Qhuinn. It's not fair to your daughter."

It was on the tip of Qhuinn's tongue to tell the guy that he didn't understand, but yeah, no. He wasn't going that route.

Blay jabbed a finger across the way. "She's a good baby, and as long as you don't fuck up the next twenty-five years or so, she's going to turn into a spectacular female. And I don't care if I'm not on their birthing charts and have no right to them—"

"No offense, but enough with that. It doesn't hold water anymore."

As Blay's eyes narrowed like he was getting good and ready to blow a gasket, Qhuinn reached into the diaper bag and put a sheaf of papers on the granite countertop.

Sliding them across at the guy, he said, "I've taken care of all that."

"What?"

Exhaling long and slow, Qhuinn dragged himself over to the table and dumped his weight in a chair. Fiddling with a crumpled napkin, he nodded at the documents.

"Just read 'em."

Blay was clearly in the mood to argue, but something must have reached him, some kind of vibe, or maybe it was Qhuinn's expression.

"Why?" the guy demanded.

"You'll see."

As the other male picked up the papers and unfolded them, Qhuinn tracked each and every nuance of that handsome, familiar face, the twitches of the brow, the tightening—and then loosening—of the mouth and jaw, the utter shock and disbelief that replaced the anger.

"What have you done?" Blay asked when he eventually looked up.

"I think it's pretty self-explanatory."

As Blay went on a reread, Qhuinn stared at the pair of carriers, at the babies in them, at the two sets of eyes that were starting to droop.

"I can't let you do this," Blay said finally.

"Too late. That's the King's seal at the bottom."

Blay came across to the table and seemed to fall into the chair his mother had been sitting in. "This is . . ."

"You have my parental rights. You're now their father legally."

"Qhuinn, you don't have to do this."

"The hell I don't. I'm putting my money where my mouth is." He pointed at the paperwork. "I declared myself incompetent and unfit—and what do you know, when you discharge a firearm in your kids' bedroom, that's an easy argument to win. And Saxton did the case law research. We took it to Wrath and he approved it."

Not readily, of course. But at the end of the night, what could the King do? Especially when Qhuinn explained the point of it all.

"I can't believe . . ." Blay shook his head again. "What does Layla have to say about this?"

"Nothing. It's got nothing to do with her."

"She's their *mahmen*."

"And now you're their father. Tell her if you want, or not. I don't care." As Blay frowned, Qhuinn tossed aside the napkin and sat forward. "Look, I'm their sire forevermore. My blood is in their veins. Nothing and no one will ever change that. I'm not giving away the fact that I sired them or the reality that I will always be in their lives. What I am doing is giving you a legal say-so. When I lost my damn mind in that damn bedroom? That was emotion." He pointed at the documents again. "That is reality."

Blay just started at the paperwork. "I seriously can't believe you did this."

Qhuinn got to his feet and started strapping in the kids, Rhamp first. When he turned to Lyric, he tried to be quick. Tried not to look her in the face.

As an unsettling emotion percolated through him, he shook it off. "I have to let Layla take them at nightfall tomorrow. I'm supposed to be out in the field and so are you—I checked the schedule. So unless you want to change it, I'll see you at the mansion tomorrow night before we all go out."

He paused before he picked up the carriers. "Unless you want to come with me now."

When Blay shook his head, he wasn't surprised.

"Okay, I hope I'll see you tomorrow. Come earlier if you want to hang with your kids before she takes them."

He knew better than to suggest that Blay might like to see him.

With a quick lift of the twins, Qhuinn turned on his heel and headed for the front exit. As he went down the hall, he hoped that Blay might have a sudden epiphany and come racing to the front of the house.

When that didn't happen, he opened the door and let himself out.

FIFTY-ONE

The delays were unacceptable. Unfathomable. Impermissible.

As Throe extracted himself from his lover's arms, he was ready to scream. First of all, he'd been unable to find all the ingredients for the spell or whatever he was doing, in the pantry the night before. This meant he'd had to go out—in the *hellren* of the house's Bentley, no less—to town to try to find black licorice and saffron and black candles.

Attempting to locate those candles in Caldwell at two a.m. had driven him mad.

He'd hit three open-all-night supermarkets and none of the stories had had them. And he'd tried a CVS. Two of them, actually. Nothing. And then, by the time he'd gotten back, Little Miss Stamp Her Louboutins and Pout went on a full bender of hysterics.

He'd nearly walked out on her. But it had been getting close to dawn by that time, and besides, he'd still needed the damn candles and the motor oil.

After watching her turn a relationship talk into performance art for at least two hours, he'd had to fuck her three or four times. Then had come the crying jags and the godforsaken regrets and recriminations. Followed by declarations of love that he didn't buy for a second.

By the time he'd been able to get free and go find a *doggen* to give a directive to, it had been four in the afternoon.

The *doggen* hadn't come back until six, and First Meal had been interminably long—and now, finally, after another round of sex, he was free: She was out like a light and going to stay that way because he'd slipped her seven Valium from the prescription bottle she kept in her bathroom.

The pills had been quite undetectable in the espresso she'd had with what the humans would have called breakfast.

Getting to his feet and moving quickly in her dim bedroom, he found his silk robe, covered himself, and rushed to the door. Out in the corridor, his footsteps bounced with an anticipation that he more typically possessed only when approaching a new lover.

And indeed, when he was at long last back in his own suite, he raced to the bed, cast the pillows aside, and brought his book to his heart.

As it warmed to the contact, he smiled. "Aye, it was too long. Aye. But here we are. Let us work the now."

It seemed appropriate to keep the lights off, as he felt as though he were doing something in secret, something sacred—or perhaps those were the wrong words.

He didn't much care for the right ones: Dimly, in the back of his mind, he knew this was evil, this stuff. And verily, as he sat in the southernmost corner of the bedroom and placed The Book upon the carpet, it seemed that all was dark and full of shadow.

Yet he would not dwell on that. He would focus only on his goal.

"I have my faith and my faith has me," he murmured as The Book flipped itself open and the pages began to fly. "I have my faith and my faith has me . . ."

When it found its proper place, the pages began to glow as if sensing his eyes needed assistance. "How kind of you," he said with a caress of its wide-open spine.

Down on the parchment, the symbols in the Old Language appeared, and he performed a quick review of the task ahead. Right, the ingredients. He needed the—

A rattling sounded out from beneath the bed. And then also in the closet.

The things he had gathered from the pantry and the market, the kitchen and the garage, migrated of their own volition across the Oriental carpet, the jumble of spice packets, that glass bottle of red wine vinegar, the plastic Coke container he'd filled with motor oil from the vintage Jaguar, and all the other provisions, moving in jumpy, skippy fashion toward him. The black candles were the last of the lot, and halfway across, they broke free of their boxes and rolled forth unto him like logs, clearly preferring freedom over containment.

All of it formed a circle about him, rather as if they were schoolchildren eager to be called upon.

"Well, such a convenience is this—"

A clattering noise brought his head around. Something was making noise in the bureau drawer, the sharp, *rat-a-tat-tat* like a knocking.

With a frown, Throe got up and went across. When he opened the appropriate drawer, he saw that one of his daggers, from his old life, was begging to get out.

"And you, too."

As he gripped its handle, and felt the hilt against his palm, he thought of his fellow fighters. He thought of Xcor.

The triggered sadness he felt was unexpected, but not unfamiliar. When he had first conceived of the plan to overthrow Wrath, he had stunned himself with his boldness and become half-convinced it was madness. But then he had reached out within the *glymera*, and found support, commitments, and resources to fight again the "improvements" that the Blind King had been making.

None of which served the aristocracy.

Riding that wave of alienation and dissatisfaction, and then manipulating it to further inflame the *glymera* unto his will, he had gotten addicted to the sense of power. Indeed, he'd enjoyed such a thing once prior, back before everything had fallen apart with the tragedy of his sister and him ending up with Xcor and the Band of Bastards. In the Old Country, before his destiny with that group of rogue fighters he had been a male of station and worth, not a servant of anyone—and he realized now that all of his animus against Wrath came from wanting to return from whence he had fallen.

A bit of an overcorrection to try to secure the throne for himself, he supposed. But one could not be faulted for reaching for the stars, no?

Refocusing on his book, Throe reread the directions. Twice. And then he took the copper pot and made a paste of the spices and the vinegar and that oil in it. The smell was unpleasant, but needs must and all that—and when that was done, he took one of the candles and coated it in the stuff, ensuring that all but the wick had been attended to. Then he palmed what was left, turned the pot over, and made a pile of it on the bottom. Standing the candle up in the little mound he'd created, he finished by rolling back the carpet, transferring his strange sculpture over to the bare floor, and making a little trail of the paste down the side and off about six inches from the pot.

With a quick scan, he double-checked that he'd done everything correctly thus far.

Blood was required next, and he provided it by streaking the blade of the steel dagger across his palm. The pain was sweet and the sanguine rush fragrant in his nose. Holding the wound over the candle, he allowed it to drip down the shaft, but was careful to leave the wick dry. More was required on the smudge over the floorboards.

With a lick of his palm to stop the bleeding, he took a gold cigarette lighter and flipped the top open, striking the flint with a flick of his thumb. Then he lit the candle.

The flame that caught hold was beautiful in its perfect simplicity, the translucent yellow light forming a teardrop shape at the head of the wick.

Mesmerizing, really.

Throe watched it for a while, and saw in its sinewy dance the movements of an erotic female.

A voice entered his head, from where he knew not: *I am waiting for you, my love.*

Shaking himself, he rubbed his eyes and felt his fear renew. But there was no going back—nor did he want to abandon this ritual or whatever it was. He was going to return to who and what he had been, and he was going to command the race with an army that followed him and him alone.

Leaning down, he put his palm in the trail of paste.

"I have my faith and my faith has me—"

With a decisive stab, he drove the point of the blade into the back of his hand, piercing the flesh, slicing through bone, burying the tip in the floorboards.

Panting through the pain, he gritted his teeth to keep from yelling out as his vision flickered.

When it came back online, he blinked and looked at the dagger. Looked at the flame. Looked at . . .

Nothing special happened. Not one damn thing.

He waited a little longer, and then started cursing. What bollocks was this?

"You promised me," he snapped at The Book. "You told me this would . . ."

Throe let the sentence drift as something caught his eye.

He had been searching in the wrong place. It was not the candle, nor the flame, not the palm nor the knife where he found what he had created.

No, it was in the shadow that the hilt and shaft of the weapon threw in the candle's illumination that was the thing: From out of the black outline cast upon the floorboards, something was boiling up, taking shape . . . emerging.

Throe forgot all about the smell and the pain as he watched an entity emerge before him, the contours of it fluid as water, its body formless and faceless and transparent as it rose from the shadows thrown, growing bigger and bigger—

Actually, it *was* a shadow.

And it appeared to be looking at him, waiting for a command.

Its size ceased to increase when it reached the dimensions of a fully grown male, and it waved gently from side to side, rather like the candle's flame, as if it were tethered to the floor . . . tethered right at the spot where the dagger's point pierced through Throe's own flesh.

With a grimace, Throe yanked out the knife and took his hand back.

In response, the entity floated about a foot off the ground, a balloon on an invisible string.

Falling back on his arse, he just sat and stared at it. Then he took the bloody blade of the dagger by the tip . . . and threw it so the weapon struck the shadow point first.

There was a hiss and sizzle, but the knife landed on the floor beyond as if it had passed through naught but air.

Clearing his throat, Throe commanded, "Pick up the dagger."

The shadow swirled around and the weapon was retrieved from the floor, gripped by an offshoot of the larger whole that was an arm of sorts. And then the entity simply waited, as if prepared for another command.

"Stab that pillow."

When Throe pointed at the bed, the thing moved with lightning speed, so fast eyes could barely track it, its body elongating and then snapping to like a rubber band.

And it stabbed the precise pillow Throe had focused on, even though there were eight lined up against the headboard.

Then the entity simply waited by the bedside, doing that balloon thing where it waved gently above its base.

"Come here," Throe whispered.

The compliance was magical. The power undeniable. The possibilities . . .

"An army," Throe said with a smile that made his fangs tingle. "Yes, an army of these will do very well."

FIFTY-TWO

Standing in the staff room at Sal's, Therese was tired, but satisfied by the end of the night. As one a.m. rolled around, and she had her tables reset and her tips collected and a backup tux to take home with her, she was happy with the way things went. She'd screwed up three orders, but not badly: One side had been incorrect, a roast beef slice had been medium instead of medium rare, and she'd confused a semifreddo with a tiramisu.

She'd had eight four tops, a six top, and three couples. Which had been an amazing haul for tips. This kept up and she was going to be out of that rooming house by the middle of January. All she needed to do was save up for a security deposit and first month's rent for something halfway decent and she was good to go—no moving expenses; it wasn't like she owned much.

"So it is done."

As Emile came up to her, she smiled at him. "Yup, and I'm still standing."

"You did well." He smiled back. "We're going out. Would you like to join us?"

"Oh, thanks, but I'm exhausted. Maybe next time?"

He took his things out of his locker, the flannel coat and the scarf simple, but of good quality. "It's a date—I mean, not a date. You know."

She nodded in relief. "I know. And that's perfect."

"Until tomorrow, then, Therese."

Emile said her name in the French fashion, and on his tongue, it sounded exotic and fancy. And she did take a minute to note the color of his eyes. So blue.

"You ready, E?"

The human woman who spoke up from the doorway was in her late twenties and had an edge to her voice, her stare, her body. Liza? Lisa? Something like that. She had dark hair that was ombre'd, dark eyes that had enviable natural lashes, and legs that made that set of jeans she'd changed back into a work of art.

She hadn't shown much interest in Therese, but it was clear who she was looking out for. "Well?"

Emile nodded. "Ready. Bye, Therese."

Liza/Lisa/whatever just turned away.

"Bye, Emile."

As Therese closed her locker, she draped the replacement tux over her forearm. She'd left on the one she'd served in and put her street clothes in her backpack because she just too tired to change. All she wanted to do was go to bed and close her eyes, because if there was one thing she knew about waitressing, it was that the next shift was going to come faster than her feet stopped pounding if she didn't rest up.

She had to admire those humans who were out for a good time.

Turning to leave, she—

Stopped dead.

"It's you," she whispered as she looked up, way up, into the face of the male who had been on her mind constantly since the night before.

Trez, the Shadow, the owner's brother, the . . . devastatingly attractive fantasy-in-the-flesh she had been preoccupied with, filled the doorway like none of the humans could have, his broad shoulders taking up all the vacant space, his incredible height bringing his head almost to the top of the doorway. He was dressed in a dark gray suit that brought out the deep color of his skin and a blindingly white button-down shirt that seemed to glow blue like moonlight on snow.

His face was more handsome than she remembered.

And that made her wonder if that lower lip of his was even softer than she recalled.

"I tried to stay away," he said in a low voice. "I made it over twenty-four hours."

She slowly lowered her backpack to the bench. "Well . . . hi."

Trez shifted his weight and put his hands into his pockets. "You have anything to eat?"

"Ah, no. I mean, I tried the dishes at the start of the night, but . . . no."

"You want to catch a quick meal with me?"

"Yes."

The fact that she didn't hesitate probably made her look desperate. She didn't really care, though: When you were deliberately overriding what was good for you, you didn't want to leave much time for introspection.

"Come on." He nodded over his shoulder. "I brought my car."

As they walked through the kitchen, she kept her head down. She had some sense that his brother, Sal's owner, wasn't going to appreciate this—and the guy was cooking right over there at the stove. Then again, eyes up or lowered, there was no way they were being inconspicuous.

When they got to the rear staff door, Trez held the thing open for her, and she was not at all surprised that there was an identical BMW parked right by the exit—just a different color. She was also not surprised that he came around and helped her into the passenger seat.

As he got in, the car interior seemed much smaller, and she didn't mind that because, God, that body. And jeez, he smelled good, the scent of his cologne, or perhaps it was just him, tantalizing her nose.

"Where would you like to go?" he asked as he started the engine and put them in reverse.

Sirius/XM was on The Heat channel, and she smiled. "We like the same music."

"Do we?" he said as he brought them around to the patron part of the parking lot.

"Yup. Oh, I love Kent Jones."

"Me, too." He paused at the main road they'd tried the night before. "Hey, I know a great all-night diner. It's nothing fancy—"

"I'm not a fancy kind of female. Basic is way okay with me."

"You're not basic."

Funny how that statement, coming from a male who was dressed like that, who looked like that, who was handling this fine automobile as he did, felt pretty much as though she'd been given the Miss America crown, a Nobel Peace Prize, and the keys to Buckingham Palace all at the same time.

Okay, fine, maybe that was hyperbole, but her chest was suddenly singing and her head was bubbly as a glass of champagne.

"So how was your first night on the job?" he asked as if he wanted to fill the silence.

Clearing her throat, Therese started to answer the question on the surface, leading with her three mistakes, but he was so easy to talk to, pretty soon she was going deeper than that.

"I was so worried I wasn't going to be good enough. I really need the job, and the other two I was looking at didn't pay as well."

"Do you need an advance or something? I could loan you—"

"No," she said sharply. "Thank you, though. I came into the world alone and I will deal with my problems alone."

As his head turned her way sharply, she dialed it back. "I mean, I don't want to be a burden on anyone."

Oh, bullshit. The truth was, she wasn't going to allow herself to be vulnerable anymore to anybody for any reason. But that was going to sound waaaaaay defensive and weird in the current context.

"So how about that Syracuse game," she said. "We were checking our phones in the kitchen while we were waiting on service."

"Oh, my God, I was glued to my phone, too. That zone defense was *insane . . .*"

And he's into college hoops, she thought with amazement. This male was seriously, like, a unicorn.

The diner turned out to be a whole lot of awesome, the front part of the establishment a converted railcar, the rear a proper restaurant with tables. The vibe was very New York, with the waitresses something you might have seen on *Seinfeld* back in the day, all wearing matching, cheerful unis, with attitudes like you'd broken into their houses and defecated on their living room sofas.

Fantastic.

"So the specialties here are pies, coffee, and the potato wedges," Trez said as they sat in the back right next to an exit sign. "And french fries. They do a good hamburger, too. Oh, and the chili is great."

As he opened his menu, his eyes roamed around. "I forgot, they also make a mean Reuben. Also the roast beef."

Therese cradled the menu to her chest and just smiled. "Any chance you missed First Meal?"

His black eyes flipped up to hers. "What? Oh, ah, yeah, I was opening tonight."

"Do you own a restaurant?"

"No, a club. Well, two."

Tilting her head, she nodded. "You know, I can see that. You look sleek and sophisticated."

Their waitress barreled up to the table with a pair of waters that she all but threw at them. "What do ya want to eat."

Trez indicated to her. "Therese?"

"The Reuben. Definitely the Reuben. I don't have to look at the menu."

"Fries or chips," came the bitchy demand.

"Fries, please. Thank you."

The waitress looked at Trez. "You."

None of the woman's statements were questions. It was more like what a mugger would say as he put a gun in your back and wanted your wallet.

Trez put the menu aside. "Cheeseburger. American. Medium. Fries. Two apples, two Cokes, and a refill on the soda before dessert. Check, please, cash no change."

The waitress flicked her eyes in his direction. Then she nodded like she was knuckle-pounding him in her head. "That's what I'm talking about."

As the woman walked off, Therese laughed. "Clearly, you know your way around the females."

"At least human ones who are serving at close to two in the morning and have another four hours before they can go home, at any rate."

They chatted until the woman came back with the Cokes and then didn't miss a beat as they were left alone again.

"Oh, yes, I've always been a hoops fan. Spartans all the way. Huge Izzo fan." Therese took a test sip of her soda and had to sit back with a moan. Oh, the ice cold, and the sweet, and the carbonation. "This is seriously the best Coke I've ever had."

"Long night, probably thirsty." He smiled. "Perspective is everything."

True. And then there was also the fact that this amazing guy was sitting across the table from her.

"How is it you're not mated," she blurted.

As his eyes popped, she thought, oh, crap. Had she said that out loud?

Abruptly, that dark stare went elsewhere, roaming around the interior full of empty tables and chairs. There were only two other couples in the place, both at the counter in front, and Therese was almost certain that if they had not been within eyeshot, he would have gotten up to pace.

"I'm sorry," she murmured. "That's none of my business."

"It's, ah, it's okay. Yeah, I guess you could say that love just didn't work out for me."

"I can't imagine why any female would leave the likes of you." With a wince, she closed her eyes and shook her head. "Okay, I'm going to stop talking now. I keep putting my foot in it."

As he sat back, that smile returned for a second. "I find your candor refreshing, how about that?"

"Hey, I have an idea. I like to be proactive about things, so can we just chalk this whole meal up to my being exhausted? You know, excuse everything that comes out of my mouth in advance? I think we'll both feel better about this when it's over."

"You have nothing to be embarrassed about."

"Wait for it. The food hasn't even arrived yet."

"I like honesty."

"You do? Well, you're in luck with me. My parents always said . . ."

As she let that drift, he murmured, "What?"

Therese shrugged. "Oh, you know, that I don't have a filter."

"Are they back in Michigan?"

"No."

"Have they passed?" he asked with a frown.

How to answer that one. "Yes," she said. "My *mahmen* and father are dead."

"Oh, God, I'm so sorry." He seemed so very sincere, his lips thinning, his brows dropping. "That's got to be so hard."

"It's why I came to Caldwell."

"Fresh start?" When she nodded, he made a move like he was going to put his hand over hers. But then he stopped himself. "It can be hard to go on when you're the one left down here."

"Let's talk about something cheerful." She cracked her neck and then smiled with determination. "You know, anything else but families and past loves that didn't work out."

He returned her smile. "That leaves us with a lot of possibilities."

"Doesn't it just."

"Hey, listen, will you do me a favor?"

"Sure."

"Will you let me find you a place other than that rooming house to stay in?" He put his hands up. "I know, it's none of my business, but that is a really shady part of town, and I'm not saying that you can't take care of yourself. It's clear that you're an intelligent, perfectly capable individual who can run her own life. But, I mean, really. It's that dangerous."

"You're sweet."

"Not sure that that's quite the descriptor most people would apply to me."

"Okay, so what would they say?"

Yes, she was trying to change topics, but not because she was creeped out by his offer. More because she had a strong inkling to take him up on it.

"Nice pivot."

"I'm sorry?" she said.

"That's a very deft way of telling me to mind my own business."

At that moment, their waitress came over and slid their plates into place. Holy crap, Therese thought as she took a gander at her Reuben. The last time she'd seen slices of bread that big was on a box spring. And there had to be a half a cow's worth of corned beef between the rye mattresses.

"This is the most beautiful thing I've ever seen," she said.

"I told you," Trez agreed.

The waitress just grunted, but Therese supposed they were lucky she didn't empty the side plates of fries on their heads.

"Tell me," Trez said as the woman stalked off, "are you a ketchup girl?"

"I am, I am."

He twisted off the cap of the Heinz bottle and handed the thing to her. When she was done, he went to town on his cheeseburger with the stuff.

"So about my offer to help you."

Therese carefully picked up one half of her sandwich. "I don't know, I'll be out of there by the middle of January as long as I can keep the job at Sal's. That's not much more time."

"See, I have some friends who have a bunch of real estate in town. Members of the species, you know. The houses are in good neighborhoods and they're monitored by . . . well, it's state of the art. They have good security systems and the added bonus of no heroin addicts in the front hall."

"But how much will something like that cost?" She shook her head. "I don't have a security deposit saved up and I won't be able to afford—"

He waved a hand. "Don't worry about that."

"Sorry, but I have to. I'm taking care of myself, remember."

On that note, Therese stretched her mouth wide and took a bite. Oh, yeaaaaaaaah, talk about your heaven. And the rye was soft as Wonder Bread, but with a tang to rival the Russian dressing.

As she moaned, Trez nodded. "Good, right? I'm glad."

As he ate his hamburger, she was impressed with his table manners. Nothing sloppy or rushed, and plenty of napkin wiping. He also managed to not spill anything on that suit jacket, which was seriously impressive.

"Is that silk?" she said as she nodded at his torso.

"The suit or the shirt?"

"Um . . . both?"

"Yes."

"Well, they're beautiful." *And I'll bet what's underneath that shirt is even better looking—*

Abruptly, his lids got low. "I'm not sure what to say to that."

Therese lowered her sandwich and slumped in the banquette. "Oh, my God."

"It's all right." His eyes went to her mouth. "Don't worry about it."

Putting down the wedge that was left of the first half of her Reuben, she wiped her hands on the paper napkin. "You know what, I think maybe I should go."

"Don't talk crazy."

"That's apparently all I can do tonight."

"Tell you what," he murmured. "Make it up to me. Stay at one of my friends' places so I don't have to feel guilty if something bad happens to you."

"Why would you feel guilty? I'm not your problem."

"Any male—any person—who doesn't step up when someone needs help is doing something wrong."

"But what about the security deposit and first and last month's rent and—"

"They'll work out a schedule for you. You know, for payments." He shrugged. "Look, this is just members of the species taking care of each other. We have to stick together in this world. Between the humans and the *lessers*, we're outnumbered."

The waitress came back over, replaced the Cokes with new ones, and pitched down two dessert plates with gigantic slices of apple pie on them. À la mode. Then she took out her old-school ordering pad and tore the bill off like it had insulted her mother.

She slapped it facedown on the table. "Pie's on the house." She nodded at Therese's tuxedo. "You work at Sal's?"

Therese's brows popped. "Yes, I do."

"Professional courtesy. Night."

The woman marched off as if she were on a campaign to shut down the kitchen.

"Wow," Therese said. "That was nice of her."

"I don't have any problem with people who are crispy because they're making an honest buck for an honest shift's work."

"Me, neither. And I would have thanked her—"

"But you were worried she'd put a gun to your head? Good idea."

They both fell into silence as Therese thought about going back to that hovel. "When could I move?" she blurted.

Trez stared across at her and smiled slowly. "Let me make a couple of phone calls and I'll find out."

She ducked her eyes. "Thank you." And then she immediately looked back up at him. "But I pay for everything myself. I don't want any discount or anything. This is just like any other tenant, okay? I would rather stay right where I am and get mugged than—"

Trez put his palm forward. "Understood. Completely understood. You'll just be moving to a place where you don't have to prove your independence by getting stabbed."

"That's right." She reached forward and snagged the check. "And on that note, I'm paying for this meal and you're going to let me, graciously."

As he opened his mouth, she feigned putting a hand over her heart. "Oh, you're so welcome. Really, it's my pleasure and a great way to pay back your kindness. And you know, may I just say, I love a secure male who can let a female be his equal. It's really sexy."

He closed his mouth. Leaned back. Leaned forward.

"Wow," he said eventually.

"What?"

Trez cleared his throat and straightened the open collar of his shirt. Which was perfectly straight. "This is a great cheeseburger. Ah, yeah. Really . . . nice fries, too."

Therese started to smile. "Wait'll you get to the pie. I think we're both going to love it."

FIFTY-THREE

At the appointed hour of four a.m., Xcor transferred his corporeal form to the top of the Caldwell Insurance Company building. As he re-formed in the stiff gusts that barreled through the air space high above the city, he took in a deep, bracing breath.

And when he looked over his shoulder, one by one, his males appeared: Zypher, Balthazar, Syphon, and Syn. When they were all standing before him, he felt a moment of pride, for he had assembled them by choice, cherry-picking from among all at the war camp those whom he felt were the best of the best. This group of fighters had followed him into countless battles, and together they had bested so many slayers, their kills would be impossible to count—

Abruptly, the image of all those jars in that cave of the Brotherhood's came back to him. For truth, if the two groups had been able to work together? Mayhap the war would be over by now.

Zypher stepped forward, clearly prepared to make some kind of statement for the whole.

"Whate'er you speak," Xcor said into the wind, "I accept and—"

The great fighter sank to his knees and stared up at Xcor mutely.

As the wind swirled around and the hair on both their heads blew this way and that along with their winter clothes, Xcor found himself blinking quickly.

And then he reached into his coat and withdrew a knife that he had lifted from that safe house's kitchen and kept within the folds of the black parka he wore. Curling his dagger hand into a fist around the double-sided blade, he squeezed hard . . . and as he withdrew the weapon from his grip, blood flowed.

Xcor offered his bleeding palm to his soldier, and Zypher lowered his mouth and drank from what welled forth. Then he swiped his mouth on the back of his arm and rose to his feet. After he bowed, he stepped back.

One by one, the other males repeated the pledge of fealty, a ceremony they had done so many, many years ago, back in a forest in the Old Country. Syn was the last to come forth, just as he had been during the first swearing—and after he partook and stood once more, he took something from off his back.

When Xcor saw what it was, he was momentarily struck dumb. But then he ran his own tongue up the wound upon his palm to seal it . . . and reached out to what was being offered to him.

It was his scythe. The one that had protected him against those males of the Bloodletter's in that forest. The one that he had claimed and used as his own for centuries. The one that was as much a part of him as his arms or his legs.

"Where did you find it?" he whispered as he accepted the grips.

It was like coming home.

Zypher looked at the others and then spoke. "At the Brownswick School for Girls. It was the only remnant we e'er located of you."

Xcor shifted his weight back and swung the great blade around. It was an old habit joyfully renewed, and with the way it moved under his power . . . it was proof that water wasn't the only thing that could exist in different states.

A blade in the right hands could also be both a solid and a liquid.

Except then he stopped. "I shall not use this against the Brotherhood. Do you understand my position."

Zypher glanced around at the group. And then over the brisk, cold wind, he said, "We are prepared to follow you. And if you follow Wrath, then we are prepared to follow Wrath."

"He is expecting you to swear unto him your fealty. On your lives so that you may remain alive."

"We follow you. If you follow Wrath, we are prepared to follow Wrath."

Xcor looked at Balthazar. "What say you?"

"The same," the male said.

"And you?" Xcor asked the next one. When there was a nod, he asked the next.

This was not the agreement the Blind King sought.

"If this costs you your lives," Xcor intoned, "if this makes you hunted, what say you then?"

"We are warriors," Zypher spoke up. "We live and die by the dagger, and we are hunted already. Naught will be different to us save the integrity of our long-held service unto our one true lord. We are at peace with our station in this manner. In any other, we are not."

They had clearly discussed the matter at some length . . . and arrived at a position that was unified and unwavering, not subject to alteration or negotiation.

Xcor felt a swell in his heart, and he followed an instinct to bow low. "I shall present this unto the King and we shall see whate'er he says."

As a unit, they bowed back to him.

"Tomorrow at midnight," Xcor announced. "I shall present you with the conclusion to all this."

"And then we shall go home," Zypher tacked on. As if that was another unalterable.

"Aye," Xcor said into the wind. "We go home."

Layla left the ranch by the sliding door, slipping out into the cold and bundling herself in the coat she had taken from the closet. As she closed her eyes to dematerialize, her heart was pounding and she knew a rage that was close to unholy.

When next she re-formed, it was out on a peninsula that jutted into the Hudson River, about fifteen miles up and across the waterway from where she had spent a good two hours pacing around. The hunting cabin that was her destination was small, and as modest and enduring as an old shoe well-repaired, situated such that it faced the city from its shore. Farther out on the jutting of land, a glass mansion of great size and elegance sat like a museum exhibit on wealth, its glow reaching all around the point as the sun's radiance fortified the solar system.

But that other structure was not her business nor her care.

Fates knew she had enough to contend with as it was.

As she marched through the snow toward the cabin's back door, her footprints were the first to disturb the pristine blanket. But there was an inhabitant within the structure, and he opened the way inside before she could knock.

The Brother Tohrment's huge body was silhouetted in the light behind him. "Hey! So this is a surprise! Sorry it took a little bit to get back to you, I—"

"Which one of you did it?" she snapped. "Which one of you shot him?"

As the Brother stopped speaking, she didn't give him a chance to answer. She shoved past him to enter the warmth of the interior and promptly took to pacing around the minimal, sparsely furnished space.

She kept her eyes on him as he closed them in together and leaned back against that which he had shut.

"Well," she demanded. "And don't fucking tell me I've got this wrong. He said it was a *lesser*—and then told me he hadn't seen one since well before you bunch of monsters kidnapped him—"

"Monsters?" Tohr shot back. "You're calling us monsters? After that piece of shit put a bullet into your King?"

Layla stopped in front of him and put a finger right in his face, punctuating her words with it. "That 'piece of shit' gave up the opportunity to sell your ass down the river. So watch what you call him."

Tohr jerked forward on his hips. "Don't make him a hero, Layla. It didn't help you out before, and sure as hell won't make things better for you now."

"FYI, I don't hear you denying that it was you. Was Qhuinn with you or did you decide to go out after him alone—and before you tell me to be a good little female and mind my own damn business, I was there when Xcor got on one knee and kissed the King's ring. I saw him make the oath, and I know damn well that Wrath told all of you to make sure he was safe. But you didn't listen, did you. You think you're more important than that—"

"This is none of your business, Layla."

"Fuck you, it isn't. I love him—"

Tohr threw up his hands. "Oh! Right, right, right, you fell in love with a murderer and a thief and a traitor, and suddenly all that tarnish is wiped clean, all those happy little details going poof! because you've got a case of the crushies! Okay, good to know, I'll just erase the fact that Wrath almost *died* in front of me because you want to suck some male's cock—"

She slapped him so hard she felt the sting all the way up her forearm. And she felt absolutely no regret whatsoever in the aftermath.

"I will remind you of my station," she snapped. "Whether you like it or not, I have been a Chosen and you will *not* disrespect me. I have earned the right through my years of service to be treated better than that."

Tohr didn't even seem to notice she'd hit him. He just leaned forward again and bared his fangs. "And may I remind *you* that it's my fucking job to protect the King. Your love life doesn't interest me in the slightest on a good night. When it conflicts with me keeping alive a male of worth like Wrath? I will mow you and your precious little delusions down faster than an arterial bleed will solve this problem."

"You"—she jabbed her finger at him again—"are the one who's going to be a murderer if you kill him, and so will Qhuinn."

She waited for him to deny that Qhuinn was involved. And was not surprised when he didn't.

Tohr just shrugged. "I have an executive order that says I can be the one who puts him in his grave."

"Which clearly was revoked." She shook her head and put her hands on her hips. "I don't know what you're going on about, but this is clearly nothing to do with Xcor—"

"The fuck it isn't!"

"Bullshit! Wrath's moved on. Wrath was the one who almost died. You're the person hanging onto what happened, and that's why there has to be another agenda at work here. If it were actually about Xcor and what he did to Wrath, it'd be as over for you as it is for him."

Tohr bared his fangs at her. "Listen to me, and listen to me good, because I will only say this once. You may be a Chosen, and you can swan around in your white robes and your holier-than-thou attitude all you want, but you are *not* in this war. You never have been and you never will be. So go home and sit on your fucking tuffet and eat your curds and whey, because *nothing* you can say to me is going to change my mind or my course in the slightest. You are not that important to me, female, and more to the point, this role that you demand respect for is not that significant when it comes down to the race's survival."

High-octane fury raged through her veins. "You sexist *blowhard*. Wow. Does Autumn know how condescending you can be? Or do you hide it from her so she'll still sleep next to you during the day?"

"Call it what you want. Label it how you do. But between you and me, there is only one of us who knows what he's talking about."

Layla blinked once. And then twice. And then a third time.

She had some inkling that where she was about to go was probably not the best idea. But he was the one who'd brought a "cock" into this showdown.

"I know what your first *shellan* was like." As the blood drained out of his face, she kept going. "While you're putting me in a box because of my ovaries, you might consider, just for a moment, how Wellsie would have reacted to your saying any of this to a female. I'm pretty sure she wouldn't have been impressed."

As the words sank in, the Brother seemed to swell in front of her very eyes, his body increasing in size, strength, and mass to that of a deadly monster.

Tohr's fists curled, and as he raised them, his face screwed down into a mask of absolute violence. In a voice that trembled, he said, "You need to go. You need to leave right now. I've never struck a female before and I'm not starting tonight."

"I'm not afraid of you. I'm not afraid of anything." She lifted her chin. "When it comes to protecting the lives of my young and the male I love, I will lay my life down in the path of their destiny, and if you beat me to death because of it, I will rise from the dead and haunt you to the point of insanity. There is nothing you can do to me that will make me back down. *Nothing.*"

For a moment, the Brother seemed so stunned he could not speak. And she supposed she could understand why. Here she was, facing off with the most fearsome kind of male the species had to offer, a trained killer who was armed and had at least two hundred pounds on her . . . and she wasn't even shaking.

Yes, she thought. The one who had always felt a little lost had found her footing and her voice.

And it turned out both were that of a lion.

Tohr shook his head. "You're crazy. You're really . . . totally out there, you know that. You're willing to sacrifice your young, your chosen family, your home, your relationship with Qhuinn and Blay, your King—anyone who's ever been there for you—all for a male who committed a war crime that was most likely one of the least offensive of all the things he's done over the course of his life. So, fine, you want to know what my Wellsie would say about this? I'll tell you. She'd say that you're a traitor, and a betrayer, and that you should never see those young again because the first thing you do with children is protect them from harm."

Okay. She was done arguing in the hypothetical here.

"I'm warning you right now, Tohrment—you need to ask yourself what you're really doing here." Layla shook her head again. "Because you're going rogue. You want to talk about betrayal? I'm very certain that Wrath went back and told all the Brotherhood what he was doing with

Xcor and the Band of Bastards and what he hoped to accomplish. And you're not following orders, are you. Does that make you a traitor, too? I kind of think it does. So maybe you and I should get matching bestie armbands or something."

"Fuck you, Layla. Hope you enjoy your life with that asshole of yours. I mean, I can only guess after all this posturing that you're going to the Old Country with him—if he lives long enough to make the trip. Yeah, female like you, you'll leave those young behind and just head off with your lover. And you know what? It'll no doubt be the only time in my life when I think desertion of a person's kids is a great idea."

"You stay away from Xcor."

"You are not in a position to give orders, female." He laughed in a hard burst. "Jesus Christ, I can't believe this is all over someone like him. Who the hell is that piece of shit anyway—"

"He's your fucking *brother*," she snapped. "That's who he is."

FIFTY-FOUR

There were times in life when you could be in a car accident without even being behind the wheel. Or on a road. Or in any kind of motorized conveyance whatsoever.

As Layla's words left her mouth and entered Tohr's brain for processing, he felt a spinning sense of being out of control, and then, yes, there was a shock of impact as he realized, yes, she had just said that. Yes, she did just mean that. Yes . . . she was still looking him in the eye.

He's your fucking brother.

"You lie," he heard himself say.

"I do not. It's in the library up in the Sanctuary. Go read it for yourself."

"I have read my book. There is no mention of a brother—"

"It's in your father's volume. Xcor is the blooded son of the Black Dagger Brother Hharm. Just as you are."

Tohr stumbled over to the old couch in front of the cold hearth and fell down on the hard cushions. "No."

"As I said, go up there and read it for yourself. And then process the fact that not only are you going against one of Wrath's direct orders, you'll also be killing your closest blood relative."

He had no idea how long he sat there. He was too busy sifting through his old life, before he had come to the New World, for any snippet or telltale sign, any clue . . . or . . . anything.

"How could I not have known?" He shook his head. "How could something like this have been kept quiet?"

"Xcor was rejected by his *mahmen* at birth. His father, your father, did the same."

"Because of his lip."

"Yes. From what I understand, he lived with a nursemaid who hated the sight of him and treated him terribly until she left him." There was a pause. "He told me he was chained outside of the place where he stayed. Like a dog."

Tohr closed his eyes.

And as if Layla sensed his changing mood, her voice grew less strident, less angry. "He doesn't know about you. As far as I'm aware, no one does."

Tohr looked up sharply. "You're keeping this from him?"

"No, he knows I have the information. But he says he doesn't want it. That it doesn't change the past and won't impact his future."

"This . . . it doesn't alter what he did."

"No, but I'm hoping it will alter what you do."

Tohr fell silent. And as he stared off into space, it was hard to categorize his emotions into neat bundles like shock, sadness, anger, grief. Hell, was shock even an emotion? And shit, he couldn't even figure out why he felt anything. It wasn't like he'd been all father/son tight with Hharm, so why would finding out his sire had had yet another son matter? And as for Xcor? Not like there was any connection there.

Other than the proclamation he had to kill the bastard.

Which Layla was right, had been rescinded.

Lifting his head, he focused on the Chosen. Layla was staring at him from over by the door, her face as composed as a portrait even as her eyes were a little too shiny from their argument.

From their knock-down-drag-out fight.

"I'm sorry," he said remotely. "For what just happened between you and me."

She shook her head sharply. "I'm not going to apologize for who I love. In fact, I'm grateful this destiny is mine. If I had fallen for another, I wouldn't have been forced to be this strong—and there is nothing wrong in this world or the next in finding out your own power."

Amen to that, he thought.

"You do the right thing, Tohr," she said. "Do you hear me? You make this right, and you make sure Xcor is not hurt out there."

"I can't control the whole world."

"No, but you can control yourself. It's a lesson I'm just learning."

Layla returned to the ranch right away. As she entered through the slider, she closed herself in and listened. Xcor wasn't back yet, and this was good. She didn't want him to know what she had deduced about who had shot him, or for him to know that she had confronted a Brother on his behalf.

And then there was the whole thing about her revealing the information about his father.

Dearest Virgin—um, Oversexed Lassiter—she hoped Tohr kept his mouth shut. But she had done what she had to in order to get a cease-fire out of the Brother.

A male who knew the pain of losing his *shellan* and unborn young was not going to kill his blooded brother. He just wasn't.

Going down into the basement, she went into the bathroom with the idea of taking a shower. But she stopped as she saw herself in the mirror over the sink. She was still dressed in the Chosen robe she had put on after Xcor had left her, the white folds as familiar to her as her own hair, her own body.

Reaching up to the tie, she loosened the sash, parted the two halves, and shucked the weight from her arms and shoulders.

As she held the robing in front of her, she thought of the many years she had spent wearing the uniform. Even after Phury had freed them all, she had still used the robes more than regular clothes. They were convenient, easy to move around in, and comforting in the manner a young might cling to a favorite toy or snuggie.

They were also a symbol.

Not just of the race's past, but of her own.

Layla was careful as she folded the thing, respectful with her hands. And then she placed it on the marble counter and stepped back.

In her heart, she knew she would never put one on again. There would be other sartorial constructs, she was sure, that would remind her of them: long dresses, long coats, even a blanket wrapped around the torso and dragging on the legs.

But she was a Chosen no more, and not just because the Scribe Virgin Herself was no more.

The thing was, when you served another, when you lived a role determined by someone else . . . you could not go back to that constriction once you found out who you truly were.

She was a *mahmen*. She was a lover. She was a proud female, a strong female, a female who knew right from wrong, family from stranger, good from evil. She had lived through two birthings and stood up to a Brother just now, and she would take on the King if she had to. She was fallible and could get confused and might well flounder from time to time.

But she would survive. That was what the strong did.

Meeting her eyes in the mirror, she looked at her face for what felt like the first time. She had spent all those years waiting in the Sanctuary to be called into her role as *ehros*, her existence at once totally dictated and yet groundless, for there was no Primale to pleasure. And then she had bumped and bounced around on earth after she and her sisters had been freed, tiptoeing timidly in the unfamiliar ways of modern life. There had been the desperate needing with Qhuinn, and then the anxiety as the young had grown within her—during which her life had been split in half with Xcor. Following that? The birth that had nearly killed her and

now the agony of the disintegration of her family unit . . . and the pend-
ing loss of Xcor.

Yet she was still alive and she was here. Looking at herself in the mirror.

And for the first time in her life, she respected what she saw.

Bowing to her reflection, she said softly, "Pleased to meet you."

FIFTY-FIVE

nnnnnnd buh-bye.

As Vishous deleted yet another YouTube video, he thought, yup, like shooting fish in a barrel. And if it were any easier to hack into these accounts, you'd get popcorn and Milk Duds for free with your efforts. Next. And . . . next. And . . . next.

In a way, he had Jo Early, a.k.a. Damn Stoker, to thank for the efficiency of all this. Her links section was a treasure trove of content in multiple destinations posted by a good dozen or so people. So after he was finished with his broom in the YouTube-iverse, he was going to do Insta and then Facebook.

Zuckerberg's little sandbox was going to be a little more difficult to hack, and as with the other two, there were multiple accounts on the platform, but he'd get through them.

And next. And next . . .

Man, this user, *vamp9120*, was a heavy-volume kind of guy. Lot of content that was tied to him.

V really should have stayed on top of this shit better. Then again, he'd been busy living life instead of sublimating his issues through sports and the Internet.

When Bruno Mars came on satellite, he switched the channel to

Shade45. It wasn't that he didn't think "24K" was magical, but the whole upbeat club shit was not on his playlist tonight. Jeezy/Bankroll Fresh's "All There." Fucking perfect. And as it bumped out the speakers, he took another drink from his Grey Goose and ice, and debated taking a break so he could hand-roll some more of his Turkish tobacco. After that, he was going to grab another bottle from the half dozen he'd ordered from Fritz. And then come back here to—

"What the fuck?" he barked.

Leaning in toward his screen, he frowned at the image that was on it. "Wait, I remember this, true?"

Yeah, he was talking to himself. It was what you did when your room-mate, who was off rotation like you were, was banging his female down the hall—and you were a lame ass in an office chair in the front of the house.

Rewinding the video, V watched again as the action unfolded. The footage had been taken from a relatively high viewpoint in a building downtown, as if the asshole with the cell phone had been looking out a third—or maybe a fourth-floor apartment. The focal point was on an alleyway below—and a figure that was walking forward.

Into a hail of bullets.

The figure was Tohrment. The bullets were coming from a slayer that was crumbled in the far corner. And the scene was straight-up suicidal.

V hadn't been there to witness the sheer stupidity firsthand, but he sure as shit had heard about it from multiple fighters. It was back when Tohr had been losing his mind, and determined to show everyone exactly how much of a death wish he had. Yes, he was shooting back at the *lesser*, his gun up, all kinds of lead pumping out of its muzzle . . . but he'd had no vest on, nothing covering him, and twelve different kinds of vital organs that should have been hit.

FFS, if he had wanted to get shot, the only way he could have been more successful was if he'd turned his own weapon on himself and pulled the trigger.

And yet he'd survived—

"Hold up . . . what is that?"

Abruptly, Vishous rubbed his eyes. Leaned even closer to the monitor. Wondered if the footage wasn't in the grassy knoll camp.

Adjusting the contrast on his screen, he ran the shit back again. And once more.

Someone else was shooting from the building across the way. Yeah . . . there was a figure up there on the roof and they . . . uh-huh, they were leaning right over and plowing a bunch of bullets into that slayer who was trying to kill Tohr.

It hadn't been a brother, that was for sure. V could pick out his own fighters in a fog bank a mile away, and it was easy to isolate them in this case even though the footage was a little grainy. Besides, there was no way one of their own would have been anywhere than right on the ground with the brother.

So who the fuck was up there? Not a human. There was no way one of those rats without tails would have gotten involved in that kind of business in that kind of way. No dog in the fight, so why risk the arrest? They were more likely to call 911 and take cover—

As his cell went off, V jumped—and shit, he couldn't remember the last time he'd done that. Especially over a phone call.

But given what wheels he had set in motion . . .

He watched as his hand reached out for his phone. He'd put it facedown on his desk, and turning the screen over took a degree of courage.

When he saw who it was, he snapped back to all business. "My Lord," he said with relief as he answered. "What can I do you for?"

Wrath was to the point, one more reason to like the guy. "I need you. Now."

"Roger that. Where are you?"

"I'll be in the foyer in five minutes."

"Tell me that we're not going to Disney World and I'll be there."

"No, this is not vacation time."

"Good."

As V hung up, he went to delete the footage and close out, but something told him to save the shit, so he did. It wasn't like he didn't have space on his hard drive.

Goddamn him, he was so fucking relieved to have something to do.

Just like earlier in the evening, he didn't tell anyone he was leaving, but this time it was because Butch and Marissa were busy getting busy. But he did shoot his best friend a text—and then he thought about texting Jane.

In the end, though, he just put his cell down, armed himself, and left.

Xcor was hanging up the house phone and starting to take off his borrowed parka when Layla ascended from the basement.

The instant he saw the tension in her face, he had regrets. "I'm sorry," he said. "I know I'm late."

She seemed surprised, and then simply shook her head as she came up to him. "I'm glad you're back. I was worried."

As her eyes lifted to his, he hated the sadness in them, especially because he knew he was the cause—and not for the first time since he left her earlier did he despise himself and the positions he put her in.

"Come here," he whispered as he drew her against him.

Cradling her into his chest, against his heart, he rested his chin on the top of her head. And he would have been content to stay like that forever, but he had things he had to tell her.

"My love," he said, "Wrath is—"

At that very moment, the slider opened and cold air rushed into the little kitchen. The Blind King was the first through the door, and Vishous was right on his heels.

"You rang," Wrath said dryly. "And hello, Chosen."

"Just Layla, please." As Layla spoke, they all looked at her.

"What?" the King asked.

"I am just Layla, please, my Lord."

The King shrugged. "Whatever you like. So Xcor, do you have an answer for me?"

"Aye." Xcor glanced at Vishous, who watched every move he made with those diamond eyes. "And I fear you are not going to like it."

"They said no, huh. Pity." Now the King looked at the Brother. "Guess this means we're going to war."

This was uttered casually, as if it were naught of consequence, and Xcor had to respect the attitude. Warriors fought. It was what they were bred and trained for. If the Brotherhood thought that conflict with a band of five soldiers was of any particular note, they needed to retire their daggers.

"No," Xcor interjected, "they did not say no. But they will not give you the oath."

Vishous spoke up, his voice low, aggressive. "What the fuck does that mean?"

Xcor addressed Wrath. "They have sworn their oaths to me. I have sworn mine to you. They will follow you, but only because that is where I have placed my fealty. They will be led by no other than myself. That is the way of it."

"Not good enough," the Brother Vishous snapped. "Not by half, ass-hole."

Xcor ripped off his glove and flashed his palm. "It was a blood oath. And those males will die for you, Wrath. Upon my orders."

"That's goddamn right," Vishous barked. "When we slaughter—"

"Enough," Wrath cut in.

There was a tense silence, and Xcor could feel Layla stiffen beside him. He would not try to tell her to go, however. She would not depart from him any more than his soldiers would.

Standing a'fore the King, Xcor met Wrath straight in the eye, even though the male was blind. Indeed, he had nothing to hide, no fight to present in this instance, no subterfuge or agenda to bring forth. And no matter the outcome tonight or any other, it was good. He was not afraid of death; the Bloodletter had taught him that. He had also discovered what love was, and she was standing next to him. Thus he was prepared to go forward with calm resolution, according to a fate that was out of his control.

So this was what peace felt like, he thought as he took off his other glove. When he reached for Layla's hand it seemed apt that it was not with the one he used a dagger with.

"You believe this," Wrath remarked. "You honestly do."

"Aye. I have been through the war with these fighters of mine. They have followed me across the ocean—"

"Are they prepared to follow you back there?" Vishous muttered. "In body bags?"

"Aye, they are." Xcor looked at the Brother. "But they have no war with you if I have none."

Wrath crossed his arms over his chest, and Xcor had to respect the sheer size and musculature of the male. He was enormous and deadly, and yet his brain civilized him.

He was going to see the logic in this, Xcor thought.

And sure enough, a moment later the King nodded once.

"So be it," Wrath said with a nod. "That is good enough for me—"

"Are you fucking *kidding* me—"

The King's hand shot out so fast the eye could barely track it, and somehow, even without sight, he got the trajectory right, clamping a hold on the throat of his fighter. He didn't even look in Vishous's direction, his focus remaining on Xcor.

In response, Vishous didn't defend himself, even as he was forced to gasp for breath, his goateed jaw dropping open.

"Don't you love it when people know their places," Wrath said to Xcor tightly. "When they understand those moments when they need to keep their fucking mouths shut."

Xcor had to smile. Wrath and he were kin in some ways, weren't they.

"Aye, my Lord," he murmured.

Wrath dropped his hold. "Like I said, this is sufficient for me. But as you can tell, my boys are going to require a greater proof of concept." The King touched the side of his nose. "I can scent you. I know this is what you believe, and our past conflicts aside, I don't think you're a fucking moron—nor do I believe for an instant that you would put those males of yours in the path of death."

"He did once before," Vishous cut in with a sneer. "That's how Throe ended up with us."

"Sounds like he got rid of the right one, though."

Xcor nodded. "Aye. Which was why I warned you of him."

Wrath inclined his head. "That was much appreciated. And we'll deal with him after we settle this with your people."

"You're not going to have a problem with that, are you?" Vishous demanded of Xcor.

"No." He shrugged. "That male goes his own way, and it is incompatible with yours and therefore mine. How you choose to address that is up to you."

"Then that is settled as well." Wrath smiled, revealing his tremendous fangs. "But as I was saying, my boys are going to require some proof. So we're going to have ourselves a good old-fashioned swearing ceremony with witnesses."

"I thought you were going to do this one on one," Vishous said in a low voice—while he pointedly stepped out of choke range.

"The Band of Bastards will not attack us." Wrath shook his head. "Not going to happen. He holds their chains, I can feel the power in him. A male like him isn't this calm for no good reason, ain't that true, Xcor."

"Aye. They will not raise a weapon against any in the Brotherhood. I will gather them at midnight on the morrow and bring them to you wherever you command. It cannot be before then, however, as I have no way of reaching them until that time. We are out of communication for their safety in case"—he glanced at Vishous—"things go awry. You understand."

Wrath chuckled a little. "Yeah, I feel you. So it is done—"

"What about your safety, Xcor?" Layla said with anger. "How will *you* be safe?"

The King fielded that one, speaking gently. "He'll be fine, not to worry—"

Layla wheeled on Xcor. "Why don't you tell him about how you were shot last night. And by who."

As his female interrupted her ruler, Xcor deliberately did not change his expression. "I told you, my love, it was a *lesser*—"

"No, it was not." Her eyes swung to Wrath. "They shot him last night."

"No," Xcor countered as he squeezed her hand, trying to silence her. "It was naught but a slayer."

Across the tidy kitchen, Wrath's brows dropped down behind his wraparound sunglasses, a chill hitting the air. And then he said, "I'm going to ask you this once, and you better be fucking honest. Did one of my males raise a gun to you at any time since you gave your vow to me?"

Xcor met the King's blind stare and projected confidence. "No, they did not."

By this time, he was gripping Layla's hand so hard he was positive he must be hurting her, so he relented his hold. But he prayed she stayed quiet.

Wrath's nostrils flared. And then he inclined his head once. "So be it. Midnight tomorrow. You will meet us downtown, Fifteenth and Market. There's a vacant warehouse. You can't miss it."

"We will be there at twelve fifteen. I am seeing them at midnight and we shall need to come to you."

Wrath walked forward and put his dagger hand out into thin air. "You and your males have my word. Provided they offer no threat to my boys, no one will get hurt."

Xcor took hold of what he was offered and they shook.

"*Until the morrow,*" he said to the King in the Old Language.

"*Until the morrow,*" Wrath repeated.

As Wrath and Vishous took their leave, departing out the slider, Xcor could only hope that that promise which had been given was one the King could keep.

"They're going to kill you," Layla said in a dead voice. "You will not live through that meeting."

Xcor looked over at her. He hated the fear in her pale face, the trembling in her body. In the quiet of the safe house, he wanted to lie to her.

He wanted to know how she'd found out the truth. He wanted . . . to stay with her forever.

But destiny had already answered that last one.

Reaching out with his hand of peace, not of war, he touched her smooth cheek. Brushed her lower lip with his thumb. Stroked the vital vein that ran up the side of her throat.

"He cannot guarantee your safety." With a desperate curse, she turned her face to his palm and kissed his war-hardened skin. "Not when it comes to Tohrment or Qhuinn. And well you know it."

"How?" he breathed. "How did you know?"

"Does it matter?"

No, he supposed, it did not.

"Why didn't you say something?" she begged. "Why didn't you tell Wrath?"

"Because ultimately it matters not. Safety in times of conflict is an illusion that can only be peddled, never promised. He and I both know that. If one of them decides to solve a problem that does not exist independently, nobody will be able to stop that. Free will is a universal truth, just like gravity."

"But it's not fair. It's not right."

"And that is why I must protect myself and expect no one, not even the great Blind King, to do it for me."

"Xcor, you need to—"

"Shh," he said as he put his forefinger to her lips. "No more talk of war. There are far better things we must do with our time."

As he brought her against him, he rolled his hips, proving his arousal even though she could no doubt scent it.

"Let me be in you," he said as he kissed her. "I need you the now."

She did not immediately respond and he gave her the time she required to sort out the difference between what was hope and what was reality, what was principle and what was fact. She was a smart female, not versed in the ways of fighting, but not naive, either.

And at the end of the night, she knew that whether he lived or died the following evening, their future was not together. If he survived, he was going back to the Old Country and she was staying in Caldwell. If he died? Well, that was him over and done with, likely in *Dhunhd.*

"I love you," she whispered when she finally tilted her head back for more of his kiss. "Always."

Xcor stroked her blond hair back. "You are more than I deserve and everything I have ever wanted."

With that, he sealed their mouths and tried to forget that time was running out for them. It was hard not to remember, however.

And he knew it was the same for her.

FIFTY-SIX

As Vishous and Wrath arrived back at the Brotherhood's courtyard, V was shaking his head. Oh, this was going to be a fun time. Yup, right up there with getting gutted while you were still alive.

The King wheeled around and was so furious there was proverbial smoke coming out of those ears of his. "You tell that mother*fucker* to get up to my study."

"You want everybody or just—"

"Tohrment. You fucking get that asshole right now and bring him to me! What the *fuck* was he thinking?"

Wrath pivoted away and headed for the stone steps to the mansion's entrance, clearly so pissed off he'd forgotten he couldn't see. And yeah, for a second, V was tempted to let Mr. Personality learn the hard way he was still blind.

He caved, though, jumping forward and catching the King's arm. "Shut the fuck up," he muttered before Wrath could jerk them apart. "You want a head injury on top of all this shit?"

It was like cozying up to dry ice, the King's mood so bad he turned the air around him even more arctic. But at least V was able to get the guy in through the vestibule and out the other side to the foyer. He knew better to hold on after that, though.

Dropping his grip on that thick biceps, he got out his backup phone and hit Tohr's number as Wrath thundered across the mosaic depiction of the apple tree in full bloom, relying on memory and stride count to find the lowest step—

A ringing sounded out. And not only in V's ear.

It was emanating from high above the foyer.

Vishous lowered his cell phone as Wrath took the stairs two at a time.

"Perfect timing," V muttered as he rushed to catch up.

Sure enough, Tohrment was sitting in one of the chairs right outside Wrath's study, as if he had seen the future and knew he was going to get his ass chewed for shooting Xcor. And clearly, the guy wasn't feeling too good about things, although whether that was because he'd disobeyed a direct order on a whim or was about to catch shit, it was hard to know. In any event, the brother's head was down, his shoulders caved, his body uncharacteristically self-contained.

"No reason to answer your call, my brother," the guy said as he turned around his cell phone. "I'm right here."

Wrath bared his fangs and hissed. "Get in there. We are not doing this shit in public."

As Tohr rose to his feet and complied with the order, V didn't ask permission to join the pair of them. He walked right in behind Wrath, shut the doors, and leaned back, holding the handles together.

Wrath didn't waste a damn second. "You're out."

Tohr shook his head. "What?"

"You're out of the Brotherhood. Out. I'm removing you, effective immediately."

Okaaaaaaaaaaaaaaay. That was not the way this was supposed to go, V thought.

No, see, Tohr was the glue that held the Brotherhood together. Save for that time right after Wellsie had been killed, he was always the one who was steady and sure, the quieting force that had kept people's heads together.

"And you shut the fuck up."

It took V a minute to realize that Wrath was addressing him. No time to respond, though, because Tohr grabbed the mic.

"He's right, V. I disobeyed a direct order. I shot at Xcor last night when I saw him out in the city. There have to be consequences."

Wrath seemed a little taken aback at the easy acquiescence.

Tohr just shrugged. "It was the wrong thing to do. It was in direct conflict with your position and what you hoped to accomplish. Guess being a traitor runs in my family."

"What?" V said sharply.

The brother waved a dismissive hand. "It doesn't matter. Autumn and I will move out first thing tomorrow. Unless you want us to leave tonight."

Wrath frowned. And then went over to his desk, circumventing the sofas and finding the throne.

As he lowered himself into his father's seat, he seemed utterly exhausted, and sure enough, he popped up his wraparounds and rubbed his eyes.

"Why?" he said. "What the fuck is such a big deal about Xcor? Why can't you let this shit go?"

"I will now. That's all that matters. I have . . . no interest in pursuing murder."

"What's changed?"

Tohr just shook his head. "Nothing of consequence. In the larger scheme of things."

Something rang in the back of V's head, but he couldn't put his finger on it, and man, that was really fucking irritating. But he was tired, and not just because his body was exhausted from lack of sleep.

Wrath sat forward. "Listen to me. The war is grinding down, we're so close to ending this. I don't want the distraction for you people. I don't want you bunch of hardheaded assholes chasing after five douchebags just because they once had a political agenda that included my head on a plate. Xcor knows where we live. He hasn't done shit about it. He's been staying with Layla for the last forty-eight hours and I feel their connection. He is also fully committed to this brokered peace and getting the fuck out of Caldwell. There is no more conflict and not just because I say so."

"I know." Tohr walked over to the fire and stared into the flames. "I, ah, my Wellsie would have been two hundred and twenty-six years old three nights ago. My young that she carried would have been two and a half years old. I think that's getting to me."

"Fuck," the King breathed. "I'd forgotten."

The brother shrugged. "It doesn't excuse my actions. What I did is not worthy of you or myself. But I will say that . . ." He cleared his throat. "I've been in search of some kind of vengeance for quite a while, and I found it in an inappropriate goal. The real target of my anger is fate, and that is nothing you can stab or shoot. It just is—and on some nights, that is harder to accept than others."

Wrath sat back on his throne and let his head loll onto the high carved back of the grand chair. After a moment, he pointed to the door. "Leave me. Both of you. My skull is about to fucking explode and I don't want the dry-cleaning bill for your goddamn shirts."

Tohr bowed low. "As you wish, my Lord. And Autumn and I will depart—"

"No offense," Wrath muttered, "but stop fucking talking, okay? Just leave me. I'll see you first thing tomorrow night—and bring the rest of the brothers with you. Go. *Go.*"

Outside the King's study, Tohr paused as his brother V closed the doors and looked over with hard eyes.

"FYI," the male said, "Xcor denied it."

Tohr frowned. "I'm sorry, what?"

V lit up a hand-rolled and exhaled smoke like it was a curse. "I was right there when Wrath asked him who had shot him, and he refused to give you up. Does he know it was you?"

"Yeah."

"Who else was there with you?" When Tohr didn't immediately answer, the brother leaned in and pointed with his hand-rolled. "I knew it. And you tell Qhuinn to cut the shit, or I will. I got no love for Xcor, I could give a fuck about him and the Band of Bastards. Kill 'em, leave 'em breathing, I don't care. But Wrath's right. We've fought a millennium to deliver the *Dhestroyer* Prophecy right up the Omega's ass, and the timing is getting ripe. No distractions, true. Enough with this petty shit."

"I can't control Qhuinn. No one can. We all saw that a couple of nights ago, didn't we."

"That motherfucker. He needs to reel himself in."

As V looked down the hall like he intended to go to the guy, Tohr put himself in the way. "I'll talk with him. I may be out of the Brotherhood, but your delivery sucks."

"I'm not that bad."

"Compared to a chainsaw, that's probably true. But we don't need any more hotheads going off right now. Everybody's about to blow."

V used his cigarette tip as a pointer. "You fix this shit, Tohr. Or I will."

"You're the second person who's said that to me tonight."

"Then get on it."

On that note, V took his leave and descended the grand staircase like he had a job to do—which involved putting someone who annoyed him in a choke hold.

When Tohr was sure there was no one around, he went to the hall of statues and strode down, passing by the contoured depictions of humans in war poses. At the third door, he kept his knock quiet, and when an answer came, he looked both ways once again.

Slipping into Qhuinn's bedroom—or rather, the one Layla had stayed in—he closed the door quickly and almost locked it.

Qhuinn was over by the youngs' bassinets, doing something with a bottle. "Hey," he said without glancing up.

"We need to talk."

"Do we?" The brother looked over. "Did you kill him?"

"No, but I did just get kicked out of the Brotherhood."

Qhuinn straightened and turned around. "What?"

"Wrath was right to do it."

"Wait, so Xcor ran like a little fucking coward to the King and—"

"He lied. For you and me. Xcor refused to give us up. He refused to tell Wrath what we did."

"Well, isn't he a fucking hero." Qhuinn frowned. "But if he didn't spill, who did?"

"Layla figured it out. She came to me—she saw that he was shot and didn't believe him when he said it was slayers. I didn't deny it to her."

"Ah, yes, the Chosen paragon." Qhuinn refocused on the young. "How tight is she, huh? She's always willing to stick up for her man. Too bad that kind of loyalty doesn't run in our direction."

Tohr shook his head. "Don't do it, Qhuinn. I may be out, but you'll be there tomorrow night."

"Tomorrow night? What's going on?"

"The Brotherhood and the Band of Bastards are meeting. You'll hear about it first thing after sunset tomorrow. Wrath is going to call the brothers together and take you all out to meet with them so you can witness their oath to Xcor."

"Why the fuck would I care about that?" The brother took the bottle into the bathroom and came back out wiping his hands with a towel. "Xcor's boys want to circle jerk with that bastard, it's not my business."

Tohr shook his head and felt like he was hopping on Wrath's skull-plosion train: In the space of about thirty minutes, he had nearly gotten violent with a female for the first time in his life, found out he had a long-lost brother, and been kicked out of the Brotherhood.

It was too much to comprehend, too much to process.

All he wanted to do was find Autumn and talk to her, tell her that he was sorry . . . but that courtesy of his piss-poor decision making, they were going to have to find another place to live.

Jesus, was this his life?

"Don't do it," he heard himself say. "Please, I've let this go. You need to as well."

"I don't have to do shit." The brother pointed at the bassinets. "Except take care of those two and try to convince Blay to come home to me and them. That's all I owe anybody."

"Including Wrath? The Brotherhood? The people in this house?"

As Qhuinn fell silent, Tohr pointed to the corner where the bullet holes had been, the evidence of Qhuinn's temper obviously having been replastered and repainted. "Everybody's lost their damn minds lately. And that is what happens when emotions run hot and logic goes out the window and stress rules the night. You're right, you have to take care of your kids. So do it by not getting yourself killed. You discharge a firearm at Xcor before, during, or after that meeting, and people are going to die. Maybe most of them are Bastards, maybe you even take out Xcor, but bulletproof vests only protect the heart, and if you want to do right by those two kids, you make it so you come home at dawn. Because I will guarantee you we will lose some of our people, too, and one of those casualties might just be yourself."

Qhuinn turned back to the bassinets, and it seemed incongruous, inappropriate, just all around bad, that they were having this kind of conversation anywhere near such innocents.

"This is not a bunch of civilians," Tohr pointed out. "You're not meeting the Bastards in a drawing room tomorrow night and trading paperwork back and forth. I'll say it again, people are going to get killed if you decide to take matters into your own hands. And if that happens, and it will, you're going to have to look those two kids in the eyes when they're older with those deaths on your conscience. You will turn their father into a murderer, and you're going to put Wrath in a horrible position— again, assuming the two of you survive. Think about it. Ask yourself if vengeance is worth the price."

Tohr turned away to leave, but then stopped. "I was almost a father once. It was a job I was looking forward to, praying for. I would do almost anything to be where you stand now over those young of yours. Sacrifice is relative . . . and you got a lot to lose over a male who's really not of consequence to your larger life. Don't be an asshole on this one, my brother, just don't."

FIFTY-SEVEN

"Well, this rather settles things, doesn't it."

As Throe stood over the bloody bed, he looked at his balloon, as he had come to think of the shadow, and smiled.

"You are efficient, aren't you."

The thing waved a little from its tether above the carpet, and one could surmise it was pleased with the praise. Or perhaps not. But what did it matter; his shadow had not denied him when he had ordered it to kill his lover's mate and had been quite accomplished at the task: The entity had readily taken the dagger Throe had provided, followed him down the hall like a dog after its master, and then when Throe had opened the door and pointed to the old male sitting up against the head-board, the death had come about quicker than the beat of a heart.

Which was something that *hellren* did not have anymore.

"What have you done!"

As a shriek sounded out behind him, Throe pivoted on his velvet slipper. "Oh, hello, darling. You're up early."

Before his lover could respond, Throe lunged forward and caught her around the neck. As he started to squeeze, her eyes popped wide and that talented mouth of hers cranked open in a scream that had no sound.

Dragging her into the bedroom, he kicked the door shut as she clawed at his hands and gaped like a fish.

The entity approached from the side as if in inquiry, and Throe smiled at it again. "Oh, how kind of you. But I've got this."

Switching his grip to her face, he gave a quick jerk and snapped her neck. Then to avoid making a noise, he escorted her gently down to the carpeted floor.

Standing over her, he noted that she was in that baby-doll nightgown he liked, the one with the lace bodice and the flouncy skirt that reached just below her panties.

"Such as shame, really. She was a bit of fun."

Throe straightened his silk bathrobe. He'd popped free of one of his slippers and rectified that problem by stepping over the cooling body of the female and stuffing his foot back where it belonged.

"Well, this is just fine." He looked around the very well appointed bedroom suite. "You know, I think I'll move in here. Once we get rid of that mattress."

Except then he thought of the *doggen* in the house. There were at least fourteen of them.

It would take them some time to eliminate that lot, and it rather seemed a waste. Good help was very hard to find.

And then there were matters of security and finance that needed to be addressed. Fortunately, he had set the identity theft in motion weeks ago, getting into the *hellren's* computer downstairs, putting tracers on things, gaining access bit by bit to accounts, data, and permissions.

He considered briefly giving the staff the option to stay. But then he looked at the mess on the bed. If his shadow friend could kill like that?

It was a good guess it could work a fucking vacuum.

They were going to need more of them, however. Throe had checked The Book to see if there were some kind of reproduction that could be brought to bear with the shadows, but it appeared that if Throe wanted an army, he was going to have to make them one by one. The hard way.

Very inconvenient. And his hand was still recovering from its puncture wound.

He was going to require more supplies. And time. And . . .

Alas, it seemed uncharitable, indeed, ungrateful, to despair over aught. He had money. He had a home he liked. And he had a weapon that was better than any gun, knife, or fist.

"My destiny," he murmured to the silent room, "is within my reach."

Throe brought up his palms—but as he nearly rubbed them together, he stopped himself. One did not want to turn oneself into a caricature of a villain. It was quite unseemly.

"Come," he said to his balloon. "I must needs get dressed and you shall help me. And then we need to go out."

Testing his toy against a *lesser* was going to be important and there was no reason to wait. The thing had performed admirably just now, but that had been against a nearly incapacitated geriatric. If it was going to face the Brothers and the Omega's fighters, even the Band of Bastards, it was going to need to perform at a very high level.

Just as Throe stepped out into the corridor, he heard the floor polisher running downstairs. If any of the staff found these bodies, there was going to be pandemonium. And with the King accepting audiences the now, the Brotherhood could descend before he was prepared for them and ruin everything.

Fates, he hated these delays. But a proper strategist recognized that there were necessary sequences to things.

As with chess, it was one move at a time.

"Come on," he said in a bored voice to the shadow. "We have to clean house first. And I must insist that you do so with a certain reserve this time. I don't want to ruin any of the art or textiles. Besides, whatever mess you make, you're going to have to tidy up."

With that, the pair of them headed off together, toward the stairs and the *doggen* who was doing his or her job down below.

The pink slip that was about to be delivered unto them was going to hurt.

FIFTY-EIGHT

As the sun set and darkness came over Caldwell, Layla stirred in the bed she and Xcor had put to such glorious use during the day. Against her back, her warrior was nestled in close as her own skin, his body seeking hers even as he slept on.

"Do not think of it, my love," he murmured.

Turning in his embrace, she stroked his hair. His face. His shoulders. "How do you always know?"

He didn't reply to that, just kissed her throat. "Tell me something."

"What?"

"If I had been another male, if my face had been different, if the course of my life had been upon another path, would you . . ."

"Would I what?"

It was a long while before he answered her. "Would you have mated me properly? And lived under the same roof with me . . . and borne my young and raised them with me? If I had been a cobbler or a farmer, a horse trainer or a mead maker, would you have stood beside me and been my *shellan*?"

She touched his upper lip. "I am your *shellan* now."

As he exhaled, his eyes closed. "I wish it had all been different. I wish that that one night, so long ago, I had picked another campfire to visit, another forest to walk through."

"I don't. For if you hadn't gone there, wherever it was, we never would have met."

"Maybe that would have been the better course."

"No," she said firmly. "Everything is the way it should be."

Except for the part that he was leaving her.

"Maybe in the future," she whispered, "after Lyric and Rhamp are grown and on their own, I might come to find you? After their transitions are over and—"

"They will always need their *mahmen*. And your life will always be here in the New World."

Even as she wanted to argue with him, she knew he was right. It was going to be decades before the young were truly independent, and who knew what the state of the war was going to be then? If Rhamp followed in his father's footsteps and became a Brother, Layla would not rest while he was out in the field even if she were in Caldwell itself. Over an entire ocean? She couldn't fathom it.

And then what if Lyric wanted to fight? There were females in the training center program. Lyric could well decide to pick up a dagger.

She could have two young out there in the war.

"There is grace in not fighting that which cannot be changed," he said as he kissed her collarbone. "Let it go. Let me go when the time comes."

"But maybe there's another solution." Although she couldn't imagine what it might be. "What if . . ."

"Qhuinn will never accept me around your young. Even if the Brotherhood and your King were to embrace me and my males, the father of your son and daughter will ne'er have me in their presence, and if I am not in your life, things between you and him will ease. Or at least that is my hope and my fervent prayer, that someday he will accept you back into his life."

But that will never happen, she thought. Qhuinn's fury knew no bounds nor any time limit. Some things, like ink on parchment, were indelible.

"Make love to me?" she whispered.

With a now-familiar surge of power, Xcor moved on top of her, their bodies so at ease with each other by now that his sex entered hers with no positioning, just a smooth glide.

As he began to thrust inside of her, she thought of the sex they'd had during the daylight hours. Her *ehros* training had come to the fore in ways that had shocked, titillated, and surprised him—and he had not complained. But that was not to say it had been a happy time. For both of them, the hours had held a desperation, a rush to the touching and kissing and penetrations, much as one would consume quickly that which was on a plate about to be taken away.

And yet now, as Xcor found his rhythm and she echoed it with her own, this was a different sort of lovemaking. This was not even about sex, per se.

This was the closest their souls could come to merging, the body parts secondary to their hearts being joined.

Just before she found a bittersweet release, she whispered in his ear, "You'll be safe out there tonight?"

When he didn't answer her, she wasn't sure whether it was because he had started to orgasm . . . or because he knew he couldn't promise her that and he didn't want to lie to her.

At the Pit, Vishous sat back in his padded chair and stared at the image on his computer monitor. The combination of pixels, of the light and dark, the gray and green and deep blue, had taken, ohhhhhh, eight hours to isolate and process to the point where you could see this much of them.

And as he looked at the face of the mystery shooter, the one who had saved Tohr's life in that alley some time ago, all he could do was shake his head.

"Too fucking weird."

The features were fairly clear now, but yeah, that distorted upper lip of Xcor's was the dead giveaway. Without it, you might have struggled to

say who it was, as all fighters with short hair, heavy brows, and hard jaw-
lines were like dimes in a sock drawer.

Pretty indistinguishable.

But no, you add that hare lip, and you got yourself a traitor. Who
actually wasn't much of a traitor as it turned out—

"Hi."

As V heard an unfamiliar voice, he snapped his head up. Jane was
standing in front of him, her scrubs wrinkled, her Crocs stained with
blood, her hair sticking straight up as if it were trying to get away from
her brain. She looked worn out, worn down, dragged through a rat hole.

He opened his mouth to say something to her, but then his phone
went off.

When he saw who was calling him, he felt the blood rush out of his
head.

"You can get that," she said with a yawn. "I'll wait."

V silenced the ringer and heard nothing but his heart pounding. "It's
nothing important."

Jane went over to the leather couch and collapsed into its far corner
of cushions. "I don't know what to do about Assail. It's a complete psy-
chotic break. I've never seen anything like it, and I don't want to again."
She rubbed her face. "And I can't help him. I can't bring him around. I've
been out to Havers's a hundred times, combing through his back cases,
talking to his staff and him. Manny's reached out to people in the human
world. All we're getting is dead ends and it's killing me."

She was staring off into space as she spoke, her eyes rapt as if she were
replaying conversations in her head, ever searching for an angle or an
answer she might have missed.

She rubbed her no-doubt-aching temples. "I can't tell you how hard
this is. Watching the suffering and not being able to do anything about
it."

As V's cell phone rang again, he nearly knocked the thing on the floor
as he went to put it on mute.

"Are you sure you don't want to get that?" Jane said. "Sounds urgent."

"What can I do to help you?" he asked.

"Nothing. Just let me go to sleep. I can't remember the last time I rested." She looked over at him. "Even ghosts need a recharge as it turns out."

Even as she said the words, her corporeal form began to disappear, the colors of her eyes and her skin, even the clothes that warmed to her immortal body temperature, fading out.

Disappearing before his very eyes.

She said some other things, and so did he, nothing earth-shattering, everything logistical, like when he was heading out, when she was heading back.

And then she was on her feet again and shuffling over to him. As he looked up from his chair, he saw her lips moving and he told his own to smile in response even though he had no clue what had come out of her mouth.

"Well?" she prompted.

"What?"

"Are you all right? You seem off."

"Lot going on right now. You know, in the war."

"Yes, I heard. Payne and Manny were talking about it."

"You better get to bed before you fall over."

"You are so right."

But instead of leaving, she reached out to him and ran her ghostly hand through his hair—and as she did, he thought there was a reason he didn't like people to touch him.

And that was true on levels other than the literal.

"I love you," she said. "I'm sorry we haven't been able to spend much time together lately."

"It doesn't matter."

"I think it does."

Vishous extended his gloved hand and took her hand away. Forcing another smile, he said, "You've got your work. I've got mine."

"True, and we're going nowhere."

He was well aware that she meant that in the reassuring, our-relationship-is-solid kind of way, and as he nodded, he was also well aware that she would take his apparent affirmation in the same vein.

As she wandered off down to their bedroom alone, however, he knew that he was agreeing with the statement in an entirely different way.

And that should have made him sad.

But he felt nothing.

FIFTY-NINE

When someone started to knock on Qhuinn's door, he was not about to get up from bed to answer the attention-seeker. He had another hour before it was time to go to the meeting in Wrath's study and most likely get his ass chewed—also maybe get kicked out of the Brotherhood as Tohr had been—and aside from him having managed to get himself showered and dressed, he was too much of a basket case to do anything else.

Like, you know, attempt civil discourse. Or do anything other than breathe.

The knock got louder.

As he lifted his head and bared his fangs, he opened his mouth to issue a fuck-off—

But burst to his feet instead.

Rushing over, he yanked the door wide like there were Girl Scouts with Do-si-dos order sheets on the other side.

Blay was standing there in the corridor looking so edible it was nearly illegal, his body clad in leather and weapons—which happened to be Qhuinn's favorite outfit on the guy. Other than buck naked.

"Mind if I come in?" he said.

"Yes. I mean, no, shit, please. Yeah, come in."

Man, if he were any smoother, he'd be a Brillo pad.

Blay shut the door and those beautiful eyes of his went over to the bassinets.

"Do you want to see them?" Qhuinn said, stepping aside, even though he wasn't in the way.

"Yes, I do."

Blay walked over, and although he was facing away, Qhuinn could feel the smile on the guy's face as he greeted one and then the other.

But when he turned around again, he was all business.

Here it comes, Qhuinn thought as he went across and sat on the bed. The answer to the rest of his life. And he knew without being aware of the specific details that this was going to hurt.

Blay reached into his leather jacket. "I don't want this."

As he took out the documents that Saxton had prepared, Qhuinn felt his heart drop. He didn't have much to offer aside from his own god-damn children. If Lyric and Rhamp couldn't bring the male around, nothing would—

"I love you," Blay said. "And I forgive you."

For a split second, Qhuinn couldn't decipher the syllables. And then, when they did sink in, he was sure he must have heard them incorrectly.

"I'll say it again. I love you . . . and I forgive you."

Qhuinn leaped up and crossed the distance between them faster than a match lighting. But he got strong-armed before he could kiss the guy.

"Hold on," Blay countered. "I have some things to say."

"Whatever it is, I agree to it all. Anything, everything, I'm in."

"Good. Then you'll make it right with Layla."

Qhuinn took a step back. And another.

Blay tapped the documents in his open hand. "You heard me. I don't need any parental rights to be legally granted. You don't have to pull some showy bullshit like this—although I appreciate the sentiment, and honestly, it did convince me you were really serious about what you said. But you told me you would do anything, and I'm taking you as a male of your word. You're not going to be right with me until you're right with Layla."

"I don't know if I can do that, Blay." Qhuinn put his palms up. "I'm not being an asshole here. I'm really not. It's just . . . I know myself. And after she put them in danger like that, and lied for so long to cover it up? I can't come back from that, not even for you."

"I think you need to focus more on who Xcor is rather than on what she did."

"I know who he is. That's the issue."

"Well, I just spoke with Tohr, who told me everything—"

Qhuinn threw up his hands and walked around. "Oh, come *on*—"

"And I really think you need to recast things."

"I'm not going to forget what happened, Blay. I can't."

"No one's asking you to do that."

As Qhuinn paced around, he decided these conversations about that Bastard were turning things into fucking *Groundhog Day*. Without Bill Murray. So yes, it sucked.

"Look, I don't want to debate you," he said as he stopped and looked across the room at Blay.

"I don't want that, either. And we're not debating this because I'm not discussing it any further. You make it right with Layla, or I'm not coming back."

"What the hell, Blay—how can you make you and me about her?"

"I'm making you and me about this family. The two of them"—he pointed to the bassinets—"and the three of us. We're a family, but only if we stick together. Blood only means so much, and after the shit your parents pulled, you know this firsthand. If we can't—if *you* can't—forgive and love and move on, then you and I aren't going to last, because I'm not going to sit by and pretend I'm okay with you resenting that poor daughter of yours just because she looks like her *mahmen*. Or waiting until I do something that you can't get over. You challenged me to forgive you for what you did—and I have. Now I'm expecting you to do the same for Layla."

Blay went back to the door. "I love you with everything I've got, and when you and Layla had those kids? You gave me a complete family. And I want my family back, the whole thing—and that includes Layla."

"Blay, please—"

"That's my condition. And I'm going to make it stick. See you out in the field."

As Xcor got ready to leave the ranch just before midnight, he let his *shellan* check the fastenings on the bulletproof vest. She was very thorough, to the point where he had a feeling if she could have strapped herself to his chest, she would have.

Capturing her hands, he kissed her fingertips one by one.

"I am a lucky male, to be cared for thusly."

Fates, he hated her distress. Would have done anything he could have to replace it with joy—especially as he feared that only more sorrow was before her. If he lived through tonight, if the Brotherhood held true to what Wrath wanted, they were still out of road for their journey.

"I fear I can't let you leave," she said through a wobbling smile. "I fear . . . I cannot bear you to go."

As her voice broke, he closed his eyes. "I will be back home here soon enough."

He kissed her so that they couldn't talk about it anymore, and as she fiercely returned his embrace, he tried to remember every detail about the way she felt against him, and how her lips tasted, and what it was to have her scent in his nose.

When he finally inched back, he stared into her pale green eyes. His favorite color, as it turned out. Who knew he had one?

And then he stepped away and didn't look back. He didn't dare.

Going over to the slider, he could smell her tears, but again, he did not stop on his way. There was no stopping any of this now.

The door made no sound as he pulled it open and stepped through, and he was careful not to turn around as he closed it behind himself.

Progressing outside the glow of the porch's security lights, he went around the far corner of the garage. There was an old shed there, one that was big enough for a riding mower, and tall enough for the handles of hoes and shovels.

As he opened the flimsy door, its hinges let out a squeak of protest.

Reaching into the darkness, he retrieved his scythe and flipped it onto his back, securing it with a simple rope tie that ran across his chest. He hadn't wanted to bring it into the house with Layla there. It had just seemed wrong.

With the knives and the guns he already had on him, he was ready for war no matter who brought it, be it *lesser* or Brother.

As he closed his eyes and prepared to dematerialize off to meet his males, he prayed for two things.

One, that he made it back here to see Layla one more time before he left.

And two, that Wrath had as much control as he seemed to think he did over the Brotherhood.

Funny how the two were intimately connected.

SIXTY

As Tohr sat alone in the bedroom he shared with Autumn, he held a black dagger in his hands. The blade had been both fashioned and maintained by Vishous, the weapon constantly kept sharp, its handle perfectly fitted to Tohr's grip, and Tohr's grip alone.

It was unfathomable to think he would never wield it again.

When he had told his *shellan* what had happened, and why, she had been saddened. It was the first time, he realized, that he'd really let her down—and given that he was still only half a male because of all the Wellsie shit? That was really saying something.

At least the two of them had somewhere to go. Xhex was going to let them crash for the next couple of nights at that hunting cabin of hers—the one where he and Layla had had their showdown.

He was sooooo happy about returning there.

Turning the knife over, he angled the black blade so that the light from the bedside table hit the tiny nicks on the sharp edges. He'd been about to suggest V do a little polish job on the thing—it wasn't as if Tohr would be allowed to. That brother worked so hard crafting the weapons that he got shirty if anyone tried to hone one themselves.

But guess all that was moot now—

Okay, why the hell was fucking Simon and Garfunkel going through his frickin' head? *Helllllllloooooo darrrrrknesssss myyyy ollllllld friiiiiend—*

"Fuck me."

Hard to know what was worse. That god-awful sixties music refraining through his gray matter, or the fact that he'd been fired from the only job he'd ever done, ever wanted to do, ever been good at.

Although come on, how hard could it be to work a deep fryer? There was that to look forward to.

And meanwhile, his beautiful female was down in the basement with Fritz trying to find boxes for their shit—

The knock on his door was a welcome diversion. At this rate, he was going to end up on Prozac and M&M's to deal with the depression he was rocking.

"Come in?" Maybe it was a *doggen* with a bunch of containers. "Hello? Come in?"

When there was no answer, he frowned and got up to go to the door. He had put his leathers and shitkickers on when he'd gotten dressed because that was just what he did. Maybe now he'd swap them out for a bunch of cardigans and loose grandpa khakis that pooled in the butt and stayed in place thanks to suspenders.

Yeah, 'cuz that was hot—

As he opened the door wide, words failed him.

Wrath was standing there, looking like the King he was, all dressed in black with those wraparounds on. Behind him, in a semi-circle, the Brotherhood, and Blay and John Matthew, were like a war waiting to happen, all those males armed and ready to fight.

"Hello, my old friend," Wrath said as he offered his hand. "Want to come to the party?"

Tohr swallowed hard. "What, ah . . . um . . . I'm sorry?"

Wrath just shrugged. "Saxton is all up my ass about human resources policies and procedures. Apparently in these times, you gotta warn someone before you can 'em. You know, bring 'em in, offer them retraining, wipe their ass for them, you know, this type of thing. Before you fire them."

Rhage piped up. "Also, let's face it. You're the most reasonable one in this group."

"A full cock going off," somebody chimed in. "Instead of a half cock like the rest of us."

"Quarter cock in Rhage's case—"

Hollywood wheeled around and glared at V. "Okay, fuck you—"

"With what?"

Wrath put a hand over his face. "Jesus, will you people stop!" Dropping his arm, he said with exhaustion, "So let's just put your ass on probation, all right? Great. I'm so glad we can move forward from this."

The King grabbed him and yanked him forward into a hard hug. "Now let's go sort this Xcor thing the right way, okay? And Beth has gone to tell Autumn. There isn't time for you to, we have to go now."

Dazed, but getting less confused by the second, Tohr ducked his eyes and pulled a manly wipe of them. Long, long ago, he had been chosen to join the Brotherhood, and it had never once occurred to him that, short of death, he would ever find himself looking in from the outside. But he had certainly deserved that and so much more for what he had done.

And although he couldn't put this reprieve on a par with losing his mate and son? It was a reminder that destiny was not totally cruel.

In a hoarse voice, he said, "Yeah, all right. Let's do this."

There was a general cheer and some serious backslapping. And yes, he wanted to go find his mate and talk to her, but the grandfather clock down the hall started chiming.

There was no more time. It was midnight.

The Brotherhood and the Band of Bastards had to go try and make peace. And he had to go look his brother in the face.

As V re-formed in front of the abandoned warehouse, he tested the air with his nose and gave his instincts as much breathing room as they wanted.

Natch.

Fifteenth and Market was a good setting for this historic and potentially dangerous meeting, he decided, the old barn-y building adequately deserted, with enough broken panes in its capitalist version of a clerestory that if they had to bail once they got inside, it was a quick trip to a number of exits.

Walking forward, he had Rhage on his right and Butch on his left, and it felt fucking awesome to be heading into possible conflict. He really wanted to fight something, and he figured if the Bastards didn't prove to be total assholes, then after this was done, he and his brothers could go find some slayers.

Or maybe he went off on his own and did something else.

Whichever it was, he knew he didn't have to go back home for a good six hours and he was going to make use of the time.

Fuck, was he actually going to—

Whatever, he thought as he shut down his case of mental seizures. One thing that you didn't have to be a genius like him to know was that if you went into a fight distracted, you weren't going to have to worry about anything, because you were gonna wake up dead the next morning.

The warehouse was your bog standard forty-five-thousand-square-foot deserted birdcage, not much left aside from its rotting, rusted exoskeleton and a metal roof that was a crash helmet on someone with a death wish. There were a number of doors, and after the troika walked down the side of the building they'd been assigned, they waited for the signal to enter after the sweep inside was completed by Phury and Z.

With his back flat against the building's pitted siding, and his guns out and up, V scanned the area. Visibility was fantastic, no trees to block his view, nothing but more vacated buildings, rubble, and pavement for blocks and blocks and blocks, the neighborhood a wasteland from the industrial era that had sustained this part of the city for so long—

Just as everyone's cells went off announcing it was clear in the interior, five figures appeared, one by one, in the vacant lot across the street.

V took out his phone and texted an audible: *We have them. Going to approach.*

He didn't have to tell Rhage and Butch what the fuck to do, and that was why he loved them. The three of them just strode forward, crossing over the crusty snow before mounting the snowbank and walking into the center of the road. As if the Band of Bastards had the same playbook, they likewise came forward from their position, their big bodies moving in unison, their weapons out, but not up, Xcor in the center.

The two groups met in the middle of the road.

Vishous spoke first. "Evenin', boys. How we doing?"

He sensed neither hate nor love coming out of the other fighters. Well, except for the guy on the end: That one on the far left was giving off a vibe like maybe he wanted to get aggressive, but V had the impression that that was his idling speed and not anything specific to this situation.

V did not lower his guns, but he did not demand that they disarm, either, even though it made him twitchy as shit. The drop-your-load was going to happen inside.

"We are prepared to follow you," Xcor said in clearly enunciated tones.

"Good." V met the eyes of each one of them. "Here's the way we're going to do this, true? We'll escort you in. You'll meet everyone, and we'll have a little cocktail mixer with passed *hors d'oeuvres* and drinks. Then we'll go see a show, and we'll cap the night off with a shopping spree at Saks and a round of mani-pedis. Sound all right? Great. Walk on, motherfuckers."

Xcor didn't hesitate, and V took that as a good sign.

And the others were right on his heels.

This, he took as an even better sign: If those boys were willing to show their backs, there was some kind of trust going on here.

Falling in line behind the Band of Bastards, V followed along, going back over the low snowbank, across that "lawn" of snow and ice, and over to the door.

V put his lips together and whistled in a short burst. As soon as he did, the metal panel broke open and John Matthew held it wide.

You want to talk about tense? The Band of Bastards, as they filed into the drafty interior, were about as relaxed as prisoners going to the electric chair. But they held their position as they looked around and no one started shooting as they continued to walk forward.

V was willing to bet they assessed the same exits in the open space the Brotherhood did. The same doors. The same rafters. The same empty window panes.

"Stop here," he told them. And they did.

Showtime, V thought as he came around to stand in front of the lineup.

"Now, gentlemen, before we bring the King in, I'm afraid I'm going to have to get you naked." He pointed to the concrete floor. "All your weapons go here. You behave yourselves and you get them back. You don't, and we'll leave you bleeding all over them."

SIXTY-ONE

ohr's heart was pounding as he stepped out from where he'd been standing against the warehouse wall. He was supposed to keep his position by this western door, but he couldn't stay put. His feet took him inexorably forward, his eyes on Xcor.

"Where are you going?" Blay hissed after him.

"Just a little closer. Stay there."

Little closer his ass. He walked all the way over to where the Band of Bastards had lined up in the center of the warehouse wasteland.

V was addressing them, the brother's voice echoing through the high ceiling. "Right there," he repeated while nodding to his feet.

In the back of his mind, Tohr knew that this was going to tell a lot. If the Bastards balked at disarming, or getting searched, then it was a good bet this was an ambush of Trojan Horse proportions. But if they—

One by one, each of Xcor's fighters complied with the order, dropping guns and knives to the concrete slab and kicking them in Vishous's direction. Even Xcor took that huge scythe of his off his back and sent it over to V.

"You want to help search 'em?" V said. "Or did you come here to give me another coat of lip gloss?"

It took a moment to figure out that Vishous was talking to him. "I'll search."

As the brother nodded, and Butch and Rhage stared at the Bastards like the males were grenades with the pins out, Tohr walked right up to Xcor and met him in the eyes.

God, why hadn't he noticed before? They were the exact color of his own.

"Tohr?" V said sharply. "What are you doing, my man?"

And that jaw. It was the shape of his. The dark hair. That lip was a distraction that made you not consider the rest, but now that he looked past it?

Tohr felt a heavy hand land on his shoulder. And then V's voice was loud in his ear. "I'd really prefer that if someone does something stupid, it's one of them. Let's not have it be one of us, true?"

Xcor stared back at him calmly, without fear or aggression: He was a male who was resigned to his fate, unafraid of whatever was before him, and you had to respect that.

"Tohr. Remember that whole probation thing?"

Tohr nodded absently, not really hearing anything. The thing was, he had wondered, ever since Wellsie had died with his son still in her womb, what it would be like to look into the eyes of a blood relation. The loss of that possibility had been one more thing to mourn.

He had never considered that some night he would meet the stare of his brother.

Xcor spoke softly. "What are you going to do?"

That was when Tohr realized that he hadn't put his guns down. But before he could rectify that, V said, "FYI, I'll have you know you're alive today because of him."

That got Tohr's attention and he looked at Vishous. "I'm sorry?"

"I found a little video clip of this motherfucker right here, defending you against a *lesser*. It's a real classic. I watched it on a loop for hours today."

"Wait, what?"

"You remember, when you were trying to turn yourself into a screen door by walking into a shower of bullets? Good times." V rolled his eyes. "Hey, I have an idea. Why don't you friend him on Facebook, and then you can look forward to the day when you get a memories post with him in it. Great stuff. Just so fucking Hallmark. Now either disarm him or get the fuck back into position."

Tohr knew exactly what craziness V was referring to, remembered precisely the moment when he had ignored his own mortality and all the laws of physics and had stepped out into the enemy's line of fire.

Frowning, he said to Xcor, "Is this true?"

When the Bastard nodded once, Tohr exhaled. "Why?"

"It is not important now," the Bastard replied.

"No, it's everything. *Why?*"

Xcor looked to V as if trying to sense whether the brother was going to completely lose his patience with all this.

Too late on that, Tohr thought. But fuck it, he might never get this chance again.

"Why?" he demanded again. "We were enemies."

When Xcor finally answered, his voice was steady and very heavily accented. "You were so brave. You walked out into that gunfire unafraid. Regardless of our positions at the time, I didn't want a warrior of that courage to be killed in that manner. In honest conflict, yes. But not like that, a sitting duck. So I shot the shooter."

Tohr blinked and thought of everything he would have missed if he had died that night. Autumn. The chance to be a part of this brokered peace. The future.

Out of the corner of his eye, he saw something move—

No, it was just Lassiter. The fallen angel had come, and that was no surprise. He was like the neighborhood busybody who was looking over the fence anytime there was drama.

Tohr refocused on those navy blue eyes, so like his own. And then he lowered one of his guns and put the other one back in its holster.

Reaching out with his dagger hand, he offered his palm.

Xcor looked down at it.

After a long moment, the Bastard accepted the gesture . . . and two brothers shook hands for the first time.

Although only one of them knew it.

From Qhuinn's vantage point in the far corner of the warehouse, he watched things unroll: the Band of Bastards entering the abandoned building, stopping in the middle, listening to V and disarming on his command. All of that was planned. But then Tohr walked forward.

As the brother shitkicker'd his way into the center, everyone else in the whole fucking place held their breath, but Qhuinn didn't. The brother wasn't going to be stupid. It wasn't in his nature for one thing, and for another, he had honor—

"Say *what?*" Qhuinn sputtered as V started talking and ended up at something about Xcor having saved Tohr's life.

Oh, he'd witnessed firsthand that little suicidal interlude, that insanity. It was one of those stories that the Brotherhood whispered about when they were drunk and it was three in the afternoon and nobody else was around, an entry in the catalog of the past that made the cost of war trauma so very real.

But what the fuck? How had V gotten footage? A security camera? Some human on the sidelines?

What did it matter—

When a figure materialized from out of nowhere right next to him, Qhuinn nearly pulled his trigger, but the blond and black head of hair was unmistakable.

"Do you want to get shot?" Qhuinn demanded.

In a Darth Vader voice, the angel shot back, "Your weapons are nothing against me."

"For fuck's sake—"

All of a sudden, Lassiter's face was right in front of his, and there was absolutely no jokey-jokey in those strange colored eyes. "Get ready."

"For what?"

At that moment, Wrath re-formed in the center of the warehouse, right by Vishous. And that was why they'd chosen the vast empty space. Factoring in the King's blindness, there was nothing to get in his way, nothing to trip him, nothing to make him struggle or look weak by having to rely on the brothers to get him around.

Man, Qhuinn thought as he measured the Bastards' big bodies. He really didn't like them so close to the King, even if they were unarmed.

"So this is really going to happen, huh?" Qhuinn shook his head at the Bastards and the Brotherhood standing so closely together. "I never thought I'd see this night, I'll tell you that."

When Lassiter didn't reply, he glanced over. The fallen angel was gone.

Qhuinn refocused and listened, which wasn't hard. Wrath's voice carried like a church organ.

"I understand the oath you have is to your leader. That's fine. But he has sworn allegiance to me, and as such that binds the lot of you. Is there any dissent here?"

One by one, the Bastards spoke a resounding no, and it was obvious by the way Wrath's nose was flaring that the King was testing their scents.

"Good," Wrath said. Then he switched over to the Old Language. "*I thereby command this assemblage that they shall pledge their oath unto their leader in the presence of the King he has sworn himself unto. Proceed the now upon bended knee with bowed head and faithful heart.*"

Without conversation or hesitation, one by one, the Band of Bastards knelt before Xcor, lowering their heads and kissing the knuckles of his dagger hand. And all the time, Wrath stood right next to them, testing the air, searching for, but evidently not finding, any subterfuge.

When it was done, Xcor turned to Wrath.

Qhuinn's heart pounded as he looked at the male's face. Although there was quite a distance between them, he traced those features, those shoulders, that body. He remembered the two of them trading punches, going those rounds in the Tomb.

He thought of Layla, pregnant with Lyric and Rhamp.

And then he heard Blay telling him to make it right with the Chosen so they could be right. So their family could be whole. So the past could be viewed with logic, not emotion.

It was with the image of his young squarely in his mind that he watched as Xcor went down on bended knee before Wrath.

Wrath put out the black diamond, the symbol of the throne, the ring that had been his father's and his father's father's before that.

The ring that perhaps L.W. would wear someday.

"Bow your head before me," Wrath commanded in the Old Language. *"Swear unto me your service from this night forward. Let there be no conflict e'er between us."*

Qhuinn took a deep breath.

And then he released it as Xcor lowered his head, kissed the stone, and said, loud and clear, *"Unto you I pledge my life and my blood. There will ne'er by any ruler above you for me and mine, ne'er any conflict between us until my grave claims my mortal flesh. This is my solemn oath."*

Qhuinn closed his eyes and lowered his own head.

Just as *lessers* broke through every door there was.

SIXTY-TWO

The doors of the warehouse opened in quick succession, *blam!
blam! blam!* and the slayers that burst in moved fast.

It was Vishous's worst nightmare.

And the first thing he did was go for Wrath. With a quick lunge, he
tackled the King and covered him with his body.

Which turned out to be like keeping a bucking bronco on the ground.

"Will you lie the fuck down!" Vishous hissed as fighting broke out.

"Give me a weapon! Give me a fucking weapon!"

Gunshots. Cursing. Slashing knives. All as Brothers counterattacked
and the Bastards dove for their armaments to help.

"Don't make me knock you out!" V growled as he wrapped his arms
around Wrath's upper body and tried to become heavier. "For fuck's
sake!"

Going on the theory that you couldn't keep a good fighter down—
even if the dumb shit's motherfucking life depended on it—Wrath actually got his feet under them both and stood up, in spite of the fact that V
was wrapped around his head and neck like a scarf, torso to the back, legs
kicking in the front.

It was the fireman's hold from hell and about as herky-jerky as a Jeep
going over a riverbed.

The good news? Guess they were testing out the binds of all those frickin' oaths tonight—and the shit was holding: The Bastards were fighting against the slayers side by side with the Brotherhood, and yeah, wow, they were some lethal SOBs all right.

But V wasn't about to go Dana White on this makeshift octagon. He had the idiot King to keep alive—

As a bullet sizzled right by his bobbing, spinning head, Vishous lost it. "Will you fucking get—"

"Forgive me, my Lord."

Huh? As V glanced back, he saw Xcor crouching right next to them.

"But this is not safe for you." On that note, the head of the Bastards went linebacker on the King of all vampires, catching Wrath's thighs in a bear hug and pile driving the guy down to the concrete. Which meant V went right with him—

—and landed so hard on his head that he heard the crack and felt a terrifying numbness radiate down his body.

With a moan of pain, V felt his arms loosen of their own volition; even as he commanded his muscles to stay contracted, they fell useless to the concrete.

Xcor's face appeared over his own. "How bad?"

"This is payback for me"—V gasped a breath—"hitting you over the head at that prep school, isn't it?"

Xcor smiled a little and then ducked his head as another bullet went flying. "Was that you, then, mate?"

"Yeah, it was me."

"Ah, you have a helluva good swing, then." Xcor got serious. "I need to move you."

"Wrath?"

"Tohrment took him. The Brother Tohrment."

"Good." V swallowed. "Listen to me, I'm about to lose consciousness. Don't move me. I could have a broken back and I don't want any more spinal damage than I might have already."

He fought against the tide that was claiming him, his vision fuzzing in and out.

"Tell Jane . . . I'm sorry."

"Is that your mate, then?"

"Yeah, people will know who she is. Just tell her . . . I don't know. I love her, I guess. I don't know."

An incredible wave of sorrow carried him off to total blackness, the sounds of the fighting, the pain, the low-level panic that came from him thinking, Oh, shit, I've really done it now, receding into a deep void of nothingness.

In the end, V didn't so much lose the will to fight . . . as put down his sword to stay alive.

When another wave of the enemy came in through the doors, Qhuinn ran out of his fourth clip of bullets—and as his semiautomatic started clicking instead of shooting, he cursed and slammed himself back against the warehouse wall.

Kicking out the empty, he put his last fresh one in and then squared off at the door he was covering, picking off three rushing slayers one right after the other, the writhing, stinking bodies obligingly piling up into an obstacle the others had to slow down to get over.

But he was out of bullets again too fast, and he pitched the gun away. It was getting too dangerous for bullets anyway, the Brotherhood fighting everywhere along with Bastards, the warehouse's emptiness now a problem, for there was no cover to be had—

The knife blade came out of nowhere, but it hit in just the right place.

His bad shoulder. In the meat.

"Mother*fucker*—"

Just as he was about to try and lunge forward at the slayer who'd played round peg to his square hole, one of the biggest, meanest vampires he'd ever seen swooped down from out of thin air and tackled the *lesser* into the wall. And then . . .

Oh. Myyyyyyyyyyyyyyyyyyy.

To channel George Takei.

The Bastard in question bared his fangs and bit the slayer's face off.

Like, literally, just Hannibal Lecter'd the nose and most of one cheek from the bone. And after spitting that out, he tore into what was left until there were flashes of white showing through the black blood and muscle.

Then the male cast the thing aside as you would an apple core.

As the Bastard turned to Qhuinn, there was a dripping black stain running down his chin and chest, and the guy was smiling like he'd won a Nathan's Famous contest.

"Do you need help getting that knife from your flesh, then?"

It seemed ridiculous that the guy was asking something so shockingly civilized.

Qhuinn grabbed the handle, grit his teeth, and yanked the blade free of his shoulder. As pain made him want to vomit, he choked out, "Actually, I was going to offer you a nice Chianti."

"What?"

"Watch out!"

As a slayer came at the Bastard from behind, Qhuinn went into action, leaping up and switching the knife out of his dominant hand, which was tied to that now really fucking bad shoulder.

Fortunately, he was ambi-daggerous.

Qhuinn plowed that blade right into the eye socket of the offending slayer, and then he twisted the hilt so hard the thing broke off and stayed in its nice new cozy home.

He and the slayer landed in a heap, just as Qhuinn's shoulder announced that enough was enough. As he turned and retched, he did it in the sight line of a huge pair of combat boots.

The slayer got lifted off of him like the pinwheeling, undead POS weighed nothing more than a rubber band. And then that big-ass Bastard crouched down.

"I'll move you, then," it said in a heavy accent.

Qhuinn was thrown over a shoulder that was the size of a house, and then there was a bumpy ride to God only knew where.

As he and his new BFFL went on a wander, he got a good look at what was doing, albeit from an upside-down perspective. Brothers, Bastards helping each other, working in concert, fighting a common enemy.

And there was Xcor, right in the middle . . .

Tears sprang to Qhuinn's eyes as he realized that the fighter, that head of the Bastards, was side by side with none other than the only redhead in the place.

The two of them were back to back, moving in a slow circle, trading stabs and punches with the swarm of *lessers*. Blay was as spectacular as always, and the Bastard more than just kept up.

"I'm going to pass out now," Qhuinn said to no one in particular.

And as he did, that image of the love of his life and the male he'd made an enemy of lingered, crossing the barrier between reality and dreams.

SIXTY-THREE

ayla was pacing around the fountain up in the Scribe Virgin's—make that *Lassiter's*—private quarters when suddenly she was not alone, and not just because her young were asleep in soft blankets by the tree full of birds.

As the fallen angel, now deity-in-charge, materialized out of thin air, her first thought was that he was the bearer of terrible news.

In all the time she had known him, he had never looked so bad, his skin so sallow it was gray, his aura diminished such that he was but a shadow cast of his usual self.

Layla rushed to him and barely made it as he fell to his knees on the white marble. "What ails you! Are you injured?"

Had he gone to the meeting of the Brotherhood and the Bastards? Had something gone wrong—

"Lassiter," she cried out as she sank down with him. *"Lassiter . . ."*

He did not respond. He just put his head in his hands and then went all the way prone on the white marble as if he had lost consciousness.

She looked around, wondering what to do. Mayhap call Amalya—

Except then he rolled over onto his back and she was stunned to see silver tears leave his eyes and fall as diamonds onto the stone beneath him.

"I can't do this . . . I can't do this job . . . it's not me . . ."

"What is happening?" she breathed with terror. "What did you do down below?"

In reply, the words that came out of him were mumbled, so indistinct she had to bend closer to try to decipher them: "The war has to end. And there is only one way to destroy the Omega. It was foretold. The prophecy must be realized and that can happen but one way."

As his eyes met hers, fear turned her cold. "What did you do?"

"The *lessers* must be eliminated. They have to kill all of them and then take out the Omega. The war has to end."

"What did you do!"

"They are my family," the fallen angel choked out as he covered his face with his hands. "They are my family . . ."

As a horrible thought dawned on her, she said, "Tell me you didn't—"

"The slayers must be eliminated. Every single one of them. Only then can they go after the Omega . . ."

Layla fell back on her bottom and put her hands to her cheeks. The Brothers and the Bastards in one place. An oath of loyalty given and accepted.

Such that if the Lessening Society would show up, the two previously opposing sides would fight their common enemy together.

"Will any of them die?" she demanded of the angel. "Who is going to die?"

"I don't know," he said in a broken voice. "That I cannot see . . ."

"Why did you have to do this?" Even though he had already shared the reasoning. *"Why?"*

As her eyes began to water, she thought about going down to earth. But she couldn't depart from the young. "Why now?"

Lassiter stopped mumbling, his eyes fixating on the milky white sky above them—to the point where she wondered if he couldn't see what was happening down below.

Leaving him as he was, she crawled over to where Lyric and Rhamp were blissfully asleep, utterly unaware of what might well be changing the course of their lives forever.

Lying down with them on the soft blankets she had folded up so they would be warm and cozy, she let her tears do what they would.

She would have prayed.

But the race's savior was not in any kind of condition to hear requests. Besides, it was clear that he already knew what she would have begged for—and shared her fears.

It was also obvious that of all the gifts he could grant and powers he had, ensuring that no Brother or Bastard fell in the fighting was not among them.

SIXTY-FOUR

In the end, the battle at the warehouse proved that wars were ultimately subject to the same rules about beginnings, middles, and ends as everything else on the planet.

The harbinger of it being over was not silence. No, nothing was silent in the cold, man-made cave. There were too many groans and broken shuffles across the concrete floor, the battlefield strewn with bodies moving and not, the air thick with gun smoke and blood.

"Is it over?"

As Wrath spoke, Tohr loosened his hold on the King a little. But not by much. He had his arms and legs wrapped around the other male's huge body, the pair of them wedged into a corner formed thanks to the only delineated space in the tremendous, bare interior: The King's back was to the juncture of walls, and Tohr was a mortal shield protecting vital organs even though Wrath was wearing a bulletproof vest.

They didn't always do the trick, after all.

And Wrath's life was nothing that anybody was prepared to gamble with.

"Is it?" Wrath demanded. "I don't hear any more fighting."

Tohr's head had been cranked to the side, and as he straightened it a bit, his neck cracked. Looking around, he tried to identify bodies, but there was no making sense of the carnage. There were twenty-five dead, maybe more, on the cold concrete floor, and there was both black and red blood everywhere.

He truly feared there had been casualties in the Brotherhood—

From out of the masses of bodies, a lone figure stood up.

It was covered in blood and moving badly. And it had a gun. But things were too smoky to tell whether it was a slayer or a brother or a Bastard.

"Fuck," Tohr breathed.

He didn't want to get up to fight and leave Wrath defenseless, because the guy was just stupid and pissed off enough at the ambush that he might well try and take up arms again—

The whistle that echoed up was like a benediction.

And Tohr whistled right back.

Vishous turned in the center of the battlefield and started limping over; his gait was bad and one arm hung at a horrible angle. But he was tougher than all that, and determined to get to his King—

It was not Vishous.

As the figure got closer, Tohr realized . . . it was Xcor. Xcor was the one coming over.

When the Bastard was in range, it was obvious he was very badly injured, all kind of red stuff leaking from wounds that seemed to affect almost every part of his body.

"We must get the King out," the Bastard whispered in a hoarse voice. "I will go scout."

"Wait," Tohr said as he grabbed for the male's arm. "You're hurt."

"And you are the shield of our King. It's too dangerous for him to be left unattended. If I die, it will not matter. If he dies, all hope is lost for the race and the Omega wins."

Tohr stared up into his blooded brother's eyes. "If you can get outside, there's help. Four blocks over to the west. They were told not to come unless someone called on them. We didn't want to sacrifice the doctors."

Xcor nodded. "I will return."

And then in an unbelievable show of will and strength, the male ghosted into the thin air. In spite of the fact that he was brutally wounded.

"We're going to have to buy that motherfucker a gold watch or something," Wrath muttered.

"Isn't that what you get when you retire?"

"You think he's fighting again after this shit?"

Tohr waited. And waited. And waited. And tried to contain his panic that people he loved were dead or dying around him and he was tending to none of them.

He told himself that as long as he didn't hear any bullets or anything, Xcor might have made it to the—

The sound started off faintly, a growl in the distance. And then it grew louder, and louder . . . and louder still until the roar was so close it shook the flimsy walls of the warehouse—

The black Mercedes S600 exploded into the interior about twenty feet from where Tohr and Wrath were huddled together, debris going everywhere, sheets of metal knocking Tohr on the head and shoulders.

As Xcor burst out of the backseat, Fritz lowered the driver's side window, his wrinkly, sagging face full of concern. "My Lords, do jump in. I fear the human police will be coming soon."

Tohr went to get up, but his knees gave out from cramps.

Xcor was the one who grabbed the King and all but threw him into the backseat.

"I'm getting really fucking tired of being manhandled like this!" Wrath hollered.

Tohr was next on Xcor's list, the Bastard taking hold of him with astonishing strength and going javelin on him.

But Tohr wasn't having it. He knew exactly what was coming next.

Snagging the Bastard's arm, he dragged the male in with them and yelled, "Hit it, Fritz!"

The *doggen* with the NASCAR lead foot punched the accelerator, wrenched the wheel, and with a tire-screeching hard turn, swung them around so the door shut itself. And then they were exiting through a different panel, going all *Fast & Furious* as the Mercedes plowed through the warehouse's outer wall again and hit the snow on the far side like it stole something.

Xcor's eyes were wide with shock as they bounced around the backseat. "You didn't have to save me."

Tohr thought about things for a second. And then decided, Fuck it. Who knew how many were dead back there and whether Xcor was even going to live, given his injuries? Whether Fritz would be able to get them out of downtown, to safety?

"I wasn't about to leave my brother behind."

At first, Xcor was determined to reinterpret the words spoken unto him. Surely there was some translation problem, although it certainly appeared that English had been uttered.

"I'm sorry . . . what did you say?"

Wrath leaned forward as well, such that Tohr, sandwiched between them, was the only one sitting back against the seat.

"Yeah," the King said as the engine roared and they got thrown around. "What was that?"

The Brother looked right into Xcor's eyes. "I am Hharm's son. So are you. We are brothers by blood."

Xcor's heart began to pound so hard his head hurt. And then he felt his stare narrow of its own volition on Tohr's face.

"It's the eyes," the Brother said. "You'll see it in the eyes. And no, I didn't really know him, either. I gather he was not a good male."

"Hharm?" Wrath muttered. "No, he wasn't. And that's all I'll say about it."

Xcor swallowed through a tight throat. "You . . . are my brother?"

And yet was confirmation truly needed? Tohrment was right, those eyes . . . were the same shape and color as his own.

"I am," Tohr affirmed roughly. "I am your blooded kin."

All kinds of things went through Xcor's mind, snippets of images, echoes of sadness, memories of loneliness. In the end, as the Mercedes reached a cruising speed that suggested they were on a highway, he could only lower his stare and fall silent.

When one was granted something that was both secretly yearned for and utterly unexpected, when a sudden revelation seemed to darn a hole in one's life, often the response was of a shock not dissimilar to when one was injured gravely.

Or perhaps he was just that. Injured gravely and losing mental function.

They were silent for the rest of the trip to where'er they were traveling, Xcor passing the time watching out the blackened window as he bled all over himself, the seat, and his . . . brother.

Sometime later, a lifetime, it seemed, they began to stop and go, stop and go, stop and go. And eventually, they came to a halting that stuck. Wrath opened his door immediately, as if the King knew where they were was safe, and Tohr followed their ruler out of the back.

Xcor went to get his own door—

His hand flopped uselessly at the latch. Even on the second try.

Tohr opened the way for him and leaned in. "We're going to get you treated. Come on."

As the Brother, and the brother, held out his hand, Xcor commanded his body to move. But it rebelled. He seemed to have . . .

A rousing dizziness made him feel as though he were going to lose control of his stomach, but he shook his head to clear it and demanded that his flesh obey him. And so it did this time. His broken-down, beat-up, shot-at body, managed to rise out of the back and ambulate forward.

For one step.

As he collapsed, strong arms locked around him and a powerful stance kept him from hitting the floor of what appeared to be a parking garage.

Tohrment accepted his weight easily. "I've got you," came the rough affirmation.

With a halting series of ungainly movements, Xcor held onto the male's shoulders and pushed himself back a little. Meeting Tohrment in the eye, he whispered, "My brother."

"Yes," the male said hoarsely, a sheen of tears making that blue stare glow like a pair of sapphires. "I am your brother."

It was hard to say who embraced who, but suddenly they were both holding on, one upon another, warrior to warrior.

There had been many consequences of the night that Xcor had contemplated, many contingencies and probabilities that he, like any good leader, had assessed and reassessed.

Finding family had never been on his radar.

And though his sire had not proven to be the brave warrior on horseback come to rescue him . . . his blooded brother certainly fit the bill quite readily.

SIXTY-FIVE

When Cormia appeared in the courtyard, Layla was up on her feet in an instant. "Tell me."

Lassiter had long since left, fading away in a shower of golden sparkles, leaving her alone with her terror.

The Chosen was frantic. "You must go down now. They need blood and I have given all I can. I shall stay with the young."

The two of them hugged and then Layla took off, traveling between the two realms in a rush, and re-forming outside the mansion, for she could not get into the interior for the steel mesh.

She didn't notice the cold as she ran up the front steps, yanked wide the vestibule's heavy door, and threw her face into the security camera—and as she waited, she wanted to scream.

It was Beth who opened things up.

"Oh, thank God," the Queen exclaimed with a hard embrace. "Go, go now to the training center. That's where they all are."

Layla started off and then called out over her shoulder, "Has anyone died?"

"Not yet. But, oh . . . just go. I have to wait for Wrath and then take him back down again."

Layla made it through the underground tunnel and out the other side into the training center in record time—but as soon as she broke into the corridor, she stumbled to a halt.

The smell of blood was overwhelming, and so were the number of males down on the floor in various stages of injury and wound care.

It was not only Brothers. In fact . . . what she assumed were all of Xcor's fighters were lined up shoulder to shoulder with the Brotherhood, Ehlena, the nurse, and all of the other Chosen, tending to them.

While Manny and Doc Jane were no doubt in surgery.

"I am here," she said to no one and everyone.

In her mind, she was yelling at them all, demanding to know what had happened to Xcor, for she didn't see him and couldn't sense him, and that terrified her.

Yet she went to the first of the injured she came to, yanking up her sleeve and putting her wrist out.

She recognized the male. It was one of Xcor's.

Zypher shook his head at her. "I am honored, sacred Chosen. But I cannot take your vein."

"You must," she breathed.

"I cannot. You are the female of my leader. I will die before I know the taste of your blood."

One of her sisters came up. "I shall feed him. Go down to Rhage."

And so Layla did, offering her vein unto him. When the Brother had taken what he needed and thanked her, she went to the next male in line.

But he was a Bastard and he, too, shook his head and refused her. "I cannot know your blood. You are the female of my leader."

And so it was down the line, until she focused only on the Brotherhood and didn't even try with the others.

So many wounds, some so deep that she could see anatomy that terrified her. And all the time, she worried about Xcor, and panicked over what Lassiter had done, and prayed that no one died.

She was about to move on to Phury, who needed another vein, so grave were his injuries, when she felt her elbow get taken in a grip.

As she looked up, Tohr's face was grim. "Xcor needs you. Now."

Layla got up so fast that she grew light-headed and Tohr had to help her down the corridor.

"You would have been proud of him," Tohr said as they came up to the closed door of the second OR. "He was unbelievably brave, and he was the one who got Wrath out of there."

"He was?"

"Yes. And he knows. About him and me. I told him because . . . why the fuck not after a night like tonight?"

Tohr opened the way in, and Layla gasped. Xcor was on the operating table, his stomach cut open, his intestines showing—and yet he was conscious.

He turned his head and tried to smile. "My love."

His voice was so reedy, and oh, his coloring was bad. And yet he still tried to sit up.

Manny's tone was sharp. "Okay, that's not working for me. Not while I'm stitching up your bowel."

"Do not look," Xcor commanded her. "You do not look at my body."

In a vivid flashback, she remembered him not wanting to take his clothes off around her.

Layla raced to him and held her wrist to his mouth. "Drink. Take of me."

"We did this once"—he winced and coughed—"once before when I was dying. Did we not."

"Twice, actually. And both times it was colder," she said through tears. "Oh, God, don't die on me. Not tonight. Not ever."

"You are the most beautiful thing I have ever seen." His eyes were fading, the light dimming. "I shared my body with others, but I was as a virgin with you, for my soul had been given to no one. You alone . . . you alone have me . . ."

A machine started beeping.

"Someone better fucking start CPR here!"

Tohr came over in an instant, and as he formed a fist of his combined hands, he said, "Breathe for him! Breathe for him!"

Even though Layla's heart was pounding out of control and she felt like she couldn't stand, she sealed Xcor's lips with her own and blew a great breath of oxygen down deep into his lungs. And then Tohr set about pumping.

"Breathe! Now!"

She dipped down again and exhaled everything she had.

And still the alarms continued to go off . . .

"Again!" Manny yelled as his bloodied, gloved hands worked fast with sutures and a needle.

SIXTY-SIX

When Qhuinn came back around, for a minute, he thought he had returned to the beginning of the nightmare, that fantasy of Blay sitting across a hospital room in a chair presenting itself once again.

"Oh, thank God."

"What?" Qhuinn mumbled.

Blay jumped up and rushed over even though he had one arm in a sling and was limping like someone had dropped a toolbox on his foot.

Qhuinn was about to ask if the male was okay when those beautiful lips were on his and that familiar bonding scent was in his nose—and oh, *fuck,* this was so much better than that fantasy—

"Ow!"

As Qhuinn let out the holler, his arm flopped back down on the bed and pain, red hot and deep as an ocean, lit off along his entire right side.

Blay pulled back and smiled. "Look at it this way. You finally got that shoulder fixed. When they stitched up that knife wound, they went in and took care of your bursitis."

As soon as he could, Qhuinn returned the grin. "Two for one."

"BOGO."

Except then he got serious. "Did we lose anyone?"

"Not from our people, but we got a lot of healing up to do. This was nearly a massacre."

"What about theirs. The Bastards."

Blay looked away. "Xcor's not doing so good. And if you've got anything to say about that you better keep it to yourself. He was the one who got Tohr and Wrath out. And Layla is in the corridor feeding people, FYI—and I don't want to hear about that, either. This is an emergency."

Qhuinn closed his eyes.

"I'm so glad you made it," Blay whispered. "I would have died along with you if you hadn't."

Popping his lids, Qhuinn blurted, "I'm sorry."

"For what?"

"I don't know." He nodded to a piece of machinery by the bed. "Is that a morphine pump?"

"Yup."

"I think I'm babbling, then."

"It's okay. Babble all you like."

Blay sat on the edge of the bed gingerly, and as Qhuinn felt his hand getting taken, he squeezed back.

They stayed like that for the longest time, just staring at each other. And yes, eyes were watering and throats were scratchy . . . but hearts were full, oh so very full.

"I don't ever want to be without you again," Qhuinn said. "Nothing is worth that."

Blay's smile was hauntingly precious. "I couldn't agree more."

The male leaned down again and they brushed lips once. Twice.

"Mmmm, you know what I can't wait for?" Qhuinn murmured.

"Peeing without a catheter?"

"Makeup sex." Qhuinn lowered his lids. "I want in you right now, as a matter of fact."

The blush that hit Blay's face was a criminal turn-on—when you were hooked up to an opium dispenser. "Then rest up," the male drawled. "And take all the fluids you can. You're going to need them."

. . .

Vishous opened his lids and wondered for a moment where he was. The white ceiling above him didn't give a lot away, and—

Jane's face, right above his, was such a surprise he jerked back into the pillows.

"Hi," she said in a wavering voice. "You're back."

"Where did I go—" Goddamn, his throat hurt. Had they intubated him? "What happened?"

And yet even as he asked, that goatfuck scene in the warehouse came back to him . . . him falling and hitting his head, and then lying there paralyzed as guns had continued to go off. Given the distribution of pain all down his body, he concluded a couple of things: one, he was not, in fact, paralyzed; two, he had been shot in a couple of places, having clearly caught some of the crossfire; and three—

"We almost lost you," Jane said, her forest-green eyes shimmering with tears. "I've been in this room for the last two hours praying you were going to come around."

"Two hours?"

She nodded. "As soon as I was finished operating, I came in—" She frowned. "What's wrong? Are you in pain? Do you need more morphine?"

"Why—"

As she brushed under his eyes, he realized he was crying—and the moment that registered, he sucked up his emotions and slapped them into submission. No crying. Nope. He was not going there.

"Here, let me call for Ehlena."

Jane was across the room and at the door leaning out faster than his heart was beating—which actually wasn't saying much. And as he heard her demand more meds for him, and then start answering questions about other people, all of his aches went away.

Except for the one at his sternum.

And that was the one that, yeah, wasn't going to respond to any kind of drug.

He watched her tilt even farther and nod to someone, and then step all the way out. Just as the door was easing shut, she looked over her shoulder, her eyes full of worry.

"I'll be right back."

No, he thought, I don't think you will be.

And sure enough, five minutes later, Ehlena came hustling in with a vial and a needle for the IV.

"Hey," she said with a warm smile. "Jane's just checking some dressings. She didn't want you to have to wait for her."

"It's okay, and I don't need that."

"She said you're having breakthrough pain."

With a grunt, Vishous sat up and swung his legs off the side. As he started to remove his IV, Ehlena recoiled.

"What are you doing?"

"I'm checking myself out. But don't worry, it's not AMA or anything, because I'm pretty much fully trained at this point. Now I'd like some privacy, if you don't mind. Unless you want to watch me take my Foley out?"

"How about I go get Jane?"

As the female started to head for the door, he said, "There are more patients out there than you guys can handle, so I'm guessing you could use this bed. And my vitals are stable, I'm already healing, so some Chosen had to have been through and fed me. I really think you need to be critical-pathing your time rather than waste any of it trying to talk me out of leaving—or bothering Jane when she needs to be with more important patients."

Right on schedule, Manny poked his head in. "Hey! Check you out all nearly-vertical. Listen, Ehlena, I need you, right now."

V shot the female an I-told-you-so. And then he gathered by her curse and disappearance that she bought into his unassailable logic.

Getting the catheter out was a bitch. His cock hadn't been used much lately and it really didn't appreciate the disrespect when he finally did touch it again.

Shifting off the hospital bed and onto his feet, he held his hospital gown together in the back and walked out.

All of the Bastards were in the corridor, and all of them were injured. He didn't see any of his brothers, but he could catch the lingering scents of their blood, and inferred that they had gone up to the mansion to recover.

Or at least the ones who were not in hospital beds had.

Jane was nowhere to be found.

As he started walking, he nodded to the Bastards, shaking hands that were offered up and pounding knuckles, the battle they had all shared in aligning them more than any formal oaths or bended-knee shit ever could.

Funny, he marveled, this was how you made steel. You took iron, applied tremendous heat, and cleared away all the impurities. What was left was pure, undiluted strength.

Like when two groups of fighters eliminated needless conflict and banded together to form a unit against their enemy that was capable of far more than they could ever have accomplished separately.

Continuing on, he thought he heard Jane's voice behind him. And he did. She was talking to Manny, trading information.

V thought for a moment she would notice that he was walking away and come after him. But she didn't.

And again, he thought as he limped to the office and headed for the tunnel alone, he was not surprised.

SIXTY-SEVEN

"Wake up, my love."

As a deep voice entered her ear, Layla's eyes popped open and she sat up in a chair—which brought her face to face with Xcor.

"You're alive!" she exclaimed. Except then she looked at all the wires and the IV tubing that had been disconnected and was hanging loose from him. "What the hell are you doing out of bed—"

"Shh," he said. "Come on."

"What?"

"We're leaving."

"Wha—"

He nodded and stood up straight. He was covered with bandages, still in a hospital gown, and pale as a ghost, but the look in his eye told her that he wasn't going to listen to anything she had to say.

They were, in fact, leaving.

"Where are we going?" she asked as she got to her feet.

"To the little ranch house. There's a car waiting for us."

"But shouldn't you stay here where there are doctors—"

"I just want to be alone with you. You're all I need."

As he stared down at her, a feeling of love spread throughout her body. "I can't believe you're alive."

"It's because of you. On so many levels."

A brief flashback of her and Tohr giving him CPR robbed her of speech. But it didn't take away her ability to hitch herself up under her male and help him to the door.

The corridor was empty, nothing but a *doggen* with a mop and a bucket getting rid of bloodstains to attest to the injured.

"Where did your soldiers go?" she asked as they started down for the parking lot. "How long was I asleep?"

"Hours, my love. And all were treated and released. Dawn is about thirty minutes away."

"Are they going to be okay?"

"Yes. All of them, and all the Brothers, too. The medical staff here are amazing."

"Oh, thank La—" She stopped herself. "Thank goodness. Fate. Everything."

It was then that she noticed a figure standing way down the hall by the exit, and as they closed in, she realized it was Tohr.

When they finally stopped in front of the Brother, the two males just stared at each other. And that was when the similarities between them became truly evident to her. Same height, same build, same jaw . . . and those eyes.

"Thank you for saving my life in that alley," Tohr said roughly.

"And thank you for saving mine on that operating table," Xcor intoned.

The two smiled a little, and then grew serious.

It was then that a chill went through her—one that intensified as Xcor unhitched his arm and leaned into the Brother.

As the males embraced, she realized with dread . . . this was it. This was going to be her and Xcor's last day together. That was why he was so determined to leave the clinic, and that was why Tohr was helping them.

Also why the Brother looked at her with such compassion when the two males stepped back from each other.

Tohr opened the exit wide and waited off to the side.

No one said anything as she and Xcor proceeded to Fritz's Mercedes. Even the butler was grave as he got out and came around to open their door.

Layla ducked down and slid across the seat, and then Xcor followed suit and Fritz shut them in.

Xcor put the blackout window next to him down and lifted his dagger hand as the car was put in drive—and Tohr returned the gesture as they headed off, the good-bye as permanent as the ink in one of the Sacred Scribes's volumes up in the Sanctuary.

It doesn't have to be this way, she yelled in her head. We can make this work. Somehow, we can . . .

But she knew she was fighting a battle that had been lost nights ago when Xcor had given his oath to Wrath and the agreement for the return to the Old Country had been set.

Looking down at her hands, because she didn't dare meet him in the face, she whispered, "I heard you were so brave."

"Not really."

"That's what Tohr said."

"He is being generous. But I will tell you, my males fought with great honor, and without them, the Brotherhood would have been lost. Of that I am well sure."

She nodded and found herself biting her lip.

"My love," he whispered, "do not hide your eyes from me."

"If I look at you I will break down."

"Then allow me to be strong for you when you feel that you are not. Come here."

In spite of his injuries, he pulled her into his lap and wrapped his arms around her. And then he was kissing her collarbone. And her throat . . . and her lips.

That now-familiar heat rose again, and when he eased her up and over his hips, she split her thighs to straddle him and was glad the partition was up for their privacy.

Shifting around awkwardly, she took one side of her leggings down and moved her panties out of the way as he pulled up the hem of his hospital gown.

"I'll be careful," she said as he grimaced from pain.

"I won't feel anything but you."

Xcor stood his erection with his hand and she slowly slid herself onto it.

"My love," he breathed as his head fell back and his eyes closed. "Oh, you make me whole."

With aching gentleness, his hands slipped under her shirt and cupped her breasts, and she eased herself into a rhythm on him, wrapping her arms around the headrest, putting her lips to his.

As the stop and the start of the car going through the gating system commenced, a sweet, sad orgasm rolled through her body . . . and took her heart along with it.

It felt as though the end of them had come just at their beginning.

SIXTY-EIGHT

The following evening, as Layla walked up from the ranch's basement, she felt like she aged a hundred years with each step of the ascent.

Xcor was already at the stove, cooking eggs, bacon, and again, running another entire loaf of bread through the toaster.

He looked across at her. And the way his eyes went over her still-wet hair and the sweatshirt she'd put on and the jeans she'd found in the dresser, she knew he was memorizing every detail about her.

"I wish I were wearing a ball gown," she said hoarsely.

"Why?" he said. "You look incredible right now."

She lifted the hem of the sweatshirt and read the letters on it. SUNY CALDWELL. "A bit of a mess, really."

Xcor slowly shook his head. "I don't see your clothes, I never do, and a fancy dress wouldn't change that. I don't see wet hair, I feel the strands between my fingers. I don't see pale cheeks, I am tasting your lips in my mind. You offer me all my senses at once, my female. You are so much more than any one thing about you."

She blinked away her tears and went to the cupboard. Trying not to lose it, she said, "Will we need plates and forks and also knives?"

It turned out they required none of any of that.

After he was done preparing the food, they brought it over to the table . . . but it just sat untouched, going cold and scentless. And she knew when they were really starting to run out of time when he began to continuously check the clock.

Then it was over.

"I have to go," he said roughly.

As their eyes met, he reached across the table and took her hand. His stare was luminous, for he was so emotional as well, his navy blue eyes glowing with both sorrow and love.

"I want you to remember something," he whispered.

Layla sniffled and tried to be as strong as he was. "What?"

In the Old Language, he said, "*Wherever I go, you shall ne'er be far from me. Wherever I sleep, you shall be beside me. What I eat, I shall share with you, and when I dream, we shall be together once again. My love, you are not gone from me ever, and I shall not take another. Till the very night I die.*"

It was on the tip of her tongue to tell him that that was impossible.

But as if he knew what she was thinking—as usual—he just shook his head. "How could I be with anyone but you?"

She got to her feet in a shaky, disorganized rise, and when she came to him, he widened his knees so she could stand between them.

As she bent down to kiss him for the last time, her tears fell on his cheeks. "I love . . ."

She couldn't get out the last word. Her throat had closed up.

Xcor's hands shifted up her body until he cupped her face. "It was all worth it."

"What?" she choked out.

"All that came before this one moment where I am loved by you. Even though we must part, I can say that what I feel for you made it all worth it."

And then, with one final kiss . . . he was gone.

SIXTY-NINE

n hour later, Layla went to the Brotherhood mansion. She felt too light on her feet, as if the inside of her had been emptied of her vital organs—and she supposed that was true. There wasn't much to her anymore.

Funny to have found herself and lost herself in such a short period of time.

And yet, as she mounted the mansion's stone steps and approached the great door into the vestibule, she knew that that was just the mourning talking.

Or at least, she hoped it was.

If this was what every night for the rest of her life was going to be like? She was in a world of hurt. Literally.

Opening things up, she put her face in the monitor and waited for someone to answer the summons. Technically, it was Qhuinn's night to take the kids, but he was still in a hospital bed, so she'd been told by Beth at around five in the afternoon that she could have them if she wanted them.

As if she would say no.

According to what she'd been told, Rhamp and Lyric had been brought back from the Sanctuary by Cormia a couple of hours ago, so they were upstairs—the hope had been, of course, that Qhuinn would be further along in his recovery. But apparently not.

She hadn't asked what his injuries were. It was not really her business, and that made her sad. But what could you do.

"Oh, good evening, Chosen."

As Fritz's cheery voice greeted her, she realized she hadn't even noticed that he'd opened the door. "Hello, Fritz. How fare thee?"

"Very well. I am so happy all are well."

"Yes," she said numbly. "Myself, also."

"Is there aught that I may do for you?"

Well, you could turn around whatever airplane the love of my life is on right now and bring him back to me. Make him stay here with me. Have him—

She cleared her throat. "No, thank you. I'll just go up and get the young."

The butler bowed low and then Layla walked slowly toward the grand staircase. As she lifted her foot for the first step, she recalled her trip up from the basement at that charming little house—and worried whether this was her new lot in life.

Tearing up all over herself every time she took to a set of stairs.

And yet she managed to keep going.

That was, after all, what you had to do, even though your heart was breaking. Dearest fates, she had no idea what she was going to do with herself on the nights she didn't have Lyric and Rhamp, but she was going to have to find something. Left to her current devices, she was liable to get swamped by her sadness at Xcor's—

She stopped halfway up as a male came to the head of the stairs.

Putting her palms forward defensively, she said to Blay, "I'm allowed to take them. Beth told me so. I'm not here without permission."

It felt like forever since she had seen the male, and she hated the necessary distance between them. But how else were they going to proceed? And oh, God, what if he didn't give her the young? What if Qhuinn had heard she was getting an extra night and had mandated from his hospital bed that she not get the time?

On tonight, of all nights, she needed a visceral reminder of what she was going on for—

Before Blay could say anything, the chimes went off with someone else who had arrived at the mansion's entrance. But Layla didn't pay any attention to that. Why should she? She didn't live here anymore—

Layla wheeled around.

And blinked at the impossible.

Qhuinn was coming in from the vestibule . . . with Xcor by his side.

Layla blinked again and rubbed her eyes, her brain incapable of comprehending what she was looking at. Surely Qhuinn, of all people, couldn't . . . wouldn't . . .

Wait, why wasn't her male on an airplane?

Xcor lifted his stare to her and took a step forward . . . and then another. He didn't focus on anything but her, all of the grandeur and the color of the foyer seeming to mean nothing to him.

Screw the whys and hows, Layla thought as she exploded into action, tearing down toward him, figuring if this was a figment of her imagination, she might as well find out right now.

And if she landed flat on her face on the mosaic floor?

She wouldn't be in any more pain than she already was.

"My love," Xcor said as he caught all of her weight and held her from the ground.

As she started to cry in total confusion, and some sort of tentative joy, she looked over his shoulder.

Qhuinn was staring at the pair of them. And then he shifted his blue and green gaze up to where Blay was standing at the head of the stairwell—and started to smile.

Layla eased herself out of Xcor's hold. Approaching the father of her young, she had to clear her throat and sweep her face. "Qhuinn—"

"I'm sorry," he said to her in a rough voice. "I'm truly . . . sorry."

All she could do was stare at him in shock.

With another quick glance to Blay, Qhuinn took a deep breath. "Look, you did the best you could, and this has been hard on everyone. I'm sorry I reacted like I did—that was beyond wrong of me. But I just . . . I love our kids, and the idea they might have been in danger? It terrified me right into insanity. I know that your forgiveness can't come right away and—"

Layla jumped at him and put her arms around her youngs' sire, and as she held onto him so hard she couldn't breathe, she suspected neither could he. "I'm sorry, too, oh, God, Qhuinn, I'm so sorry . . ."

Messy, tearful apologies were the best kind, especially when they were accepted with open hearts on both sides.

When they finally broke apart, she fit herself under Xcor's arm and Qhuinn put his hand out to the other male.

"Like I told you in the car coming here," he said, "not that you need it or want it, but you two have my blessing. One hundred percent."

Xcor smiled and shook what was offered. "For your support, I am more honored this night than any other."

"Great. That's real great." Qhuinn leaned into Layla. "Turns out he's not such a bad guy, after all. Go fig."

As she laughed, Qhuinn clapped her male on the shoulder. "So come on, time to meet the kids. And see where you'll be staying."

The world went wonky on Layla again and she looked between Qhuinn and Xcor. "Wait, what is . . . what are you . . ."

"If the two of you are going to be properly mated"—the Brother put up his forefinger—"and I will tell you that I'm an old-fashioned male so I want the mother of my children to be properly mated, he's got to live here."

At that moment, chimes went off again, and Fritz, who was blotting his eyes with a white hankie, hustled back over to the door.

The butler let in Tohr—which wasn't a surprise—and then all of the Bastards filed into the foyer as well. Every single one of them.

She looked at Xcor and Qhuinn in shock. "They're coming here, too?"

"Kind of a package deal," Qhuinn said with a grin. "Plus I heard they suck at pool, so that's a bonus. Grab your shit, boys. This is Fritz. You will learn to love him, especially when he irons your socks."

Layla was in an absolute daze as the fighters began to bring in all kinds of duffels. And then she was escorted up to the top of the staircase by two of the three most important males in her life.

Blay, the third one, smiled at her and gave her a big hug. And then it was the trio of them heading past Wrath's study toward the hall of statues.

Which made her ask, "And Wrath is okay with this?"

Qhuinn nodded as Blay answered, "More fighters is always best. And God knows we have the room. Plus Fritz will be over the moon—more to cook for, more to clean up after."

"And damn, those males are good in the field." Qhuinn glanced over at her. "Last night? It would have been a tragedy for the history books without your male."

Xcor showed no reaction to the praise. Well, unless you counted the tinge of red that hit his cheeks. "Well, the same could be said for the Brothers."

As they came up to the suite where the kids were, Qhuinn was the one who stepped forward and opened things up.

Blay went in first and then Xcor hesitated . . . before putting a tentative foot over the threshold. And then another. Like maybe he was scared there was a monster under the bed or something.

Layla looked at Qhuinn. And then she took his hand. "Thank you. For this."

Qhuinn bowed so low he was nearly parallel to the floor. When he straightened back up, he placed a kiss on her forehead and murmured, "And thank you, for our kids."

Layla gave his forearm a squeeze, and then she went in.

Xcor had halted in the center of the room and was staring across at the bassinets like he was terrified.

"It's okay," she said, urging him over. "They're not going to bite."

She took him to Rhamp first, and as Xcor looked down in awe at the little infant, he got a frown in response.

Xcor laughed in a rush. "Dearest fates, that is a warrior right there."

Qhuinn and Blay came over, arm in arm, and Qhuinn said, "Right?

That's exactly what I think. He's a tough number, aren't you, Rhamp? Also poops out toxic waste. You'll learn that later."

Xcor's eyebrows shot up. "Toxic—"

"Figure of speech. But wait'll you smell it. Put hair on your chest, and vampires don't have that."

"And this is Lyric," Layla said.

Xcor had a bemused expression as he went to look at the other bassinet—but then everything about him changed.

His eyes welled up, and this time, tears did fall from his eyes. Glancing over at Layla, he said, "She looks . . . exactly like you."

As Xcor struggled for composure, Blay and Qhuinn came up behind him.

"Isn't she just beautiful?" Qhuinn said in a hoarse voice. "Just like our Layla."

Layla watched the three huge warriors leaning over the tiny little female . . . and was overwhelmed by a sense of love and completeness. It had been a hard, long road, with many times that all could have been lost. And yet here they were, together, as a family of both blood . . . and choice.

At that moment, she realized Lassiter was standing in the doorway to the bedroom.

Putting his forefinger to his lips, he made a show of going shhhhhh-hhhh. And then he winked at her and silently disappeared.

She smiled at the sparkles that fell in his wake. "That angel may be better suited for the job than he knows."

"What?" Xcor asked her.

"Nothing," she murmured as she leaned in and kissed him.

Or maybe it was everything. Who was to say.

"Do you want to hold her?" Qhuinn asked.

Xcor recoiled as if someone had inquired whether he'd like a hot poker in his hands. Then he recovered, shaking his head as he made a manly show of scrubbing his tears away like they were permanent marker on his cheeks.

"I don't think I'm quite ready for that. She looks . . . so delicate."

"She's strong, though. She's got her *mahmen's* blood in her, too." Qhuinn looked at Blay. "And she's got good parents. They both do. We're in this together, people, three fathers and one mom, two kids. Bam!"

Xcor's voice got low. "A father . . . ?" He laughed softly. "I went from having no family, to having a mate, a brother, and now . . ."

Qhuinn nodded. "A son and a daughter. As long as you are Layla's *hellren*, you are their father, too."

Xcor's smile was transformative, so wide that it stretched his face into something she had never seen. "A son and a daughter."

"That's right," Layla whispered with joy.

But then instantly that expression on his face was gone, his lips thinning out and his brows dropping down like he was ready to go on the attack. "She is *never* dating. I don't care who he is—"

"Right!" Qhuinn put his palm out for a high five. "*That's* what I'm talking about!"

"Now, hold on," Blay interjected as they clapped hands. "She has every right to live her life as she chooses."

"Yes, come on," Layla added. "This double-standard stuff is ridiculous. She's going to be allowed . . ."

As the argument started up, she and Blay fell in beside each other, and Qhuinn and Xcor lined up shoulder to shoulder, their massive forearms crossed over their chests.

"I'm good with a gun," Xcor said like that was the end of things.

"And I can handle the shovel," Qhuinn tacked on. "They'll never find the body."

The two of them pounded knuckles and looked so dead serious that Layla had to roll her eyes. But then she was smiling.

"You know something?" she said to the three of them. "I really believe . . . that it's all going to be okay. We're going to work it out, together, because that's what families do."

As she rose up on her tiptoes and kissed her male, she said, "Love has a way of fixing everything . . . even your daughter starting to date."

"Which is *not* going to happen," Xcor countered. "Ever."

"My man," Qhuinn said, backing him up. "I knew I liked you—"

"Oh, for the love," Layla muttered as the debate resumed, and Blay started laughing and Qhuinn and Xcor continued bonding.

But it turned out she was right.

Everything worked out just as it was supposed to, and love triumphed over all kinds of challenges. And years and years and years later . . . Lyric did actually date someone.

Except that is another story, for another time.

ABOUT THE TYPE

This book was set in Garamond, a typeface originally designed by the Parisian type cutter Claude Garamond (c. 1500–61). This version of Garamond was modeled on a 1592 specimen sheet from the Egenolff-Berner foundry, which was produced from types assumed to have been brought to Frankfurt by the punch cutter Jacques Sabon (c. 1520–80).

Claude Garamond's distinguished romans and italics first appeared in *Opera Ciceronis* in 1543–44. The Garamond types are clear, open, and elegant.

TURN THE PAGE
FOR MORE FROM
J. R. WARD

BLOOD KISS

The legacy of the Black Dagger Brotherhood continues in a spin-off series from the #1 *New York Times* bestselling author . . .

Paradise, blooded daughter of the king's First Advisor, is ready to break free from the restrictive life of an aristocratic female. Her strategy? Join the Black Dagger Brotherhood's training center program and learn to fight for herself, think for herself . . . be herself. It's a good plan, until everything goes wrong. The schooling is unfathomably difficult, the other recruits feel more like enemies than allies, and it's very clear that the Brother in charge, Butch O'Neal, a.k.a. the Dhestroyer, is having serious problems in his own life.

And that's before she falls in love with a fellow classmate. Craeg, a common civilian, is nothing her father would ever want for her, but everything she could ask for in a male. As an act of violence threatens to tear apart the entire program, and the erotic pull between them grows irresistible, Paradise is tested in ways she never anticipated—and left wondering whether she's strong enough to claim her own power . . . on the field, and off.

THE BOURBON KINGS

The #1 *New York Times* bestselling author of the Black Dagger Brotherhood delivers the first novel in an enthralling new series set amid the shifting dynamics of a Southern family defined by wealth and privilege—and compromised by secrets, deceit, and scandal . . .

For generations, the Bradford family has worn the mantle of kings of the bourbon capital of the world. Their sustained wealth has afforded them prestige and power—as well as a hard-won division of class on their sprawling estate, Easterly. Upstairs, a dynasty that by all appearances plays by the rules of good fortune and good taste. Downstairs, the staff who work tirelessly to maintain the impeccable Bradford façade. And never the twain shall meet.

For Lizzie King, Easterly's head gardener, crossing that divide nearly ruined her life. Falling in love with Tulane, the prodigal son of the bourbon dynasty, was nothing that she intended or wanted—and their bitter breakup only served to prove her instincts were right. Now, after two years of staying away, Tulane is finally coming home, bringing the past with him. No one will be left unmarked: not Tulane's beautiful and ruthless wife; not his older brother, whose bitterness and bad blood know no bounds; and especially not the iron-fisted Bradford patriarch, a man with few morals, fewer scruples, and many, many terrible secrets.

As family tensions ignite, Easterly and all its inhabitants are thrown into the grips of an irrevocable transformation, and only the strongest will survive.